DRAGON NEMESIS

DRAGON NEMESIS

DRAGONS OF BOSTON BOOK 2

CHRIS A. JACKSON

Cover Design by Melissa McArthur

This novel was written before the pandemic of 2020 that has taken so many lives and shattered so many families. I had no notion that such a future loomed as I wrote of the potential global catastrophe of an outbreak of the infection Aleksi suffered. Serendipity, it seems, is both poignant and cruel. I dedicate this story to all of those whose lives were affected by the COVID-19 pandemic. There is hope, however. Science and medicine offer a light at the end of this dark and dreadful time. Until that deliverance arrives, please be safe.

1

Her evolution was complete. The ancient infection that had reforged Aleksi Rychenkna's fragile human flesh into something else, something new or perhaps very old, had finally finished its course.

Monster... Inhuman... Freak... But flying doesn't suck.

The night skies of Boston were hers, but that was all she had.

I'm still Aleksi... I'm still me... But, as her wings caught the warm night air and she wheeled around the ornate cornices of a church's lofty bell tower, she wasn't so sure of that.

Dragon...

She caught a stone spire with one clawed wing and swung around to hunker down in the shadows. *Wait... Listen... Hide...* Those three things, her own holy trinity, had kept her alive as winter blossomed into spring and then summer. She knew they were still watching for her, if not actively hunting. Hiding in plain sight had proven impossible with everyone in the greater Boston metropolitan area walking around in spring dresses and short sleeves. Heavy coats drew stares. Aleksi had risked a few forays wearing the head-to-toe coverage of full niqab, but that also drew too much attention, mostly racial profiling. She longed for winter when she could once again walk among crowds of humans unseen.

Spring was supposed to be a time of renewal, life, budding trees, and warmth. It had brought Aleksi only fear and loneliness.

And hunger... Dragon's gotta eat, after all.

Food was another problem. Now that her evolution was complete, her ravenous appetite had eased, but she still had to eat, and fresh meat was hard to come by outside of grocery stores into which she dared not venture. Even when closed, stores had security cameras. She had tried lurking behind supermarkets, knowing they threw away vast amounts of food every day. Sometimes that yielded beautiful steaks or roasts still wrapped in plastic and barely past the "best by" date. But rooting through dumpsters for food disgusted her. She had learned when the small butcher shops got their deliveries, when they threw out their older stock, and when shipments arrived at meat-packing plants, but every time she scavenged or stole, she risked her life.

Something primal within her longed to hunt. Unfortunately, there was only one type of prey walking the streets of Boston.

No...I won't kill. I won't murder people for food. I'm not a cannibal...

Aleksi breathed in the scent of four million humans in the night air and suppressed the urge to feed. She'd been successfully suppressing that urge for half a year, and still it plagued her. She might not be a murderer, but she was certainly a predator. Whatever had changed her into this —*Dragon? Is that what I am?*—had been unknown to science until she dug it up. Aleksi was a scientist, and there were new discoveries in paleontology all the time, but no one had ever found anything like this. The specimen they'd discovered had been encased in a pyroclastic ash deposit, but its DNA, and the virus-like infection that had transformed her, had survived the heat. Its skeletal structure, however, had not. Only a few teeth had been recovered; the ash cast had contained only degraded remnants.

Do dragon bones decompose when they die? Is that why there's no record?

Dr. Bornstein, an old classmate of Dr. Hutchinson's—*"Hutch, or it's two demerits!"* She smiled at the memory—had said her bones resembled something between cartilage and bone after he dug a bullet out of her scapula. She was certainly lighter and more flexible than she'd been before. But why? Birds had hollow bones to aid flight. Why didn't she?

Reminder to self: Google pterosaur skeletal structure.

Aleksi had too many questions and no answers. Hutch had searched every paleontology database known to man for her and had gotten nothing. There were legends of dragons in almost every culture, but no hard evidence, no skulls mounted on walls, no trophies. There was also no record of any kind of infection that changed humans into monsters—legends of lycanthropy aplenty, but no solid evidence. Nothing like her.

How such a thing had evolved, she had no idea. The only hypothesis she had, and precious little evidence to support it other than her own feelings, was something to protect humans from other predators. It had to be some type of deeply coded activation of dormant human genes, but she had no way to confirm that it wasn't entirely alien. The reason it wasn't found in genetic databases might be because it had always already been there, walking around on two legs, driving cars while texting, ordering coffee at Starbucks, living and dying with no knowledge of the dragons within each and every one of them.

Preliminary analysis of the samples showed human DNA and other sequences previously uncategorized, sequences that were undoubtedly the result of recombined human junk DNA. Unfortunately, Bob Tomlin, the young man who was doing the analysis, had been murdered, and the entire sample stolen before any meaningful theories could be formed. Aleksi was alone, the only dragon in the world.

The phone duct-taped to her hip vibrated, snapping Aleksi out of her musing and stretching her scaly lips into a smile. Only one person ever called her. Only one person had her number: *Hutch.* Harvard professor, her former advisor, briefly her lover, and the only human in the world she trusted. She peeled the tape away from her scaly hide and looked at the text.

Where R U?

Aleksi grinned, teeth like razors gleaming in the shadows. She tapped, "At Church" and hit send.

Really?

"Really," she tapped, then added. "Well, on one, anyway."

Ha! Feel like company? Can't sleep.

Aleksi checked the time, three-twenty a.m., and frowned. "Too dangerous."

Bullshit. Come over. Got a steak 4 U.

Damn... Hutch knew what she longed for: food, company, and comfort. He worried about her, and provided what he could: a meal, conversation, a shower, and sometimes even a bed to sleep in during the day, but she was afraid. She still had nightmares of her claws rending his flesh, her teeth descending to tear out his throat. When he was close to her, when he held her, she felt a confusing conflict of visceral emotions—

hunger, need, love, and the urge to protect him. She was afraid that one day the hunger would win.

You still there?

"Yep," she tapped, then, "I'll come, but can't stay."

Door's open. He added a heart emoji.

Love... Aleksi affixed the phone to her hip, checked the street for onlookers, and launched herself into the sky. She stayed low, weaving in and among the buildings, keeping to the shadows, never sure if the government was looking for her with night vision scopes and radar. They knew she existed, and wanted her, but they hadn't been foolish enough to try to kill her again.

Hutch had found a few conspiracy theory websites that posted blurry pictures of her, and had even seen a "Dragons of Boston" webcomic and graphic novel by some geeky artist. The websites never lasted long, probably hacked and crashed by the government. The graphic novel, however, had gotten out in print. A few hundred copies had sold before the production closed down and the artist moved on to other things. Hutch had offered to look the guy up and ask questions, but Aleksi had told him not to. Right now, the government was helping keep her existence a secret, so she'd let them.

She banked over the Esplanade and swooped down over the Charles River, the tips of her wings creasing the water, ground effect pressing against her chest. At the Western Avenue bridge, she banked hard, flying beneath it in shadow across the river. The pedestrian paths were empty, and there were only a few cars on Memorial Avenue. She banked again, swooping low along the shore and watching the headlights. When there was a gap, she pulled up hard, gaining altitude to just above the street lights to cross the avenue, then dove back down into the shadows of Cambridge. Even if someone caught a glimpse of her, they wouldn't believe their eyes.

Aleksi loved flying, but she would trade it in an instant to be human again.

Hutch's condo building loomed ahead, and she swooped around to the north side. His window was dark, of course, but the big sliding glass door was open.

Aleksi billowed her wings and clutched the rail of his balcony with clawed toes, pausing there for a moment to listen and scent the air. One heartbeat, the scents of Hutch, raw meat, and a thousand other smells of human habitation: soap, aftershave, coffee, toilet bowl cleaner, fabric softener, antiperspirant, her friend and former pet iguana, Iggy, and another scent…familiar, but not. She experienced a flash of memory—red cashmere, a bright smile, laughter, friendship.

No, it's just some cologne or perfume on something. She hopped down from the balcony rail and walked into Hutch's home. The drapes closed behind her, the hum of the electric motor loud in her ears.

"Hungry?" a low light flicked on, and Hutch sat in his armchair, a steaming cup on the arm beside his hand. He wore a robe with an Asian dragon embroidered on it, his favorite, he said. He got up and put his cup on the end table.

"Ravenousss," she admitted. "Thanksss for the invite." She hated the lisp she'd developed with the changes. The shape of her lips, mouth, tongue, and throat had been altered enough to make enunciating certain sounds difficult. *Just another part of being a monster.*

"Any time." He came to her, his fragile arms enfolding her, his scent filling her.

Aleksi wrapped him in her leathery wings, clawed fingers interlaced behind his back to keep from piercing his thin skin. *Longing... love... comfort...* God, he felt good. She still loved him, but she knew they could never be together. She could, however, hold him occasionally. She breathed deeply of his scent, flicking her sensitive forked tongue over his neck, tasting him… Again, she caught that hint of another, a faint musky floral scent that reminded her of someone else. But he tasted good…

Hunger...

She broke the clinch before the urge fully manifested. "That steak smells wonderful."

"Two-pound porterhouse, fresh from the butcher." Hutch grabbed his coffee, and she followed him to the kitchen. A huge slab of meat lay on a plate on the counter. "I know you like it warm, so I put it out last night."

"You knew you'd be up at this hour?"

"I'm always up at this hour." He poured himself a coffee and leaned back against the counter.

"You drink too much coffee." Aleksi picked up the knife and fork beside the plate. She hardly needed them, but eating like a monster would be rude. She cut a piece and slipped the meat off the fork with the razors her teeth had become, chewing in bliss.

He didn't answer, just shrugged and sipped.

She ate another bite. "How's the research?"

"Going well. Vince and Beth are making good progress on the bone bed. They've gotten solid genetic data, and Alvarez is already massaging the stats." Vince and Beth were his two new graduate students; Aleksi and Bob Tomlin's replacements. "But neither of them is you."

"I hope not." She ate a bite and smiled at him. "I wouldn't wish *another* neurotic recluse on you."

"You weren't…" Hutch paused and shrugged.

"I *was*…" she raised a clawed wing, "…before this."

"Did I tell you that Lonnie got a post-doc position in Boston?"

It was an obvious effort to change the subject from what both of them had lost with her transformation. Aleksi decided to accept it. "No. Who's she working with?"

"Jim Bornstein, at Harvard Med." Hutch smiled over his coffee cup.

Aleksi swallowed her bite of steak, and her jaw dropped. Jim Bornstein had agreed to help Hutch look for some cure for her condition. She didn't think he would ever find a way to reverse the transformation, but to have someone actually doing research on it gave her a sliver of hope. But there was danger in looking into things that powerful people wanted kept secret.

"Hutch, tell them to be careful. Homeland Security will be all over them if they publish anything."

"Jim knows that. He's got a ton of grant money for looking into all kinds of genetic diseases. They can do the work under the guise of Lonnie's new project: Retroviral Infections in Ancient Humans."

"That sounds right up her alley." Lonnie Westinghouse was a brilliant paleontologist and an accomplished geneticist. Her doctoral dissertation had been an analysis of human genetic markers in pre-human hominids.

"Yes, and there's a real chance they could find something." He put his cup down and stepped over to her, raising one hand to brush his fingertips down the smooth scales of her shoulder. "So, eat your steak and don't despair. We're working on this."

"Thanks, Hutch." Aleksi suppressed a shiver of pleasure under his touch.

She felt a pang of wanting, a need she knew he couldn't fulfill. She was too changed. She didn't even wear clothes when she came to visit him anymore, unable to fly with anything restricting her wings. She had several robes and heavy coats and hats stashed away for forays into humanity, but to fly, she needed to be free. Her nudity, however, resembled nothing human, let alone feminine. Her breasts had flattened, her hips narrowed, her waist slim and muscular. Fine scales covered her everywhere, and the only hair on her body was a thin ridge that ran from the crown of her head, between her shoulder blades, to the cleft of her butt.

Unfortunately, that didn't mean she didn't want him.

"Hutch...please." She nudged his hand away with the back of one taloned finger. "I can't..."

His smile fell. "I still love you, Aleksi." He looked her in the eye, as if into her soul. "I miss touching you, being with you."

"I'm not *me* anymore, Hutch. I'm not even human." She turned away, leaving the rest of the steak on the plate, her appetite gone. "You need to find someone else. I can't...be with you that way."

"Why not?" He stepped up behind her, and his arms encircled her. His fingertips made tiny circles on the scales of her chest, gentle, delicate.

"Hutch, don't. It's...wrong." But she didn't stop him. She could have, easily, but didn't. It felt so good to be touched.

"What's wrong with it?" His fingertips caressed the smooth scales, questing for a hint of the swell of her breasts. A tiny trickle of sensation, like a faint shock of electricity, shot down from his fingertips to her pubis.

"Hutch..." *Stop him! Don't let him do this!* But her body wasn't listening.

"Please, Aleksi. Just let me touch you." His fingers quested down her flat, hard abdomen, brushing the scales where her legs joined.

Aleksi shuddered. "Hutch, I don't..." But she *did*. A flood of tingling warmth spread out from his touch.

"I think you do, Aleksi. You need this as much as I do." He slipped one finger down lower...an unexpected wetness there told her that he was right.

Wrong! No! Don't!

Aleksi pulled away and turned to face him, her knees quaking with the ripples of sensation his touch had elicited. "Hutch! No. It's...*bestiality*!"

"No, it's *not*!" His vehemence caught her off guard. "You're *not* a beast! You're Aleksi Rychenkna, and I'm still in love with you!"

"And I'm still in love with *you*, Hutch, but I can't..." She bit her lip and tasted blood. The pain cleared the fog of desire clouding her mind. "I'm afraid to let you... You might contract this thing from me. I caught it from the specimen, but that doesn't mean I'm not infectious."

"Then we'll be *careful*." He took a step forward, but she backed away.

"No, Hutch. I'm sorry, but I can't risk it. I *do* want to, but I can't." She turned away and started for the door. "I should go."

"Aleksi!" She heard a clank and turned to see him holding her plate out. "At least stay to eat your dinner. I don't want to throw it away."

Eying the steak for a moment, then him, Aleksi knew she had to protect him from his own misguided desires. She made a decision. "I'm *not* the woman you fell in love with, Dr. Hutchinson." She moved in a burst of blinding speed, snatching the meat off the plate before he could even blink. She wolfed it down in two bites, bone and all, her teeth crunching and shearing. She swallowed and licked her lips with her forked tongue and saw the flash of shock on his face. She'd scared him. *Good...* "I'm not a woman at all. Find someone else to fuck."

"Aleksi, you—"

But she was already gone, out the door and off the balcony, her wings catching the warm night air in a rush of sound that drowned out his words.

Mary Buckmann showed her DHS ID to the security guard at the O'Neill Federal Building in Downtown Boston and submitted to the fingerprint and retinal scan. The guard smiled at her from behind his monitor and waved her through the detector.

"Welcome, Dr. Buckmann."

"Thank you." Mary retrieved her briefcase from the scanner and wondered if the upgraded security was really doing any good. Whoever had impersonated her six months ago had passed fingerprint scans. *Let it go. Get back to the job.*

The bitterness of being abducted still lingered, her identity stolen, impersonated, her project destroyed, her good reputation tarnished. She'd proven beyond the shadow of a doubt that she had, indeed, been impersonated. Video evidence of the culprit, although convincing on the surface, didn't hold up under scrutiny. Mary had a tiny scar behind her left ear from a childhood accident that the doppelganger had not possessed, and personal mannerisms didn't quite match. When she'd regained consciousness in a motel room with three weeks of her life missing, she reported to the Director with a raging hangover, ten pounds lighter. They'd done a full health workup and found degradation products of anesthetic and amnestic agents in her blood. After a week of tests, they'd released her, but the debriefing, interviews, and investigations had taken months. She was still under scrutiny, in fact, and only now was being given a real assignment.

Mary got off the elevator and passed through yet another checkpoint, this time handing over her sidearm and jacket to undergo a mass-density scan—because the fear of surgically implanted explosives was the latest phobia, and the government didn't give a damn about anyone's cancer paranoia—and picked it all up on the other side. Finally, she stood at the Director's reception desk.

"Buckmann. I have a five p.m. with the Director."

"Yes, Doctor. Good to see you again." The young man waved her on with a smile. "You're good to go in."

"Thank you." Mary strode to the Director's door, and the light on the latch turned green as she reached for it. She stepped in to find the Director and three others already waiting for her. They all stood, and the three visitors turned to face her. She recognized two security specialists she'd worked with before, Larry North and Sharice Kosta, and one other scientist, Blake Withers.

"Mary, good to see you." The Director waved to the single empty chair. "Have a seat. You know everyone here, so I'll forego the pleasantries. We should be able to wrap this up quickly."

"Thank you, sir." Mary took her seat and fished a tablet from her case.

"So, you all know this is pretty much a rubber stamp approval. We've gone over every molecule of data we could find, and there's *zero* doubt in my mind that Mary *was*, in fact, impersonated. What I need is everyone's off-the-record opinions of what happened and how we can prevent it from happening again." He looked at his watch. "It's technically after hours, and I'm hereby stating that we are *all* off duty, so not a word of what's said here will be recorded or can come back to bite anyone on the ass."

Of course, that didn't mean shit, but it might encourage a modicum of honesty.

"You first, Larry."

"Sure." Larry shifted and made brief eye-contact with Mary. "From an IT standpoint, I still don't understand how anyone got Mary's passwords. The print scanners can be fooled, sure, and the disguise…well, not my bailiwick, but her passwords were written down nowhere, transmitted nowhere, and were basically available only through multiple layers of encryption or from Mary directly. Our systems were either hacked without our knowledge, or her *brain* was hacked without hers. Frankly, *both* those possibilities scare the shit out of me."

"As they should," the Director agreed. "As of now, our encryption has been upgraded, which we *hope* has addressed the first possibility. We're working under the assumption that the information was delved directly from Mary under the influence of various drugs."

"Sir, I—"

He held up a hand to forestall her. "I've read your report on that, Mary. No fault of yours if this happened. We need to know how to defend against it happening again." He turned to the next security specialist. "Sharice?"

"Yes, sir. We're working on a bio-monitoring chip that transmits constant data. It's still in development, but variances in biometric data should tell us if any of our people are compromised for more than twelve hours." She shrugged. "Of course, there's nothing to prevent someone transplanting the chip into an impersonator, but the gap in data should be detectable. The analytics software's still in development. How they managed to fool voiceprint is still anyone's guess. They didn't use a recording, and the analysis matched Mary's closely enough to get by."

"Keep on that." The Director turned to the only other scientist in the room. "Blake?"

"Direct DNA testing would have caught this impersonator, sir, but it takes time, and it would cost a bucket-load of money to implement." He shrugged helplessly. "It'd be virtually impossible to put in place in all our installations, but we might consider placing it in key facilities."

"That's a budget nightmare, but I'll pitch it. What about our current upgrades?"

"Retinal scans are good, but they're not foolproof. Surgically implanted lenses can fool them."

"But these lenses would be detectable with our mass-density scanner, right?"

"Not really. The use of polymers that are barely more dense than human tissue would probably fool it." He shrugged helplessly. "Mary's impersonator had matching fingerprints, and facial recognition software didn't penetrate the disguise. However it was done, they knew their shit."

"No doubt there." The Director frowned and turned to Mary.

"Well, Mary, your honest opinion?"

As if she would give a dishonest one. "*Honestly,* I'm still pissed as hell, sir." That got some shocked stares, but a wry smile from the Director.

"Frankly, if someone could snatch me out of a coffee shop, impersonate me, and fool everyone in the Laurence Street facility, they could do the same to anyone else in this room, including *you*, sir. We know the impersonator wasn't wearing prosthetics, and I can't believe they planned to mimic me far enough in advance to have someone undergo surgery. If they had, they would have trained them to mimic my mannerisms better." Mary nodded to the tech people. "I've suggested pattern recognition software, like facial recognition but to analyze full body motion, hand gestures, gait, posture, but all I've gotten back is blank looks."

"The software to discern someone's identity from gait has been a failure from the get-go, sir," Larry countered.

"He's right, Mary. I've seen the reports," the Director said.

"I'm not talking *identity* recognition, sir, but *pattern* recognition in comparison with baseline data we probably already have for every employee." She pulled up a video on her tablet. "Look here. This is me and my impersonator on video walking away from a CCTV pickup." She Bluetoothed the video to the flat-screen on the wall and played it for everyone. "If *I* can see the difference between us, a computer should be able to."

They all watched the video of two Mary Buckmanns, both dressed similarly, hair similar, body shape similar, walking away from the camera. The one on the left bounced and swung her hips much more than the one on the right.

"I'm on the right. The software wouldn't have to say that was me, only that the *other* one was different than expected."

"Larry?" The Director pinned him with a flat stare.

"I'll get my people on it, sir." He sounded contrite, but Mary knew better. Larry was pissed that he'd been shown up by a lab geek.

"Do that." The Director scanned the faces. "Anything else?"

"Only that I'm eager to get back to work, sir." Mary shut off the video. "I'm sick to death of watching video of my impersonator."

"Then you're not going to like the assignment I have for you, I'm afraid." He stood, so everyone else did. "We're done here, as far as the rest of you go. I expect reports from you all within the week. You don't need to know the details of Mary's assignment."

They all left the room, and the Director went to a credenza opposite the video. "Something to drink? We're off the clock."

"No, thank you, sir." She put her tablet away, unsure whether to be offended or reassured by his offer. He knew she didn't drink, but he was being polite. It didn't matter; she braced herself for the news. "What's my assignment?"

"Let me first assure you that you're not going to receive any serious black marks on your record for what happened." He shoveled ice into a glass and poured something over it. A peaty aroma filled the room. "I'm also sorry I can't assign you to the project that you were intended to take over. We've already reassigned it."

"The Johansen Project?" DHS projects were often nick-named after the fictitious names of their project heads. "There *is* no project, sir. Penningly's body *and* the sample were both stolen. We had some backups of the digital data, but..."

"Oh, there's a project, all right." He turned to her and smiled as he sipped his drink. "We sequestered backup samples from the specimen *and* Penningly, and the DNA's been fully sequenced and compiled. You didn't think we'd put all of our eggs in one basket, did you?"

A thrill of hope flared in Mary's gut. "Sir, I'm intimately familiar with that project, I really should—"

He waved her to silence. "We already moved to another facility, and the work's well underway."

Mary's hope died like a moth in a flame. "They've made progress?"

"Significant progress, yes. It's strictly need-to-know, but I'll keep you in the loop. What I really need from you is to keep digging into what happened before. I want you to find out who impersonated one of my best supervisors right down to her goddamn fingerprints!" He raised his glass to her. "I want you to find these fuckers, Mary. They hacked us hard and stole a significant asset."

"Very well, sir." Mary considered her progress, or lack of it, and decided to dangle one more hook in front of him. "I may have a line on the *other* subject in the Johansen Project, sir, but things are still in development."

"Rychenkna?" The ice clinked in his glass, and his brow furrowed.

"Yes. Whoever stole my identity also stole Penningly's corpse *and* the original sample. If they were interested in those, they'd be interested in Rychenkna."

He nodded. "How?"

"The only lead we ever had, sir. Dr. Hutchinson."

He frowned, then nodded. "All right, Mary, but be careful. We don't need a media shitstorm, and if Rychenkna finds out you're digging into Hutchinson, she'll be pissed. I *don't* want her pissed. Is that clear?"

"Crystal clear." She gave him a subtle smile. "Don't worry, sir. I've got someone on the inside."

T*hat scent...* Aleksi had been right, it was familiar, and now she knew why she'd smelled it in Hutch's place.

Julie Parks left her bike chained to the rack of Hutch's condo building and bounced into the foyer, skin-tight yoga pants girding her shapely legs. Her pink sports bra and fluorescent green tank top were more of an emphasis of her stunning figure than they were covering anything. *So, Hutch is seeing my old roommate.* Suppressing the cold knot of jealousy in her gut, Aleksi told herself this was a good thing. Julie was fun, sexy, vivacious, and nice. She enjoyed men like other women enjoyed chocolate. She was exactly what Hutch needed, nothing serious, just fun.

...find someone else to fuck! She wondered if he already had, and felt that surge of jealousy again.

Aleksi hadn't gone home to her subway hideaway that day, but stayed in the heights of a huge oak tree north of Hutch's condo building. The thick foliage afforded concealment and a good view of his window. He hadn't gone to bed after she left, but stood on the balcony drinking coffee. He'd gone to work at the usual time and come home early. Now she knew why. She waited and watched.

Dragon ears picked up the tone of Hutch's doorbell, and Aleksi watched him cross in front of the windows to answer the door. He wore his jogging clothes. She couldn't quite make out their voices over the rush-hour traffic noise, but watched them as Hutch went to his kitchen and retrieved a water bottle from the fridge. Julie leaned against the counter, her eyes on his ass as he bent down into the fridge.

Yep, she's hunting all right. Aleksi grinned without humor, knowing where this would go. Her teeth chirped together, and she tried to relax. This would be good for Hutch, and she liked Julie. *You're in for quite a treat, Julie...*

She watched them leave the condo, then emerge from the foyer. They stretched for a few minutes—more Julie watching Hutch's ass, but not so much him watching hers—then jogged off. Aleksi stayed where she was, forced to wait for nightfall. She hadn't moved a muscle all day, long practiced in the art of patience, waiting, staying perfectly still...the skills of a predator.

But I'm not hunting, she reminded herself. She let her eyes sag closed, her ears attuned to her surroundings, wary, and drifted off to a light sleep.

"Want to come up for something cool to drink?"

Hutch's voice snapped Aleksi's eyes open. He and Julie were stretching again, both drenched in sweat, skin glistening in the fading light of sunset. They'd been out for more than an hour.

"Sure!" Julie dragged her mop of blonde curls back and bound them in a scrunchie, still breathing hard. "I ran out of water at three miles."

"Hope I didn't push you too hard." Hutch went to the door and held it open for her.

"Not at all." Julie went through, and Hutch followed, but before the door swung closed, Aleksi heard, "I need someone to push me."

That didn't sound very seductive. Julie wasn't usually subtle with men; if she wanted something, she asked for it and usually got it.

Except with Bob Tomlin, Aleksi reminded herself. When Julie and Bob were going out, she hadn't pushed him into anything physical. He'd been murdered before they did anything more than kiss, and Julie had been a complete wreck. Now, maybe, she'd found another nice man. *Maybe he'll be good for her, too.* Aleksi wondered how long they'd been working out together. They didn't interact like they were intimate yet.

Aleksi looked at the sunset, longing to move, to leave, to not witness what might happen in Hutch's home, but she had another hour, at least, before it would be dark enough.

Through Hutch's balcony windows, she watched them come in. Hutch went to the fridge and pulled two drinks from the door, and the clatter of Iggy rattling his cage came through clearly. The traffic noises were lower now, and Aleksi could make out their voices. Julie bent down and said hello to the iguana.

"Ice?" Hutch held out a bottle of iced tea.

"This is fine." Julie stood up, cracked the bottle, and drank. Then she pressed the cold glass to her forehead and then her upper chest. "I don't know whether to drink it or poor it over my head. I think I overheated."

"Here." Hutch turned back to the fridge, and Aleksi heard the ice machine in the door grinding. Then the water ran, and he turned to Julie holding a dish towel wrapped around a bundle. "Press that to the back of your neck."

"Thanks." Julie took the bundle and pressed it to her neck. "God, that feels good."

"Old trick." Hutch tilted his bottle of iced tea and drank.

"I've been meaning to ask you something, Hutch." Julie pressed the cold compress to the front of her neck.

Here it comes...

"Sure."

"About Aleksi."

Aleksi tensed. *She's asking him about me? What the...*

"What about her?" Aleksi could hear the tension in Hutch's voice.

"I wondered if you two…if you ever got together with her." Julie put her drink down and lifted her shirt to run the cold compress over her stomach. "She seemed different after she met you."

"Once, yes, right after Bob was killed." Hutch put his drink down. "You'd gone out of town, and she asked me to be her alibi, just to watch over her. She was pretty freaked out, and so was I. We…she stayed the night here, but then vanished."

"Huh. I thought it would have been before that. She just seemed so…*different.*" Julie finished with the cold compress and handed it to him. "Thanks."

"No problem." He dropped it in the sink.

"You don't know where she went?" She sat on one of the counter stools and sipped her drink.

"No idea." Hutch evidently wondered the same thing Aleksi was thinking. "Why the interest?"

"I get calls from her parents every so often. They're crushed. It'd be nice to be able to tell them something."

Aleksi felt a pang of guilt for not contacting her parents, but she knew it was too risky. There would be questions she couldn't answer, and her mother would never relent. *But why is she asking about me?* Aleksi could tell by Julie's body language that she was flirting, but Julie always flirted. She did it subconsciously. But what was coming out of her mouth wasn't flirtatious at all. *What's she up to?*

"We were pretty close, and you know how…shy she was. I just wondered, like, why she changed so all-of-the-sudden. I figured if you two were doing it, it might have given her some confidence. You know?"

"No, we just got together once, then she left." Hutch finished his iced tea and turned to rinse the bottle. He said something low, but Aleksi couldn't hear it over the running water.

"I'm sorry, Hutch." Julie rounded the counter. "I didn't mean to—"

"It's okay." Hutch turned around with a sad smile, and Julie was right there. "I've been told that I should move on with my life."

Yes...by me.

"Are you?" Julie put a hand on his chest and looked up at him. "Moving on, I mean? Because my shrink's been telling me to get over Bob for six months, and all I can do is feel like I'm cheating on him."

What the... Julie Parks, stuck on a man for six months? A dead man, at that? Aleksi could barely believe it.

"I'm trying to." Hutch cleared his throat. "But yeah, I pretty much feel the same way."

"Do...you think we could...help each other?" Julie leaned in.

"I think we could try." Hutch bent down.

Aleksi heard the crunch of wood, her claws piercing the hard oak as she watched them kiss. The urge to fly into the room and rip Julie apart surged up in her so profoundly that she felt she might explode. They kissed deeply and fondled each other in a fumbling, groping rush of sweat and skin. She watched Julie fumble Hutch's sweaty shirt over his head, then her own, then her jog bra.

I told him to... Aleksi made herself watch every moment of it. Her teeth ground together when Julie pulled his shorts down and knelt before him, her head bobbing and weaving enthusiastically. The ecstasy on Hutch's face felt like a knife in her heart.

I told him to find someone... She stared, transfixed when Hutch swept Julie into his arms and carried her to the couch. He flung her down almost violently, jerking her stretch pants off and burying his face in her manicured tuft of pubic hair. Julie cried out, clenching her hands in his hair, arching and bucking.

Do it! I told you to do it! Aleksi flexed her talons deep into the tree limb, envisioning herself there as Julie Parks writhed and cried out, arms and legs shuddering.

I could have had that...would have had that...but I made him stop.

Finally, Julie clutched Hutch by the hair and pulled him up, breathless. "Condoms!"

Not very romantic, but at least she was being safe.

"Bedroom," Hutch replied.

Julie locked her legs around his hips. "Take me there!" She squealed as he lifted her and carried her out of Aleksi's view into the bedroom.

The drapes there were thankfully drawn, but Aleksi forced herself to listen, telling herself that it was her fault. When the sounds of their lovemaking finally subsided, it was well past dark and safe for Aleksi to move. She retracted her claws from the hard oak one at a time. *Quiet...careful...*

"I'm sorry if I hurt you," Hutch said, and Aleksi froze, feeling for an instant like he was talking to her.

"You didn't." Julie sounded more spent than after their run. "Well, maybe a little, but sometimes you have to hurt to heal."

"There is that." The bed creaked. "Shower?"

"Sure." The bed creaked again, and Aleksi heard the hiss of water.

"I told him to do it…" Aleksi removed her last claw from the tree and checked for people down on the street. "I'm glad he did it. Julie's right. Sometimes you have to hurt to heal…"

She launched herself into the night, her wings filled by the sultry summer air, taking comfort in the notion that Hutch was finally getting over her. Julie would be good for him. She was everything that Aleksi wasn't: happy, vivacious, funny, pretty…and human.

"I *told* him to…" Tears streaked down her scaly cheeks, but she blamed the wind, not her breaking heart.

There was still a ball of jealousy and longing in her gut as she soared over the Charles River back toward the concealing concrete canyons of Boston, but she knew she'd been right. Hutch needed someone. He needed a woman who could fulfill his human desires.

He needed someone…not me.

2

After the shower, and another far more inventive and less enthusiastic coupling with Julie, they dried each other off, and he wrapped her in a spare robe. As they gathered up her scattered running clothes, guilt rose up from his gut like a sickening tide, both for betraying Aleksi and for deceiving Julie. All the time they'd made love, he'd been thinking of Aleksi. Julie didn't deserve that.

"Something to eat?" He opened the fridge and grimaced. "Or we could order in."

"No, I should go." She pulled on her sweat-damp yoga pants with a grimace.

"You don't have to, Julie. Really, I don't..." Didn't what? Want her to leave? He realized that he did, and that she knew it. "I'm sorry."

"Hey, don't be *sorry*, Hutch!" She smiled and came to him. "I wanted this. I *needed* it. I think you needed it too. We've both been sleeping with ghosts for too long."

"Sleeping with ghosts..." *Or with a dragon.* He closed his eyes and shook his head. "I can't get her out of my head. Even when we..."

"I *know*, Hutch, and it's okay." Her arms snaked around him, and she squeezed. "I *wanted* this, and you *gave* it to me. This doesn't have to be anything more than you want it to be, but I don't want to...just throw it away."

He held her, amazed at her frank honesty. "No, I…I don't want to throw it away either, but…"

She pulled away and looked up at him, a smile on her lips and tears in her eyes. "But you can't stop thinking about Aleksi. I get it. She was lucky to have you, Hutch, for a friend *and* a lover. It wasn't fair for her to just leave without ever calling you or anything."

He felt guilty again, this time for lying to her, but he couldn't betray Aleksi's trust. "Maybe it *was* fair, from her standpoint."

"From *her* standpoint? I don't get it."

"She didn't want to risk my career. She said so, even before we…were together. When the warrant for her arrest came out, I think she just snapped. If the cops found out we were sleeping together, it would have been…complicated."

"Yeah, I get it, but she could have at least *called* you."

"Not without the cops tracking her down. I'm pretty sure my phone was tapped."

"Your *cell*?" Julie's brow furrowed. "They can *do* that?"

"Pretty sure they can, and it was a murder investigation."

Her face fell suddenly. "Yeah, I remember."

"Sorry, Julie. I didn't mean to dredge that up." He took her by the shoulders. "So, honesty time. I like being with you, Julie. You're pretty, and funny, and sexy, and you make me feel alive. I don't want to throw that away, but I want you to know that I'm not…feeling for you what you might think I am."

"Wow, that *is* honesty!" She laughed, however, and poked him in the stomach. "So, Dr. Hutchinson, can *I* ask *you* something?"

"Anything." *If she asks about Aleksi one more time…*

"Would you mind terribly if I come over occasionally and fuck you silly?" She fondled him under the robe. "Even if it's only physical?"

"No, I—" He caught his breath as her skilled fingers teased him. Guilt rose up again, but Aleksi's words also returned to him. *Find someone else to fuck.* She'd told him to, and he had. And the truth was, he *had* needed this. "I'd like that."

"Good!" She gave him a squeeze and let go. "Maybe not again tonight. I've been celibate too long, and I'm a little sore." She doffed her robe and wiggled into her sports bra and shirt.

"Can I at least drive you home? It's dark."

"Sure! Thanks!"

So, Hutch got dressed and drove Julie home. They didn't talk a lot on the way, but it wasn't far. When he pulled up in front of the apartment and helped her take her bike off the rack, he remembered the night he'd dropped Aleksi off after the evening with Congressman Twain, the night she'd propositioned him and he'd refused her.

"Hey."

He turned to find Julie staring at him.

She reached out and gripped his shoulder. "Where'd you go?"

"Just memories." He smiled and squeezed her hand. "No worries."

"Okay." She didn't look convinced, but accepted the evasion. "Go for a run with me on Saturday?"

"Sure." She leaned in, so he kissed her again, trying not to think of Aleksi. "And thanks, Julie, for being honest with me."

"And thank you, Dr. Hutchinson, for being an *amazing* lover and so *ridiculously* nice!" She gave him another peck and wheeled her bike toward her door. "Give me a call."

"I will!" Hutch got in his car, watched her go into the apartment building, and drove away, wondering what he was getting himself into.

He'd never been much for casual sex, but Julie was all the things he'd said: interesting, pretty, funny, sexy, and… He let himself think it. *And human.* Aleksi was human; he knew she was, but she was also right about the risk of them being intimate. Whatever had changed her so dramatically could be infectious. If he contracted it from her…

What?

Maybe they could be together for real, two dragons flying through the skies of Boston. But Aleksi would feel responsible. She would think she'd ruined his life. Then again, Hutch was the one who had brought her into the bone-bed project in the first place. If she had turned him down, she would never have contracted the infection. She would still be human.

But there was hope. Maybe, someday, she could be fully human again.

On a whim, he tapped his phone. "Call Lonnie."

It rang and she answered, "Hutch! It's late. What's up."

"Nothing really. I just wondered if you might like to catch lunch this week. I'd love to know how your new project is going."

"Oh, sure. Why don't you come into the city tomorrow? We'll grab some sushi, and I'll show you what we're working on."

"Cool! Ichiban around one? They're always crushed for lunch."

"See you there."

"Thanks!" He disconnected and tried to concentrate on the drive home.

He thought he should probably eat, but the notion of food couldn't compete with the last three hours of memories. Julie, Aleksi, sex, love, honesty, lies, secrets, and hope all whirled around in a tornado in Hutch's mind. Of all those things, however, hope was what kept him breathing.

Mary Buckmann was a biologist, not an investigator, but she was also the agent most intimately involved with the unsolved mystery of her own impersonation. Consequently, the investigation was hers, and she couldn't refuse. After all, the Director had pointed out that she'd already been investigating it unofficially for months, so she might as well continue, and anything she could dig up on Aleksi Rychenkna would be invaluable to the Johansen Project.

The Johansen Project, *her* project. It was moving forward, and someone else had been put in charge of it. Secretly, Mary wondered if she'd been given this assignment because there was still a lasting stigma of mistrust hanging over her head.

Regardless, continue the investigation she would. She was a team player and went where she was told to go. Consequently, she sat at the very same desk in the Laurence Street facility where her doppelganger had given the orders to box up and ship out the project's samples.

The facility as a whole had been repurposed, but this floor of the building was ground zero of a serious security breech, and the scene of an active crime investigation. DHS took its violation personally and wouldn't close the investigation until it was solved. As such, the floor where the impersonation had taken place had still not been repurposed. Forensics had gone over every millimeter and had precious little to show for it. They had gotten a lot of Penningly's DNA, and had recovered samples of hair, skin, saliva, and other less savory bodily fluids, from almost every employee who had worked in the facility. They also had two other samples. One was from Dwayne Hutchinson. The other, she hoped, was from her impersonator.

She reviewed the best video they had of those two people together, the interview where the Buckmann look-alike grilled Hutchinson right here in this facility. She'd watched it a thousand times, and would watch it a thousand more, but each time, anger smoldered beneath her calm, analytical scrutiny.

Mary was a biologist, and had been focusing on those aspects of the case, playing to her strengths. The mystery DNA sample had already been analyzed, but she knew little about its owner: female, predominantly Anglo-French heritage, and the individual's DNA had never been sequenced by any family history service, intelligence service, or police department. If the DNA of any new suspect matched that sequence, however, Mary had her doppelganger. So far, she had zero suspects.

Mary still had no memory of her abduction. She'd picked up a coffee at her favorite shop and continued on her way to work. CCTV cameras had recorded her at the shop and leaving it, but she had no recollection of the walk or speaking to anyone. Street cameras had glimpsed her here and there, then...nothing. She had the area of the abduction nailed down to a five-block radius, but that was huge, and hundreds of vehicles had come and gone through that area in the minutes after the last recording of Mary. Someone had called in sick for her, and her assistant had simply logged it without suspicion. The next recording of her, or rather, of her impersonator, had been when she'd arrived at the Laurence Street facility a few days later. The woman had driven her car, worn her clothes, lived in her apartment, eaten her food, and slept in her bed. Hell, she'd even used her credit cards and done her laundry. For the first time in her life, Mary was grateful that she lived alone, for if she'd had a husband or boyfriend, she felt sure that the imposter would have filled that role as well.

Mary had awoken in a Worchester motel room, fully clothed, weak, and hung over, the tiny wound of an IV in her left arm. All of her things were on her person, and, seeing the date on her phone, she'd immediately called the DHS emergency line. The medical examinations and debriefings had been grueling, but she hadn't complained. Her life had been stolen. She wanted answers as badly as everyone else.

Whatever those answers were, she felt sure they were tangled up in this bizarre fossil that had infected Derrick Penningly and Aleksi Rychenkna. The list of organizations and rival states who would be interested in stealing the sample was long, but they had no leads that any foreign government or terrorist group had been in play. *So, who?*

All their sparse evidence pointed to a small, covert organization with considerable resources, both financial and technical. Mary had a list of known groups that fit that profile, but none of them had ever shown interest in paleontology. But this sample was more than a fossil, it was a weapon, or could be, if it got into the wrong hands.

Find it, and you find your impersonator, Mary told herself, replaying the recording of the Hutchinson interview once again, watching every nuance, memorizing every word.

Two things the impersonator had said during that interview struck her every time she watched it. First, when Mary's doppelganger slid a paper cup of coffee across the table, she said, "Strong and dark with milk, no sugar, right?" This told Mary that the woman knew Hutchinson far better than DHS did. Their file on Hutchinson was extensive, but didn't go so far as to list his beverage preferences. Secondly, when the woman called him "Hutch" instead of by his name, further suggesting familiarity. It was well documented that Hutchinson's friends, students, and coworkers called him by the nickname, and one interviewee had mentioned that he disliked "Dwayne," and had picked up the moniker in high school. That opened up a huge number of possibilities, but it lent credence to the theory that the impostor knew him.

Which narrows the list of possibilities from millions down to mere thousands!

A message icon blinked in the corner of Mary's monitor. She paused the recording and opened it. It was from the Director and had several large attachments. The message itself consisted of only two short sentences. "Need-to-know only. You are now in the loop."

The attachments were all labeled with the primer "Johansen."

"Yes!" She opened the Project Summary file and started to read.

The project was broken down into phases. Phase One was Derrick Penningly, and although that had ended badly, they'd gotten a lot of data from him. Mary had already read most of it.

Phase Two was the genetic analysis of the original sample itself. That analysis was complete and frustratingly inconclusive. There were inconsistences in the data, sequence variances from sample to sample. The best working theory was that the specimen was transitional, that it had been encased in a pyroclastic ash fall while still in its infancy, halfway between human and the endpoint. They were calling that endpoint *Homo draconis*, which seemed a bit theatrical to Mary. The basis for this theory was the similarity in the sequence variances between the sample and those collected from Derrick Penningly while he was in transition. They had no sample of the endpoint, of course, and as far as anyone knew, there was only one place they could get it: Aleksi Rychenkna.

But that didn't mean they couldn't manufacture a new source.

Phase Three, animal trials, had been going on for three months, but none of the trials had gone to fruition. There were no viable results. All subjects had died in various stages of infection. Most, the rodents, canine, feline, and bovine—*They put this in a cow? Really?*—had died in very early stages, before any outward changes had taken place. Primate testing had yielded better results, but still offered no viable endpoint. She followed the link to the best-result study and stared at the images of the two-year-old female chimpanzee they'd inoculated. The twisted half-chimp, half-something else, turned her stomach. Whatever this was, it had evolved specifically in humans after the evolutionary split with other primates. That it didn't work in chimpanzees, even considering the high degree of genetic similarity between the species, supported this theory. Interestingly, the chimp had progressed far enough to show significant skeletal and organ changes, and upon its death, the altered bones had degraded with astonishing rapidity. Some had been preserved, of course, flash frozen in liquid nitrogen, but most had crumbled to dust, dust not unlike that found inside the original sample.

Which is why we haven't found this in the fossil record, Mary thought.

Although they had not had any successful trials, they had isolated the infective agent. The original sample, besides the organism's semi-transformed DNA, was packed with ultra-short segments of RNA that were similar to viruses and had sequences prevalent in some cancers. These segments attacked the subject's cells, hotwiring ribosomes to initiate a cascade of gene-switching proteins. These, in turn, activated segments of the genome, previously considered "trash" regions, that in turn coded for more gene-switching proteins. Changes in the subject's actual DNA sequence began with normal cell replication, but transformative protein production began almost immediately upon inoculation. This initial phase was where most of the animal subjects had died due to a brain inflammation similar to encephalitis. Penningly had reported a three-day fever with some flu-like symptoms, including a headache, after his initial infection, which corroborated these findings.

Then Mary saw the header, "Phase Four: Human Trials," and her heart skipped a beat.

Who the hell could they find to volunteer for that?

But as she read on, she found there were no shortage of volunteers. Most were former soldiers, covert ops specialists, or government operatives in their fifties or early sixties and sporting steadily declining performance ratings. They'd all been told up front that the project would likely end their careers as operatives and was dangerous in the extreme. The exclusion criteria were rigorous, the foremost being psychological stability.

"Well, *that's* good at least." Putting this into another psycho like Penningly was a non-starter.

They'd narrowed the candidates to five, all of whom were former soldiers and male. That niggled in the back of Mary's brain like a silent alarm. Something she'd watched clicked into her mind, and she opened a screen on her display, searching through her video files. She found the one she wanted and called it up. She'd only watched this one a few times, since it was poor quality from a security goon's body cam.

The shaky frame included three figures: the Buckmann imposter, Dwayne Hutchinson, and the dragon, Aleksi Rychenkna. The background showed a row of floor-to-ceiling windows and the nighttime Boston skyline from the top of the Prudential Tower.

Mary fast forwarded to the segment she wanted, and hit play.

"You want to create some kind of...weapon out of this." Aleksi gestured to her own face with one clawed hand. The imposter flinched back. "You're playing with a fire you can't control. It's more dangerous than anything the human race has ever discovered. It'll destroy civilization if you let it loose."

Mary hit pause. "Destroy civilization…" She ran the recording back to near the beginning. There was one more thing Aleksi had said. She hit play again.

"...evolved to protect humans, but in him*...it didn't. It may work differently in men than women. Whatever he is, the changes, his violent impulses, are out of control."*

"Different in men than in women?" Could it have been that simple? Could the transformation amplify typical male aggression to the point beyond reason? If so, how could it evolve at all? Penningly had been a borderline sociopath to begin with, a serious egotist with a long record of relying on his family's money to get him out of trouble. He'd treated women like shit all through college, and had stolen another student's senior project, which was probably what he'd planned to do to Aleksi.

The Director had undoubtedly seen this recording and heeded the warning. Veteran special ops agents were some of the most psychologically stable people in the world. The project leaders knew what they were doing and would take every precaution. Mary knew this, and yet her heart pounded in her chest at the notion of putting this infection into a soldier.

"Relax, Mary. They're on this." She closed the summary and got back to work. She had her own investigation to do.

3

God, I honestly hate her sometimes, Mary thought as Julie Parks bounced into the packed Cambridge restaurant.

The young woman wore a red beret, a white blouse off one shoulder showing one pink bra strap, a wide black sash around her hips, ripped jeans, and a pair of low-heel red sling-backs. Mary wouldn't have been caught dead in the outfit. Parks not only made it work but drew half the eyes in the place as she spotted Mary and waved. She worked her way through the crowd effortlessly, a blazing smile painted on her face.

"Aunt Mary, you look *awesome*!"

Mary stood and played her part. "Hi Jules. Glad you could make it." She had dressed as casually as she could, considering her wardrobe, but her jeans and a green polo shirt had drawn zero looks when she came in. After enduring a sisterly embrace, she sat and motioned to the other chair. "So good to see you!"

"You too!" Julie slung her micro-purse over the back of the chair and sat. "So, how's the new job?"

"Oh, it's good. My supervisor's a dick, but you know how it goes."

Julie laughed genuinely and waved a waiter over. Mary had to admit, the woman could act. Of course, drama was Julie's field of study. She might look like a bimbo, but she wasn't just another brain-donor. Harvard didn't accept fools into graduate studies, and Julie could not only act, but write, direct, and produce, and was probably looking at a serious career in either the film or theatre industry. Mary hated her a little more as the waiter took their orders, his eyes fixed upon Julie the whole time. They chit-chatted until people stopped paying attention to them, then finally got down to business.

"So, I got my loan statement." Julie sipped lemon water and smiled thinly. "I suppose I should thank you."

"You're welcome." The government student loan forgiveness program had seen fit to miraculously wipe Julie's student loan away. Of course, it had hardly been a miracle. Mary had pushed it through as compensation for services rendered to the Department of Homeland Security. "How is Dr. Hutchinson?"

"Really nice, actually." Julie's eyes went flinty. "*So* nice, in fact, that I truly feel like shit doing this."

Oh, you poor thing, Mary thought venomously. "We *all* have to do things that are distasteful, Miss Parks. Get used to it."

"Nice." Julie made a face and lowered her voice. "But call me Julie or Jules, Aunt *Mary*. Or is it too *distasteful* for you to act like a human being for ten minutes?"

Mary gritted her teeth at being taken to task by a civilian. "Point taken. So, any progress with the location of our friend?" They'd agreed to refer to Aleksi by that ambiguous designation.

"No. Total stone wall. I did coax out of him that they'd at least had a relationship, but it was like a one-night stand. They did it for the very first time the night the cops put out the murder warrant on her, then she vanished."

"They were intimate?" Mary wondered how Hutchinson hadn't contracted the transformative infection. An exchange of bodily fluids, even saliva, should have done it. Analysis of cheek swabs from Penningly during his transformation had yielded the infective RNA strands. Somehow, Hutchinson had evaded the infection. Mary wondered if he could somehow be immune.

"Well, *yeah*! What do you *think*?" Someone called Julie's name from across the restaurant and she turned to wave, then turned back. "I mean you can't blame her for *that*. Hutch is a catch. He's *also* still *totally* in love with her."

That, Mary could use. "He told you that?"

"Not in so many words, but he is. Can't stop thinking about her, you know, the usual." She made a vague motion with one hand and looked away. "He's really hurting. It sucks."

Cry me a river, Mary thought. "And did he admit that he's in contact with her?"

"No. He said he hadn't spoken to her since she vanished. I told him that wasn't fair, that she should have at least called him, but he didn't budge."

"He's lying, Julie," Mary said.

Julie cocked a plucked eye brow and pressed a hand to her heart. "No! Say it isn't *true*!"

"Save it for the theatre, Jules." Mary paused as the waiter delivered their salads, then continued. "He's spoken to her on multiple occasions and met with her at least three times since that night. What we really need to know is where she's staying."

"So, no offense to your investigative prowess, Aunt Mary, but why don't you just ask him for her number? Why all this cloak and dagger bullshit?" Julie speared a piece of romaine and popped it into her mouth.

"Because he's already told us he won't cooperate with us. He thinks we want to put our friend in a cell." Actually, isolation and medical examination would be the least distasteful thing they would probably do if they ever captured Aleksi. Right now, however, the identities of the people who had impersonated Mary were higher priorities. In the end, Aleksi would be a much greater asset helping them with that investigation rather than strapped down to a dissecting table. "The *theory* is that he might confide in a friend."

"Well, he didn't, okay?" Julie kept eating.

Mary drenched her salad in dressing and tried a piece of tomato. "I want you to keep trying. Maybe in time he'll open up to you. Misery loves company."

"Well, he's certainly miserable enough." Julie shook her head. "So, I don't get it. Why is our friend still hiding out? The charges were dropped. Everybody knows Penningly killed Bob. She could probably pick up her enrollment if she came clean about what happened, though she'd probably have to find a new advisor if she got back together with Hutch."

Mary choked on an olive and coughed. "*Probably?*"

Julie made a dismissive gesture. "Okay, the faculty council would have issues with her sleeping with her advisor, but she's like *brilliant*. She could take her pick. Why stay a fugitive?"

Mary had to keep reminding herself that Julie had no idea the changes Aleksi had gone through. She didn't know about the dragons, the battle that had destroyed Hutchinson's home, the mutilations and cannibalism

Penningly had descended to, the lucky shotgun blast from a Cambridge cop that had ended it. And Mary wasn't about to tell her. She had to tell her something, however.

"Your friend has changed, Julie. She's not the person you knew."

"But Hutch is still in *love* with her." Julie shook her head and pushed her plate away. "It's not fucking fair. The *least* she could do is come back and be with him."

Time for a little truth, Mary decided. "We know they're in contact, but she's probably still unwilling to trust the police. We know Hutchinson's helping her, giving her money, food, maybe even paying her rent, but it's all cash, so we can't trace it. We're not interested in hurting or arresting her, Julie, I just need to speak with her. We need her help with another investigation, something that involved Penningly. I'm sorry, but I can't give you any details."

"Right, well you should probably pitch that directly to Hutch, then." Julie leveled a cold stare across the table. "Take me out of the middle of this. I like him too much to pry into his pain like this."

"You think you've done enough to compensate us for what we've done for you?" Mary barked a laugh. "No, Jules, you'll keep seeing Dr. Hutchinson. You owe us. Be careful, but keep up the act. You're good at it. You *are* an actress, after all."

Julie's face flushed, and she leaned over the table. "I told you I *like* him, *Mary*! It's not a fucking act!"

Wow! Touched a nerve there! Mary wondered just how far Julie had gone with Dwayne Hutchinson. "Okay, sorry. That wasn't necessary, I admit it, but we *do* need you to keep seeing him, Julie. He trusts you. Eventually, he'll open up."

"He doesn't trust me enough to betray the woman he loves." Julie dropped her napkin on her plate and stood. "Thanks for lunch." She walked out, drawing more stares.

Mary finished her salad and paid the bill, invisible in the lunchtime crowd. She strolled back to her car, wondering if she might be able to pitch a plea directly to Hutchinson. But she'd watched too many recordings of his interview to think for a minute he'd cooperate without some coercion.

F*riday night and the natives are restless.*

Aleksi peered down at the pulsing Boston nightlife from her vantage atop one of the downtown buildings. She loved downtown, the seething pulse of humanity, the canyons of steel and glass, the constant thrum of motion. It was nothing on the scale of Manhattan, of course, but Boston had its charms. Once again, she longed for winter, when she could disguise herself and mingle with the weekend crowds, but the summer heat had exiled her to the rooftops, shadowed alleys, and trees. Still, she enjoyed watching people, and she found that enjoyment strange.

Prior to her transformation, Aleksi had been largely asocial. Social Anxiety Disorder was the clinical term, and she'd been enough of a scientist to understand she wasn't normal, but she'd never sought counseling or treatment. Taking medication or telling a psychologist her feelings never appealed to her. It had been easier to simply avoid human interaction. Even in her relatively isolated career as a paleontologist, however, other academics expected her to interact, to teach, make presentations, even socialize. She'd dreaded all of it...before the changes.

Now, her isolation wasn't anxiety-based, it was survival.

Curiously, now she actually *enjoyed* watching people, listening to their conversations, reading their body language, making up stories in her mind about them. After months of watching the weekend rituals of the downtown Boston social scene, she probably could have written a thesis on primate mating behavior. The tight groups of men and women, couples, and foursomes in and around the bars and clubs fascinated her. And the clothes, especially around the dance clubs, made her laugh. Always the scientist, she wondered about mating displays in various species, and how backward humans seemed. In most species, it was the male that put on the display, bright plumage, colors, antlers for dominance contests, and the like. In humans, the females seemed more flamboyant, with tight clothes, colors, makeup, ridiculously high heels, jewelry, and near-indecent neck and hemlines to attract the attention of men, or sometimes other women.

Maybe I'll write a paper and have Hutch submit it, she thought with a silent laugh.

Aleksi's stomach growled, and she checked the time. One-thirty, and almost closing time for the bars and clubs. The last trains on weekends ran at two-thirty to take intoxicated party-goers home. The earliest meat packing shops started taking deliveries at three-thirty, and she planned to pick up dinner at one before she flew home. She hated stealing, but the meat distribution centers had little security, and one or two hams or beef loins going missing generally didn't even raise an eyebrow. She'd seen supervisors stuffing whole crates of packed meat into the trunks of their cars on a daily basis.

Wherever there are people, there's crime...

Aleksi launched herself from her rooftop and flew through the dark canyons, above the street lights and security cameras but below the skyline. Her safe zone. She started south—most of the larger packing houses were near the freeway south of downtown—but she still had time to kill. So, she wheeled up to cling to an overhanging cornice near a nexus of dance clubs west of Tufts Medical Center, one of her favorite people-watching perches. They used to call this area the Combat Zone, but it had been cleaned up a lot from the days of seedy strip clubs and dives. It was still pretty seedy, but the clubs were now mostly for dancing and drinking. People would begin leaving for home in crowds soon, and she enjoyed watching them pair up or cling to their tiny groups on their way to the subway stations or parking garages. Sometimes fights broke out. Consequently, there was always a thick police presence, too, so Aleksi kept hidden.

At ten of two, the exodus began.

Aleksi watched the drunken stumbles, the tippy heels, the posturing and posing, the blustering men and giggling women, and wondered why people participated in this bizarre ritual. She'd never understood it—the clothes, the dancing, the hooking up with strangers. It seemed inane, dangerous. Maybe that was the draw: pathological risk-taking behavior. There had to be easier and safer ways to meet people, have fun, and get laid. Even Julie, one of the most social women Aleksi had ever known, had shunned the club scene. She'd declaimed it as too chancy. "Way too many gropers," she'd once said with a grimace. "Those "intimate dance-floors" are way too intimate." Julie preferred a movie or a play, and maybe a small social gathering after with friends. Aleksi had always preferred staying home with a book, work, maybe an Irish coffee, and her boyfriend, Iggy.

Now she was just as alone, above the crowd, watching others touching, fondling, and stumbling down the street. She picked out conversations, watched hands, faces, mannerisms, analyzing and categorizing. *Primate behavior. It's like watching a National Geographic special.*

Then one foursome caught her attention.

All four wore clubwear, the women in tight dresses and heels, the men in dress shirts and tight pants. What caught her eye was the degree that the men were supporting the women as they wove their way down the sidewalk. Aleksi had seen many drunks stumbling, falling, even puking outside the clubs, but the two men looked to be almost carrying the women, guiding their every step, both to a startlingly similar degree. And the men weren't stumbling at all.

Aleksi left her hiding spot to fly closer, another overhanging cornice where the two couples would pass. She clung there, claws gripping the rough concrete, easily supporting her weight. Poised there, she cocked her head to listen, filtering out the background noise to pick out the couples.

"...to go home. I don't feel so good. Where's Brenda?" The woman in the first couple didn't sound drunk; her words weren't slurred, but her gait and manner spoke of serious impairment. She could barely walk, and kept touching her face with her free hand and looking around as if bewildered.

The man with her kept up a constant comforting narrative. "Don't worry. I'm taking you home. You had too much to drink is all. You'll be fine. Brenda's right behind us."

Brenda, presumably the second woman, remained focused on her friend, gripping her escort to stay on her feet. Her escort, however, also kept reassuring her. "We're taking you home. It's okay. You'll be fine. Our car's right over there."

Don't get in the car, Aleksi thought. *Pull out your phone and dial a ride. Don't get in the car.*

But they couldn't hear her thoughts.

The four reached a late-model Taurus sedan, and the guy in the fore unlocked it with a fob. "We'll take you home. Just get in and slide over. You can sleep all the way. Don't worry."

Aleksi felt like screaming as the two men helped the women into the car and then exchanged a victorious grin and a fist bump before following them in. Anger rose up in her, and she considered dropping down to intervene, but there were too many people around, even a pair of cops only a few yards away. Nobody had noticed the men ushering the impaired women into the car, but if Aleksi fell from the sky, they would certainly notice her.

The Taurus pulled away from the curb and turned west at the corner.

Suppressing her more violent urges, Aleksi followed, soaring high and keeping the car easily in sight. The traffic was thick for so late, cars leaving parking structures to join the lanes. Aleksi stayed high enough to keep out of the light, pausing here and there to let the slower Taurus catch up. She didn't know what she intended to do, but she knew in her gut what was going to happen to those two women, and it made her blood boil.

Then the Taurus turned into a parking garage.

"Shit!" Aleksi would lose them in a multi-level maze of cars packed in like sardines in a can. But she could only see one way in, through the ground-level drive up, flooded with light and in plain view of the street. And the automated ticket dispensers were usually covered by video cameras.

She banked into a climb and gripped the building's decorative facing six floors up. She scrabbled around until her head pointed down, finding easy purchase in the bricks with her claws. She watched for a lull in the traffic.

The internet was good for random facts, and Aleksi had done extensive research on video surveillance. Survival compulsion had altered her fields of interest somewhat. Outside of military facilities, CCTV cameras rarely recorded even 30 frames per second, regular commercial ones far less. If she shot through the entrance fast enough, she'd only be a blur in the CCTV pickup. But she couldn't be spotted by a driver or pedestrian, either.

A very long minute ticked past, her heart pounding in her ears, claws grating on the soft mortar between the bricks. *Come on...come on...*

The lights changed and traffic paused. Aleksi released her grip on the building and plummeted toward the street. At the last instant, she banked hard and shot through the entrance into the parking structure. Past the gate in a flash, she had to swerve to avoid walls, pillars, and parked cars. Pulling hard around the first corner ramp, she folded her wings with no collisions and landed in a crouch between two SUV's. Here, she stopped and listened for the Taurus' engine or the squeal of tires on smooth concrete.

Nothing. She'd lost them.

The sounds of the city hummed in the background, masking other noises. Aleksi stepped into the open, cocking her head to listen, straining to parse through the sounds, filter out the background. She turned slowly, concentrating to pick out the faintest anomaly.

"...wanna go *home*!" The faintest whisper of the plea reached her above the background hum of the city, and she snapped into motion, the senses of a predator locking onto direction and distance innately.

She dashed up the levels, wings billowing, rounding corners by latching onto support pillars with her claws and wheeling around them. One level, two levels, then, on the third, she heard another whimpering plea and spotted the Taurus. The car was jostling from the motion inside. The driver's side window was half open, and the woman's moan of misery cut through the sultry air like a knife.

Rage took hold of her, a visceral urge to kill, rend, protect.

Aleksi scrabbled onto the roof of the car and smashed a fist through the driver's side window into the front seat. Her claws latched onto the leg of the man there—he was lying face down on top of one of the women, so his calf was in easy reach. As she yanked him out through the window, his other leg bent wrong, the hip popping out of joint. He flailed and screamed, but then his head met with the edge of the car parked beside the Taurus, and he went limp.

"What the *fuck*? Larry?"

Aleksi dropped him and whirled, her hind claws cutting furrows in the roof. She plunged both fists down through the back window into the rear seat, claws piercing the other man's bare ass, biting deep. She hauled him screaming out.

His shrieks, the blood, the scent of his terror, almost drove Aleksi over the edge. She wanted to plunge her teeth into the back of his neck, sever the spine, taste the salty, warm blood. But the primal urge to kill clashed with everything she cherished as her last vestiges of humanity. She wasn't a killer, a murderer, a beast.

She was, however, *exquisitely* pissed off.

Aleksi flung the screaming man face down onto the torn roof of the car and latched onto the back of his skull with her talons. She pulled him up, hissed in his ear, "Fucking rapist!" and bashed him down hard enough to damage both the sheet metal and his face, but not hard enough to smash bones. Well, not too many bones, anyway.

He went limp.

The dragon crouched there for a moment, heaving breaths, struggling to control the impulse to eviscerate these vile creatures. If these were examples of humanity, maybe it wasn't such a bad thing not to be human any longer. A mumbled cry from the front seat snapped her out of her trance.

"I wanna go *home*!"

The pitiful cry tore at Aleksi's heart and quenched her rage. She hopped down to check on the women, but knew if they saw her, they might panic. There was little doubt that they were either drugged or inebriated to the point of incapacity, but drunk and panicked would be worse. The woman in the back seat lay unmoving, eyes closed, curled in a ball, her breathing slow. Rage boiled in the pit of Aleksi's stomach. In the front seat, her companion was slightly more conscious. She'd rolled onto her side and pulled her knees up, hugging them to her chest, rocking in the seat, muttering her plea to go home over and over.

Drugged certainly, Aleksi thought. *But what the hell am I going to do with them?*

The answer, fortunately, sat in a cradle mounted to the dash—a cell phone, still on, its navigation program active. Aleksi reached in and snatched the phone from the cradle, minimized the map, and pulled up the phone app, her fingers leaving bloody smears on the screen. As she did, she noted barely one bar of service, probably due to the parking structure. But one bar was enough. She punched 911 and waited for an answer.

"Nine-one-one, your call's being recorded. Where is your emergency?"

Aleksi didn't want her voice on the recording, so she put the phone on speaker, leaned through the window she'd smashed, and put it near the muttering woman's mouth.

"I wanna go *home*!" she pleaded.

Aleksi heard the operator's response. "Where are you, ma'am? What's the emergency?"

"I wanna go *home*!" she said again.

"We can take you home if we can find you, ma'am. Where are you?"

"In a car. They said they'd take us home."

"Where's the car, ma'am?"

"Parked," the woman muttered, rocking back and forth. "They said they'd take us home."

"Parked where, ma'am?" Aleksi had to admit, the operator was good, calm and persuasive. He undoubtedly knew he was speaking to someone intoxicated and traumatized. "Can you tell me where you are?"

"We were dancing. At the Guilt. They said they'd take us home."

"Okay, you're in a parked car. On the street or in a structure?"

"It's dark. I can't see out. It's quiet. The window was broken."

"Okay, ma'am, we're sending squad cars to search for you. Can you tell me what street you were on?"

"They turned left from the Guilt. I don't… I want to go *home*! Please! Brenda!"

That would bring the cops looking for a parked car with broken windows in a structure. Or maybe they could track the phone call directly. Aleksi didn't know if the police had that capability, but she knew DHS did. They'd found her that way once, and it had cost her a bullet wound.

To make the search easier, Aleksi pulled the unconscious man off the roof of the car and dumped him between the rows of parked vehicles. Both he and the other were still breathing, but they were cut up and unconscious. Honestly, she wouldn't care if they lived or died—she even toyed with the notion of castration—but she couldn't wait around for a confrontation with the cops. Unfortunately, getting out of the parking structure proved just as challenging as getting in.

She was still looking for a stairwell when she heard sirens echoing up from the street. Then the siren went silent. Tires squealed below. *Score one for the BPD*, she thought, looking for a place to hide.

Vanishing was easy; you either went someplace nobody looked, someplace they couldn't look, or someplace they wouldn't see you if they did look. In her experience, people didn't look up. They looked left and right, and even under cars, but never over their heads. *Bad evolution*, she chided. Leaping up to the ceiling between two thick concrete supports, her clawed fingers and toes gripped the piping of the sprinkler system. Her thoughts drifted to evolution, wondering if search behaviors might reinforce certain human evolutionary theories, when flashing blue lights painted the far wall of the structure. *Focus, Aleksi. Stop being a damned scientist for five minutes!*

The squad car rounded the corner, lit up like a Christmas tree: headlights, spotlights, and flashers. The tires chirped to a stop, headlights gleaming off the bare and bloody ass of the man she'd left lying in the open. The searchlights scanned the parked cars—left and right, not up—and found the damaged Taurus. Both doors opened, and the cops leveled pistols at the unconscious man.

"Police! Don't move!"

Don't think he's moving, Aleksi thought, wondering if they'd shoot him anyway. She really didn't care if they did. She held perfectly still, her body in shadow. They'd *certainly* shoot her.

The officers advanced, moving to the opposing rows of cars to cover each other and keep the unconscious man in sight. They reached the Taurus, and one cop shined a light on the car.

"Got another guy down. Blood. Leg's torn up."

The other cop called in the information on his shoulder mic and advanced on the man lying in the drive. "Multiple stab wounds on both. Alive but unconscious."

"Ambulance in route," the dispatcher responded. "Backup ETA two minutes."

Two minutes to get the hell out of here, Aleksi thought.

"Jesus, Gary, this guy's face is like *flattened*!"

"Yeah, looks like this one took a hit to the head, too, but he's breathing. Check for weapons, but don't move 'em. They're not bleeding out. Leave it for EMS."

"Right." The other bent to check, then Aleksi heard the woman in the front seat.

"I wanna go *home*!"

The cop nearer the car raised his pistol. "Someone in the car, Mike."

"Gotcha!" The other cop left the unconscious man to cover his partner.

They found the two women, and cursed loudly and fluently.

Time to go. Aleksi slipped from hiding while their attention was fixed on the inside of the car. She took some solace in the stream of expletives the cops used. Evidently, they didn't like rapists any more than she did.

She finally found a stairwell and hurried down to the ground floor, trying not to leave bloody handprints on anything, though it was a little late for that. Another siren blared. Cracking the door open half an inch, she peered out. There was way too much light and traffic for her liking. Then another squad car rounded the corner and raced down the street, lights and siren blazing.

Reasoning that every eye on the street would be watching the squad car, Aleksi waited for it to pass, then slipped out the door and scrabbled up the side of the building. Three floors up, she paused to look back.

The squad car slowed and turned into the parking structure she'd just escaped. Backup had arrived, and more sirens were approaching. She was done here. She'd been too late to save the women from being assaulted, but she'd stopped it and kept herself from killing, which was a win, at least.

Aleksi launched herself into the air and soared through the canyons of

Boston, thinking about what she'd done, whether it had been justified. Yes, it had been. A bit of excessive force, maybe, but she'd managed not to kill them. Her stomach rumbled, reminding her about dinner once again. Her claws were still bloody, so she should probably wash her hands first. No telling what kinds of diseases guys like that might carry. She wheeled north toward Boston Common; the lake there would suffice for a quick rinse.

As she flew through the dark, she watched the herds of humans walking toward the Chinatown T station and wondered how many other women would be assaulted tonight. The pit of rage smoldered in her stomach, but she felt a little better about her recent intervention. The cops would find the evidence of what the two rapists had done. The women would get help, and would have their blood tested for drugs. The men would be arrested.

And she hadn't killed them. She'd resisted the dragon's instincts. She was still Aleksi Rychenkna.

4

Mary read the report and tried to keep from grinding her teeth. The department had search programs that scanned police reports, and one had found this from the previous night. What had seemed a simple case of a thwarted sexual assault—one reason for her grinding teeth—had turned up some disturbing details. The two women were recovering from the assaults and the drugs that had incapacitated them. They'd tested positive for alcohol, though minimal, and GHB, a popular date rape drug. That term, "popular date rape drug," added to the teeth grinding. Like violating women was a popular pastime. Of course, she knew from the statistics that it was.

The two men were suffering from lacerations and head trauma. One was severely concussed, with a cervical spine injury and dislocated hip. The other's face had been smashed in, nose and jaw broken, top and bottom front teeth knocked out.

Serves the fuckers right, Mary thought, but she tried to look past the far-too-familiar details of sexual assault to the other information.

What had flagged the report was the pattern of the stab wounds, one in the first man's leg, three deep punctures, and both of the other man's buttocks, three stabs each, and three more in the back of his head. X-rays of the second one's skull showed actual gouges in the bone. There were also distinctive punctures and tears in the sheet metal of the car's roof. Forensic reports suggested a knife or claw weapon, but the pattern of the injuries and the damage to the car was too familiar to be anyone but Aleksi Rychenkna.

Unfortunately, the police saw similarities in the wound patterns, too; similarities with a series of murders from six months ago that had been perpetrated by Derrick Penningly. There were no suspects yet, but someone at BPD had brains enough to point out the differences from the Penningly murders, too. Neither of the men had been killed or mutilated, and the attacks looked like someone coming to the aid of the two victims. The women showed no injuries similar to the men's, and so far, recalled nothing of the attacks and little about the assaults.

That was a blessing in disguise, both for the women's sake, and for Aleksi's.

The Director had dispatched a medical team to get blood samples from the men and another to get statements from the women. The blood was being tested for the transformative RNA, but the results would take another six hours. If the men were infected, DHS would have to step in. None of the injuries looked like bite wounds, so maybe they had a chance.

Aleksi, what the hell are you doing? Mary thought, reviewing the data once more.

But the answer was obvious: she'd spotted the men abducting the women and had intervened. Too late to save the women from the assaults, but early enough to catch the rapists in the act and beat them senseless.

"Lucky she didn't kill them." Mary sipped her coffee and reviewed the data once again, reconstructing the scene in her mind.

Aleksi had followed the car from the club, got into the parking garage without being spotted—though the CCTV recordings were still being reviewed and sanitized by department IT specialists—found the car, and dragged the men out one at a time. In Mary's opinion, Aleksi had shown remarkable restraint in not killing the men. She doubted if, given the same situation, she would have showed the same restraint. After dealing with the men, she'd made a 911 call on the driver's phone—luckily no fingerprints there, just some blood smears—and gotten out again without being spotted.

Like a damn special forces operative, Mary thought.

She wanted more than ever to speak to this remarkable woman, if she really *was* still a woman. This event, this delve into vigilantism, might give her just that opportunity. Mary picked up her phone and called Dwayne Hutchinson. He answered on the third ring, sounding slightly breathless.

"Hello?"

"Dr. Hutchinson, this is Dr. Johansen. We met about six months ago in relation to the Derrick Penningly incident." Actually, she'd never met him, but her impersonator had, so she'd have to play like she had.

"Hang on a second."

Mary heard some muffled sounds, a woman's voice, then Hutchinson came back on the line.

"What's this about?" He didn't sound happy.

"It's about Aleksi Rychenkna, Doctor. She's done something very dangerous. I'd like to meet with you today to discuss it."

"What's happened?" Tension edged his voice like a razor.

"As far as I know, she's alive, but she attacked a couple of men. This is serious, Doctor. The police are drawing parallels with the Penningly killings. I need to show you the details and talk about what to do. This can't happen again."

"Fine. Where and when?" The tension had been replaced by irritation.

"How about this afternoon? We can meet anywhere you like."

"Okay, how about Peet's Coffee in Cambridge, the one just south of campus. Three this afternoon okay?"

"That'd be fine, Doctor. I'll see you there."

"Fine."

Before Hutchinson disconnected, Mary heard a woman's voice in the background. "Who was that, Hutch?" She recognized Julie Parks's voice and smiled. No doubt, Julie was still working him for information, and probably more. Well, she couldn't blame the girl for sleeping with him. He was attractive, and sex would help him trust her more. Of course, if this ploy of Mary's worked, she wouldn't need Julie Parks any longer.

Persephone Terris stirred from sleep to the buzz of her phone vibrating on the nightstand. The man lying beside her moaned and muttered something. She reached over her bedmate and snatched it up. A swipe and a tap brought up the message app, and the short text read, "GG - ASAP."

Shit!

If there was one thing that could get her out of bed with a hot young man, it was an all caps summons from her great-grandmother. She tapped "15min," slipped out from under the sheet, and dashed for the bathroom. A five-minute shower, another minute to struggle back into her dress from the night before, a scrawled note to leave on her still-warm spot on the bed, and she was out the door.

Gi-gi really should know better than to text her with an emergency on a Saturday morning. Persephone had the life of a Boston socialite to live up to, and it was summer. There were parties, fundraisers, gallery openings, dedications, and even sporting events to attend. There was champagne to be swilled, caviar to be eaten, and young artists to seduce. *Work, work, work...*

The elevator took her to the lobby, and she jogged past the gaping hotel doorman to her car. Firing up the Jag, she squealed tires out of the lot and onto the street. Six minutes, two blown red lights, and one swearing pedestrian later—*That'll teach you to jaywalk, moron!*—she skidded to a stop at the gate to the family home, swiped her card, and punched in her code. With everything that had happened in the last few months, they'd recently upgraded their security.

"It's me. I'm home." The light flashed green, and the gate rolled away. She parked by the front door and tossed the butler her keys. "Thanks, Freddie."

"My pleasure, miss." He cocked an eyebrow at her as she passed. "Your panties are hanging out of your purse, miss."

"Fuck! No *wonder* the doorman gave me a look. Thanks!" She stuffed them away and hurried downstairs.

Through the wine cellar to the Sanctum door, she punched in the code and pressed her palm to the ID pad. It beeped green and popped open. Taking a deep breath to calm her heart, she entered the high-tech lair of the mistress of her family.

Gi-gi lay, as always, in her bed, her torso elevated forty-five degrees, her frail chest rising and falling faintly, oxygen cannula under her nose, wizened hands poised over the remote controls set into the armrests of the bed. The only real sign of life in the ancient woman was in her eyes. Blazing lavender irises darted around like a pair of fireflies, absorbing data from the array of flat screen monitors at the foot of her bed.

"Is there an emergency, Great-Grandmother?"

"Possibly." The woman's voice, barely audible, scratched like sandpaper on stone. Those intense eyes flicked to Persephone, then back to the screens. "The dragon has arisen."

Persephone turned to the screens. Text scrolled down one, police and medical reports, from the look of it, and photos flicked past the others.

Blood, injuries, X-rays, then a picture of the roof of a car, parallel furrows cut in the metal. She'd seen marks like that before.

"Aleksi?"

"So it would seem. She evidently intervened in a sexual assault in the city last night." The slide show stopped, and Gi-gi turned to face her great-granddaughter. "She injured two men, and left some impressive evidence behind. This could be problematic."

"That girl's got a temper, that's for sure." Persephone peered at the pictures. "But she didn't kill anyone, at least."

"No. She showed some restraint." Gi-gi flicked a finger at the displays. "I've sent all this to you. Review it. We may need to intervene. If Aleksi continues to play vigilante, she's going to draw too much attention, perhaps even get hurt or killed."

"That would be bad," Persephone agreed. So far, the notion of dragons prowling the greater Boston area consisted only of unsubstantiated stories, and both Homeland Security and Persephone's family had done all they could to stifle or denounce them as fantasy, hallucinations, or outright fakes. So far, it had worked. If Aleksi started ripping up cars and rapists, covering up her existence would become impossible. The cops, well *most* cops, wouldn't back down from the investigation. She knew one who had met Aleksi personally; he'd blown Derrick Penningly's head off with a shotgun. Sergeant Jasper was a believer. He was also under orders from DHS to keep what he knew quiet, but if too many learned the secret, it would eventually get out into the mainstream.

Then people would start hunting Aleksi Rychenkna.

Mankind liked its spot on the top of the food chain, and the idea of a sentient creature, even if it was a changed human, displacing them from that position would spark a storm of fear-based hysteria. Eventually, someone with a high-powered rifle and a night scope would put a bullet into the only dragon in the world.

"I want you to make every effort to contact Aleksi," Gi-gi said. "She must be more careful."

"I'll see what I can do." Persephone knew of only one person who could contact Aleksi. She hadn't seen Hutch in months. "I'll call Hutch and see if I can find out what's going on."

"Be careful, Great-Granddaughter. He must not learn of us."

Persephone shot her a disgusted look. "I was *married* to the man for two years, and he didn't find out. I think I can make it through a lunch without spilling the beans."

A faint smile tugged at the corners of Gi-gi's razor-thin lips. "Good. Go."

Persephone nodded and turned away. She had work to do.

Hey, Dr. H! The usual?" The barista reached for a cup.

"Hi, Doug. Please." Hutch didn't really need a coffee, but he did need a reason to be here. The day had started out nearly perfectly—a run and yoga with Julie, and then she'd all but dragged him to bed. The warm afterglow had been ruined by Johansen's call. He'd spotted her sitting in the corner table when he came in. Accepting the coffee and handing Doug a five, Hutch waved off the change.

"Thanks! Not working on Saturday, are you?" Doug asked.

"Always working, Doug." He sipped his coffee. "Don't ever get a PhD. You don't get to do *any* of the fun stuff anymore."

"No worries there, Dr. H. I'll be happy with my BA."

Hutch walked to the back of the café and sat down across from Johansen, resisting the urge to tell her she was overdressed for Cambridge on a weekend. The place was virtually empty, so he wasn't worried about being overheard. "So, what's happened?" He couldn't believe Aleksi had attacked anyone without provocation.

"This." She slid a tablet across the table. "Two men were attacked while in the act of sexually assaulting a couple of women. They weren't killed, but there's little doubt it was Aleksi."

Hutch flipped through the photos of the injured men and the mutilated car. He tried to keep a straight face at the photo of the man's buttocks sporting six deep puncture wounds. "Looks to me like they got what they deserved."

"I'm not disputing that, Doctor, but playing vigilante is not acceptable."

Hutch narrowed his eyes at her. "Doesn't look to me like she was *playing*."

"You know perfectly well what I mean! This was *dangerous*!"

Something about Johansen seemed different than he remembered, more blunt, harder, less familiar than he remembered. "For her, or for asshole men who sexually assault women?"

"Both, actually, but I'm much more concerned for Aleksi than any sexual predators. The police aren't *stupid,* Doctor. They've already made connections to Penningly's handiwork."

Johansen was certainly acting differently than she had before, less solicitous, and the mannerisms he'd thought familiar before were completely absent. She'd even called him Hutch in the interview room, now he was Doctor. She seemed stiff, as if cut from cardboard.

"Then they should be smart enough to see the *dissimilarities* to Penningly's attacks." He pushed the pad back across the table. "Nobody was killed, and a crime was stopped. I'd call that justice. If your so-called 'good guy with a gun' had done that, he'd be getting a medal."

She glared at him. "And if the police arrived half a minute earlier and put a bullet in Aleksi's head? Would *that* have been justice?"

He returned her glare without rising to the bait.

"Come on, Doctor, I *know* you care about her. I'm not asking for anything but some cooperation here."

"I do care about her, *Doctor,* and I won't lie to you, this worries me, but there's not a hell of a lot I can do about it. I don't *control* her."

"No, but she'll listen to you. I'm only asking for you to talk to her about this. Tell her you're worried for her safety. Tell her *I'm* worried. The very last thing I want is for her to get killed."

"What exactly *do* you want from her, Dr. Johansen?"

She looked mildly surprised. "Eventually, I'd like her to grow to trust us. We might be able to help her, and she's already helped us once by neutralizing Penningly. Oh, and my real name's Buckmann, Mary Buckmann. The Johansen Project is still underway, but there's a new supervisor. I'm not involved in it anymore."

That sounded like something the government would do, but if she wasn't involved in the project, asking about Aleksi didn't make sense. "So, Dr. Buckmann, why are you even concerned about Aleksi?"

"Because I'm conducting a secondary investigation that she might be able to help me with. I can't go into details."

Of course, he thought, *they're only interested in what she can do for them.* "And what are you willing to offer her for her help? Have you found a cure yet?"

"No, but they've isolated the infective agents."

"Agents? There are more than one?"

"Yes, but they're all very similar, RNA segments that take over cellular protein production. They code for transcription binding proteins that unlock dormant genes, which in turn code for major changes in morphology and even genetic alterations during cellular replication. The cascade compiles new genes, and the expressed genome changes drastically." She cocked her head curiously. "It's truly a wonder that you weren't infected. We found these RNA segments in cheek swabs we did on Penningly when he was still changing."

Hutch's stomach dropped. He took a sip of coffee and swallowed hard. "I guess I dodged the bullet."

"We're thinking she might not have been infectious yet when...you were with her."

The flash of discomfort on her face struck him as odd. Did she think people didn't have sex or something? "Lucky me. Look, I'll talk to Aleksi and tell her everyone's worried about her, but I can't control her actions. We're...not as close as we used to be. She's changed a lot, and I don't mean just the physical transformation."

"That's not surprising. She's had to become self-reliant."

"She always was, but now it's about survival, not just her academic career."

"True." Buckmann put her pad into her bag and lifted her coffee. "Look, I'd like you to give a message to Aleksi for me. Just please tell her to be careful. An outbreak of this infection would be disastrous."

"She knows that better than *you* do, but I'll relay the message."

"Thank you." She stood, then stopped. "Also, please tell her I'd like very much to speak with her." She fished a card from a pocket and put it on the table. "That's my personal number. You can call me any time, and so can she. We can set up a meeting anywhere, any time she likes, in private, no cops, no guns, no surveillance."

Hutch picked up the card. "I'll tell her, but I can't guarantee she'll call you."

"I know you can't." She nodded once and walked out.

Hutch watched her go and wondered again what had happened to her since their last meeting. She seemed very different, even walked differently. It was like she wasn't the same person at all.

5

Aleksi's phone vibrated, snapping her out of a sound sleep. She considered silencing it and rolling over, but reconsidered. Hutch knew she was nocturnal; if he called during the day, it was usually important. She also hadn't spoken to him since she'd spurned his advances.

She opened the call and said, "Hey. What's up?"

"Sorry if you were sleeping, but I thought you'd like to hear this. I just had a sit down with the former Dr. Johansen."

The last vestiges of sleep vanished. "What? The *former* Johansen?"

"Yeah. She said her real name's Buckmann. The project was named Johansen and whoever's in charge wears that name, evidently."

That sounded like a typical government thing. "Okay. What did she want?"

"She wanted me to tell you to be careful. Your stunt last night drew some attention."

"My *stunt*?" Her temper flared, and she vaulted out of bed to her feet, pacing the tiny space of her lair.

The long-disused section of the Boston subway was her home, such as it was. She had a nest of blankets with a sleeping bag, and several coolers to keep food fresh and safe from rats and cockroaches, though both had now vacated the premises. The former didn't like her scent, and the latter responded well to insecticide and traps. It wasn't much, but it was the only home she had.

"My *stunt* saved two women from being *raped,* Hutch! I think it was worth the risk!" Well, she'd been too late to really save them, but she'd tried.

"Hey, don't kill the messenger. I'm not saying you didn't do the right thing, but she was right. What you did was *dangerous,* Aleksi."

"Being *female* is dangerous in this city, Hutch!" She bit back her temper. He was just concerned for her, but he also didn't understand. "Did you know there are over seven *hundred* reported sexual assaults on college campuses alone in the greater Boston area per year? That's like two every *night,* and those are just the ones being reported!"

"No, I... Holy *shit,* Aleksi. That's...staggering." He sounded truly appalled.

"Google it if you don't believe me."

"I *believe* you, but this isn't about whether what you did was right or wrong, it's about the *danger* of what you did. You've *got* to be more careful."

"Look, Hutch, I know you worry about me, but don't. I can take care of myself."

"Okay, *wait.* Back up. I didn't make myself clear. I *am* concerned about you, Aleksi, but the danger isn't just about you! It's about the whole human *race*!"

She stopped pacing. "What?"

"Buckmann confirmed what you suspected. You're infectious, Aleksi. Actually, it's a wonder *I* wasn't infected, but the point is, you can pass this on. Think what would happen if this broke out into the population. If you infect someone while you're trying to save a victim from being hurt, you could spread a plague that could change the face of humanity."

"I..." Aleksi felt like she might throw up. "Do they know if the two men I hurt were infected?"

"So far, they're showing no symptoms, but there's no cure for this yet." He paused, and his voice calmed. "If you infect someone, they'll become like you, and they could infect others. You took epidemiology as an undergrad. You know the numbers."

She did. If the incubation time of this infection was about a week, and it went misdiagnosed, as hers had, the infection could spread like a strain of COVID. In a month there could be five thousand infections across the globe; in two months, a million; in three, fifty million.

"I'm sorry, I…" She'd been only thinking of herself, of the immediate need to intervene, to help, to protect. "I couldn't just stand by and do nothing, Hutch. I *had* to help."

"Okay, and maybe this need to protect people from violence is some part of the changes you've gone through, but you have to think it through, Aleksi. Is it worth risking millions to save a few?"

The cold hard truth said no, but she didn't know if she could just stand by any longer. Not with what she knew she was capable of. Besides, taking down those two rapists had felt *good*. She felt like she'd finally found a purpose, a calling, some reason for the torture she had gone through.

"Then I'll be careful."

"Okay, let's assume you're perfectly careful and don't infect anyone. What happens if you make a mistake?"

"What do you mean?"

"You're playing judge, jury, and executioner here. What if you hurt or kill someone who doesn't deserve it? People have all kinds of inclinations. You might mistake some kink for abuse and hurt the wrong person."

He was arguing for her to stop trying to help people entirely, and it ignited a flame of suspicion in her heart. Hutch loved her. He was painting the worst picture he could in an attempt to protect her. She couldn't blame him, but she also hated being manipulated, even by him.

"I couldn't do much worse than the criminal justice system."

He snorted a dry laugh. "Well, okay, maybe not, but you're the one who would have to live with it."

"Then I'll live with it."

Silence… It dragged on for a very long time. She could hear him breathing on the other end.

"Aleksi?"

"Yeah."

"I didn't mean to start a fight. I'm sorry."

"Yeah, well, maybe you shouldn't have opened up by calling what I did a *stunt*." She was still pissed about that.

"Shitty choice of words. I apologize."

"Apology accepted."

"Buckmann did say you showed remarkable restraint not killing those two assholes."

The sound of the man's scream, the scent of blood, the desire to bury her teeth in the back of his neck rushed back into her. "Yeah, well, I *really* wanted to."

"I could tell by the pictures. I'm glad you didn't."

Silence again. This time she broke it. "You ever think that maybe this is the reason I exist?"

"What?"

"This…mutation, or evolution, or whatever you want to call it. I think I'm beginning to understand the evolutionary basis for it. I mean, look at human evolution. We're weak, slow, and tasty. How the hell did we ever get to the tool use stage?"

"Big brains from a higher protein diet than other primates," he said.

"Sure, while hyenas, jackals, lions, and other big cats pick us off. It would have worked a lot better if we had an alpha protector, like baboon and gorilla troops do." She sighed and laughed dryly. "Besides, I felt such a *rush* when I took those two rapists down, Hutch. It was like I was doing what I was *made* to do. Saving those women. Protecting them." Aleksi heaved another breath. "God, it was so *right!*"

"Maybe. Who knows? I *do* know if there's an outbreak of this infection, we'll have thousands of people like you thinking the same thing, and they'll probably have a lot less restraint."

"Point taken." She heaved a breath and let it go. "So, if this thing's infectious, what's the vector?"

"Oh, so Buckmann really is a scientist, or so it seems. She filled me in on some of the mechanisms Lonnie hasn't considered yet. The infection itself is RNA-based, almost like a filovirus, or one of the RNA strands that mediate some cancers."

"Shit! You mean like Ebola?"

"Well, not the same mechanism exactly, but the same type of vector, yes. It hotwires the cellular ribosomes to produce transcription proteins that alter the DNA during replication. It starts a cascade effect."

Aleksi felt like she would throw up again. "Fuck, Hutch. It's a miracle you weren't infected!"

He chuckled dryly. "Yeah, well, I must be living right."

"That healthy vegetarian lifestyle."

"Right. So, I asked Buckmann if there was a cure yet, and she said no, but that they're working on it. There's *hope,* Aleksi."

Suspicion rose up again. "And you believe her?"

"Well, not really, but maybe a little. She said she was taken off the project, which made me wonder why she was concerned about you at all, but she told me she was conducting another investigation that had something to do with Penningly. She asked me to give you her number. She'd like to speak to you."

"Yeah, I call, they find me through my phone, and the next message I get is tied to a bullet."

"I'm not telling you what to do, Aleksi, but she said you could meet in person if you'd prefer. Any time you like, anywhere. She offered to help you as much as she could in return. They *are* still working on this. They might find some way to reverse it."

"Hutch, you're a scientist. Do you *really* think this could be reversed?"

"Biotech is the biggest breakthrough science in the world right now, Aleksi. We still only understand about two percent of how things actually work! Jesus, that makes astrophysics like rock-solid and evidence-based in comparison. There's so much to learn. They *could* find something."

"Maybe, but I don't think I could trust the government to stick a needle in my arm. I'd wake up in a cage."

"True." After a short silence, he added, "but just talking to her might not hurt. She seemed different than I remembered her."

"She wanted something from you, Hutch. She was acting nice to get it."

He snorted another laugh. "Just the opposite, actually."

"What?" That didn't make sense. "What do you mean?"

"She was pretty solicitous when I met her the first time, even though I was being detained. She seemed stiffer now, defensive, less familiar. She kept calling me Dr. Hutchinson, and I remember her calling me Hutch before."

"Huh, that *is* weird."

"So, if you want to talk to her, I can set it up for you. That way they don't get your number and can't locate your cell. I can call her at the last minute, so they won't have much time to set up a trap. If you pick someplace that works to your advantage, you should be reasonably safe."

"Maybe." Aleksi tried to think of someplace safe from sniper rifles, and failed. Then she reconsidered; it might be better if she picked someplace open that she could surveil, watch for activity, listen for engines or helicopters. And she did want to talk to the woman, if for no other reason than to call her a lying bitch to her face. "Okay, I think I want to do this, Hutch."

"Okay. How can I help?"

He was always so willing to step into harm's way for her. Love wasn't just blind, it was pretty stupid, too. "Call her at around two-thirty a.m. Monday, and tell her Parkman Bandstand in Boston Common at three."

"That's a pretty open area, Aleksi."

"I know. Trust me. That'll work more to my advantage than theirs. Tell her to show up alone. No cops, no surveillance, no guns, no helicopters, or I won't show. Also tell her if she tries any bullshit, she'll be the first one to die."

After a short silence, he said, "Okay. I'll make the call."

"Thanks, Hutch." A pang smote her heart. "I'm...sorry about the other night, but..."

"I know, Aleksi. I love you, you know. I'd like to see you."

Visions of Julie in his apartment surged up out of nowhere. "No, Hutch. They might be watching your place again. I can't risk it."

"Okay. Just be careful with Buckmann, please. I don't trust her."

"Neither do I."

"So, do you need anything else?"

"Not that I can think of. Maybe after I meet with her you can do some shopping for me and we could meet somewhere secluded."

"Sure. Just text me a list."

"Will do. Thanks Hutch. Bye."

As she ended the call, she heard him say, "I lo—" but he was cut off.

Maybe that was best.

Minutes after he hung up with Aleksi, Hutch's other phone rang. For a moment, he wondered if Buckmann had been somehow listening in on their conversation, but when he picked it up, caller ID told him differently.

"What the..." He took the call and answered, "Persephone! Long time!"

"Yeah, sorry about that, Hutch. I was travelling for a while. You know how it is."

"Europe, the Med, Monaco... Yeah, I... Oh *wait,* no I *don't* know how that is." He laughed.

"Oh, you filthy liar!" she countered.

"Hey, I'm a scientist. I *never* lie!" But he had. In the two years of their marriage, he and Persephone had had some wonderful vacations, more than he could ever have afforded on a professor's salary. His trips usually consisted of sleeping in a tent in Wyoming or Utah.

She scoffed at him. "Never trust a man who says, 'I never lie.' Liar."

"Busted again. So, you're back from trotting the globe, and you decided to call. What's up?"

"Nothing really. I just wanted to say hi and see how you were doing, maybe grab dinner and chat. I think about you a lot, Hutch."

"You're worrying about *me*?"

"Well, I do sometimes, you know. I'm not *always* a cold-hearted, rich, self-centered, um…oh, beautiful, don't forget that one…Hmm, what else?"

"Humble. Try that one."

"Nah, I don't *do* humble."

"There's a shocker!"

They both laughed, and Hutch found himself enjoying it.

"So, dinner? My treat," she said.

"Okay. Tomorrow night okay?"

"Sunday's open for me. Sure."

"Nothing too fancy, and not too late, either. I've got an early meeting on Monday."

"Oh, I forgot you do that *work* thing! Such a drag."

"Well, it keeps me busy. What do you feel like?"

"Oh, anything but bar food. Maybe someplace outdoors? The weather's just *wicked* nice."

"The Daedalus has a roof-top, and everything's in bloom. No white tablecloths, but the food's good."

"Perfect! You said early. Is six okay?"

"Fine. I'll see you there."

"Oh, I can pick you up if you like."

"Okay, then. See you downstairs at six."

"See you!" She ended the call.

Hutch stared at his phone for a moment and shook his head. It was just like Persephone to call out of nowhere when they hadn't spoken in months and take him out for dinner.

"Impulsive," he muttered, "that was the other one."

Tony Jasper and Marty Willis sat staring at the screen of Tony's computer, their attention rapt. The two homicide detectives weren't strangers to scenes of bloodshed, but these photos strummed chords of familiarity in their memories.

"Gotta be her," Jasper said.

"That or Edward Scissorhands is playing in town, and one of the cast went totally Rambo," Willis replied.

Tony chuckled and flipped to the next image, a concrete post with three parallel scratches across it. "Or Freddy Krueger."

"All claws, no teeth. You notice?" Marty pointed to the scratches. "Even the injuries on those guys. Nothing like Penningly."

"Oh?" Jasper turned and touched the faint scar on his partner's neck where Penningly had torn Marty's throat open with one swipe of his claws. "I seem to remember some claw action going on somewhere." The surgeons had saved Marty's life and had even reduced the scarring, but the marks of the attack would stay there forever, as would the memory.

"Well, sure, but Penningly would have gotten around to chewing on me *eventually* if you hadn't shot at him. I was thinking of the other victims. He definitely had an oral fixation."

"Or just a healthy appetite," Jasper countered. Many of the bodies they'd found during Penningly's rampage had been missing pieces.

"So, this was either Aleksi Rychenkna, or some kind of freakishly strong, claw-wielding, vigilante." Willis leaned back and looked at his partner.

"Yeah. Pretty sure it was our girl." Even though Jasper had been ordered by his chief and DHS not to speak of Aleksi's condition to anyone, he'd broken that confidence twice. Once with Dwayne Hutchinson, who already knew about Aleksi, and again with Willis, because he deserved to know, and Tony trusted him with his life.

"Well, all things considered, she did one hell of a job remodeling a crappy Ford, and managed not to kill anyone. I call that a wiener. And speaking of wieners, it's a wonder she didn't take those two rapists' dicks as trophies." Willis was always cracking wise, which was one reason Tony liked him so much.

"Yeah, that would have been appropriate." Jasper flipped the screen to the next photo, a close-up of a man's ass that had six deep claw wounds. He winced. "Maybe if she had, these fuckers wouldn't roofie-rape any more women."

"Oh, I think they'll be out of commission for quite a while. The women are both pressing charges, and they've got solid evidence for felony sexual assault, felony kidnapping, and possession and use of GHB." Willis snarled an evil grin. "I hope they get some nice boyfriends in prison. See how they like it."

"Right." This wasn't their case, and hadn't even gone down in their jurisdiction, but all the greater Boston area departments shared reports, and Jasper had been watching for any sign of Aleksi for months. It looked like she'd finally crossed the line. "I hope she doesn't make a habit of this."

"Might thin out the rapist population a little," Willis said.

"Or end up with our girl lying dead on the street with a bunch of cops scratching their heads wondering what the fuck they just shot." Jasper shook his head.

"Well, that *is* a danger, but I don't want to be the one to tell her to stop. She might get pissed."

"No, I think there's only one person in the world who could tell her that and not earn an ass-kicking."

Willis looked at him sidelong. "You gonna call him?"

"I think so, just to let him know what's happened, if he doesn't already know."

"Okay, but be gentle. You're right about one thing: you *don't* want to piss off his girlfriend."

"Damn *straight* I don't," Jasper agreed. "But Hutch is our only connection to Aleksi."

6

Persephone pulled the Jag up into Hutch's condo building parking lot and spotted him leaning beside the vestibule door. She tapped her horn, and he waved. Watching him approach, she thought he looked thinner, but he was smiling as he opened the door and got in.

"Hey! You cut your hair!" Hutch leaned across and gave her a peck. He smelled good.

"Oh, yeah." She fluttered her cut and pulled the car out of the lot. "Getting older, you know. Old ladies don't have long hair. It's a rule or something." She'd actually cut her hair short to impersonate Mary Buckmann, but she'd found someone to give her a proper do. Mary had the worst haircut she'd ever seen.

"Oh, bullshit!" He reached over and fluttered the back of her hair. "It looks good, and you're not old."

"Thanks." Persephone smiled at him and drove on. Seeing Hutch always brought back memories, and she was glad they'd stayed amicable. The casual touching of a formerly married couple still on good terms always set her hormones raging, but she wasn't about to tell him to stop. "You look good, too, but you've lost weight. You're not training for another stupid marathon, are you?"

"No, and I don't *think* I've lost weight. I haven't stepped on a scale in months."

"I hate you." She shot him a playful glare.

"Oh, quit it!" He laughed at her. "I'm letting you take me to dinner, and I promise to clean my plate, okay?"

"Deal."

She drove the few blocks to the Daedalus, found a parking spot nearby, and they walked in. He held the door for her, but he'd always had that chivalrous streak. Upstairs, the hostess showed them to their table. The place was packed, but Persephone had called ahead. They didn't take reservations, but her name still carried some weight in this town.

After ordering drinks, she said, "So, how have you been? And tell me the truth."

"Oh, good enough. Working and trying to stay sane pretty much take up all my time." He sipped water and shrugged. "Life goes on."

"Yes, it does." She watched his face and saw the evasion. This wasn't going to be easy. "I'm sorry I kind of dropped off the radar, Hutch, but with everything that happened, I just couldn't handle it. You know me, when the going gets rough, I get the hell out of town."

"It's no problem."

"And thanks for the check, but you could have kept it." After the loss of the specimen and the disaster of losing two of his graduate students, Hutch had returned the unspent portion of the money she'd given him. "You could have spent it on one of your other projects."

He shook his head. "Everything else I've got is fully funded, and I didn't want any improprieties. After the specimen was stolen, the faculty council was looking at me under a microscope."

"And nobody ever found out what happened to that mystery specimen?"

"Nope." The waitress arrived with their drinks, and they ordered food. When she'd gone, he continued. "No, it just vanished. Neilson's *still* pissed at me for that."

"And Aleksi? Jesus, Hutch, what the hell *happened* to her?"

"No clue. I think she just freaked out and left. I mean, she wasn't the most *stable* young woman in the first place, right? When Bob was killed and the cops put a warrant out on her for it, I think she just snapped."

Again, she saw the evasion, but she doubted anyone else would have. Persephone knew him very well. "But Penningly's dead, and she's exonerated. Why not come back?"

"No idea. Maybe she went back to New York. If she wanted to vanish, that'd be the place to do it." He sipped his beer and shrugged again. "Hell, she could change her name and get a job at any one of a dozen museums with what she knows."

"Damn it, she was so *brilliant*, Hutch."

"Yeah, I know." He drank some beer and shook his head. "But I've got two new students and the bone-bed project is back on track, so here's to moving on and putting things back together." He raised his glass.

"I'll drink to that." Persephone lifted her glass in toast, they sipped, and she decided to go for broke. "You seem…different, Hutch. Sad or something."

"Sad?" He arched his brows at her. "Do I?"

"Yes."

"Well, it's taken me a while to recover from this, I guess. I've never had one of my students murdered, another one vanish into thin air, and a priceless artifact stolen from my lab all in the same *week* before." He fixed her with a narrow stare. "You seem different, too. More serious or something."

"Well, I'm trying to turn over a new leaf. Spoiled bitch wasn't working so well anymore."

He laughed at her. "Well, maybe we've *both* changed a little then."

"Everyone does, one way or another." She reached across the table and put her hand on his. "If you need someone to keep you company, I'm right here, Hutch."

He squeezed her hand and chuckled. "Funny you should say that. Everyone's been telling me I should move on, find someone, even if it's just a casual thing."

"Oh?" Her heart skipped a beat.

"Well, not everyone, but some. And I did."

"You're seeing someone?" She forced a smile and released his hand. "Good for you! Anyone I know?"

"No." He smiled and actually blushed. "Strange turn of events, but I bumped into Aleksi's old roommate, Julie Parks, at the gym, and we started working out together. Turns out she's into yoga, and runs to keep fit. One thing led to another."

Persephone gaped at him, honestly shocked that he was seeing anyone new. As far as she knew, he was still stuck on Aleksi like a bug on a windshield. But Julie Parks? "Wait! Isn't she the girl who was dating Bob Tomlin?"

"Yeah." He cocked an eyebrow at her. "How'd you hear about that?"

"Oh, probably a news story. You know how they're always going into people's personal lives." She waved it off. "But she's a student, isn't she?"

"Yes. Graduate in the drama program."

"You *dog*!" She laughed and swatted his arm. "No fallout about that from the faculty council, I hope."

"Not yet. We just got serious the other day, as a matter of fact, and it's nobody's business. It's pretty casual, actually." He shrugged again and sipped his beer. "She's nice, and funny, and I'm... She was pretty stuck on Bob, and she suggested we...help each other move on."

"Well good for you!" Persephone had seen pictures of Aleksi's roommate and knew that she was probably *very* good for Hutch. The woman was a knockout. Then again, it was probably very good for Julie, too. Persephone enjoyed sex and had experienced quite a few lovers, but Hutch had a certain something that most men lacked. He took serious pleasure in pleasuring. She'd watched his face through innumerable intimate encounters, and the greatest rapture she'd ever seen in him had been when she felt *her* greatest rapture. There weren't many men like that. "You deserve something casual, Hutch, and I *mean* that!"

"Thank you." He smiled like he meant it.

"And you still haven't heard a word from Aleksi?"

"Nope." He disguised the evasion with another sip of beer. "Her parents have called me a couple of times. That's all."

"Oh, they must be devastated."

"Yeah, it was pretty hard on them. Her father drinks, and her mother... well, you can imagine."

"No, I don't think I *can* imagine losing a child." She frowned and sipped her wine. "God, how did we get on such a depressing subject? Tell me about this Parks woman. She's in drama? Is she an actress?"

He barked a laugh. "Acting, singing, dancing, directing, writing, producing, Julie does it all. Harvard, you know."

"Wow! And I bet she's blonde and beautiful, too!" Of course, Persephone knew she was.

"As a matter of fact..." He blushed again and smiled.

Persephone swatted his arm again and laughed. "Well, I hope you two have fun! You deserve it."

And she wasn't lying; Hutch did deserve it, but Persephone found it a little too coincidental that Aleksi's old roommate would bump into Hutch out of the blue. Maybe she would have a closer look at Julie Parks. Not that she was jealous or anything, but because Persephone Terris didn't believe in coincidences when they happened anywhere near the dragon of Boston. There were too many people out there who wanted Aleksi.

Aleksi kept Buckmann waiting for half an hour while she carefully circled the area looking for government spooks. In the dark, she could fly in and among the trees without being seen, while watching Buckmann and looking for threats at the same time. She paused again to listen for motors and helicopters, but the roads and sky remained clear.

Buckmann stood dead center in the bandstand. She wore a sport jacket, jeans, and sneakers. Aleksi couldn't tell if she was armed, but her hands were visible and empty.

Finally satisfied, Aleksi gained altitude briefly and landed atop the domed structure of the bandstand, hunkering in the shadowed ledge around the rim, her claws click-clicking on the hard stone. Pausing to listen again, she heard Mary Buckmann breathing and the impatient shuffle of her feet. Then Aleksi inhaled her scent—a faint whiff of cheap perfume and cloying body lotion, and, beneath it, something totally unfamiliar.

The scent screamed "Wrong!" in her mind. This was not the scent of the woman she'd met atop the Prudential Tower six months ago. She remembered Hutch mentioning how the woman had changed, how she seemed different. He'd been right. This was a different person entirely.

What the fuck is going on here? A scant peek over the edge confirmed that the woman remained oblivious to her presence. It looked like the same woman, but her scent didn't match.

Aleksi edged to the opposite side of the structure from where Buckmann was facing and dropped down behind one of the pillars. "Who the hell are you?"

The woman whirled like she'd been poked with a cattle prod, her eyes wide. "Jesus!"

"No, just a dragon. Now, *tell* me. Who *are* you?"

"I'm...Mary Buckmann. We met once before, Aleksi, when you—"

Aleksi moved, wings billowing, claws scratching furrows in the concrete. She was on the woman before Buckmann could even gasp, talons resting on either side of her face, the needle tips barely touching the skin, her teeth bared. "Bullshit! You're not the same woman I met at the Prudential Tower. You look like her, but you don't *smell* like her. Now, if you like your face still attached to the front of your head, tell me who you are."

"I really *am* Dr. Mary Buckmann!" The woman trembled under her touch, her breath reeking of old coffee and breath mints, her heart hammering in her throat. "The woman you met that night was an imposter. Someone abducted me, replicated me perfectly, and put that woman in my place. They stole the specimen from us, Aleksi. I swear, I'm telling you the truth."

"*Replicated* you? How?"

"We don't know. That's what I want your help with. I'm investigating my own abduction and impersonation. They stole a priceless artifact from the federal government."

"And you stole it from my lab." Aleksi lowered her talons, but kept them ready. "I find the fact that someone stole it from *you* amusing. Why do you think I can help find out who did it?"

"Because whoever did this must be interested in *you*, too. They managed to fool fingerprint scanners, facial recognition software, hair, voiceprint, clothes, and even got my passwords from somewhere, passwords that weren't written down *anywhere*. The only place they existed was in a heavily encrypted government network, and my head." A curious mixture of anger and awe edged her tone. "I've watched every frame of recording we have on this woman, and the only ways that she didn't mimic me perfectly are her mannerisms and the way she walks."

"Okay, that's interesting," Aleksi admitted. "Are you saying they created some kind of fully grown *clone*, and implanted it with your *memories*? I'm not buying that."

"A clone? No, but the woman's face wasn't a mask. Even top of the line prosthetics aren't that good. She sweated, ate, drank, and put on *my* makeup. The disguise was physical, flesh and blood."

"Plastic surgery?" Aleksi tried to recall the scent of the woman she'd met atop the Prudential Tower, but couldn't place it. All she could say was that it was different than this Mary Buckmann.

"Possibly. We don't know for sure." She took a deep breath and let it out slowly, examining Aleksi head to toe for the first time. "You're... different than the pictures we have of you."

"I've matured." She raised a clawed wing and extended her talons. "The changes are complete. But tell me more about this imposter you're searching for. Why did they do it, just to get the specimen?"

Buckmann nodded. "And to neutralize Penningly, it seems, yes."

"And they took the dragon specimen? Everything?"

"They *tried* to get everything, but there were samples sequestered away for safe keeping." She shrugged. "If the government's good at one thing, it's covering their own asses. I didn't even know they had backups until recently."

"And what are they doing with it?"

"I don't know. I'm no longer on that project."

Aleksi saw the lie in the woman's eyes, heard it in her heartbeat, smelled it in her sweat, but didn't call her on it. "So, do you have any suspects?"

"None. Whoever did it had the resources and skills to infiltrate our facility with a convincing copy of me. That narrows the field considerably. If the disguise was truly a physical copy of me, they have resources that we don't. Technologies in biochemistry, genetics, and biology that we can't match. Frankly, we didn't think anyone in the *world* could match us there, and it's sparked some serious concerns."

"I imagine it has." It also sparked considerable interest from Aleksi, for if someone could manipulate human flesh well enough to mimic a human being to the degree Buckmann suggested, they might be able to do something for her. "But I have no idea where to start looking."

"Whoever did this is also interested in *you*, Aleksi. If they have the sample, and the skills and abilities we *think* they have, they could be making more like you even now."

"And you're telling me the government isn't?"

"Honestly, I don't know if they are or not. I hope not. I've warned them, shown them the footage from the Prudential where *you* warned them, but I'm not in the loop." Again, Aleksi spotted the lie. People tended to look away when they lied, and Buckmann had only done that twice. "With your recent activities, these people may be prompted to contact you, as I have, to warn you to be more careful."

"I *am* being careful, Doctor." Aleksi was tired of people telling her what to do. "I didn't kill or infect anyone the other night, and those rapist assholes deserved far worse than what I gave them."

"I can't argue with that, but vigilantism's too dangerous. Please, consider the risks."

"Consider this." Aleksi raised a claw again and, faster than Buckmann could blink, placed the tip on the woman's nose. "This is what I was *made* for, Doctor. You telling me not to do it is like me telling you not to fuck around with the most dangerous thing the world has ever discovered. We're both going to do it anyway, and to hell with the risks."

Buckmann swallowed, her eyes fixed on the claw at her nose. "That's a valid point. I'm just urging you to be careful. An outbreak—"

"An outbreak would fuck humanity right up the ass. I know." She lowered her claw. "But from where *I'm* standing, watching men prey on women like wolves preying on deer is already fucked up beyond tolerance."

"Again, I can't disagree," Buckmann said, and for once, Aleksi believed her.

"If I find anything out, I'll tell Hutch to set up another meeting."

"That's all I can ask."

"Goodbye Doctor. Thank you for not trying to have me killed tonight."

"You're welcome."

"I would have hated to murder you...or anyone." She whirled and dashed out of the bandstand into the darkness, her wings catching the sultry night air and vaulting her into the sky.

As Aleksi soared through the canyons of concrete, glass, and steel, she began to wonder who on Earth had the skills to do what Buckmann had suggested. If someone could mold flesh and bone into the likeness of another human being, what might they be able to do for Aleksi? Hope ran through her veins like a drug, but it was a drug that had burned her before.

For once, Aleksi vowed to take the advice she'd been given. She was going to be careful.

7

Hutch sat at his desk in the Northwest Science Building, conducting his usual Monday morning ritual: coffee, a Danish from Buckminster's—actually his second breakfast; his first had been a protein shake at five a.m. before an hour at the gym—working out his week's schedule, dealing with emails, checking on his four graduate students, and trying to get some work done on his next grant proposal. Both the coffee and the Danish were gone when his phone vibrated.

He snatched it up without looking at the screen. Everyone used cell phones for work during the week, so he answered, "Hutchinson."

"Good morning, Doctor. Tony Jasper here. How are you?"

"Tony?" Hutch hadn't spoken to the detective in more than a month. They'd had a beer together a couple of times since the Penningly incident, but the friendship hadn't really jelled. He liked Tony, but all they had in common was Penningly and Aleksi. "What's up?"

"I'd like to talk to you, if you have a few minutes to spare. I know you're busy."

"Is this police business?" Hutch thought about the pictures Buckmann had shown him and her warning that the police were drawing parallels to Penningly.

"Unofficial police business. I just want to chat."

"When?" Hutch pulled up his schedule.

"Now would be good. We can come to you."

"Okay. I'm in my office in the Northwest Science Building. You know where that is?"

"Yep. Be there in ten minutes."

"Okay." The call ended, and Hutch stared at the phone.

This had to be about Aleksi, either her attack Friday night, or something had happened with Buckmann this morning. He tried to regain his focus on work until Tony arrived, but failed. When someone rapped on the frame of his door, he looked up to find Jasper and his partner, Marty Willis, filling the doorway.

"Hi, Tony, Marty. Come in." He waved to the other chairs.

"Hey, Doc." They came in, and Willis closed the door behind them. "Sorry to bother you."

"It's Monday morning. Isn't that what they're for?" Hutch pushed his screen out of the way and leaned back in his chair. He'd seen Willis only once since the incident that had left him in the hospital, and the scars of Penningly's attack were much reduced but still visible. "So, is this about Aleksi, or something else?"

"It's about an attack on two men early Saturday morning." He pulled his phone and started to tap the screen.

Hutch held up a hand. "I've seen it, Tony."

His eyebrows arched, and he traded a glance with his partner. "How did you—"

"The feds," Willis interrupted. "They beat us to it." He sounded slightly resentful.

Hutch nodded. "I was contacted by the same woman you met after the incident in my home, then again the night you shot Derrick Penningly. She told me to tell Aleksi to quit playing vigilante. I relayed the message."

Jasper frowned and put away his phone. "She seriously fucked up two men, Hutch. You make it sound like a traffic ticket."

"She seriously fucked up two rapists who had drugged and were in the middle of assaulting two women. Tell me *exactly* what she did wrong."

"Well, that's a thin line to walk, Hutch. She didn't just stop a crime, she committed several. My personal opinion is that these fuckers got less than they deserved, and I hope they have a nice long stay in the concrete Hilton. I don't give a damn for them, but if she starts acting like some kind of avenging angel, we've got a problem."

"Yeah, I know. The feds said the same thing. I relayed the message, but..." He shrugged helplessly.

"But what, Hutch? What'd she say?"

"I don't know if I should tell you, Tony."

"Why not? It's not like either of us have her on a leash or anything. I understand you can't tell her what to do, but if she's going to start ripping people apart under the guise of vigilantism, I need to know."

"Why?" Hutch countered. "So the police can put snipers out there to shoot her?"

"No. Because it's our fucking *job* to protect people. Unfortunately, that includes rapist assholes. Stopping a crime isn't illegal, but tearing someone's ass off to stop a crime is." The muscles of his jaw bunched and relaxed. "Like I said, it's a thin line, and she crossed it."

"So, you're here to tell me I should warn Aleksi that she's breaking the *law*?" Hutch snorted a laugh. "Come on, Tony. We both know her very existence trumps that bullshit."

"Look, Hutch—"

Willis put a hand on Jasper's arm. "Hey, enough with the pissing contest, guys. Okay?"

Jasper shot a glare at his partner, but then nodded.

"So, we're not here to warn you, or threaten you, or piss of Aleksi, we just want to let you know that the Boston PD is working under the theory that some sick fuck is copying Penningly's MO." Willis held up a hand before Hutch could interrupt. "We *all* know that's bullshit, but if she continues this, she's gonna get hurt."

"*She's* going to get hurt, or more rapists are going to get hurt?"

"Well, both, but like Tony said, our concern for the asshole rapists can only be measured in micro-give-a-shits. We *do* care about Aleksi. If she's bent on continuing this crusade, tell her to lay off ripping up cars and leaving claw marks all over the place, okay?"

Hutch nodded. "I've already told her to be careful, but I'll relay your message."

"Good." Jasper nodded to Willis, and the two stood. "Thanks for the chat, Doc." He held out his hand.

"No problem, Tony." Hutch stood and shook their hands. "I know you can't control the police, but you might mention that she didn't kill anyone. She's not a murderer. Not like Penningly."

"Oh, there are cooler heads prevailing in the Boston PD, Hutch, but they *are* looking for the perp." He shrugged and followed Willis out. "I have about as much control over their investigation as you have over… your friend."

"*Our* friend, Tony."

He nodded. "I hope so. I wouldn't want her as an enemy."

After they'd gone, Hutch stepped around his desk and closed the door. He pulled his second phone and tapped a call in to Aleksi. She answered after one ring.

"Hey."

"Hey. Sorry if I woke you."

"Nope, I'm surfing."

"How did your meeting go?"

"Yeah, I need to talk to you about that."

"Well, the feds aren't the only ones concerned. I just got a visit from our two favorite Cambridge homicide detectives."

"More warnings?"

"Basically, but it boiled down to be careful, and try not to leave as much physical evidence that points to…someone like you. Boston PD's investigating, but they're not freaking out and calling for SWAT quite yet. Not killing anyone helped."

"Well, that's good anyway."

Silence hung for a moment. "So, what about your meeting with Buckmann?"

"Yeah, that's going to take some explaining. Mind if I come over?"

His heart leapt. "I'll thaw a steak! What time?"

"Around two? I hate to break up your night, but this is pretty weird."

"No problem at all, Aleksi. I'll see you tonight."

"Okay. Thanks, Hutch."

"I love you," he said, but the call had already been cut off.

Persephone wasn't much of a burglar, but with her family's resources, breaking and entering was about as hard as polishing her nails. She used to own Hutch's condo, and even though she'd given it to him outright in the divorce, she'd kept her swipe card to get into the vestibule and elevator. These places never changed their security, and even if they had, Gi-gi could have hacked the system in moments, just like she'd hacked the video feeds to ensure that the entry wouldn't be recorded.

The elevator door opened, and Persephone strolled down the hall to Hutch's door. They'd decided the middle of the day would be the best time to do this, as most residents worked and wouldn't be home for hours. Hutch's door lock had been changed, so she resorted to a high-tech pick; just slide the little blade into the lock, apply just a little pressure, slide her finger down the bar, a little more pressure, another slide, and *click*!

She stepped in, wiped the handle, closed the door, and donned a pair of driving gloves.

The place wasn't exactly as she remembered, but an extensive remodel had been necessary after Aleksi and Derrick fought here. Half the furniture, shelving, and appliances had been destroyed. Even the stone countertop had been cracked and replaced. The new decor was okay, but could have used a bit more panache.

A rattle from the kitchen startled her, and she stared for a moment at the large green lizard in a cage there. Then she remembered. *Aleksi's pet iguana.* Hutch had adopted it after she'd been forced into hiding. She leaned down to the cage and pressed a finger to her lips.

"Shhhh."

Iggy just stared at her.

But she wasn't here to judge Hutch's décor or socialize with his lizard; she was here to spy. Their dinner together had been nice, but getting any real information about Aleksi from him had been impossible. Besides, if Hutch was actually having a relationship with Julie Parks, maybe he wasn't as close to Aleksi as they'd hoped. Still, he spoke to her occasionally, and they might discover some way to contact her with some simple surveillance.

Delving into her purse, Persephone retrieved a tiny Ziploc bag. She opened it and slid a transparent sticker with a tiny dot barely bigger than a pencil eraser into her palm. The wireless micro-camera would be activated when she turned on the receiver. She peeled off the plastic backing, picked a spot on the bookshelf, and stuck the camera in a position where the wide-angle lens would cover the dining room and kitchen. She placed another camera in the living room covering Hutch's favorite chair and the couch, another in the office, and, finally, one in his bedroom, high in the corner to cover the entire space. She decided against putting one in the bathroom. Let him have a little privacy.

Persephone also snooped a little as she placed the cameras, searching his desk, kitchen cabinets, and fridge. The stack of individually frozen steaks in the freezer caught her off guard. Hutch was a vegetarian. Then she realized they were for Aleksi. She also spotted two used condoms in the bathroom trash. *Well, well...you naughty boy.* She wondered if Aleksi knew he was fucking her former roommate.

Lastly, she withdrew the small base station for the cameras from her bag. It was barely bigger than a makeup compact, but had an impressive range and a month-long battery life. She activated the Wi-Fi receiver, and all four indicators blinked green for a moment, telling her it was working. Dropping it behind the clothes dryer—*nobody ever cleans back there*—she left the condo and locked the door behind her.

Hutch might not be willing to talk to her about Aleksi, but Persephone's family might be able to track her down with some good, old-fashioned spying.

8

His name was David Gilford, but he'd used many others throughout his career. He'd held many ranks, visited dozens of countries, and spent forty years employed by the US government, the last twenty-five of which he served as a covert operative. He was fifty-eight years old, and he was just about done.

Between training and combat injuries, his body had endured more trauma than any two NFL running backs during their entire careers. Bullet wounds, broken bones, skull fractures, cervical spine injuries, joint dislocations, compressed spinal discs, concussions, and torn muscles and tendons had left him incapable of continuing his profession. He'd been offered early retirement or participation in this new project; the choice of another decade of worsening pain and decrepitude or the chance to be reborn.

David had signed up without hesitation. Of course, the project might kill him, but that risk was nothing new.

He stood as the interview room door opened. Two men and a woman came in. The woman and one of the men wore lab coats. He'd met them for blood samples during his workup. The other man he recognized as the Director.

"Sir." He didn't salute; that habit was long dead.

"Gilford, how are you feeling?" The Director held out a hand.

"Ready, sir." David shook it. It was soft. The Director was former military but had been a desk jockey for twenty years.

"Good. I'm here to congratulate you and to thank you for volunteering for this project." The man's face went suddenly grave. "You're our primary candidate, and I want to make sure you know *exactly* what you're getting into."

"I've been fully briefed, sir." At first, David hadn't believed what they were telling him, that some long-lost fossil had infected people with a disease that changed them into...something else, something not quite human. High-resolution video of one of the previous subjects, the woman who had first been infected, had convinced him that it was true. Humans with wings, claws, teeth like razors, strength and speed unmatched... *A chance to be reborn.* "I'm one-hundred percent on board, sir."

"Yes, so you've stated in your interviews." The Director held out a hand, and the male lab geek handed over a pad. "Your skill set is impressive, but let me tell you the real reason we chose you from all the other applicants." He flipped through pages. "Throughout your exemplary career, your psych evaluations have always been rock steady. No signs of PTSD, no drug abuse, no alcoholism or behavioral issues. No insubordination either, which is unusual, considering some of the clusterfucks you've been thrown into. The only instances where you refused to carry out orders were later determined to be unlawful orders in the first place. You not only have discipline, but you have a brain, Gilford. *That,* even more than your skills, is what we need."

David didn't know what to say, so he stood mute. The Director wasn't praising him, just stating why he'd been chosen.

"The most important thing I need you to understand is that there is *absolutely* no turning back from this. The moment we inoculate you with the sample, you'll have no choice but to become something other than what you are. We don't know if you'll survive, but I feel that your chances are good. I want you to be completely honest with me. Are you ready for this?"

David answered without hesitation. "Ready and willing, sir."

"Tell me *honestly* why you want to go through with this."

The question took him aback for a moment. The truth was the only response he could give.

"My body's fucked up like a bipartisan bill in Congress, sir. I can't do my job anymore, won't sit at a desk, and *despise* the idea of retiring." He set his jaw and twisted his neck, eliciting several pops and a jolt of pain down his arm. "Better a chance like this than dying in a puddle of my own piss and shit, drooling on myself. This is a chance to live again. My *only* chance."

"I understand."

David doubted if he really did, but it didn't matter.

"You've met Doctors Price and Baker." He gestured to the woman and man wearing lab coats in turn. "They'll be helping with the initial phases. We'll need baseline samples before the inoculation."

"I understand, sir." David nodded to the two doctors. "I'm ready."

"Follow us, please, Mr. Gilford." The woman, Price, gestured to the door.

As David followed them out, the Director paused and held out a hand again.

"Thank you again, Gilford. I'll be observing from the command center. You won't be alone."

"No problem, sir." David shook his hand once again. Truth be told, he doubted he'd have one private moment for the rest of his life. He'd be under constant surveillance. But he'd be reborn, too. That seemed like an even trade.

He followed the two medics to another room, a treatment room with a padded table. The table was equipped with restraints.

"Please take off your clothes and put this on, Mr. Gilford." Price handed him a medical johnny and turned to wheel a portable monitoring system closer to the bed.

"Call me David. This mister stuff's gonna get old after a while."

"Sure, David. I'm Linda, and Dr. Baker is Bill. You'll be seeing a lot of us."

"I imagine I will." David stripped.

Forty years in government service had inured him to modesty when it came to medical exams. He had difficulty reaching behind his back to secure the johnny's ties; the cartilage of both of his shoulders had long since been shredded, rebuilt, and shredded again.

"May as well leave the top one undone." Baker held up a tangle of leads and gestured to the table. "We're going to wire you top to bottom, and we'll need to roll you on your side for a spinal."

"Fine." David climbed up, and Baker started attaching a twelve-lead heart monitor.

Price placed more leads on his head to monitor his brain waves, he imagined. She also started an IV. Her hands were cold but steady. She took several vials of blood, each one with a different colored top, inverting each once before putting them on a tray. Baker got the monitors recording and pronounced everything ready.

"Spinal next, but that's just a stick, not a catheter. We need some fluid for baseline measurements." Price pealed open a spinal tray and donned a pair of sterile gloves. "Roll onto your left side, please, and pull your knees up. I'll numb you first, so this shouldn't hurt much."

"Sure." He rolled over and pulled his knees up.

Baker untied the gown and swabbed his back. "You've got some impressive scars, David."

"Price of doing business. You know my lumbar is fucked up, right?"

"Yes, we've seen your files. Don't worry," Baker said.

"Not worried, just saving you the trouble." David held still while they prepped him, numbed the area, and put a needle in his spine. It only took a few minutes.

"Done," Price said. "That wasn't so bad, was it?"

"Didn't feel a thing." He rolled onto his back.

"Well, I can't promise this next one won't hurt." She pulled another tray from a shelf. "We need a bone marrow sample."

"Hip or thigh?" he asked.

"Hip. You've had one before?"

"Yep. We get exposed to some pretty weird shit now and then, and they always want to test us for toxins." He rolled over and pulled the gown aside. "Hurts less than getting shot. No worries."

"I wish we could just put you under for this whole thing, but they want your input on what you're feeling." She swabbed his hip and felt for the right spot. She numbed him again, then put the biopsy needle in, rotating it to get into the marrow.

David held still through the procedure, wincing only when she aspirated from the needle. Again, it only took a couple of minutes.

"Okay, that's all." She put a small bandage on the site and tapped his leg. "Roll onto your back, and we'll put some soft restraints on you. We don't know how you might react to the infusion."

"Sure." Again, he held still.

The straps were padded and warm. They girded his arms, wrists, chest, and legs. Lastly, they put a strap over his forehead, careful not to dislodge any of their telemetry. Baker put a blood pressure cuff on his right arm and cycled it once.

"Everything's recording," Baker said.

"Okay." Price donned protective gear and retrieved a red plastic container from a shelf. From inside she withdrew a single ten-cc syringe labeled with a long number and barcode, as well as biohazard tape. "This is the magic bullet, David. Last chance to back out."

"No, I'm good. Let's do this." A flutter of pre-mission adrenaline tweaked his gut.

"Don't be nervous, David," Baker said, obviously watching his brain and heart.

"Not nervous. Just hyped. I'm good."

"Okay then." Price crimped the IV, uncapped the syringe, and twisted it onto the injection port. "This is inoculation of substance *Homo draconis*-twelve to test subject, David Gilford. Injecting now."

"Tell us what you feel, David," Baker said from his monitors as she pushed the plunger.

"A little cold, like any IV," David said.

Price opened the IV to flush the line. "That's just the fluid."

David suppressed a shiver and felt his heart skip a couple of beats.

"A couple of PVC's on the heart monitor. Nothing abnormal," Price said.

"Feeling some warmth in my hands and feet," David informed them. "Yeah, it's a rush, tingling, moving up my arms and legs."

"Peripheral vasodilation." Price cycled the blood pressure cuff. "BP's a little low, but heart rate's compensating. Vasovagal reaction."

"Any light headedness, David?" Baker asked.

"Not bad. A little dizzy. Some fading, now...gray around the edges of my vision. I might...pass..." He shivered again, and the darkness that was pressing in faded back. "It's easing off. I'm good. The tingling's going away."

"Heart rate's coming back down." Baker cycled the cuff again. "BP's back in range."

"Let's give it another minute," Price said. "Let us know if you feel anything new."

"Feel pretty normal now." David waited but felt no new symptoms. "Nope, all good."

"Good. How's telemetry, Bill?"

"All normal."

"Okay, we'll call it good. I'm going to pull the IV." Price pulled the catheter from his arm and pressed a ball of cotton to the tiny wound. "Restraints off." She unbuckled him from the top down. "I'd like you to sit up slowly, David. If you get light headed, let me know."

"Sure." He did but felt fine. "Nope, I'm good."

"Excellent." She went to the shelving again and brought back two more packages. "We're going to keep the telemetry on for a little while, so I'll rig the leads to transmitters you can wear on your belt."

"How long?"

"Oh, just a few days. You'll probably start feeling flu-like symptoms and spike a fever within six hours."

"Yeah, I read the brief." He held still while she wired him up to the little transmitters and accepted her help getting dressed. Baker remained glued to his monitors.

They made sure the data was being recorded, and Price smiled at him. "Thanks, David. You're a model patient."

"No sweat, Linda."

"We'll walk you to your room, and you can relax."

"Sure." David followed them, following orders, as always. He wasn't sure what all the fuss had been about.

They showed him into a well-appointed room, complete with a living area, comfortable furniture, entertainment system, and a separate bedroom and bathroom. They told him to relax.

"You're being monitored." Price pointed to the cameras mounted here and there. "If you start feeling symptoms, just say so. If you want anything, food or something to drink, let us know. We want to make you as comfortable as possible."

"Sure. Thanks, Doc." He looked around, but for some reason couldn't remember how he'd gotten here. He remembered signing up for the project, what he was in for, even going to the treatment room, but after lying down, it was all fuzzy. "So, this is home?"

"For now. There are extra clothes in the closet, blankets, and heating pads for sore muscles. We can bring you coffee or tea or whatever you like to eat or drink."

"I'm fine for now, thanks." But he wasn't. He felt weird, like he couldn't remember the last half hour.

They left him alone, and David tried to shake of his unease. He's had short term memory loss before, but that had been due to head trauma. Other than the fancy rig attached to his scalp, he felt no injuries other than a spot of pain on his hip and the prick of the IV. He had a look at the amenities. He flipped through channels on the television, then turned it off. The game system was standard, but he'd never played much. He checked out the books they had on a tablet reader, picked one at random, and settled down in an armchair to read. After reading the same page four times without remembering what the story was about or why he was reading, he put the tablet aside and tried to relax.

Keyed up, he thought, assessing himself. *Fidgety, pre-mission nerves.*

This was nothing strange to David. He'd been on hundreds of missions of every conceivable type, and at the beginning there was always the niggling apprehension. Once things started happening, he was always fine, working the job, on task, focused. Now he felt like he was standing on the ramp of a C-130, staring out at the darkness, waiting for the green light to send him hurtling out into space.

But I've already jumped, he realized, fingering the bandage on his left arm. *It's already in me. There's no turning back now.*

David Gilford leaned back and closed his eyes, focusing on his future, recalling the high-resolution images he'd seen of the woman who had become a dragon.

Homo draconis, they called it, and it was in him. He was going to be reborn.

9

Aleksi landed on Hutch's balcony and melded into the shadows. She paused to listen, to scent the air, scan the darkness, all her dragon senses attuned to the night. People were looking for her again: police, feds, and probably someone else she didn't know anything about, someone with the resources to infiltrate a secure government facility and impersonate a federal agent. The notion both thrilled and scared her, these secret people who could mold flesh into any shape they wished. All this because she'd saved two women from human predators. All things considered, pulling those two rapists screaming from their car had been totally worth it. She'd felt alive, useful, focused for the first time in months.

The night was still, only distant city sounds and an occasional car passing on Memorial Drive. The air was warm and thick with scents, most of them human-related. The door to Hutch's condo stood open an inch, the scent of him clear, clean, tantalizing. She could see the warm glow of him sitting in the dark, a cup on the arm of his chair, heat rising from it in swirling eddies.

She slipped inside and closed the door, crouching low. "Hello, Hutch."

"Hi." The drapes closed with the hum of the electric motor, and a lamp filled the room with warm yellow light. Aleksi's eyes snapped to accommodate the illumination as he rose from his chair. "How are you?"

"Fine." She straightened from her crouch and breathed deeply through nose and mouth, taking in the scents: Hutch, coffee, meat, and several other things clicked through her mind. Iggy's cage, rotting fruit, the milk that had spilled on the counter when he poured it into his coffee, and Julie. There was a *lot* of Julie here—sweat, perfume, and more intimate scents. She'd known there would be, had prepared herself for it. *I told him to...*

But there was another scent, too. Something vaguely familiar that she couldn't quite put a name too.

Hutch interrupted her musing by coming to her with his arms wide for their customary greeting.

Aleksi backed away, and he froze. "What's wrong?"

"I'm sorry, Hutch, but we have to be more careful. I love you, but I can't let it be physical. Not at all. I can't risk it. Buckmann confirmed it; I'm infectious."

"I haven't been infected yet, Aleksi. There's no harm in—"

"No" She turned away. "The risk is too great."

"You keep saying that like *you're* the one at risk!" he snapped. "Why don't you let *me* asses the risk, since it's *mine,* not *yours?*"

She turned to stare at him, stunned. "You don't know what you're talking about. You don't *want* this, Hutch."

"And why don't you let me be the judge of *that,* too? It's *my* life!" He took a step toward her, but she backed away again. "If I did contract it, at least we could be together again."

"*No,* Hutch! I'm not going to let that happen. Not after what it did to Penningly." The thought of him catching this from her, transforming into a monster like her, sickened her. "We still don't know how this works, how it might change you. Penningly's behavior might have been linked to changes in his Y chromosome, or testosterone, or something we don't understand yet. If you turned into some kind of monster, *I'd* be the one responsible for..." She couldn't say it. "Drop it, or I'll leave and never come back!"

Hutch frowned, his eyes hard, but he finally nodded. "So, sit down and eat, and tell me what you wanted to say."

The rebuke hurt, but she couldn't fault him. "Thank you." She sat on a kitchen stool and picked up the knife and fork lying beside the slab of raw steak. The scent set her mouth watering. She sliced off a bite and ate as she spoke. "So, this Buckmann woman. You said she seemed different than you remembered, right?"

"Yes, stiffer, like she was cut out of cardboard." He recovered his coffee and went into the kitchen to refill it. "Did you notice?"

"More than that, Hutch. She's not the same person we met before."

"What?" He took a bottle of milk from the fridge and topped up his cup.

"I mean she's a different person. It looked like her, but her scent was all wrong."

"Her *scent*?" He sounded doubtful. "You can tell people apart by scent?"

"Yes."

"Well, maybe she was wearing a different perfume or—"

"Believe me, Hutch, I can tell!" His skepticism irritated her. "Just like I can tell your milk's going bad, Iggy's cage needs to be cleaned, and you and Julie had sex on that couch, and again in the bedroom."

His mouth dropped open and his face flushed. "How can you… Aleksi, I can explain! We've been working out together, and it just kind of happened! I don't—"

"You don't have to explain anything Hutch. It's okay." She ate another bite of steak, forcing herself to remain calm. *I told him to, and he deserves someone human.* "It's good in fact. I like Julie. She's exactly what you need."

"Exactly what I *need*? What do you mean by that?"

Aleksi swallowed and stared at him. "You really want me to answer that?"

His face flushed again, but this time it was anger, not embarrassment. "What I *need* is *you*!"

"Well, I'm not me anymore, am I?" She took another bite of raw meat and chewed. "And we take what joy we can get, don't we? Julie's nice, and I told you to find someone else. She'll be good for you, and you'll be good for her. It's okay." She forced herself to believe it.

"I didn't mean for it to happen," he said.

"I said, it's *okay*. Can we talk about something important now?" She took a deep breath through nose and mouth. "Like who was the other woman in here?"

"Other woman?" He looked a little stunned. "What do you mean?"

"There was someone else here recently, like today or yesterday." She breathed in again. "One of your new grad students?"

"No. Nobody's been here but Julie and you."

"Huh." She finished the steak and stood. "Mind if I sniff around? The feds might have sent someone in here to bug the place."

Hutch looked suspicious, like she was making fun of him or something, but waved at the room. "Go ahead."

She did. The scent seemed strongest in the kitchen, on the cabinets and refrigerator, and again on the closet door in the bedroom, but not on the bed, then again faintly in the bathroom. Hutch followed her, still looking skeptical.

"So, I thought you came here to talk to me about Buckmann, not sniff out intruders."

"I did, but..." Aleksi stopped and sniffed again. An olfactory memory exploded in her mind. "Shit! That's it!"

"That's what?"

"Buckmann!" She shook her head and closed her eyes, letting the olfactory input conjure the image in her mind. "Or rather *Johansen*! The woman at the top of the Prudential Tower. *That's* the scent I'm getting! She was here!"

"Wait. You really meant that they were two completely different people?"

"Yes, Hutch, and Buckmann confirmed it." She strode back out to the living room, and he followed. "When I met with her, she didn't smell right, and I...confronted her about it. She said someone had impersonated her. She was abducted, and someone who looked just like her, good enough to fool all her coworkers and security, took her place. They even managed to get her passwords, and she swore they weren't written down anywhere. *That* was the woman we both met. She stole the specimen, and tried to wipe all the data from the fed's system. They didn't get it all, but the imposter escaped undetected. That's the investigation she wants me to help with."

"Wow." Hutch looked flabbergasted. Then his brow furrowed. "But how does she expect you to help with that? You didn't even know about it until yesterday."

"Yeah, but whoever took her place did it to steal the specimen and Penningly's body. They're interested in the infection, Hutch, which means they'll also be interested in *me*."

He shook his head. "But how could anyone impersonate someone to that degree?"

"I don't know, and neither did Buckmann, but she said it wasn't a simple mask or prosthetics. The only way she didn't match perfectly was mannerisms and gait. It was *physical*, flesh and blood." She raised a clawed hand and turned it. "Flesh can be altered. I'm evidence of that. If these people can change physical appearances through some kind of biological or genetic intervention, maybe they could change *me*."

Hutch opened his mouth, then closed it, then said, "You really think that's possible?"

She carefully extended her wings, flexing her claws. "Would you have believed *this* was possible if you hadn't seen it?"

"No, and you're right. If you can be changed to this degree, other changes are possible. I don't know how, but..." His face lit up. "That means there's *hope*, Aleksi."

"That's what's got me worried, Hutch." Aleksi wrapped her wings around herself as if she could shield her heart from that hope.

"What?"

He didn't understand. "Hope is a double-edged sword. Coming to grips with what I am has been hard enough. Hoping for a cure, then having that hope crushed... I don't think I could do it."

"Even if it means a chance to be *you* again?" He took a step closer, but didn't try to touch her. "Even if it means a chance we could be *together* again?"

Hope pierced her thin armor and her heart beneath. "I've got to think about this." She started for the door.

"Be careful out there, please. I can't lose you."

Aleksi stopped at the curtain and looked back at him. She loved him still, but she was afraid they'd already lost each other. He opened his mouth to say something, but she couldn't stand to hear it again. Not now. She was through the curtain and into the night before he could speak.

"We're in trouble," Persephone turned away from the damning monitor and started to pace the floor of the Sanctum.

"Aleksi's olfactory capabilities *are* truly astounding, and yes, we are in trouble." Gi-gi started the recording from Hutch's apartment from the beginning, studying it closely. "We must decide how to deal with this."

"How can she even *do* that! I barely touched anything, and I wore gloves."

"Oils and pheromones on the gloves, perhaps. That she could match your scent to your encounter at the Prudential is even more intriguing. The physical changes of your disguise would mask your scent somewhat, but your sweat would carry pheromones and other components that weren't altered. She picked those out and matched them. That implies a true olfactory memory of exquisite precision."

Persephone stopped her pacing. "You don't think she could match it to when we met earlier, do you?"

"Well, she hasn't yet. Perhaps the olfactory memory doesn't go back that far. She was not yet enhanced when you met her before."

"Thank God." Persephone resumed pacing. "So, now she and Hutch know Buckmann was impersonated and there's a third player in this game."

"A fourth, if you count the police."

Persephone waved a hand. "A minor inconvenience."

"A police officer killed Derrick Penningly, Great-Granddaughter. Sergeant Jasper is a sharp one, and he's as relentless as a virus."

"Also true." *And he saved Hutch's life when I was still blocks away.*

"We must be careful, Great-Granddaughter. If Aleksi catches your scent, she could make the connection and barter your identity to Buckmann."

"For what? They can't cure her. They barely understand what they *do* have." They'd hoped to eradicate the specimen from government possession, but had known of their failure shortly after. Gi-gi monitored their communications and knew the Johansen Project was still underway. They didn't, however, know exactly how far it had progressed.

"No, but she doesn't know that. If they trick her into trusting them, they might be able to abduct her."

"I hope she's smarter than that."

"Hope is a dangerous thing, my dear. You saw Aleksi's face when your former husband mentioned a potential cure for her condition." Gi-gi stopped the recording and zoomed on Aleksi's features, her slit pupils wide, her hardened features struck dumb.

An idea niggled at the base of Persephone's mind. "But what if *we* were the ones to offer her that hope?"

Gi-gi turned to look at her, lavender eyes wide. "We might be able to offer her true hope, dear, but it would be dangerous in the extreme. We'd be *literally* meddling in the affairs of dragons."

"And she has my scent."

"Yes, and that." They stared at each other in silence for a long span. "I'll watch closely. If we can discover a safe way to contact her without giving our secrecy away, we will attempt it."

"Okay. Good." Persephone turned to go, but Gi-gi's sandpaper whisper brought her back.

"Are you sure, my dear, that you wouldn't consider this transformation yourself? Aleksi has shown us that she's stable, and her capabilities are truly astounding."

"No, thank you, Gi-gi." She smiled at the offer, but then remembered the tiny crow's feet creeping into the corners of her eyes, the sagging breasts in the mirror, the first twinges of hot flashes plaguing her sleep. "Not yet, anyway. Not until we understand it better. If we can make the changes selective, pick the evolution apart for *some* of the traits, then *maybe*."

"The transformation is vast and intricate, Great-Granddaughter. It could take decades to unravel all of its secrets."

"Then, if I'm still alive when it's unraveled, I'll consider it." Persephone turned away and left the Sanctum.

This wasn't the first time she'd felt that kind of pressure from Gi-gi. It was the way of their family to pass their gifts to the next aging generation. The benefits of longevity and genius, and now the traits of *Homo draconis*, were, so far, bridges that were burned the moment they were crossed.

Not yet, she resolved. *Not while I've still got so much living to do.*

10

The fever's broken. How are you feeling?" Dr. Baker shone a penlight into David's eyes, the brightness painful.

"Wrung out, like I had the flu." David tolerated the exam. He followed orders, but he was a little tired of being asked how he felt. He'd given them a detailed account of his misery over the last four days. "Achy still, but not bad. I'm hungry."

"Again?" Baker tapped his pad. "You've already had over two pounds of protein today."

"What can I say, Doc? I'm a growing boy, right?" He stretched his neck in an attempt to alleviate the ache and tolerated the usual shot of pain down his arm.

"We hope so." Baker put his pad down. "I've sent for a meal. Want something for the pain?"

"No, I'm okay. It'll fuck up the results, right?" They were taking blood samples twice a day now and had left an IV in his arm to make it easier. The cardiac and brainwave monitors were cumbersome, however. "A hot shower, maybe."

"Sure. You can disconnect for a while. I'll send a tech to hook you back up."

"Thanks." He stretched again while Baker checked reflexes, felt pulses, and peered in his ears, nose, and mouth. The doctor then gave David a strain gauge to squeeze and logged the results. "So, how soon do you expect to see changes."

"We're already seeing some. Your temperature's still significantly elevated, blood-pressure is up, and your white cell count is through the roof. Primary immune response, for the most part, but we're seeing new proteins in your blood already. It's progressing."

"Okay, good." David flexed his aching hands. "Mind if I stretch. If I sit on my ass too long, it starts to think I'm a civilian."

"No problem, I'm done." Baker put his tablet away, packed up his equipment, and stripped off his protective gear. They were being careful around him, of course. This thing was infectious, but it wasn't airborne, so gloves, gowns, and face shields were enough to keep them safe. "I'll see you later."

"Later, Doc." David got up slowly, still shaky from the fever. He'd contracted dengue once in Panama, and it had nothing on this bug. He twisted slowly against the aches, pushing through the pain. He was used to that, at least. Getting old wasn't for wimps.

He heard someone outside his door before the knock. "Yeah."

It opened and one of the techs he'd seen came in with a tray. "T-bone steak, medium rare!"

"Thanks." He watched her as she put the tray on the coffee table. "I didn't catch your name."

"Amy." She flashed him a brief smile. "Baker said you needed someone to reconnect your telemetry after you shower. Just say when you're ready, and I'll come hook you up."

"Thanks, Amy." The aroma of the steak made his mouth water. "See you later."

"Later." She left with a little wave.

David sat down to eat. The steak seemed a little overdone, but it was tender and delicious. Their chef knew their job, but it was pretty hard to ruin good meat. When the bone was bare, he picked it up and stripped the last bits of meat off with his teeth. After a big glass of water, and he felt sated, good even.

He stood and finished his stretches, working through the pain, refusing the weakness. It came easier than usual, like four days in bed had given his joints a chance to heal from the constant strain he put them through. When his muscles were warm and the aches had eased somewhat, he looked to the nearest monitor and waved.

"Okay, I'm disconnecting for a shower."

"Fine, David. Glad to see you feeling better."

David was surprised to recognize the Director's voice. "Good to feel better, sir."

He unplugged the leads from the pads affixed to his skin, placed the telemetry packs on the counter, and went to the bathroom. Turning on the hot water, he shucked out of his slightly funky bedclothes and looked at himself in the sink mirror. The same old torn-up soldier stared back at him, scars and tattoos unchanged. "Well, this isn't going to happen overnight, is it?"

David adjusted the water and stepped in, relishing the hot spray on his aching muscles. Soap alleviated the background irritation of so long in bed without a bath, but it was the water that felt good. He adjusted it hotter and let it pound against the back of his neck for a while. Never one to idle excessively, he shut off the shower and toweled dry. He felt good, clear-headed, sharp. The shower had given him energy.

After brushing his teeth—the toothpaste tasted funny—he wrapped the towel around his waist and went to his bedroom for fresh clothes. Knowing the tech would be hooking him up again, he just put on a clean pair of pajama bottoms and called it good. "Okay, I'm done. Ready for the hookup."

"There in a minute," came the reply. Not the Director this time, but the voice was male. Maybe Baker.

David grabbed a shirt and went back out to the living room. He poured himself a glass of water and drank it down to wash the taste of the toothpaste from his mouth.

Amy knocked and came in with a cheerful, "Room service!"

He chuckled and said, "Sorry to bug you with this, but I don't know which lead goes where."

"No problem." She put on gloves and a face shield. "All part of the job."

"Thanks." He stood still while she hooked him up and hung the data transmitters on his waistband. Bending down so she could reach the pads on his head, he caught a whiff of her. It wasn't perfume, but maybe some body lotion or something. She smelled good.

"You've seen a lot of mileage," she said.

"Got that right."

"I rotated through Iraq, but never saw any fire. Saw a lot of torn-up soldiers, though." She affixed the last lead to his scalp. "You've got all your limbs, at least. Fucking IED's took a toll."

"Yep, a bomb can surely ruin your day." David had placed hundreds of the devices himself, all over the world. He wondered if she'd treated any of his victims.

"Sure can." She smiled and turned to the nearest pickup. "Test the feed."

"All good. We're getting everything clean," came the reply.

"Excellent." She turned back and took up his clean shirt. "Let me help you with this. It'll be easier with all the leads."

"Sure." David watched the pulse in Amy's neck, the tiny hairs on her skin, her eyelashes, and breathed in the sweet scent of her. "Thanks, Amy."

"No problem, David." She went to the door and stripped off her protective gear. "Give a shout if you need anything."

"I will." David stared at the door for a moment after it closed, then turned to find something to read. *Follow orders... Part of the job...* The problem was, he had no orders, no task but to sit and relax. He tried to tell himself it was like a vacation, like leave or time off, but sitting in a chair and reading a crime novel wasn't his idea of fun. Still, the story was good, even if the protagonist was a little too hard-boiled to be sympathetic. He put the book down after about an hour and got up to stretch again.

"Are you in pain, David?" the voice asked.

"Not really, just stiff. No more than usual. Sitting makes it worse."

"We can bring in some exercise equipment if you like."

"Sure. That'd be great." It would give him something to do, too. He thought about asking for another meal, but reconsidered. Maybe later, when his appetite was sharper. Food always tasted better when he was really hungry. He stretched and did some deep breathing exercises, trying to relax, let the anxiety and restlessness leave him with every exhaled breath. *You've already made the jump, soldier. There's only one destination.* His mind wandered, the faint scent of Amy bringing visions, memories of his dreams.

David hadn't told them about the dreams yet. They were just from the fever, and nightmares of blood were nothing new for him. Still, these were different. With his experiences jumping out of aircraft, he'd had thousands of dreams of flying, but none like these. They were like looking through someone else's eyes, feeling through someone's skin, tasting through their tongue, full of swooping and diving through trees, chasing game down for the kill. He could still taste the meat in his mouth. His stomach growled.

He caved and turned to a camera. "How about some coffee and a snack. Beef jerky, or something."

"On the way."

"Thanks." David reached for the remote and turned on the TV, forcing himself to relax. Food would stop his growling stomach, and maybe Amy would bring it. He liked her. She was military and knew soldiers.

Besides, he thought as he heard her footsteps approaching from down the hall, *she smells good enough to eat.*

Hutch sat in the third row of the theatre, watching Julie on stage. He could barely recognize her in all the makeup, but there was no mistaking her.

The play was a farcical rendition of The Wizard of Oz in which the wicked witch was the protagonist. Dorothy and her vicious canine-human companion, Toto, were evil invaders who dropped houses on her sisters and stole the family's magical shoes. Of course, it was set in "Ozton," a parody of Boston. Julie had the title role of Ozwitch, the Wicked Good Witch of Worchester. Green paint, a black wig, and a beak nose disguised her to the point of absurdity, but her voice came through, and she moved with animated grace.

Hutch had never seen Julie perform before, and he had to admit, she was good. The play wasn't her creation, but the writing was good, the humor spot on, and the music and choreography played to the talents of the cast. Evil Dorothy, a comically buxom blonde made up to look like a dominatrix Dolly Parton, drew laughs and cheers from the audience for her audacity and outright evil, but when Julie took center stage, and the lights lowered, the theatre hushed, and she shone like a diamond among lesser stones. She had it all, voice, grace, poise, and perfect timing. The audience loved her.

But Hutch didn't.

He appreciated the play, and cheered her performance, but Julie didn't pull on his heart like Aleksi did. They enjoyed each other, but that was as far as it went. It was more than just sex; they took pleasure in each other's company, too, but there was no love. Julie had even said they were "fuck-buddies," once. Hutch found that a little crude, but apt.

And Aleksi knew about, and even *approved* of the relationship. He was still trying to square that away in his head without the added weirdness of a secret organization capable of identity changing genetic manipulation infiltrating the DHS to steal a fossilized dragon.

With all the absurdities that had invaded his life rambling around in his brain, the farcical play seemed downright normal.

The performance ended predictably and hilariously, with a comically tiny house dropped on evil Dorothy, the ruby slippers and a pair of comically huge boobs sticking out from under the edge. The Wicked Good Witch of Worchester and her troop of flying monkeys performed the final number, "Ding-dong, the Bitch is Dead," surrounded by adoring munchkins. The curtain came down, and the cast took their bows to roaring applause.

Ozwitch was a hit.

Hutch stayed seated until most of the crowd had filtered out, then strolled to the side door. He approached the guy at the backstage door with a smile. "I'm with Julie Parks. Dwayne Hutchinson."

"Oh, sure." He glanced at his clipboard and checked off a name. "So, how'd you like the show?"

"Loved it!" He thanked the guy and went in, thinking, *but I don't love Julie.*

Backstage was pandemonium, as Julie had assured him opening nights usually were. The entire cast seemed to be hugging one another and doffing their costumes all at once. The wardrobe team looked haggard, trying to sort out clothing, witch noses, and monkey wings, and hang it all up without damage. Evil Dorothy shucked out of her gown, fake boobs and all, and handed it over while carrying on a conversation with her evil team of axe-murder tin man, cannibalistic lion, and crow-murdering scarecrow. Fortunately, the cast wore clothes beneath their costumes.

Hutch caught a passing guy's arm and asked, "Julie Parks?"

"Sure. In the back getting degreased." He pointed to the line of lit makeup tables where actors were scrubbing of paint and peeling off prosthetics.

"Thanks." Hutch worked his way through the throng and spotted Julie at the last seat in the row. Her hair was tied back for her wig, and she wore jeans and a strapless pushup bra that gave her costume cleavage. She scrubbed at the green paint with one moistened towelette after another. He stepped up behind her and leaned down to meet her eyes in the mirror. "You were sensational."

"Hutch!" She vaulted up and whirled around to kiss him, then cringed.

"Oops. Sorry!" She snatched another towelette and wiped his mouth. "Makeup."

"It's okay." He took the towelette and gestured back to the mirror. "Go ahead. I've got this."

"Ha! Old hand at wiping off unwanted lipstick, right?" She plopped back down and resumed her work. "Never green, I'll bet."

"Nope. Green's a first." Hutch leaned down so he could see himself over Julie's shoulder and wiped at the smudges on his face.

"So, you really liked it?" Julie asked, obviously still running on a rush from the performance.

"Yeah, really. It was fun, and you were flawless."

"Well, we'll see what the critics say. Opening night's always a catastrofuck."

"I'm no theatre critic, but it looked good to me." He tossed the towelette in the trash and kissed a clean spot on her neck. "Let's celebrate with a late dinner. Wherever you like, on me."

"Oh, no, not until closing night. No celebrations until the fat lady sings!" She knocked on the edge of the table. "Bad luck."

"Okay, then let's just hit Sulmona for pizza. I'm starving, and you're keyed up like a grand piano."

"No shit. Sounds good, then you can take me home and put me to bed." She caught his eye in the mirror and winked. "Or maybe the reverse. No better way to come down from an adrenaline high, and I've *got* to sleep tonight."

"Your performance isn't until eight tomorrow. Why not sleep in?" She had still never spent an entire night at his place.

"I've got to work on my rom-com in the morning. Between school and *Ozwitch*, weekends are the only time I can write my own stuff."

Julie had told him she was working on a musical romantic comedy that she hoped to get on Broadway, or rather Off-Off-Broadway. If she did, it would be her first major production. She was working with several others, but she was the writer. It was her baby. She hadn't let him read it yet but promised to when it was finished. It was called "Up and Down" and focused on the love life of an upscale hotel's elevator attendant.

Julie finished with the towelettes and asked him. "Did I miss any?"

He checked her over. "Left ear."

When she was clean and dressed, they left through the back door of the theater arm in arm. Julie was positively bouncing with energy, and he found her exuberance infectious. In no time they were laughing and hip-checking each other on the way to his car.

He still didn't love her, but Julie was fun. Maybe Aleksi was right. Maybe this was exactly what he needed.

Aleksi watched from the roof of the theatre as Hutch and Julie laughed and joked their way down the street. She'd been internet-stalking Julie for a few days, knew about the play's opening night, and suspected she would ask Hutch to come watch her perform. Watching them together like this hit her harder even than watching them in his condo. The jealously was still there but distant now. The urge to fly down and tear Julie apart was fleeting and easily suppressed. She wasn't a beast, but she wasn't human either. She still loved Hutch, but it could never be like it was. What hurt even more was watching their easy way with each other, the companionship, the warmth, the laughter.

I never had that with him, she realized.

They loved each other, certainly, but their relationship had been shrouded in sadness. They'd gotten together in the midst of a crisis, supporting each other, needing each other, but they'd never had anything like this easy-going banter. That was what she had lost with her transformation, the chance to be best friends with the man she loved.

Unless... Hope smote her heart even harder than the loss of love. *I can't do it again. I can't think I have a chance to be human again. I'm not, and I never will be.*

With that resolve, Aleksi launched herself into the night and wheeled toward the canyons of Boston. The weekend loomed, and the city was buzzing, but it was early. She had plenty of time to hunt, but where?

College campuses had ridiculous amounts of security, cameras on every building, every lamppost, every doorway. Still, with an average of two sexual assaults every night, it was a rich hunting ground. In a city like Boston, however, there was no shortage of prey. The clubs would close at two-am, but she had hours yet. Maybe she'd check out some of the bars south of town in the rougher neighborhoods.

She wheeled through downtown, past the soaring towers, the empty offices. *Prowling for evil-doers,* she thought with a smile. *Who the hell am I, Batman? Dragon Woman?*

Aleksi pictured herself with a stylized DW painted on her chest and snorted a laugh.

Soaring past a corner penthouse, she flew within a few yards of a couple making love on a balcony. The woman gripped the railing, facing the night, her lover behind her. For a flashing instant, their eyes met, and the woman drew a gasp.

Then Aleksi was gone, past, vanished into the darkness, but the woman had seen her.

Shit! Be more careful! She dipped lower, just above the streetlights but below the balconies, her safe zone. *You're all alone now. Nobody to rely on but yourself. It's better this way. Safer...*

Aleksi kept up the litany of justifications for her solitude well into South Boston, Roxbury, and Dorchester. Here she flew among the neighborhoods, weaving in and around the trees, the mean-looking apartment buildings, the rows of single-family homes, the neon lights of TVs shining through drawn curtains. There were bars and clubs on almost every corner, and music blared. Shouts rang out, obscenities, threats, curses.

Then she heard a scream and breaking glass.

11

Okay, so maybe the bedroom camera was a bad idea. Persephone looked away from the scene of Hutch and Julie in his bed, angry with Gi-gi for bringing her down here to see this.

"What's the point of watching this?" She didn't bother keeping the barbs out of her voice. "I *know* he's having sex with Julie Parks! I don't need to *watch* it!"

"Calm yourself, Great-Granddaughter. It's not about the sex. It's what happens after that is interesting." Gi-gi's lavender eyes swiveled to pin Persephone like a butterfly. "If you can't deal with this situation objectively, I can—"

"Stop it." Persephone glared at her. "Just because I don't care to watch the man I used to be *married* to fuck another woman, doesn't mean I'm not on task!"

"Very well." Gi-gi's finger moved on the remote, and the scene went into fast forward.

The scene—Persephone couldn't help but watch out of the corner of her eye—took on a comical aspect at high speed. The couple moved so fast she wouldn't have been surprised if they spontaneously combusted from friction.

She remembered her time with Hutch, all the tenderness, his attentive lovemaking. This seemed almost mechanical in comparison, hasty—just sex. Still, she couldn't blame Hutch for hooking up with Julie. The girl was certainly hot, and enthusiastic, and inventive, and... *Maybe I could have stayed with him. God, I hate my family sometimes...* Finally, after a last shuddering climax, Gi-gi slowed the speed again.

"That was nice," Julie grabbed a towel from the nightstand and slid off. She kissed him and rolled out of bed. "Just what the doctor ordered."

Nice? Persephone thought. *That seems a little impersonal.*

"*Nice?* I think we broke the bed." He accepted the towel from her and wiped off.

"Sorry. That was a stupid thing to say." She stepped into panties and reached for her jeans. "It was great, Hutch. I'm just...feeling a little weird, I guess. Wired and tired. I need sleep."

"Stay, then." He rolled out of bed and took her by the shoulders. "Hey, you okay?"

"I'm fine, Hutch, and I can't stay." She kissed him and turned away to pick up her bra. "You get up stupid early, and I need a full eight hours."

"Well, let me at least drive you home." He reached for a shirt.

She's running away, Persephone thought.

"No, I'll Uber it." She pulled a tee-shirt over her head and shook her hair free. "I don't want to complicate things."

"Complicate things?" He grabbed his jeans and pulled them on without underwear. "What's complicated about a ride home?"

"Hutch." Julie stopped and faced him. "Look, I like you. I like you a *lot*. We have fun together, and..." She gestured to the bed. "And that's just... *God,* Hutch, you have no right to be so fucking *nice,* okay. Why can't you just fuck me and tell me to get out?"

Persephone gasped.

"Julie! Hey! Where the hell is *this* coming from?"

Julie folded her arms defensively. "It's about Aleksi, okay?"

What the... Persephone gaped, struck dumb.

"Aleksi?" Hutch looked just as floored as she. "What are you talking about, Jules? I haven't—"

"Just stop it, Hutch. I know you're still in love with her, okay? I can tell. Just don't lie about it."

"Lie about it? I haven't even spoken to her in months."

"Come on, Hutch. You may not be seeing her, but I know you're at least *talking* to her." She turned to pick a phone off the nightstand and held it out to him. "The spare phone?"

"Okay. Look, Julie, I do talk to her occasionally, but that's all." He snatched the phone away from her and tossed it onto the rumpled bed. "There's no relationship for you to be jealous about. There can't be."

"I'm *not* jealous!"

"Then what *are* you, Jules? You're certainly pissed off at me, and I can't figure out what I've done wrong. I talk to another woman on the phone occasionally. Yes, we were in love, and I think about her a lot. Do I still love her?" He shrugged. "Probably, but not the way you think."

"Why *not*, Hutch?"

"*What?*" He reeled back like she'd slapped him.

"Why not *be* with her? Why does she have to stay away? What the fuck *happened* to her?"

He stared at her for a few breaths. "I can't tell you, Jules. It's…more complicated than you can imagine."

"Does it have to do with Bob's murder?" Julie's voice shook.

"Indirectly, I suppose, but…" He sighed. "I'm not lying to you, Julie. I don't know where Aleksi lives, or what she's doing, or why she's doing it, but I promised not to tell anyone about her…situation. She's…not the same person we knew. She's changed so much you wouldn't even recognize her."

Well, that's the cold hard truth, Persephone thought, but she could hear the pain in Hutch's voice.

Julie stood silent for a while, then wiped her eyes. "I'm sorry, Hutch."

"Don't be. You don't deserve this."

"No, but neither do you." She stepped up to him and caressed his cheek with her fingertips. "Friends still?"

"Of course." He cupped her face in his hands and kissed her.

"Thanks for telling me the truth." She wrapped her arms around him and squeezed. "And thanks for putting up with the cranky witch from Worchester."

He laughed. "You mean the wicked *good* witch from Worchester."

Julie laughed. "You were pretty wicked good yourself, Doctor."

"What the hell is that about?" Persephone asked as they kissed again.

"A play," Gi-gi whispered. "Not important. Watch."

"Sure you don't want a ride home?" Hutch asked again.

"No, I'm fine." Julie pulled her phone from a pocket and walked into the living room. "One tap, and my ride's here in two minutes. No complications."

"No complications." He smiled and escorted her to the door, and the monitor shifted to another camera. "How many more shows?"

"Eight. If you want to come to closing night, there's always a party after." She opened the door and turned to him. "You might get lucky and hook up with a sexy actress."

"Already got one, but I'd love to come to closing night." He kissed her goodbye. "Be safe, okay?"

"Yes, Doctor." She smiled and left.

Hutch locked the door and went straight to his bedroom. There, he retrieved the spare phone from the bed and punched the entry code. The screen was facing the camera when he pulled up the phone app.

"This!" Gi-gi froze the recording and zoomed in on the phone. The tiny camera's resolution was just good enough to read the screen. There was only one contact: AR, and the number beside it stood there plain as day. "Aleksi's number."

"Play it," Persephone whispered.

Gi-gi zoomed back out and resumed the recording. Hutch tapped the call icon and paced with the phone to his ear, but didn't say anything. No answer. He ended the call, and tapped a messaging app, his thumbs a blur. The image wasn't good enough to read what he sent, but it was short. He tucked the phone away and left the room.

"So, we have her number," Gi-gi said.

"What do we do with it?" Persephone asked.

"We proceed with exquisite care, my dear. But there is another question we should be asking."

"Why is Julie Parks so interested in Aleksi?"

"Exactly that. There are no coincidences around the dragon, Great-Granddaughter, and I do *not* believe that a woman of Parks's charismatic qualities is so emotional about a lover's old flame. Even if they *were* roommates."

"They *were* friends, but yes, I agree. She's a consummate actress. Her performance was good, maybe even good enough to fool Hutch, but... No, I don't think Julie Parks is the type to pine over a dead boyfriend for six months, then whine about her lover's long-lost girlfriend."

"I believe I'll take a closer look at Miss Parks."

"And I get to figure out what to say to Aleksi Rychenkna, right?"

"Correct." Gi-gi touched the remote again and flicked through the pictures of the two injured men and the mutilated Ford Taurus. "Tread with care, Great-Granddaughter."

"With Aleksi?" She snorted a laugh. "Always."

God, I hate mornings," Willis muttered as they got out of the car. "Why can't we ever talk to someone at like *noon* or something?"

"Because nobody else likes mornings either." Jasper looked up at the single-family home, the peeling paint, unkept landscaping, and the blue tarp nailed up to cover the front window. "Tired people don't lie well. You know the drill."

"You and your element of surprise."

Jasper looked at Willis and laughed. "Late night last night?"

"Charles wanted to go out. God, I hate nightclubs."

"You hate everything before eight a.m."

"The world sucks before eight a.m."

They climbed the steps, and Jasper pulled his badge and knocked. Nobody answered. He knocked again and called out. "Police officers, Mrs. Wilbur."

A deadbolt clicked, and a chain rattled. The door opened a crack, and a middle-aged woman with a battered face squinted through the gap. "What do you want? I already gave my statement."

"I'm Sergeant Jasper, and this is Detective Willis, Mrs. Wilbur. We're homicide detectives." He didn't tell her they were Cambridge PD, and that Roxbury was far out of their jurisdiction. "We believe the events of last night might have a bearing on a case we're investigating."

"Homicide?" The woman made a face, and Jasper saw that several of her teeth were missing. Mrs. Wilbur had a long list of domestic violence complaints. Her husband liked to drink, and when he drank, he liked to hit things. She was his favorite punching bag. "Wasn't any murder."

"We know, Mrs. Wilbur. But the person who invaded your home last night might be involved in another incident." He gave her his most imploring look. "We're trying to prevent another person from being hurt, or even killed, ma'am. We just want to ask you some questions about what happened."

"All right, I guess." She closed the door, pulled the chain, and opened it wide. "Don't know what I can tell you. It happened fast, and I didn't see much."

"We read the report, ma'am," Willis said.

They'd also seen the pictures of her husband's injuries. He was still at Boston Medical Center, scheduled for surgery today to put his crushed hands back together. He wouldn't be hitting his wife for a while.

"Then you know everything I do. Don't know what else I can tell you." She didn't offer them a place to sit, but the living room was still pretty torn up. "Didn't see much. It happened too fast."

"Yes, you said someone smashed through your front window and attacked your husband. He was hitting you again, right?"

"Fuck yes, he was hitting me!" She pointed to her face. "He fucking hits me all the fucking time, and none of you cops ever did a fucking thing about it! Now he's in the hospital and won't be able to work for like fucking *months*!"

"He also won't be hitting you for months." Jasper had read the long file on the couple. Wilbur's husband had a rap sheet longer than a federal inquest, but his wife had always dropped charges before he did any jail time. Evidently, he was a nice guy when he was sober. "We only want to ask you about this person who invaded your home and hurt your husband."

"The *person*?" She snorted a laugh. "You wouldn't believe me if I told you."

"Your report said a person. You're saying it wasn't?"

She looked away from them. "Some fuckin' freak in a Batman outfit."

"A *Batman* outfit?" Jasper traded a glance with Willis. "Can you describe it?"

"No, I can't. It happened too fast, and I'd just been knocked flat." She glared at Jasper. "Just a big fuckin' blur. Like gold colored. Big fucking wings like a bat."

"And did you see this person hurt your husband."

"No. He turned around and the...whatever the fuck it was...just grabbed him, and he screamed." She sniffed and looked away again. "Thought it was gonna kill him, then me. I closed my eyes. When I opened them, it was gone. Ben was layin' there with his hands lookin' like he stuck 'em in a chipper."

"You said 'it', ma'am. Could you tell if it was a man or a woman?"

She stared at Jasper like he'd insulted her. "I'm not even sure it was fuckin' *human,* and before you accuse me of being high, or crazy, go look at Ben's hands. Nobody could have done that to him. Nobody *normal* anyway."

"We're not suggesting you were intoxicated, and we've seen the medical report, ma'am. We're just interested in your honest account of what happened."

"Yeah, well, you got it." She frowned. "And I got a smashed-up house, a husband who can't work, a bashed-up face, and ain't even had my coffee yet."

"I'm sorry to have disturbed your morning, ma'am. We'll be going. Thank you."

"Yeah, sure." She opened the door and ushered them out without another word.

Jasper and Willis didn't speak until they were in their car.

"Our girl. No doubt," Marty said.

"Who else?" Tony agreed.

"She's gonna kill some fucker if she keeps this up."

"Maybe." Jasper pulled his coffee from the cup holder and drank. It was cold. "Depends on who she catches and what they're doing, I think."

"Probably, but with her temper, it's just a matter of time. She catches someone hurting a kid or something, it's all over. And once she crosses that line…" Willis sipped his coffee and grimaced.

"She likes what she's doing, that's for sure." He drank the last of his cold coffee. "Hungry?"

"No, but I could use another coffee."

Jasper started the car and nodded. "Not my neighborhood. Find the nearest DD."

"Because it's always time for Dunkin'!" Willis pulled up his phone and punched the Dunkin' Donuts app. "And calories don't count if it's donuts."

Tony chuckled. "Hey, they're shaped like zeroes, right? That's the calories! It's like nutritional information right there in donut form."

Marty snorted and peered at his phone. "Four blocks, then left."

When Aleksi got back to her lair, she settled down to eat and checked her phone out of habit. She'd missed a call from Hutch at ten thirty the night before. He hadn't left a message, but had texted. It simply said, "Need to talk."

She didn't feel like talking to him. She put the phone down and took another bite of the butt roast she'd snagged from behind her favorite butcher shop. It was two days past the 'Sell By' date, but was far from old. Humans were so squeamish about food.

Her phone vibrated.

"Goddamn it Hutch, I don't *want* to talk to you!" After watching him with Julie, she was surprised he wanted to talk to her, too. He had everything he needed. She was a danger to him, nothing more. He probably had gotten word from Buckmann or Jasper about the night before and wanted to tell her to be careful again. She *was* being careful, and she wasn't going to stop.

But when she picked up the phone, the text wasn't from Hutch.

Wrong number? She pulled up the text and stared at it, cold tendrils of fear creeping up her spine.

It read, "We can help you, Aleksi."

The incoming number was blocked. That suggested the feds, but this didn't sound like something Buckmann would have sent, and she'd said they didn't have a cure yet. *The people running the Johansen Project?* she wondered. She felt like answering with a curt obscenity, but didn't want to give them the satisfaction. One thing was certain, someone had gotten her number. She needed a new phone, and if this one had been hacked, they might be able to listen in.

Oh, for a credit card and an Amazon account, she thought. Hutch had suggested she use his credit card to make purchases, but those could be traced. Besides, she didn't think a UPS driver would deliver to a disused subway tunnel. She'd have to get Hutch a message somehow. Email wasn't safe either; she had little doubt that the feds were watching him again.

"Not today." She put the phone down and returned to her meal.

The phone vibrated again. This time the text read, "Not DHS. Met you atop the P Tower. We can help you."

Johansen, Aleksi thought, recalling the scent in Hutch's home. They must have gotten her number from his phone, but he never left it lying around. This was exactly what Buckmann had foreseen; they were interested in her, and they were offering help.

But could she trust them?

The answer to that was an emphatic, "Hell, no!"

Aleksi turned the phone off and finished her meal. There was no cure for what she had become. They were just dangling hope like a lure, waiting for her to bite. Well, she wasn't that stupid.

Sated, she cleaned up, stowed the trash, and lay down to sleep. Memories of the night's activities, the brute of a man whose hands she'd crushed, the beaten woman, then, later, the stalker following a woman across the Boston College campus. That one, at least, she didn't think the police would hear about. She'd let him off with a warning and six shallow puncture wounds on the sides of his head, oh, and a puddle of piss spreading at his feet.

A productive evening...

The intervention at the college had been especially satisfying because she'd actually prevented something instead of arriving during the crime. Aleksi wondered if he would tell his friends about it. She secretly hoped he would. Maybe the threat of having their genitals bitten off would prevent men from preying on women.

What's the fun of being a dragon if you can't eat a few genitals, anyway? she thought with a smile.

Then she thought of the texts. *We can help you...* What if they could? What if she could be human again?

Visions drifted through her half-sleeping mind, snippet dreams of walking with Hutch, arm in arm, laughing, joking, being best friends, like he and Julie were. The double-edged sword of hope slid between her ribs into her heart.

12

A golden shadow flew into the parking structure like a wraith on the wind, silent and all but invisible. Aleksi landed beside a pillar and crouched to listen for a few minutes, taste the air, and feel the vibrations of distant cars transmitted through the concrete beneath her feet.

Nothing threatened.

The texts had continued to come, as did the calls from Hutch. Four of the former every day, each with a new pitch line, and Hutch texted her every evening, but only asked her to call back or come see him, that he had something important to talk to her about. At this point, Aleksi felt sure that his home was being watched and his phone was tapped. That left her few options to get a message to him.

She hadn't kept much from her former life: her old phone, which she never used but had all her old contacts, her laptop, which she only used for anonymous internet activity and some data modeling, a few pieces of jewelry that her father had made for her, and her old keys. The last item on the list finally came in useful. The Oxford Garage, the very one where Bob Tomlin was murdered, had a direct connection to the Northwest Science Building where Hutch had his office. At two-thirty in the morning on a week night, even the most dedicated graduate students had gone home.

There was one security camera on the door into the building, but she had months of experience fooling cameras. Wings precluded wearing anything with shoulder straps, so she had rigged the straps of her pack to loop over her head, and used duct tape to secure it to her chest. Her skin, tough and set with fine scale-like growths, was far less tender than human skin, so the tape came off easily. In her pack, she kept her disguise.

Aleksi slipped into the shroud of full niqab and veil, adjusting her arms in the voluminous sleeves by folding her last two fingers back along her forearm. With only her eyes showing, she could walk by the camera with her head down and pass for a student. She'd actually considered strolling college campuses like this at night, trolling for racists and sexual predators, but hadn't tried it yet.

Aleksi took short steps to the door to keep her feet hidden, her pack slung over one shoulder, head down, and worked her old student key in the lock. Inside, the smells of the place brought back memories of her former life, that first day in Hutch's office, walking and laughing with Bob. She tried to press down those memories and failed. Hope had taken root in her now. She couldn't deny it. There was a chance that she could be human again.

But not tonight, she thought. *Tonight, you're still a dragon.*

She hurried to Hutch's office door and pulled the note from her pack. She checked it, folded it, and slipped it under his door. With luck, Hutch would find it in the morning. She walked out the way she came in, crouched behind the very same pillar, and doffed her robe. After stuffing it in her bag, she applied more duct tape and flew into the night.

When she got home, there were two new texts waiting for her. One from the mysterious Johansen woman, read, "You have a chance to be human again, Aleksi!" The other, from Hutch, was shorter. "R U OK? Worried!"

She dumped her bag, turned off her phone, and went back out to hunt.

Hutch opened his office door and put his backpack down beside his chair. When the world got weird, he relied on old routines to reestablish order and breathing exercises to calm his singing nerves. He hadn't heard from Aleksi in almost a week, but his other phone had been ringing constantly with updates from Buckmann and Jasper about her activities. He'd repeatedly told them he hadn't heard from her, but that did no good. Finally, he'd stopped taking their calls.

His fuck-buddy relationship with Julie had recovered somewhat. They'd both apologized, him for lying and her for prying into his life. He couldn't ask her why she was so interested in what happened to Aleksi. That was a no-win scenario.

So, with his old routine reestablished—protein shake for his first breakfast at home, then the gym for an hour, then Buckminster's for coffee and second breakfast, then work—he felt at least grounded. He could concentrate on his grant proposal, his courses, his research, and his grad students without his mind constantly drifting to conspiracy theories and concern for Aleksi. At ten minutes of ten, his phone chimed with the reminder for the comparative zoology lecture he was teaching, and he put his computer away and picked up his bag.

Only then did he see the folded yellow post-it note on the floor beside the door. When he'd opened the door, it had been pushed aside. Now he bent to pick it up. Unfolding it, his heart hammered at the sight of Aleksi's distinctive hand.

"We need new phones. Mine's been hacked. Go for an early run tomorrow. See you under Eliot Bridge, 3 a.m. Thanks! A."

"No *wonder* she didn't call!" Hutch stuffed the note in his pocket and hurried out, mentally adjusting his schedule, mind and heart racing. He could pick up two prepaid phones after his afternoon meeting and still make it home in time for dinner and a run. That was easy. What worried him more was the signature at the bottom of the note in his pocket.

Thanks, not love... I think I've lost her.

His attempt to reestablish order, calm, and routine in his life had just been burned to the ground by the lack of one simple word.

Someone not quite David Gilford stared back at him from the steam-fogged mirror. David wiped the mirror with his towel and peered at the reflection. His eyes and hands had started to change. He wasn't complaining. The aching joints and sore muscles didn't bother him; it was less than he was used to. He felt younger, stronger, sharper, and more flexible than he had in years.

The only problem was the dreams.

David had seen combat in all its shocking grotesqueries, and had no shortage of nightmares about it, but this was different. He'd finally told Baker and Price about them, and they'd said it was normal, expected even.

Both Penningly and Aleksi had reported graphic dreams, and the theory of genetic memories had been bandied about. David had never bought the idea of inherited memories, but now he did. There was no other explanation. The visions were too vivid, too sharp, too real. Colors, smells, tastes, and sensations overflowed, and unlike true dreams, his memories of them didn't fade. He really wished they would.

He finished drying and wrapped the towel around his waist. From the bathroom to his bedroom, he spotted Dr. Price seated in the living area, a laptop in her lap.

"Didn't hear you come in." For some reason, that bothered him; not her invasion of his privacy—he had none—but that he hadn't heard her over the spray of the shower.

"Sorry." She looked up, her eyes darting over him. "You were in the shower. I thought you'd like to see the latest test results."

"I would." He'd paid for the tests with hours of needles, biopsies, scans, and psychoanalysis. The last was the worst. If someone asked him how he *felt* about his changes one more time, he swore he'd dislocate their shoulders. "Let me get dressed."

David went to the bedroom and donned loose-fitting pants and a tee shirt. They'd allowed him to remove the heart and brain telemetry leads, at least, though they took new recordings twice a day. He didn't bother with shoes. He snagged a handful of beef jerky from the jar beside his bed and went back out to the living area.

"So, what's the diagnosis, Doc?"

"You'll be happy to know that the torn cartilage in your shoulders and back is reforming at an astonishing rate. Your mobility scores are those of a thirty-year-old."

"I could've told you that." He rotated his formerly shredded right shoulder with almost no pain. "My neck feels better, too."

"Yes, that was only tendon damage, like your knees." She rotated the laptop screen for him to see and clicked through the MRI slides, pointing out the healing tissues. They'd taken four full-body scans in the last nine days, and he was due for another tomorrow. Price had put together a time-lapse 3D progression of his entire body. "How's the skin irritation?"

"Irritating." He grinned and tore off another bite of jerky. "Not bad." His skin was flaky and itchy, and his hair, even though he had shaved his head for years now, seemed to be receding.

"Good." She flipped the screen to another image, a graph with multiple up-curving lines. "So, you can see here that virtually all your physiological parameters are being enhanced by the changes. Strength, reflexes, flexibility, hearing, sight. It's harder to measure your sense of smell, but I imagine that's sharper, too."

"It is." He breathed in deeply and resisted the impulse to tell her he could smell that she was menstruating. He ate more jerky, the spicy, smoky flavor overpowering the scent of her blood.

"We'd like to start testing endurance today. Treadmill, stair climber, like that."

"I shouldn't have showered, I guess."

"There's no shortage of soap and water." She rotated the screen back and flipped to another page. He could see it reflected in the plastic of her face shield, a long list of some kind with check boxes. "Oh, right. I'd like to take some nail clippings before we go." She put the computer aside and fished a pair of clippers from her pocket.

"No problem. They're growing so fast I can't keep them short." He extended a hand.

"Don't clip them yourself. They should stop at about an inch, and you'll be able to retract them."

"Yeah, I already learned that trick." Price took his hand, and he unsheathed his nails by flexing the tiny muscles in his fingers. She strained to snip the tough nails, catching the clippings in a Ziplock. "You're going to need a pair of tin snips, soon."

"We have shears, but I didn't think they'd be so tough yet." She clipped two more and pocketed the bag and clippers. "That's enough. We're good to go."

"Lead on, Doc." He rose and followed her out to the testing room, or torture chamber, as he had started to think of it. Another exam table, MRI, X-ray, CAT scanner, and various monitors and exercise equipment. One wall was lined with shelving stacked with blue plastic trays. He'd learned to cringe when they reached for those trays; they always held needles. There were two techs here, already garbed in protective gear. David recognized them by scent before they even turned around. "Hi Amy, Jim."

Jim just nodded, but Amy greeted him more warmly. "Hello, David. Ready for a workout?"

"Anything's better than more needles." He turned to Price. "What's first?"

"The treadmill." She pointed to a machine modified with monitoring leads and a breathing circuit. "We'll wire you up first, so take off your shirt, please."

"Sure." He did, and held still while Amy and Jim swabbed him with alcohol wipes and applied leads to his chest and scalp. Amy smelled good, but Jim had bad breath, like he'd eaten garlic and not brushed his teeth. Lastly, they strapped a pulse-oximeter to a finger.

"Okay, just a warm up for the first few minutes. Baseline recording," Price said.

"Sure." David held still while Amy applied the breathing circuit. He took the mouthpiece between his teeth, and she tightened the straps behind his head. The nose clamp shut off the scents of people, the room, and the machinery like flipping a switch. He suppressed a flutter of claustrophobia. With a nod, he stepped on the treadmill and started walking as Jim pressed the start button.

They slowly increased the speed until he was jogging at an easy pace. His knees hurt less than he ever remembered, his gait steadier, balance perfect. He wasn't even breathing hard yet.

"Feeling good?" Price asked.

He gave her a thumbs up, then a twirled finger to increase the speed.

"Okay, up to twelve, Jim. We'll hold that for ten minutes."

"Yes, Doctor." Jim pressed the button that increased the speed.

David noticed Jim's hand was shaking. He also didn't make eye contact much—not very friendly, like Amy. He picked up the pace easily and started to sweat. His hip twinged a little but settled down. He felt good, strong, young again.

Reborn...

In ten minutes, David had hit his stride. When Price asked him how he was doing, he gave her another thumbs up.

"Okay, good! Up to fourteen, Jim. His heart rate and blood pressure are steady."

"Yes, Doctor." Jim pushed the button, his hand still shaking, sweat beading on his brow.

David increased his pace, and thought, *Boy's really got a stick up his ass about something.* Amy's eyes flicked back and forth from the monitors to David, her pupils wide, nostrils flaring like a deer catching the scent of a predator.

Fear? David wondered. *Is she afraid of me, or something else?* He shook off the impulse to tear the breathing rig away, to release his senses, breathe in her scent. He closed his eyes and ran faster, deeply in the zone, now, reveling in his new body.

"He's a damned machine!" Price said in clear admiration. "You okay, David?"

He gave her the thumbs up.

"Good for a little more?"

Another thumbs up. *Bring it.*

"Sixteen, Jim." The machine topped out at twenty, but that was a flat-out sprint.

"Yes, Doctor." The panel beeped and the pace increased.

David sped up, really working now. He'd never run so fast for so long, even in his prime. It was like he was on some kind of drug. His legs just kept pumping like they would never stop, like a predator chasing down a gazelle. A dream-memory filled him, closing in for the kill, wings wide, jaws gaping. But there was no scent of fear, no terror, no blood. He heaved breath after breath, but there was nothing there. The vision clashed against a wall of sensory deprivation.

Can't breathe!

In a flash of panic, David bit down hard through the breathing circuit's mouth piece. He ripped the rig away and spat out the tasteless plastic. The sudden movement made him stumble, and he faltered, stepping back off the spinning machine. He landed badly, twisting his hip, but recovered with his hands on his knees. He heaved in air laden with sweet scents of sweat, fear, blood, urine, garlic. He could *breathe.*

"Shut it down, Jim!" Price snapped. "David, are you okay?"

A hand touched his shoulder, and he resisted the urge to bat it away. He straightened and nodded. "Fine. Sorry." It was Amy who had touched him, and her eyes were as wide as saucers, her pulse pounding at her throat. He could smell her excitement, taste it on his tongue. The impulse to grab her, to take her, bite, claw, fuck—he didn't know what—surged up, and he pushed her hand away. "Don't... Sorry, I just had a moment there."

"Yes, you did. We got it on EEG. You went ballistic." Price waved Amy back. "Can you describe what happened?"

"I... The breathing rig. It felt claustrophobic. I couldn't smell anything. Then, I had a...a vision, I guess, and suddenly couldn't breathe. I had to get it off."

"A vision of what?" Price asked.

"Like something from one of my dreams, closing in on an antelope, going in for the kill, but I couldn't scent it, and felt like I was suffocating."

"An *antelope?*" Jim said, disbelieving.

"We pushed you too hard, I guess," Amy said.

"No, it wasn't that." He shook his head and took another deep breath through nose and mouth. "It was like being blind, not being able to smell things that I knew were there. Like when you have a head cold and can't taste food, but this was like…like when you can't hear after a round goes off near your head, but you can see someone screaming at you." He shook his head. "It's hard to describe."

"Maybe it'd be better without the breathing circuit," Amy suggested, looking to Price.

Price shook her head. "We need the data. We won't push as hard next time. Maybe we could put it on room air with a nose-mouth mask instead of a mouthpiece."

"Yeah, that'd be better, I think." David heaved another breath—*sweat, blood, urine, garlic, fear*—and nodded. "We done?"

"Yes. Disconnect him, Amy. Jim, log the data. Thank you, David."

"All part of the service, Doc." David held still while Amy disconnected the leads and peeled the pads off his skin. She still smelled good, but there was fear and excitement under that scent, too. "Sorry if I scared you."

"No worries." Her eyes flicked up, then down as she peeled off another sticker. "I'm used to dealing with soldiers. Shit just happens sometimes."

"It certainly does."

David breathed in her scent and felt that strange *grab, bite, fuck* urge again. He liked her; she understood him, but he couldn't parse out what he was feeling. He couldn't figure out if he wanted to fuck her or eat her. Maybe both. He couldn't tell Price about that, of course. She'd freak out, and he'd end up in another psych evaluation. He shook it off and accepted a towel to wipe off the sweat.

"I need a shower, and maybe something to eat."

"No problem. Amy, you want to bring him a steak?" Price asked.

"Sure!" She accepted the damp towel, and handed him his tee shirt. "Medium rare?"

"Rare, please." His mouth watered at the thought of food and the pulse throbbing at Amy's neck. "Thanks."

"All part of the service." She smiled and left the room.

David watched her go and recalled the vision of chasing a gazelle.

13

Aleksi heard him coming from quite a distance. There were few people out at this hour, but she would have recognized the susurrations of Hutch's breathing and rhythmic cadence of his gait anywhere. She dropped down from her hiding place when he jogged into the tunnel.

"Thanks for coming." His scent wafted to her, and she breathed him in like a drug. There was no Julie on him this time.

"Any time. I'm glad you're okay." He fished two phones out of his pocket and held one out. "I already set them up. How did you find out yours had been hacked?"

Aleksi took the new phone. "I've been getting texts." She peeled her old phone off her leg, pulled up the message app, and handed it to him. "Read for yourself. I haven't replied. I didn't dare use the phone. It's probably the feds trying to track me down."

He scrolled up through the messages from the beginning and nodded. "It's bait."

"That's what I thought, too, but it doesn't sound like something Buckmann would do."

"No, you're right. They're certainly persistent." He handed the phone back. "You don't believe it, do you? What they're feeding you?"

"No, but…" There it was again. Hope. "What if it's not the feds?"

"Who else could it be?"

"So, I've been thinking about that, and just listen. This started when I took out those two rapists. I drew interest from three places: the feds, Jasper, and this mysterious Johansen woman we both met. I smelled her in your home. She was there. Now I'm getting texts offering to help me, to make me human again."

"It's *bait*, Aleksi. It's got to be."

"Does it?" She'd been thinking about this a lot. "These people, this Johansen and whoever's backing her, changed a person's looks, their *physical* appearance, just to stop Penningly and steal the specimen from the feds. If they can do that…who knows. Maybe they're telling me the truth."

"You can't trust them, Aleksi."

"Oh, I *don't*. Not yet, anyway, but I think I might text them back. Do you think they can track me if I just text?"

"Maybe. I don't know." He took a step closer, his face etched with worry. "If you do it while you're out, then turn it off, they won't be able to follow you. Calling them would *certainly* let them track you. Don't do either one from your home."

"Yeah. I wasn't planning to." Sometimes he stated the obvious, like she hadn't been a fugitive for half a year. "Maybe you could call Buckmann. If the feds are behind this, maybe she could tell them to lay off. They'll deny it, but if the texts suddenly stop, we'll know it's them."

"Good idea."

"So, what did you want to tell me?"

"Yeah, it's…" He looked suddenly uncomfortable. "It's about Julie."

A stab of ire shot through her. "What about her?"

"She asked me about you. More than once, actually, but at first it was just in passing. You know, sharing grief. Then, the other night, she confronted me, got really upset that I'd been lying to her about you."

Suspicion tickled her senses like the scent of blood. "Lying?"

"Yeah. She spotted my other phone, said she knew I was talking to you. I'd told her before that I didn't know what happened to you, that I hadn't spoken to you at all."

"She got that from a spare phone? That's a stretch."

"It's more complicated than that, but…" He hesitated, uncomfortable again. "She said she could tell I was still in love with you, Aleksi. She's right. I am. Julie's okay that she and I are just friends, but she didn't like that I was keeping secrets."

"Friends with benefits," she said.

"Yes, but that's *all*. It's just physical, and she's okay with that."

"And she knows you're thinking about me when…you're with her? Then she sees the spare phone and makes the leap that you're talking to *me*?" The suspicion lingered. "What did you tell her?"

"Look, I had to tell her something. I said we were talking, but that I didn't know anything else about where you were or why you'd disappeared. I think she bought it, but I hate lying to her, Aleksi. Julie's nice. She doesn't deserve that."

"She doesn't deserve to get caught up in all this either, Hutch."

"I know, but… Look, I hate to add one more worry, but I couldn't get why she would be so persistent about you. I hate to be suspicious, but I kept asking myself why she was asking so many questions."

Maybe she doesn't like the idea of the guy she's fucking thinking of another woman while you're inside her. Aleksi bit back the surge of jealousy. *I told him to, and this is Julie.* "I don't think it's anything more than jealousy, Hutch. She might *say* she's okay with just a physical relationship, but she might want more. I know you don't like lying to her, but you can't tell her about me. It'll put her in danger."

"I know. I won't. She hasn't mentioned you in days, I just…thought I should tell you." He frowned. "And she was right. I *do* still love you."

Hope… She couldn't do that to him. He'd found some joy with Julie. She needed to let him have that.

"Hutch, I love you, but we *can't* be together, okay? You like Julie, and she likes you. You should let that grow." Aleksi felt like she was slipping a knife between her own ribs.

His face darkened. "Julie's nice, Aleksi, but I don't love her."

"But you're *friends* with her. You're easy with her. You enjoy each other's company, joking, laughing. We were never like that."

Surprise crossed his features. "Are you…*watching* us?"

Shit! "I saw you leave the theatre with her, Hutch, that's all. I was curious. I'm sorry, but I could tell you're good together. It's okay."

"It's really *not* okay. Please don't stalk us."

"That's not what I meant, and I'm not *stalking* you! I meant it's okay to fall in *love* with her, Hutch! Don't deny yourself that! It…just makes it harder."

"I'm not falling in love with Julie. We're friends who sleep together occasionally. She's nice, and I like her, but that's all it's ever going to be."

"And if I wasn't around?"

His face flushed with anger. "Don't *say* that!"

"Hutch, you have to face reality. I'm not who I was. I'm not even *what* I was." She spread her wings. "You can't love a monster."

"Aleksi, you are *not* a monster, and I *do* love you."

She couldn't listen to him anymore. She couldn't give him the same hope that was killing her. "Goodbye, Hutch. I'll be in touch."

"Aleksi! I—"

But she was already gone, out of the tunnel and into the sky, across the river and into the canyons of Boston before he said what she could no longer bear to hear.

Hutch went to work the following morning strung out on caffeine and punchy from lack of sleep. He closed his office door, sat down, and pulled up Buckmann's number on his cell.

"Dr. Hutchinson." She sounded surprised to hear from him. "Thanks for calling. Have you spoken to Aleksi?"

"Yes, as a matter of fact, and she's angry with you."

"Why would she be angry with *me*?"

"Someone hacked her phone and has been sending her texts, promises to help her. It needs to stop." He didn't bother keeping his irritation out of his voice.

"Sending her texts?" She sounded honestly baffled. "It wasn't me, Doctor. What kind of texts?"

"I told you, promises to help her, to make her human again. It's bait, and she's not falling for it. If it's not you, it's your department. Nobody else has the ability to do that, or would want to track her."

"I told you, Dr. Hutchinson, we have no cure for Aleksi's condition. We could offer her a secure place to stay, but little more. I'll ask, but I don't think anyone in the project would be foolish enough to try to trap her that way."

"I hope not, Doctor." He knew he couldn't believe her, but he could certainly warn her. "If they try it, she'll slaughter them."

"Aleksi hasn't killed anyone yet, even though she's continued her one-woman campaign of terror. Please tell her to stop this. It's dangerous in the extreme."

"I *know* it's dangerous. I've *told* her. I don't control her actions, Doctor."

"Okay, okay. I'm just concerned. Please, keep in touch. You're our only contact with her."

"Unless someone in your department is harassing her with these texts," he shot back.

"I'll ask. If they are, I'll urge them to stop, but I don't think it's us."

Hutch ended the call. He couldn't believe a word out of her mouth, but she made sense and sounded sincere. Putting his phone away, he tried to get to work, but all he could think about was the woman he loved being stalked by some unknown organization that could reshape human flesh. He feared for Aleksi, but he couldn't help thinking, *Maybe...*

Mary Buckmann stared at her phone for a moment after Hutch broke the connection, wondering about the origin of these harassing texts. Had the Director ordered someone to hack Aleksi's phone? Did they intend to track her down and end her vigilante rampage with a bullet? How could they have managed it?

She had only one way to try to find out.

Homeland Security's internal communications system was heavily encrypted, so all she had to do was send a message to the Director requesting a video call. She wanted to see his face when they spoke. She then went back to work reviewing her recent communication with Julie Parks; the transcript of the taped conversation scrolled past on her screen, and she made notes in the margin from memory, logging mannerisms and other details. Less than an hour later, she received his call.

"Mary! New developments?"

"Perhaps, sir. I just received a call from Dr. Hutchinson. Aleksi is evidently receiving texts from someone who's promising to help her. There have been quite a few. I need to know if anyone in our department might be behind it before I formulate any hypotheses as to who this could be."

His eyebrows arched. "As far as I know, you're the only one who has any communication with Rychenkna at all."

"That's what I was led to believe, too, sir, but I need to be sure. I thought you might have approved an effort to persuade her to stop the vigilantism. If someone *else* is trying to recruit her, we could have a problem." He knew what she meant by "someone else." If the organization that had impersonated her got their hands on Aleksi, who knew what they might do.

His curt nod and frown said it all. "Agreed. I'll make inquiries, but to my knowledge everyone on the Johansen Project *not* working to keep Aleksi's antics off the internet is fully engaged in the human trials."

"They're under way?" That familiar pit of worry opened up in her gut.

His face lit up. "Yes. Ten days in, and the subject is progressing well. He's quite astounding, actually. Surpassing all expectations."

"And this subject is a former soldier?"

"Soldier and covert ops operative, yes. Forty years of exemplary service."

"And he's stable, sir? Psychologically, I mean?"

"Solid as a rock, Mary." He sounded affronted, like she'd insulted him.

"Did you review the conversation from the Prudential Tower, sir? Aleksi was quite clear that her transformation gave her violent impulses, and she was a socially repressed scientist, not a soldier."

"I said, he's *solid,* Mary. He's the most stable man I've ever met. Frankly, he's seen shit that would put you and me into the fetal position, and he's never shown a single chink in his armor."

"That's reassuring, sir, but he's also a trained soldier. He's been conditioned to be aggressive. The changes will make him more so. Please remember what happened with Penningly."

"Penningly was a whack-job to begin with, Mary. A spoiled sociopath who thought he could break all the rules and rely on his family to pull his ass out of the fire. This man is conditioned to follow orders. He's the *perfect* candidate."

Mary could see this was a losing argument. "Very well, sir. I hope you have him well contained."

"Stick to your investigation, Mary. We've got this."

"Yes, sir. I'll contact Hutchinson as soon as you confirm that these texts didn't come from anyone on our side. Maybe I can offer to help them find who's doing this."

"Good plan. If you need anything, let me know. We want these people, Mary. No holds barred."

"Roger that, sir." She nodded and broke the connection, encouraged that she'd been given free rein to go after the people who had impersonated her with all the resources at the government's disposal.

Still, the notion of putting the *Homo draconis* infection into a solder gave her chills. Just what the Director's endgame was, she had no idea, but creating a covert military force of dragons made the Manhattan Project seem safe by comparison.

Persephone typed out, "You can be with him again, if you let us help you," and hit send. She'd been slowly escalating her assault, prying at Aleksi's emotions, her loneliness, her love, her hope, but so far, she'd received no reply. These things took time. Meanwhile, she'd been carrying on with her life, or at least the public aspects of it.

"More coffee, miss?" Freddie asked as he came into the dining room.

"Please. Thanks." She pushed her plate away and accepted the cup. "Am I the last one up again? Sorry to mess up your schedule." She hadn't seen any of her cousins that morning, but she hadn't come downstairs until after nine.

"You were the last one *in* last night, miss. Seems only fair that you were the last one up. It's no difficulty. It's the social season, after all, and appearances must be maintained."

"Appearances." She chuckled and sipped her coffee as he took the dishes away.

A large part of her role in the family was keeping up appearances that they were a normal, albeit filthy rich, New England family. Old money up here meant a social life. Persephone had been groomed from childhood to take up that role, and had played it to the hilt her entire adult life. She didn't know whether the role was getting old, or she was.

Her phone vibrated, skittering on the polished wood of the dining table.

Please, please, please, be Aleksi! But when she snatched it up, the message read "GG ASAC," which meant "As Soon As Convenient." It wasn't an emergency, at least, but she had nothing pressing, so she downed the last of her coffee and made her way down to the Sanctum.

Two of her younger cousins were there tending Gi-gi. The ancient woman suffered from skin conditions due to her immobility and required specialized care. Persephone had tended her when she was younger and had vowed at the time to die rather than succumb to such decrepitude.

She rounded the bed—the attendants had rolled her onto her side to clean her back—and caught Gi-gi's eye. "I can come back if it's inconvenient, Great-Grandmother."

"No. Have you heard from Aleksi?"

"Not yet."

"I found something interesting about Julie Parks. Her student loans have recently been forgiven. Almost two-hundred-thousand dollars."

"Forgiven? Not paid by a third party?"

"No, forgiven by the federal government."

"They're not very subtle, are they?"

"No, they're not, and Julie Parks is theirs. This explains her interest in Aleksi's whereabouts."

"It certainly does." Persephone could barely believe that Parks had seduced Hutch for money, but the evidence was irrefutable. Of course, two hundred thousand dollars meant a lot more to a young student of no particular financial means than it did to Persephone. She often had difficulty assigning value to money in terms of human motivations. People committed murder for far less, after all.

"We're finished, Grandma Gi-gi," one of the attendant cousins said.

"Thank you both," Gi-gi wheezed as they rolled her back and covered her up. Her wizened features contorted in brief pain as they positioned her, then she breathed easily. As they packed up and left, her lavender eyes focused on Persephone once again. "We need to decide what to do about this agent of the government."

"Whatever we do, we will *not* be telling my former husband of this," Persephone stated emphatically. "That would do us no good and him irreparable harm."

"Agreed. We should probably also keep this information from Aleksi."

"I agree wholeheartedly." Aleksi would likely tear Julie to pieces.

"That leaves us only the option of dealing with Parks directly." Gi-gi made a motion with her hand, and Persephone helped place her hands on the control pads built into the arms of her bed. "There are many possible ways to take her out of the equation."

"Some of them likely to do more damage than good," Persephone pointed out. Having Parks killed would be almost as bad for Hutch as telling him what she was up to. "We could also do nothing. Hutch isn't going to give Aleksi up to anyone."

"True." The multiple screens at the foot of the bed lit up with a twitch of Gi-gi's finger. "I'll perform a risk analysis, and inform you of my decision."

"Very well, Great-Grandmother."

"Please keep up your messages to Aleksi. She must at least be curious by now."

"Curious and suspicious, I imagine. Maybe even angry." Persephone bowed out and hurried up to her own room. She had to step up her game if she was going to break through Aleksi's distrust.

14

Aleksi lay atop an apartment building listening to the intermittent roar from Fenway Park and watching the masses of humanity below. If Hutch dealt with his tumultuous emotions by trying to establish a familiar routine, Aleksi did so by prowling the city. By intervening in everyday violence, she not only gave outlet to her own pent-up aggression but also, she hoped, did some good.

But word had gotten out.

The internet buzzed with talk of her actions. Police called her a "Costumed Vigilante" and warned people to be careful at night. The public had more colorful names for her, not all of them nice, and a few blurry cell phone images had gotten out. Aleksi didn't care. If the police were so concerned for the safety of rapists and wife beaters, they should pay attention to the violence plaguing the city. If the men who preyed on women were angry and afraid to go out at night, all the better. A very few had even called her a hero.

Aleksi didn't think of herself that way. *More like a trash collector,* she mused.

She heard another extended roar from Fenway. Maybe the Red Sox had pulled one out of the dumpster. They'd been down three to one when she left the game. Aleksi had never understood why people were so fanatical about sports, but the crowds were fascinating to watch. She'd lain atop one of the stadium roofs for an hour, examining human behavior and formulating theories until boredom and anxiety forced her to leave.

The texts had continued, promising to return her life to her, her education, her career, her lover. She needed a distraction, a diversion... She needed prey.

The roar faded and the foot traffic increased as people left the bars where they'd watched the game. Vehicle traffic picked up slowly as more people left the ballpark. She kept her attention on Back Bay Fens Park, knowing from experience that men preyed upon women there. Right now, there were too many people out and about for her to do anything. Sexual predators also liked quiet and solitude. She settled down to wait, attuning her hearing to the voices, the laughter, the shouts, and taunts.

Music blared from the club behind her as the door opened, a high-energy pop beat...another human interest she'd never understood.

A motor revved and tires squealed behind her from Boylston Street. Shouted obscenities rose above the city noise, the epithets clearly targeting some people who had just left the popular gay nightclub. The ugly slurs drew Aleksi's lips back from her teeth.

She moved across the roof to the north side and peered down. Two men hurried arm-in-arm up the narrow alley toward the row of parked cars behind the corner gas station. A late model car with wide back tires sat crosswise at the entry to the alley, the four men inside continuing their disparaging comments. Then one of the two men walking half turned and gave the car the finger.

That was stupid, Aleksi thought.

The car's tires burned in reverse, then again in forward. The car shot up the alley. The two men walking picked up their pace, turning off the alley into the parking lot. As the car screeched to a stop, four men got out, two of them with baseball bats, all four shouting more epithets. This was going to get ugly, and there wasn't a cop in sight to stop it.

Well shit! Aleksi scanned the alley, but nobody was paying any attention. Even if someone saw the altercation, they weren't likely to intervene. Her view of the parking lot was obscured by trees, but she could hear them well enough.

"Leave us alone!" one of the couple shouted.

"Leave our *city,* you fuckin' faggots!" one the men shot back. "Go fuck each other in New York and root for the fuckin' Yankees!"

Really? Insults with baseball references? These guys were not the brightest bulbs in the box.

"We don't want any trouble," the other of the couple said, and Aleksi could hear his fear.

"Then your faggot friend shouldn't have flipped us off! How about I fuckin' *break* that finger for you!"

Aleksi moved and glimpsed them through a gap in the foliage. The couple was backed up against a car, the four men facing them, giving them nowhere to go.

"I say we fuck these faggots up," one of the bat wielders said, smacking the stick into his meaty palm.

The four men closed in.

Enough! Aleksi leapt into the air, swooped wide around the trees, checking the alley and parking lot for onlookers. There were none. *Just another Saturday night gay-bashing; nothing to see.*

She banked and rolled, diving down under the trees behind the four men. As she pulled to a stop, the wind from her billowing wings buffeted them. Before they could turn, she buried claws into one bat-wielder's shoulder and threw him back, snatching the weapon away with her other hand. As the others turned, wide-eyed, she snapped the bat like a twig and cast it aside.

"What the *fuck?*" One man backed up, but the other bat wielder took a panicked swing.

Aleksi caught the swing and broke his arm, the elbow bending the wrong way with a satisfying crunch. He screamed and went to his knees.

The world exploded in a deafening report, and something hit her. The man nearest her held a small revolver, the smoke of the discharge hazing the air between them. His finger pulled the trigger again, and Aleksi watched the hammer come back.

Rage surged up in a red tide. She sidestepped, and felt the lesser tug of the bullet passing through her wing membrane. Her claws slashed, and the gun and the hand holding it were torn away. Blood sprayed from the ripped meat and shattered bone, and the man screamed.

"Fuck! Fuck! Fuck!" the fourth man stumbled back into the stunned couple.

Pain lanced through Aleksi's arm, delayed nerve impulses finally reaching her brain. Blood and torn muscle, hers. She'd been shot.

She whirled and tried to leap into the sky, but her arm stabbed her. She couldn't fly.

Got to get away! The gunshots would draw attention, and she was hurt. Cops would arrive with more guns.

Aleksi scrabbled over a parked car and leapt to the apartment building. She might not be able to fly, but she could sure as hell climb. With her injured arm trailing, she swarmed up the six-story building, claws cutting furrows into the brick facing. At the top, she vaulted over the edge and crouched in the shadow for a moment to examine her arm.

The bullet had blasted through her bicep, but had missed the bone. It was bleeding freely, however. She had to stop it, or they'd be able to track her. But she also had to get away, find someplace to hide, someplace police helicopters couldn't see her.

Clamping her hand onto the wound, she dashed across the roof, building up as much speed as she could manage before she leapt over Peterborough Street to the next apartment building. From there, she traversed the roof and dropped down to the next building on the corner of Queensbury and Park. Back Bay Fens loomed across the wide boulevard, a safe haven of tall trees where she could hide, but she had to get across the street; she couldn't fly, and there was too much damned traffic.

Sirens blared from behind her. BPD had gotten the call. They'd be all over the place soon, looking for her, hunting her.

"Well, you're in deep shit now, Dragon Woman." Aleksi examined her arm, lamenting her lack of duct tape. She'd left her phone at home, too. She couldn't even call Hutch. *Hutch... Oh, he's going to be so pissed at me.* But his wrath was the least of her worries. She had to cross a wide boulevard without being spotted, and she was still bleeding. The entrance wound was blackened with powder, but the exit wound was worse: muscle was torn out of the hole from the passage of the bullet.

On impulse, or perhaps instinct, she licked the wound. Her blood tasted coppery, disconcertingly like food. She poked the distended muscle back into the wound and licked it some more. The taste of gunpowder residue turned her stomach, but the bleeding slowed. She applied pressure again and gauged the sporadic traffic on Park. More sirens howled, the flashing blue and red lights illuminating the night like lightning.

You've got to move, Aleksi!

She couldn't fly, but maybe she could glide over the street into the park. Her legs were strong enough to propel her half the distance. Experimentally, she extended her injured wing. Pain shot up her arm, and the wound started bleeding again, but if she didn't flex too much, it might hold her up long enough.

"Or I'll crash into a passing car," she muttered.

Backing up to the far corner of the roof, she waited for a lull in the traffic and dashed, launching herself into the air. She gritted her teeth against the agony as her wings caught the air, buoying her up just enough to clear the Emerald Necklace walkway. Her claws left cuts in the bark of a tree as she scrambled up into the foliage. Her arm hurt like hell, but it hadn't folded.

Still not satisfied with her position, she climbed as high as she could, then launched herself again, over the pond to the thicker foliage of the trees on the other side. There, she climbed high and found a forked branch where she could rest comfortably.

Sirens wailed through the night, and her arm throbbed with her pounding heart. She licked the wound some more, and the bleeding subsided. If she'd left a blood trail, they'd follow it and know she was in the park. *Move or stay put?* she wondered. The night was her friend, so wherever she went she'd have to hole up there through the day until the following night at least. She couldn't fly and had no robes to hide her nature, so she couldn't walk home tonight, either.

The distinctive sound of a helicopter settled the argument. She'd stay put.

Worrying about infrared cameras and night scopes, she lay there listening, trying to think through the pain. The encounter with the four men replayed in her mind. She'd been a fool not to expect a gun. Worse, she had panicked. She hadn't intended to maim anyone, but the response had been instinctive. It was only luck that she'd taken his hand off instead of his head. More than anything, the surge of visceral rage bothered her, the loss of control, her mind momentarily taken over by the instincts of a beast.

"Is that what I'm becoming?" Aleksi licked her wound and listened to the night.

She tried to rest, but the pain wouldn't let her. She replayed the encounter with the men over and over, and realized that Hutch had been right after all; she needed to be much more careful.

Tony Jasper and Marty Willis entered the Brigham and Women's Emergency room into a throng of police and bleary-eyed reporters. Willis' husband, Charles, had given them a call, alerting them to the attack. Charles worked Vice, and Saturday night was prime time. He'd been working the Cambridge night clubs and received a text from an informant who tended bar at The Machine nightclub. Charles called Willis and told him where the victims were being taken, and that he'd meet them there. He waved them over, and their badges got them past the harried BPD uniforms.

"What's the story?" Jasper asked.

"Depends on who you talk to, as usual." Charles gave Marty a peck and sighed in obvious frustration. He was dressed in his work clothes, a shiny silk jacket, purple shirt, and a tie that probably cost more than Jasper's gun. "Three *victims*, if you can call them that. One shoulder laceration, one broken arm, and one with his hand torn off at the wrist. They took him to Mass Gen to have it reattached."

Willis shared a look with Jasper. "Hand *torn* off? Not cut?"

"They said torn, but I didn't see. EMTs said it was an ugly wound, like an animal attack." Charles made a vague gesture. "Brings back visions of Penningly."

"It does," Jasper agreed. "So, three injuries. And I presume these fine young men were minding their own business?"

Charles snorted in disgust. "So they say, but it doesn't hold water. There were four. One wasn't injured, but he did piss himself. He said they stopped to talk to some people and were attacked, but the couple they were talking to have another story. They'd just left The Machine, a gay couple, and this carload of assholes started yelling at them. The usual filth. Then they got out of their car with baseball bats."

"Fuckers," Willis spat.

"Where are the two from the club? Have they been questioned?"

"Barely," Charles said in disgust. "BPD's more interested in the *victims*." He frowned deeply. "I know them. Nice guys. They don't deserve this shit."

"Are they here?" Jasper asked.

"Yes. They were pretty freaked out, so BPD brought them here. You want to talk to them?"

"I do. Thanks, Charles!"

"Don't mention it." Charles led them through the waiting room to a smaller area reserved for doctors who needed to tell loved ones bad news. Two men wearing clubwear sat there clutching coffee cups, looking rattled. "Hey, guys. How you holding up?"

"Hey, Charles," one said, and they stood, eying Jasper and Willis. "Pretty freaked out, actually."

"Larry, Ben, meet Sergeant Jasper and Detective Willis. They're working a case that might have something to do with what happened tonight," Charles explained. "They want to ask you some questions, okay?"

"Sure," Larry said.

"Dunno if you'll believe us, though," Ben added in a thick Southie accent. "Some weird shit."

"We've seen all *kinds* of weird shit, guys. Don't worry. This is off the record." Technically, Jasper and Willis were out of their jurisdiction again, but there was no harm asking questions. "So, these four assholes came at you with bats, right?"

"Yeah. I really thought they were going to use them, too," Larry said.

"Real assholes," his partner agreed. "Only two had bats, though."

"But then someone attacked them. Did you get a good look at this person?"

The two exchanged a look, and the Southie guy shrugged. "It happened wicked fast."

"Like *freaky* fast," Larry agreed.

"And was this guy tall, short, stocky, armed?" Marty asked. "Anything at all might help."

"Look, you're gonna think we're crazy, but...this wasn't a guy." Larry looked to Ben, but his partner just shrugged. "It was...I don't know. Maybe somebody wearing a suit or costume of some kind."

"A costume?"

"Yeah, like a Halloween costume, or one of those cosplay dudes you see pictures of. He had a bodysuit, this cape like thing, and really long things on his fingers."

"Wings," Ben added. "Like bat wings. They were *big*, and went from the long fingers all the way to his ankles."

The description matched what Jasper had seen the night he'd blown Derrick Penningly's head off. "Okay, I don't want to scare you guys, but this isn't the first time we've gotten this description, so we believe you. Now, I know it happened fast, but can you tell us what you saw?"

They exchanged another glance, clearly disturbed that Jasper had not refuted their claim.

"So, I didn't see this...guy until he grabbed one of these assholes and threw him back like he weighed nothing. Snatched the bat right out of his hand and broke it like a twig. Just *snap*!"

"Broke it over his knee?" Tony was fine with them thinking Aleksi was a man.

"Nope, just snapped it like a bunch of spaghetti." Larry made a twisting motion with both fists. "Couldn't hardly believe it."

That sounded like Aleksi all right. "Okay, then what."

"Well, then this other dumb ass tried to swing his bat, but the dude just caught it and broke the guy's arm." Ben made a chopping gesture. "He yelped like a bitch and went down. Then one of the others shot the guy."

"Shot him?" Jasper hadn't heard anything about gunshots. "Actually *hit* him or just shot at him."

Larry shook his head. "Nope. It hit him. It jerked him around, and I saw the blood. He fired twice, but I didn't see if the second one hit."

"Yeah, but that didn't stop him from tearing the guy's hand off. One swipe and the hand and the gun went flying. Like something out of a horror movie." Ben shivered and frowned. "Wicked gross."

"You said you saw blood when the gun went off. You're *sure* it was *this* guy's blood, not from somebody else?" Willis asked.

"Pretty sure. The shot hit his arm, like here." Ben pointed to his own upper arm. "Jerked him around a little, but then he moved so fuckin' fast I didn't see what had happened until the shooter's hand went flyin'. I'll never forget that as long as I live. It still had hold of the gun."

"Then the guy like took off. He went up the side of that apartment building like Spiderman." Larry shook his head. "I tried to get my phone out, but he was gone before I could get a pic."

"Yeah, he was like wicked fast," Ben agreed.

Jasper looked to Willis, but his partner had no other questions. "I think we've got everything we need. Thank you, gentlemen." Tony held out a hand. "You've been helpful."

"Sure." They shook his hand

"Hey, maybe don't look for this guy too hard, huh?" Ben added. "He fucked those assholes up, but he saved us. Maybe he's a freak, but he's a *good* freak, you know?"

"I know," Jasper assured him, and he felt it was time for a little honesty. "The same guy saved *my* life once. I'm more interested in getting him to stop risking his life than arresting him."

"Wow." The two exchanged a startled look. "Okay. Cool."

Jasper thanked them again, then Charles. He and Willis left the ER, but didn't speak until they were in their car.

"This is escalating, Marty." Jasper sighed and gripped the wheel hard.

"You think?" Willis sipped his coffee and rubbed his eyes. "Can't believe she tackled four guys. She's got balls."

"And she was shot. I just hope BPD doesn't track her down."

"You gonna tell Hutchinson?"

"Fuck yeah." Jasper pulled his phone. "And I hope I ruin his Saturday night!"

"So, there are *rules* for these things, you know." Julie took a bite of pizza and talked as she chewed. "Stage kissing is like a whole subject. There are *classes* on it. You're supposed to *talk* about it, agree, and follow the rules, right?"

"Sure." Hutch had never imagined such things would have rules, but it seemed reasonable.

"I mean, there are even *more* rules for *really* intimate scenes, but kissing is so...you know...personal." She chased her bite with a sip of wine. "Then, right in the middle of a full dress rehearsal, this jerk sticks his tongue halfway down my throat."

"Okay, that's a little disgusting."

"You're not kidding!" She took another bite. "He was way out of bounds. I mean, we *rehearsed* this, right?"

"And what happened?" Julie was still hyped from the play, and chatty. Hutch had picked her up after the night's performance and enjoyed letting her talk, entertained by her energy.

"Oh, he *so* regretted it!" She sipped her wine with an evil smile. "I bit him."

Hutch gaped at her. "Like, bit his *tongue?*"

"Yep! Drew blood, too!" She snapped another bite of pizza, white teeth flashing, as if demonstrating her technique. "He spoke with a lisp for a week, and the director almost pulled him from the play. The guy was all pissed at me, wanted to press charges, but I told everyone what he did, and he was totally shunned."

"Serves him right." Hutch reached for his beer, but his phone vibrated in his pocket. He pulled it and saw that it was Jasper calling again. *Oh, hell no. Not tonight.* He put the phone down and paid attention to Julie.

Thirty seconds later, his phone vibrated again. He swore under his breath and looked at the text from Jasper. The three words, "Aleksi was shot," hit him like a freight train. He read it three times before he believed it was real.

"Hutch? What's wrong?"

He stared up at Julie like she'd appeared out of nowhere. "Uh…sorry, but…it's an emergency." He stuffed the phone away and pulled his wallet. "I've got to go. This is serious, Julie." He threw down three twenties. "I'm sorry."

"Hutch! Wait!" He was already out the door of the restaurant when she caught up and grabbed his arm. "Wait! What happened?"

"I can't…" Hutch gritted his teeth. "I can't say, Julie. This is an emergency. Someone's hurt. I have to go."

Julie's face went stiff. "It's *her*, isn't it?"

"I…" Hutch tried to breathe, tried to think, but those three words ran over and over in his head. *Shot. Aleksi's been shot…* "Yes. Now, I have to go. I have to find out what happened. If you can't accept that, I'm sorry. This isn't about you, or us, it's about Aleksi's *life*. Okay?"

Julie went white, then blushed. "I didn't mean… I'm sorry, Hutch. Go."

"Thank you." Hutch hurried to his car and got in. Pulling his Aleksi-only phone from the glove box, he punched the only contact in it. The phone rang and went to voice mail. "I heard you were shot. Please call me if you can. Whatever you need. I love you, Aleksi." He broke the connection and then sent a text to the same effect. He had to back up and retype it twice due to shaking hands. Finally, he hit send, and put the phone in his pocket.

Aleksi's been shot… Aleksi's been shot… Aleksi's been shot…

"Fuck, fuck, *fuck*!" Hutch hammered his palms against the steering wheel. It didn't help. He couldn't think straight, and he needed to. He needed to figure out what to do.

15

A *perfectly good Saturday night, shot to hell.* Persephone kicked off her pumps at the door to the cellar and hurried down the stairs. She'd been at a reception for a senatorial candidate—black tie, champagne, the whole nine yards—when her phone had gone berserk in her purse. Something had happened. *Why can't that woman play vigilante on weeknights?*

In the sanctum, Gi-gi's monitors blazed with images: police reports, wounds, a dismembered hand still clutching a small revolver. "Our girl's been busy, I see."

The images paused, and Gi-gi looked at her. "By three different accounts, she was shot."

"Shot?" Persephone's petulance at having her evening interrupted vanished. "Not *killed.*"

"No. The wound didn't impede her from leaving the scene. She didn't fly, however, and one observer said her arm was bleeding. We have no way to know how badly she's been injured."

"But she got away. That's something."

"Yes. The police are searching for her, however. They've found blood on the rooftops."

"She's infectious, Gi-gi! If they—"

"In the age of HIV and hepatitis, I'm sure they're taking all precautions, dear." Her finger flicked over the remote, and Google Maps came up on a satellite view with the site of the incident highlighted. A cursor winked up, tracking as she spoke. "She attacked four men who were about to assault a gay couple here. Three were injured. The man who shot her lost his hand, though surgeons are attempting to reattach it. She fled up the side of this building, and blood was found here, here, and here."

"Toward the park," Persephone said.

"Yes, but there are many hiding places. The sewers, the subway, parking structures…" Dozens of blue icons winked on in a southward arc. "They have, as yet, found no other traces of her."

"Should I text her? Offer help?"

"That may yield results, if she has her phone or reached her lair."

"Worth a try." Persephone pulled her phone and texted "R U hurt? We can help! No questions."

"Thank you, dear. I'm sorry to interrupt your evening."

"Forget it. Politics bores me." Persephone flicked a dismissive hand. "Is that all?"

"I'll continue to monitor the situation. If the police find her, we may be forced to intervene quickly. Please stay close."

"Of course." Persephone turned to go.

"And you may be glad to know that we can neutralize Julie Parks with little effort," Gi-gi added.

"Neutralize?" She turned back. "You're not going to hurt her, are you?" It wouldn't be the first time someone had vanished of the face of the Earth at a twitch of Gi-gi's finger.

"Oh, *no*, dear." The ancient woman's razor-thin mouth twitched at the corners. "We're going to fulfill her wildest dreams."

Hutch stormed into his home and turned on the late news. He'd realized halfway home that he'd been rude to Julie, but right now that was the least of his worries. He'd also realized that there was nothing he could do for Aleksi. She was on her own.

But he could find out more details. Pulling his regular phone, he called Jasper.

The detective answered on the first ring. "Hutch! Has she called you?"

"No. I've texted and called but no answer yet. Tell me she's alive, Tony."

"As far as I know. An eye witness said she was shot in the arm. She climbed a building after, so it was probably superficial. BPD's conducting a man hunt."

"How did this happen, Tony?" Hutch pulled a tumbler from the shelf and went to the kitchen. He grabbed a bottle of Glenlivet from the cabinet, and his hand shook so badly that he slopped whiskey onto the counter.

"She attacked four guys who were assaulting a couple outside a club. The Sox game had just gotten out, and there were people everywhere, but it happened in a parking lot behind a gas station. There weren't many witnesses. The guys had baseball bats. She took three of them down, but one guy had a gun. He fired two rounds, and BPD dug the slugs out of a building, so we don't think she was hit in the body. No pics so far, but there were six eyewitnesses. One's missing his right hand."

"His hand?" *Lucky it wasn't his head.*

"Yeah, the shooter. He's still in surgery. They think they might be able to reattach it."

"Jesus…" Hutch took a healthy jolt of whiskey and gasped for air. "Thanks for calling, Tony. I'll let you know if I get word from her."

"Thanks, Hutch. Sorry for fucking up your Saturday night." He didn't sound sorry.

"No problem." Hutch hung up and thought of Julie. Should he call and apologize?

Before he could dial, his phone vibrated in his hand. It was Buckmann. He really didn't feel like talking to her, but she might have more information than the police.

Hutch answered, "I already got the news."

"About *Aleksi*?" She sounded angry. "From who?"

"From Tony Jasper. You remember Tony, the cop who cleaned up your *last* fuck-up?"

"Derrick Penningly wasn't *our* fuck-up, Doctor!"

"Oh? You had him and you let him loose. I call *that* a fuck-up."

"That's neither here nor there, Doctor. Tonight's incident is *exactly* what I warned you about! She's out of control!"

"She was never *in* control, *Doctor*! She's her own person, not your lab rat!"

"I *know* that, but she's also your *friend*. I'd hoped she would listen to you."

"So did I." Hutch took another sip of whiskey and tried to swallow his temper. "And before you ask, no, I haven't heard from her."

"That's not surprising. She's gone to ground. The police are searching, but I doubt they'll find her."

"Are *you* searching for her?"

"Not yet, but after tonight, that might change."

"Then it's time for *me* to warn *you*, Doctor. Aleksi won't be your prisoner. If you try to take her, there'll be blood on your hands."

"It's not my call, unfortunately. Oh, and I have it on good authority that nobody at DHS is sending texts to her. It's not us."

"I didn't think so."

"I have little doubt that this is the same organization that was able to impersonate me and steal the specimen, Doctor. They're dangerous and resourceful terrorists."

Dangerous to you, he thought, but held his tongue. Taking the specimen out of government hands wasn't exactly what Hutch would call terrorism.

Then Buckmann surprised him. "If Aleksi will work with us, we may be able to find them. I'm willing to compensate her."

"*Compensate* her? How? She doesn't need anything but to be left alone."

"Left alone to terrorize innocent people?"

"That's bullshit, and you know it. Every single person she's hurt has been in the act of hurting someone else."

"That may be true, but it's going to eventually get her killed. We can offer her safety, anonymity, even something for her parents if she cooperates with us. We can give them closure."

"If and when she returns my calls, I'll give her your offer, but I can't make any promises."

"I understand that. Thank you."

"You're welcome." Hutch ended the call and sipped his whiskey.

An on-site commentator on the news was at the scene of the incident. There were police cars everywhere, and yellow crime tape strung around like holiday decorations. They even had forensics people rappelling down the side of a building.

Hutch topped off his whiskey and sat on the couch facing the TV, watching the report without sound, imagining Aleksi in hiding somewhere, bleeding, in pain, alone. He checked his other phone, but had missed no messages.

"Damn it, Aleksi, what the hell were you thinking?" But he knew the answer: she was protecting someone in danger. She'd found her niche, her purpose, and she wasn't going to stop.

Unless...

Hutch sipped and thought about the relative threats of the government versus these supposed "dangerous and resourceful terrorists." So far, they hadn't terrorized or hurt anyone. DHS, on the other hand, had tried to use Penningly to hunt down Aleksi and was responsible for uncounted murders when he got loose.

The lesser of two evils... He wondered at this mysterious group's motives. Did they just want to capture Aleksi to lock her in a cage, or were they sincere about wanting to help her? And if they were, could they? If they could, contacting them might be worth the risk.

But it's not my risk, he realized. *It's Aleksi's.*

16

The daylight hours were the worst. Hunkered in her tree at the edge of the water, Aleksi listened to the police combing the park. She hadn't considered that they would use dogs to track her. Fortunately, she hadn't touched the ground north of Park Street and had glided over water to her current perch. Unfortunately, they'd found the tree she'd left claw marks on.

She could do nothing but sit still and try to rest.

By nightfall, they'd given up the active search of the park. The marshy ground around her tree had yielded no scents for the dogs to follow, and the foliage was thick enough to hide her. Even after dark, she didn't dare move. Aleksi listened to the trains on the Green e-line and estimated the time. They would stop running at twelve-thirty. When they fell silent, she risked moving.

Extending her wing brought stabbing pain, but no bleeding. The wound was cool and dry, scabbed over. She could move, but she doubted she could fly.

"Gotta do this the hard way, then."

Thankfully, Sunday night was quiet. People had to go to work in the morning.

Aleksi worked her way south through the trees without touching ground, brachiating one handed from limb to limb. She made noise, but stopped to listen after each move. At Agassiz Road, the limbs of the trees reached out to meet over the pavement. Waiting for a lull, she leapt the gap and scrambled into cover, pausing again to listen.

Nothing.

Now, however, things became more difficult. She had three city blocks to traverse to get to Huntington Avenue and the subway, then another few blocks east before it went underground. The first step was to get through the park and across Fenway Street. There weren't enough trees for her to stay off the ground, but there was marshy foliage along the Emerald Necklace walkway.

She climbed down to the ground and crept along, keeping low on the verge of the foliage. Twice she heard cars, and once, a late-night jogger. Each time she hunkered in the vegetation, silent and still, until they passed. As the walkway curved west, she picked her spot to cross Fenway and waited again for a lull in traffic. She didn't have to wait long.

With a burst of speed, she dashed across the street, hurdled the row of parked cars, and vaulted off an iron railing to scrabble up the side of a building. On top, she once again hunkered and listened to the low hum of the city. No cries, no voices, no barking dogs.

Score one for Dragon Woman.

From here, her traverse from rooftop to rooftop was easier. The streets were narrower, and the buildings taller. Twice she had to scramble up to higher buildings, but nobody looked up, or if they did, they didn't believe their eyes. She worked her way southeast from one flat apartment roof to the next, pausing to listen after every leap. Finally, she reached Huntington avenue just east of Gainsborough, where the Green e-line went underground.

The gaping darkness of the subway entrance beckoned. It was too far to jump, but from six floors up, she had a decent glide path. Again, she waited. The traffic here was heavier, the streetlights brighter, and her flight path would descend into the light before she reached the cover of the tunnel. And there were also wires and the third rail to avoid.

Extending her wings carefully, the tortured muscle of her arm stabbed her. Gritting her teeth, she stretched out her longest fingers, drawing the thin membrane of her wing taut. She would have to bank ninety degrees at the tunnel, which would put real stress on her arm. This was going to hurt like hell.

You've got nobody to blame but yourself. Suck it up, Dragon Woman! She stepped back from the edge of the building. When the sounds of traffic fell silent, she dashed forth and leapt.

She'd been right: it hurt like hell.

Banking over the iron fence at the edge of the rail line, she clipped a traversing cable with her wingtip. The impact sent jolts of agony up her arm, and she overcompensated. Her claws raked the concrete wall of the descending tunnel, but she managed to land without rolling into the third rail. She hunkered in shadow and checked her arm. The scab had opened but it wasn't bleeding much.

Any landing you can walk away from...

From here, she was safe. The trains weren't running, so the stations would be empty. All she had to do was avoid the security cameras and nighttime maintenance crews, and she'd been doing that for months. The Boston subway system had become her warren, and she knew her way around. Generally, she flew. Jogging along the tracks took longer, but she reached her lair well before the first trains started to run.

Thirsty and starving, she went to a cooler and retrieved a bottle of water and a package of ham. She kept one cooler full of preserved meat just for emergencies like this. She could lay up for days without a problem. She even had some medical supplies. Aleksi applied antibiotic ointment and adhesive bandages to her arm and swallowed four ibuprofen between bites of meat and swallows of water.

Sated, rested, and nearly pain-free, she finally picked up her phones.

Three texts and a voice mail from Hutch—about what she'd expected. At least he didn't sound angry, just worried for her. Both Jasper and Buckmann had landed on him like a ton of bricks. He didn't deserve this. It was almost four in the morning, but she called anyway.

The line didn't even ring once before he answered. "Aleksi! God, it's good to hear your voice! Are you okay?"

"I'm fine, Hutch. I had to hide out yesterday. Sorry I couldn't call."

"Jasper said you were *shot*!"

"Yeah, well, it's not that bad, but I couldn't fly. I'm okay." She picked up her other phone and thumbed through the messages. She'd gotten six, all of them offering help with no questions. "I'll be fine in a few days. It's healing fast."

"Thank God." He heaved a sigh, and she could hear his stress. "I can arrange a meeting with Jim Bornstein if you need medical attention."

"No, I'm good. Right now, going out is more dangerous than staying put."

"You need anything? I can drop you a package anywhere you like."

"Maybe later. I'm good for now. Dipping into my emergency supplies.

Sorry you were grilled by Jasper and Buckmann. You sound exhausted."

"I haven't slept much. Lucky it's the weekend." He sighed deeply. "I'll go to bed after we talk, but I want to tell you, Buckmann said nobody in their department is texting you. She thinks it's the people who impersonated her and stole the specimen. She offered to compensate you if you help them find these people."

"*Compensate* me?" She stared at the last text on her other phone and hissed a laugh. "With what? Anesthesia while they strap me down and vivisect me? Right now, I trust them both about the same, but...I don't know, Hutch. What if these other people can do what they say?"

"Then it might be worth the risk to contact them, but not until you're well."

"No, and not from here. I'm going to lay low for a few days."

"Text if you need anything, okay?"

"I will. Thanks, Hutch. I'm sorry to put you through this."

"Don't worry about me, Aleksi. You're the one at risk. I love you."

Aleksi remembered her claws tearing the man's hand off, bone and cartilage snapping, blood spraying. *I'm too dangerous for him to love.* "I'll talk to you later, Hutch." She cut off the call and closed her eyes against her raging emotions.

Her other phone vibrated, and she stared at the new text. "Hope you're safe. We can help. Whatever you need. No questions. Be safe."

Be safe... Nobody's safe in this world. Aleksi turned off both phones and lay back in her nest of old blankets and sleeping bags, trying to find a position that didn't hurt her arm. Despite her exhaustion, sleep wouldn't come. She couldn't get the image of her claws ripping the man's hand off from her mind...and the taste of blood. Blood that tasted like food.

David paced the floor of his room, trying to keep his claws from piercing his palms. The changes were accelerating, the psychological ones as much as the physiological. His finger and toenails were now claws, his smallest two fingers elongating, a fine membrane forming between them and down his arm. His eyes had turned stark yellow, the pupils elongating into vertical slits, his senses so sharp he could count the hairs standing up on the back of his psychologist's neck. He quenched the desire to bury his teeth right there at the base of the pencil-pusher's skull.

"And your dreams are the same, or have they also intensified?" The psych doc scratched notes on an electronic tablet as he spoke. "More dreams of flying?"

"Flying, hunting, feeding… Yeah, the same." He hadn't told anyone about the more erotic dreams, scales on scales, teeth and claws, violent copulation.

"But your anxiety has increased, yes?"

"Yes. Mostly I'm just bored, I think. I'm sick of needles, tests, evaluations, and questions. No offense, Doc, but this shit's driving me nuts."

"But you've undergone extended periods of stress before. Special forces training pushes most candidates past the level of human endurance, both physically and psychologically. You passed those trials with flying colors."

"I wasn't *Homo*-fucking-*draconis* then, Doc!" David clenched his hands into fists and winced as his claws pierced the flesh. "Fuck!"

The psychologist looked back at the blood on David's hands. "Are you all right? You want me to call for medical attention?"

"No. I just need to get used to these fucking things." He extended his claws for the doctor to see, pleased with the man's suddenly dilating pupils, the reek of fear sweat, the increased pulse. He sheathed his claws and licked his palms. "I'll be fine. It's happened before. The wounds heal fast."

"I know it's happened before, David." He turned back to his tablet, the stylus scratching notes. "Are you sure it's accidental?"

"You think I'd hurt myself on *purpose?*" One glance over the man's shoulder at his notes confirmed that he did. "It's accidental, Doc. I clench my hands when I'm wound up. I need something to *do*! Some entertainment! TV's disgusting, and I don't play video games. I need a night out, or a night *in* for fucksake!"

"Well, we can offer you movies, alcohol, or even some mental challenges. There are strategy games on your system." He scratched more notes. "I'm sorry, but I can't offer you female companionship due to the contagion risk, but we do have erotic videos and simulations."

So, if I wasn't contagious, you'd deliver a whore to my room? He snorted in disgust. "No thanks. Well, yes to the alcohol. Bourbon. Strategy games make the anxiety worse. I need to get out, move around."

"The evaluations are scheduled to include some VR simulations. Combat scenarios. You've used those before, yes?"

"Sure." The headgear was heavy, but military technology far-surpassed the mainstream gaming industry. Covert ops ran training simulations of missions prior to deployment, the environments recreated from satellite footage and intel reports. They were certainly challenging. "That might pass the time."

"I'll put in a request to the Director." He scratched a note and stood. "I'll also send for some whiskey. Try not to get too intoxicated, however. There's no telling how it might affect you."

"Sure. Just something to take the edge off. I'll look though the movie list again. No worries, Doc."

"Good. If you need anything else…"

"Yeah, I know, just ask." He grinned, stretching the aching muscles of his changing face. "Thanks, Doc."

"You're welcome, David." The man peeled off his protective gear and left.

David sat down and flicked on the TV. He started scrolling through the movie list, but nothing caught his eye. The lingering scent of the man's fear hung in the air like a buzzing insect. He heard Amy halfway down the hall. He was up when she knocked.

"Yeah!"

She came in with a paper bag in one hand. "Drink, sailor?" She pulled a pint bottle from the bag, Jim Beam, his favorite.

"Thanks." He pointed to the counter. "Join me for a cocktail?"

"Sorry. Can't." Amy put the bottle on the counter and wadded up the bag. "Regs, you know." She turned for the door.

"Regs…" David picked up the bottle and cracked the cap. The aroma of bourbon filled his head and covered Amy's scent. He took a sip right from the bottle, letting the burn wash away his tension. "Hey, if you're not busy, I could use some company. Just someone to sit with and maybe watch a movie with. Someone who's not poking me with needles or asking me how I *feel* about shit."

She turned and shrugged. "Sure. I'll ask. I don't see why not."

"Thanks, Amy. I think the isolation's getting on my nerves." He took another sip from the bottle.

"I'll set it up, then. Shouldn't be a problem." She flashed him a smile and turned for the door.

"Good. See you later."

"Later." She left with that little wave she did.

David sipped bourbon and stared at the door for a while. He decided that he liked Amy for one simple reason. She wasn't afraid of him. He wondered how long that would last.

17

If Aleksi had learned one thing about being a dragon, it was that she did not like isolation and inactivity. Staying silent and hidden during the day was one thing. Five days and nights in her lair, venturing out only once briefly to pick up a Styrofoam cooler packed with smoked ham that Hutch had left beside a dumpster for her, was driving her crazy. She had the internet, books, audios, meditation, and music to keep occupied, but she craved physical activity. She needed to be out and around humans. And more than anything else, she wanted to fly.

Friday night finally rolled around, but her arm was still stiff. The wound was healing well, the skin fully closed over, but the underlying muscle had been badly damaged. She had tried to exercise it, looking up physical therapy for bicep injuries on the internet, but they didn't have any for dragons. She doubted she could fly very well yet, but she had to go out. It was time. She'd go nuts if she didn't.

And there was one thing she needed to do.

It was time to find out who was sending the mysterious texts. They had gotten more and more personal, more intimate. Whoever was sending them had delved into her past, the events that had precipitated her transformation, and her relationship with Hutch. How they knew so much about her, about her hope for a cure for her condition, she had no idea. There was only one way to find out.

So, with the city once again humming with the energy of the weekend and a Red Sox night game at Fenway, Aleksi donned her niqab, veil, and a pair of sturdy boots, and waited for the trains to stop running. When the last Red Line fell silent, she hurried out of her lair and through the labyrinth of disused passages to the nearest station, one of the exits she could use without being recorded by a security camera. Cracking the door, she peered out onto the platform. A few late-night revelers were stumbling by, vocally disappointed that they'd missed the last train. She slipped out and headed for the stairs to the street, head down, steps short, hands folded into her robes. The internet was good for many things, and she'd analyzed the mannerisms of traditional Muslim women at length. She had this down.

On the street, she hurried along as if she had somewhere to go. A couple of drunks slurred a racist comment in passing, but she suppressed the urge to teach them manners. She found an alley and crouched in the shadow of a dumpster to listen. The city was far from silent, but she was alone.

Aleksi pulled her old phone, opened the messaging app, and reviewed the last few mystery texts. *Time to find out.* She tapped in, "Who are you?" hit send, and waited.

This late, she expected she might not get an answer until morning, but in less than five minutes, her phone vibrated in her hand.

The screen displayed her answer. "The only friend you've got."

Aleksi's temper flared. She tapped, "Bullshit. I have friends."

The answer came immediately. "Not many, now that Hutch is with Julie."

Heat flushed to her face, and she struggled to keep her claws sheathed as she replied, "Who the fuck are you?"

"Meet me and find out," flashed up seconds later.

Just like that? No way. She tapped, "I don't trust you!"

This answer came slower. "You trusted me when we met atop the Prudential…before you flew away."

Aleksi felt suddenly cold. This either had to be the woman who had impersonated Buckmann, or it was a government trap. She tapped, "How do I know this isn't a trap?"

"You don't," came the quick reply. Then, "You pick the place and time, and I'll come alone. If I'm lying, kill me."

The woman's got balls, taunting a dragon! Aleksi texted, "I don't kill people."

"I know," they replied. "Even the people who deserve it. That's why we want to help you!"

Aleksi stared at the screen for a long moment, thinking. This person had all the answers.

Another text arrived. "A chance to be with Hutch again is worth a little risk."

Fucker, Aleksi seethed. Whoever it was certainly knew how to push her buttons. Suppressing the impulse to dash off an acerbic reply and turn off her phone, she considered where she might meet this person with the least risk. The when was easy. The less lead time she gave this mysterious texter, the safer she'd be. But where?

Someplace close to a T-tunnel, but open, where I can see. A park nearby with trees, maybe. In six months, Aleksi had learned the MBTA transit system as well as she knew the Harvard campus. She knew where every line delved beneath the street and the surrounding environs. Only one nearby came to mind that filled all her criteria.

She tapped, "Amory Park ball field. 15 min. You stand on pitcher's mound." Three blocks from the Green Line tunnel entrance, wooded, and quiet this time of night, the park would be safe.

After a short pause, she received, "I'll be there."

Aleksi stared at the reply, stunned. *Well, shit. It's put up or shut up, now, Dragon Woman.* She could get to the ball field in five minutes if she flew. Her arm still hurt, but some things were worth a little pain...and risk.

She stowed her phone, doffed her boots and robe, and climbed up the side of the building behind her. The muscles of her arm ached, but felt looser when she reached the top. There, she stared out into the night for a moment, girding her nerves. *Now or never.* Launching herself into the sky for the first time in a week, Aleksi gritted her teeth against the pain and wheeled to the west. The dragon of Boston had taken to the skies once again.

Persephone pulled the Jag onto the grassy verge beside the Amory Tennis Center and got out. The spike heels of her pumps sunk into the turf. She checked her watch, three minutes to spare. Luckily, she kept a change of street clothes in the trunk for emergencies, and the parking lot of the hotel had been secluded enough for her to slip into jeans and a sweater. The pumps didn't really go with jeans, but fuck it. This wasn't a social occasion.

No, you're meeting with a dragon. The old adage about being caught dead in a mismatched outfit came to her out of nowhere, and she almost laughed. She donned a light jacket, flipped the collar up, and strode for the pitcher's mound.

She didn't see Aleksi, but she hadn't expected to. They knew from hours of hacked CCTV footage that she was adept at staying hidden. She stopped atop the mound and checked the time. Exactly fifteen minutes had passed. Pulling her phone, she texted, "I'm here," and hit send.

No answer.

Persephone turned a slow circle, eying the trees, bushes, and buildings. Nothing moved. She yawned. *If she stands me up...*

"Who are you?" asked a voice from the shadow of the visitor's dugout.

Persephone peered into those shadows, but could see nothing. She cleared her throat. "Don't you recognize me? I'll admit, we've only met twice. Well, three times if you count the Prudential, but I didn't look like me that time."

No answer.

Persephone tried a different tack. "I'm really sorry this happened to you, Aleksi. You're a brilliant young woman and deserve the life you wanted. Let me try to give it back to you."

"Walk to home plate. Keep your hands out of your pockets."

"Sure." Persephone walked the sixty feet, trying to keep from trembling. *She's not going to kill me. She doesn't kill people.* She stopped and spread her hands wide, smiling into the shadows. "Recognize me now?"

The dragon stirred in the darkness, golden eyes reflecting the ambient light. She emerged to the edge of the shadows, eyes narrow, examining her, mouth slightly open, nostrils flaring. *Smelling me,* Persephone realized and shivered.

Then the eyes widened. "Persephone?" Another step into the light, wings folded but claws extended. "What the *fuck?*"

"Yes. Sorry for the deception." Persephone took a breath and let it out slowly. "I need to caution you, Aleksi. You can't tell anyone who I am. *Especially* Hutch. If you do, we'll have no choice but to cover our tracks and vanish."

The golden eyes narrowed again, her upper lip curling back from teeth like daggers. "What do you mean, 'cover your tracks'?"

"First, let me explain a few things that'll help you understand. My family is very old and powerful. We have more money, influence, and technical and scientific knowledge than most governments." Telling this to anyone outside the family was a serious breach of the rules, but she'd been given the okay by Gi-gi. This was a special circumstance. "We gather information, myths, biological anomalies, legends, and use what we learn to develop new technologies and applications. We root out the truth. It's made us very rich, but we've always remained anonymous, hidden from the powers of the world."

"Why? How?"

"Why is complicated, but the how is simple. One of my ancestors, centuries back, delved the jungles of the Congo, seeking legends of pagan gods. He found one."

"A *god?*" Aleksi snorted, her nostrils flaring wide. "Bullshit."

"Well, not a god, per-se, but a man changed into something else. Rather like yourself, in some ways, really. He was an invalid, but worshiped by his people. He possessed an intelligence that dwarfed that of normal humans. He learned to speak French in a matter of hours and conversed at length with the strange white man from another world." She lifted her hands and shrugged. "My ancestor learned the secret of that transformation, of the frightful intelligence, and used it. From that day forward, my family climbed the ladders of wealth, power, politics, and knowledge. At least one member of my family acts as our higher mind at all times, while the rest of us do the dirty work."

"The dirty work."

"Yes. Sometimes we...intervene in events, as we did when the government tried to...learn of your condition."

"How did you do that? Impersonate Buckmann, I mean."

"Another trick we've learned over the ages." She shrugged again. "Not all legends are myth, Aleksi. Just like the ones of dragons probably aren't. There have been sub-races of humans who had the ability to change their appearances. They're responsible for a great many stories about shape-shifters and doppelgangers, even werewolves. They've since been exterminated for their abilities, or at least we *think* they have. We learned the underlying biology, their ability to alter proteins in the human body, and we applied it. I became Mary Buckmann to take the specimen you discovered away from the government. They can't be trusted with such things."

"You failed. They still have it."

"I know." Again, she shrugged. "Sometimes we fail. The point is, we've learned a lot of things, and we use what we've learned to learn more. Not for power, but for *knowledge*. We know more about biology and genetics than anyone else on Earth. If *anyone* can help you, we can."

"So, you're a spy for your family. Why the rich socialite persona?"

"Rich socialites have access to a great many people, Aleksi. What better persona? I learn things from powerful people, and my family decides what to do with that knowledge. We influence politics, finance, governmental policy, even laws."

"So, your job is to fuck information out of brilliant men, like Hutch." Aleksi hissed the last like a curse, her claws flexing.

Trying to bait me? "Among other things, and not only men, but yes." Persephone smiled thinly at the dragon, staring her down. "I'm not going to apologize to you for marrying Hutch, Aleksi. If it's any consolation, I *did* love him. Honestly, I wish I could have stayed with him, but it wasn't possible."

Aleksi's claws retracted, her shoulders lowering slightly, relaxing. "Okay, I'm not really buying all this yet, but answer my question: What did you mean by 'cover your tracks'?"

"Exactly what you think I meant. If we're exposed, we'll be forced to eliminate anyone who knows the truth about us."

"You mean murder them."

"Yes." Persephone cocked her head at the dragon. "That shocks you? Governments murder hundreds of innocent people every day, Aleksi. When we kill, it's for self-preservation. Just like when you killed Derrick Penningly."

"I *didn't*. Tony Jasper did."

Persephone waved it away. "Semantics. You were ready, willing, and actively *trying* to kill him when Jasper pulled the trigger."

"So, you kill anyone who learns your secret. Does that include me?"

"No, Aleksi. We kill for self-preservation, only those who threaten us, and then very rarely. We want to help you."

"Sure you do, so you can learn about me."

"We've had the original specimen for half a year, Aleksi. We already know more about you than anyone. But yes, I'll admit that we want to learn more about your condition. We've done this before with other... anomalous genomes."

"And you expect me to *trust* you?" She hissed a laugh.

"No. I expect you to take the only chance you have in the *world* of becoming human again." Persephone took a step forward, her hands out and open, imploring. "The only chance you have to be with *Hutch* again.

The only chance you have for a career in science, with *us*! You're *brilliant*, and we would welcome your efforts on our behalf. If you keep doing what you're doing, some lucky asshole's going to eventually put a bullet in your head, or worse, in your spine. You do *not* want to end up strapped down on a dissection table."

Aleksi stared at her for a moment before she spoke. "I need to think about this."

"Of course. I'd be disappointed in you if you didn't. But please, don't tell anyone about me."

"I won't."

"Thank you for meeting with me. I'm sorry for what you've gone through, for what you've lost. I know what that feels like."

"You really don't." Aleksi raised a clawed wing. "Nobody knows what *this* feels like."

Persephone nodded. "True enough. Take all the time you need. You have my number."

Aleksi turned to go, but then hesitated. She looked back over her shoulder. "By the way, you were right about me."

"About what?"

"In the restaurant, when we first met, you told me… I *was* in need of… someone." Her lips quirked into something approximating a smile. "And Hutch was *way* better than just *very good*."

Persephone smiled back. "I know. As I said, I hated to let him go."

Aleksi nodded, "So did I."

"You can get him back, Aleksi. You can *be* with him again."

The dragon's eyes narrowed again. "You can't know that."

"I think we can reverse your condition, Aleksi. I can't promise, but, at the very least, I'm virtually sure we can neutralize the infectious elements. That, at least, will safeguard the human race from a plague of dragons."

"And if it doesn't work? If you can't make me human again?" The pain of shattered hopes rang in her voice.

"Then we will have tried, and we can help you stay safe."

"In a *cage*?"

"No! Never! You have my *word* on that, for what it's worth. Even in your current condition, you're a brilliant scientist. You could work with us. We could give you a purpose. Something better than vigilantism."

Aleksi nodded again. "Let me think about this."

"Of course. Take your time," Persephone agreed. Then she added, "Just don't get killed before we can save you."

18

"Scenario twelve, ready to initiate," the tech announced. "Acceleration factor four. Ready?"

"Ready." The subject raised the simulated pistol, a VR control grip made to the exact dimensions and weight of a Sig Sauer 226. The practice weapon even had an ammo counter and replaceable magazine. The only thing it didn't fully simulate was recoil. The VR environment, however, gave visual, audio, and tactile feedback that came close.

The Director, Price, Baker, and a dozen more techs and government representatives watched the monitors. Telemetry pads taped to the subject's skin gave the control center full readouts of physical and mental parameters. The video feeds covered four angles and the view through the VR headset strapped to David Gilford's head. They stared rapt, transfixed by their creation.

Gilford's body gleamed with sweat. He'd been through a dozen scenarios without more than five minutes between each. Twenty days after the fever had broken, he was looking less and less human. The faux pistol didn't fit his altered hand very well, and the membrane that stretched from his elongated fingers to his ankles interfered with clothing and equipment, but his performances in the simulations had escalated to the point where the state-of-the-art computer system could barely keep up with him. He was nothing short of magnificent.

"Commencing now." The technician started the scenario.

The monitors blurred into motion. The subject's view showed the darkened interior of a factory festooned with manufacturing equipment and stacked crates. The other monitors displayed the inside of a gymnasium arranged with movable barriers that had been set up to emulate the virtual environment. This allowed the subject to actually interact with what he was seeing, to touch walls, lean against crates, climb and leap over obstacles. The virtual environment also included twelve armed adversaries and more than thirty innocent bystanders. The goal, of course, was to eliminate the hostiles with minimal civilian casualties.

So far, David had beaten every scenario they'd thrown at him.

The hostiles were heavily armed, held hostages, wore body armor, and had the accuracy, tactics, and mobility of trained soldiers. They also had been accelerated to four times normal human speed. One might think David wouldn't stand a chance, but the reverse had actually proven more accurate.

Clawed toes cut furrows in the padded rubber flooring as David lunged from barrier to barrier, firing his weapon with deadly accuracy and moving at blinding speed. He ducked and rolled under incoming fire, exchanged magazines, avoided traps, and annihilated the hostiles, never once hitting a civilian. The encounter was over in less than one minute.

"He's astounding," one of the military representatives said in admiration. Three officers from the Joint Chiefs had been sent to evaluate the subject.

"Gilford always was a deadly motherfucker, but *Jesus*," another agreed. He looked to the Director with a furrowed brow "You sure that was real time, sir?"

"It is, and he *is* astounding, isn't he?" *More than that, he's the future of warfare.* The Director had already forwarded data of the subject's abilities to his higher ups. They wanted more. He'd assured them that this was only the beginning. "And he continues to improve. Once his evolution is complete, we'll know what we've really got here."

"Can we talk to him?" the third rep asked.

"Of course." The Director keyed his mic to connect with the simulation and the techs working the room. "We're done for now. Stand down, David. Unplug him and stow the equipment. We're coming in." He motioned for the reps to follow and led them to the gymnasium. "Please remember that the subject is infectious. We are under contact contagion restrictions. No touching, and we wear gloves and face shields."

"We've been briefed, sir," the first rep assured him.

Maybe, the Director thought. *But you've never met Homo draconis before.*

They stepped into the gym and donned protective gear. "Hello, David. We watched your performance. Very impressive."

"Didn't know I had an audience." Dragon eyes snapped up to focus on them. He stood still while Amy and Jim removed the battery pack and telemetry leads. Other techs unlocked the movable barriers and rolled them to the walls. "I'm afraid I tore up the floor a little."

"Nothing to worry about." The Director waved the reps forward. "This is Commander McCally, the Joint Chiefs rep for Admiral Henderson, Captain Flint, whom you've met and is working for General Nelson, and Colonel Jamison, rep for the Air Force's General Olson."

"Sirs," David nodded to them. "Captain, good to see you again."

"Hello, Gilford. How's the new assignment?"

"Optimal, sir!" David grinned, his teeth now markedly pointed, canines elongated. His face had changed, too—his cheekbones more pronounced, eyebrows now arched ridges of scales, and eyes larger with bright yellow irises and vertical slit pupils. "I feel better than I have in decades! Ever, in fact!"

"Your performance was nothing short of awe-inspiring," Jamison said. "I can't wait to see what you're capable of when these changes are complete!"

"Me, too, sir." David raised an arm, the wing membrane from his elongated digits stretched taut, pulling his spandex shorts away from his hip. "I won't need a chute to jump out of a plane the next time."

They all laughed politely, though the Director could hear the strain in it. They feared him.

"Here you go, David." The female tech finished with the last electrode and handed him a towel. "See you later."

"Thanks, Amy." He toweled the sweat from his torso, muscle rippling under the golden sheen of his skin.

"Any complaints, David?"

"The headset's a little heavy, but it's not a problem. My hands don't fit the weapon very well, and the shorts won't let me extend my arm over my head." He demonstrated again, and the wing membrane came taut against his stretch shorts. "Maybe we could figure out a new grip, and some kind of adhesive for the shorts, or just ditch them. It's not like the whole staff hasn't seen me in the buff anyway."

"We'll work on some modifications."

"We could take him to Natick and run him through the mill," Flint suggested. "New pistol grips should be simple enough to design, and maybe some adhesive backed web gear for equipment that doesn't interfere with your…um…"

"Wings," David finished for him with a grin. He extended both arms straight out, his elongated digits fully extended. They spanned almost nine feet already. "Don't worry, Captain. I'm not bothered by these… changes. I signed up for it, and I knew what I was getting into." He turned to the Director, dragon eyes flicking, dilating. "I'd like a trip to Natick, sir. The simulations are good, but I'd like to stretch my legs."

"I'll set it up. Right now, I imaging you're set for a shower and a meal."

"Roger that, sir."

"We'll talk later, David." The Director motioned his charges to the door, and they said their goodbyes and followed.

Outside, the reps voiced their concerns.

"Are you sure he's okay?" Flint asked. "He seems…twitchy to me. Amped up, like he's on stimulants. Not like the soldier I knew. Gilford was always stone-cold."

"He's evolving, Captain. His senses are far sharper than yours and mine. He's experiencing a sort of constant sensory overload, scents, colors, sounds, even vibrations that we can't feel. He's forthright about it, and says he's getting used to it."

"And psychologically? Is he stable?" Jamison asked.

"He's been experiencing hyper-vivid dreams since the inoculation, genetic memories, actually, but he's okay. He's one of the most stable men I've ever met. We're evaluating him constantly."

"And how long until the endpoint of these changes?" McCally asked.

"We don't know exactly. The previous subjects weren't under our control during the later stages of the evolution. Another few weeks, maybe. We know that the one surviving subject is still at large, and is healthy and psychologically stable, though she's…currently creating some problems."

"The recent spate of vigilante attacks?" McCally asked.

"Yes. We're considering intervention, but that would be risky."

"If she's anything like Gilford, I imagine it would be more than *risky*."

"So, what are you planning for field tests?" Flint asked.

The Director shook his head. "Nothing yet. We have to consider the risk of infection. We can't afford an outbreak."

"But the potential applications for someone like this… They're mind-blowing."

"I know, and we'll explore all the opportunities once he's finished evolving. Don't worry. Tell your bosses we're on this. David is an exemplary subject. He's performing well beyond our expectations." The Director escorted them back to the control center to review the recordings again, his mind filled with visions of aerial deployments over hostile territory, taking out terrorist cells, rogue governments, wet work deep in China and Russia.

Nobody will see this coming, he mused, hiding his smile. *Better than a fucking smart bomb.*

In David's quarters, the dragon stepped into the scalding cascade of his shower, letting the pounding spray drown out the sounds, smells, tastes, dozens of beating hearts, the stench of fear, blood, sweat, piss, and coffee, the whispered conversations about him out in the hallway. *Freak, monster, fucking scary...*

Damn right, I'm scary. David squinted through the fogged shower door into the mirror, raising one clawed hand and extending his claws. *I'm Homo-fucking-draconis. Reborn...*

The humans were afraid of him...as they should be.

With no one to talk to about the revelation of Persephone's mysterious family, Aleksi investigated the only way she could. Unfortunately, the internet didn't offer her much more than she already knew, and she suspected most of that was fabricated.

If she's telling me the truth and not just making it all up to have a dragon in a cage to show her rich friends. Hutch said she was a cryptozoology nut...

The woman she'd met at the ball field seemed so different than the Persephone she'd met at a New Year's Eve party and again at a restaurant when Hutch had asked her to loan them money to help analyze the mysterious specimen they'd found. That woman had been brash, flamboyant, elegant, and seemed to take pleasure in putting people on the spot. This new Persephone struck her as cold and calculating, analytical, willing to kill to keep her family secret.

A secret family organization that wielded the power to rival governments seemed like a wild conspiracy theory. Hiding that behind the false persona of a Boston socialite sounded like something out of a spy novel. But if someone could convincingly impersonate a government agent, couldn't they also impersonate a Boston socialite? Was the woman she met at the ball field really Persephone Terris?

But her scent... There was no doubt in her mind that this was the same woman she'd met on the observation deck of the Prudential Tower. Aleksi racked her brain to recall what Persephone had smelled like when they first met. She recalled perfume, but little else. She hadn't had the senses of a dragon then. Was this the same woman? There was no way she could be sure.

Her skepticism waned in time, however. The internet provided hints that something wasn't exactly right about Persephone's family. According to socialite gossip, her family was worth about four hundred million dollars. That sounded like a lot of money, but it wasn't anything near the hundreds of billions that would rival governments.

Most of the family's wealth had supposedly come from investments of three generations ago. Persephone's great-grandfather, Julius Terris, had been the only son of French immigrants, but records of his parents were elusive, just two typical French names on an immigration document that might or might not be true. They had died in a train accident in the Midwest when their son was nineteen years old. Julius took a chance on some risky investments, hit it rich, and married Francine Paine-Terris, who seemed to have no background at all, or at least nothing on paper. The family's financial successes since then had been miraculous, and Persephone had been born with a diamond-studded spoon in her mouth. She'd had private tutors, earned four bachelor's degrees before she was twenty-five in the diverse fields of business, biology, computer science, and art history, and lived a high-profile social life. Beautiful, rich, and intelligent, the young woman had become a star of the Boston social scene. Newspaper and internet articles posted pictures of a younger Persephone on the arms of media moguls, politicians, bankers, and finally, Dr. Dwayne Hutchinson.

That seemed out of place. *Why Hutch?* Had she married him for his work in paleontology, his penchant for cryptozoology, or his connections at Harvard? One thing for certain: she hadn't batted an eyelash when Aleksi accused her of having sex with men for information, and even admitted it. That actually *had* sounded like the Persephone who had asked her flat out in a restaurant if she and Hutch were fucking.

Hutch... If Aleksi told him about her, would Persephone really have him killed? The man she had been married to, who she had said she once loved?

"I hated to let him go," she'd said.

Does she still love him? Aleksi wondered.

Hutch... Hope smote her heart once again, but she pressed it aside. She had to think this through with her brain.

The simple fact of the matter was that Aleksi had no way to be sure if Persephone was really who or what she said. She had no way to tell the truth from a convincing lie. She'd seemed a little nervous talking to a dragon, but that was expected. One thing was certain, if she lived a false public life, she was a consummate actress.

But if she's telling the truth, there's a chance to be human again.

The next question loomed like a storm front: if she accepted the offer, how could she stay safe?

The answer was simple: be careful.

No time like the present. Aleksi taped both of her prepaid phones to her legs and left her lair. The trains were still running, so she crept into an active tunnel and waited for one to pass. When it did, she flew down the tunnel right behind it, gaining speed. Her arm felt only vaguely stiff now, and she'd done this a hundred times. As the train slowed for the next station, she swooped up and landed on top of the last car, lying flat, perfectly still. When it left the station, she rode along.

Three stations later, the train emerged from the tunnel, and Aleksi simply billowed her wings and caught air. She was up above the streetlights in a flash, in her safe zone. Banking up, she landed on an apartment building rooftop and stopped to listen to the night.

Aleksi pulled out her phones, and another thought came to her: *No more flying through the canyons of Boston.* If Persephone was telling the truth, she'd be human again. She stretched out an arm and looked at it. *No more wings. No more flying.* She'd miss it, but not as much as she missed Hutch.

Can't have your cake and eat it, too, Aleksi. She texted Persephone, "Let's do this. Where and when?"

Less than a minute later, she received, "We can pick you up anywhere you like at your convenience, night would be better."

She tapped in, "Tomorrow, 2 a.m. where we met before. If you try to hurt me, you'll regret it."

Persephone answered, "I promise you, we'll do our best to help you."

Aleksi wasn't about to banter with her about truth and lies. She picked up the other phone and texted Hutch, "Going to be out of touch for a while. Found someone who may be able to help me."

The reply came immediately. "Mysterious Johansen woman?"

"Yes. I met with her. She seems legit. I think I can trust them."

"Why?"

She paused, knowing she couldn't tell him the truth, that it was the only hope she had of ever touching him again, being with him, being human again. She tapped, "Dragon intuition."

"Ha! Funny. Can you come by? I'd like to see you."

The dread of what might happen if she did welled up in her. "Don't think that's a good idea. Too risky. They're watching you."

After a long pause, she received, "Please be careful. I love you."

Hope flickered in her chest, a burning butterfly fluttering against her heart. She tapped, "Always." Then on impulse, added, "Both."

19

David stepped out of the facility and looked up at the sky for the first time in twenty-five days. It was brighter than he remembered, the leaves on the trees sharper, the cascade of scents a riot in his head. He breathed deep and stepped into the van.

Follow orders. Just part of the job... And it was better than sitting in his room and getting stabbed with needles.

He wore a poncho-like garment with a hood even though the van had darkly tinted windows. He sat in the back with two armed guards, Dr. Price, and his two minders, Amy and Jim. They all wore gloves, clear face masks, and protective glasses. The scents in the van, the closeness of humanity, sang along his nerves like a bow on violin strings.

"Could you turn on some air. It's a little stuffy back here."

"Sure." The guard in the passenger seat turned the air on full, and the closeness faded somewhat. The driver pulled them through the checkpoint and headed for the freeway.

David watched the world passing outside the windows with his new eyes, marveling at the detail, the motion, and more than anything, the endless mass of humanity. The traffic seemed to crawl at a snail's pace, the drivers in their seats, yawning, talking on their phones, texting, oblivious to the monster in the van. They passed a woman jogging along a path, and David's heart pounded with the urge to chase, to hunt.

Chill, soldier, he thought, forcing calm, closing his eyes to dim the riot of sensory input. It helped a little, but the closeness crept in around him.

"You okay, David?" Amy asked beside him.

He opened his eyes to look at her, wide pupils, sweat beading on her upper lip, fear spreading from her like a bloodstain, not like before. But was Amy different or was it him? "Just a little claustrophobic, I guess. I'm fine."

She rested a gloved hand on his knee. "Not much longer. Deep breaths."

"It's okay. I'm good." He tried to ignore her. She touched him all the time. She even sat and watched stupid movies with him, laughed with him. He liked Amy. *Then why the hell do I feel like ripping her arm off?*

The feeling subsided with some deep breathing exercises, and he watched the scenery. They crossed a bridge over a small lake, boats on the water, people on the shore in bathing suits, and he recognized Cochituate Park. He'd been to Natick Soldier Systems Center before, but years ago. The driver took the exit off of the Mass Pike and navigated the ramps onto busy suburban streets. They drove past a shopping mall, the lot packed with cars full of people out buying things.

It all seemed to David like a simulation, a crazy panorama choreographed just to taunt him. He belonged out there, in the open, in the sky, hunting, stalking, feeding…

The van pulled into Natick and proceeded through a security checkpoint. The guard glanced at the driver's credentials and waved them through. Finally, they pulled up adjacent to a building and more guards beside a nondescript door. The van door opened, and he could breathe.

"This way, David." Price stepped down and flashed her badge to the guards at the door. They nodded and punched in a code that opened it.

David stepped down and looked around, the world sharper again without the tinted windows. The sun glinted on the lake, a million diamonds on a rippling sheet of blue silk. He stopped and stared.

"David?" Amy touched his arm.

He jerked, then saw her. She was scared. "Sorry. I just…" He waved a hand at the lake. "The water. It's…beautiful."

She looked, and smiled behind her plastic mask. "It is. Come on; we need to get inside."

"Sure." He followed his minders into the building, the door closing behind him, obliterating the beauty. *Do the job... Follow orders... Chill...*

They escorted him into an elevator, and he ground his teeth at the confinement as they descended. When the doors opened, they were met by a man in a lab coat with two assistants in standard army fatigues, but no weapons. They did, however, wear protective gloves and face shields.

"David, this is Colonel Winston. He'll be heading up the weapons design team." Price gestured to David. "Colonel, this is David Gilford, our subject."

"David, how are you?" The colonel nodded, but didn't put out a hand to shake. He obviously knew better. When David pulled back the hood of his poncho, however, none of them hid their shock at his appearance.

"Good, Colonel." He raised a hand and extended his elongated fingers. "Hope you're up to a challenge."

"We've already begun, actually." He waved a hand down the hall. "This way, please."

They all followed Winston down the hall, past several doors labeled with numbers and letters, and stopped at one that had an unlit red light overhead. The door was stenciled with the words "Firing Range."

"We'll leave you in the Colonel's care, David," Price said. "We're meeting with the apparel design team, just down the hall, and Amy and Jim will be setting up your quarters."

"Thanks, Doc." He gave them a nod and caught Amy's eye. "See you later."

Amy twitched a smile and followed Price.

"So, we got measurements from the Director and knocked up some prototypes." Winston led them into a standard indoor firing range, long and low, the walls unpainted concrete. "Let's give them a try, shall we?" A table had been set up beside one of the firing positions. Several familiar weapons lay there, but with grips different than any David had seen before.

Custom made for dragons... He smiled and flexed his hands. "Yes, *sir*!"

"We have a modified M4 and MK17, and four pistols, two Sigs and two Glocks. The Director thought that you might like the lighter weapons for potential aerial deployment, so we included the Glocks. Our apparel engineers are working on web gear to hold weapons and ammo, but we can start here." He nodded to his two assistants, and they handed out ear protection.

David went through a standard live-fire exercise with all of the weapons and gave the colonel his honest opinion. He was still changing, but his grip wouldn't change much more than it already had. His two smallest fingers needed more space to fold back along his forearm while firing, and the balance felt off. Also, his claws tended to catch on the trigger guards. He fired two magazines from each weapon, much preferring the pistols. His accuracy was perfect with every weapon.

"Well done, David. You're quite a marksman."

"Better than I ever was." He handed over the last weapon, a ten-millimeter Glock. "Thanks for the work. These are better than the standard issue, by far."

"We still obviously need some work for speed and safety." He gestured to the door. "We'll make some more modifications and have them ready this evening."

"You guys work fast."

"Ha! Yes, we've got an entire 3-D design team on this. Printing technology has made our job a lot easier." Out in the hall, he waved his escort forward. "Take him to the other side, please. I'll see you later, David."

"Thanks, Colonel." David followed the escort to another lab, this one clearly set up to create various types of belts, holsters, and harnesses. The officer in charge, a short, stocky Asian woman, stood talking to Price as he came in.

"Ah, David. How'd the weapons trial go?"

"Good. The colonel said he'd have some modifications for me by this evening." He nodded to the other woman. Her dark eyes widened, her mouth slightly agape, but it wasn't fear. She looked fascinated.

"This is Captain Fen. She's a combat apparel specialist," Price said.

"Good to meet you, Captain." She wore an ugly smock with pockets that hung on her like a sack. For someone who specialized in clothing, the garment seemed crude.

"And you, David." She spoke with an accent, Korean or Japanese, he couldn't discern which. "Can you please remove that garment. I need to see you."

"Sure." He pulled the poncho over his head. He wore the hated stretch shorts underneath, and they pulled as he raised his arms.

Fen's eyes lit up like beacons. "Fascinating! I received pictures and measurements, but… Yes, this will be challenging." She approached him, extending a gloved hand. "May I touch you?"

"Sure." He tried to smile, but something about the woman made him nervous. "Not like I haven't been poked and prodded constantly for the last few weeks."

"I'm sure." She sounded distracted, distant. She ran gloved fingers down his side where the wing membrane met with his torso. "Lift your arm, please."

He did, and the wing membrane tugged at the shorts.

"This clearly won't do. It chafes, yes, and restricts mobility."

"Yes." He found her intensity a little disconcerting, and something about her scent set his teeth on edge.

"Please take it off. I need to take measurements." She pulled a tape from a pocket of her smock. "Maybe something adhesive…"

David complied. *Follow orders…* He'd never been particularly modest, and Price had given him thorough physical exams twice a week since this started, but Fen's touch unnerved him. It was like she didn't even think of him as a person, just a thing, like she was upholstering a couch.

And that scent… He breathed deep. This was something different, something new, and it felt dangerous, wrong, distasteful.

He held still while she took careful measurements, clenching his teeth to keep them from grinding.

"Yes, I believe I can have something by tonight. We'll do a fitting." She nodded and backed away, smiling for the first time. "Thank you, David. You're challenging me."

"Happy to oblige." He tugged on his shorts, resisting the urge to tell her that she was challenging him, too. For some reason, the combination of her troubling scent and her brusque manner set him off.

Then she turned and walked to a workbench, and the stiff waddle of her gait clicked into his head. Fen was pregnant. *That's the scent!* He breathed deeply and wondered once again why it bothered him. He searched his memories of his dragon dreams for that disturbing scent, and found only screams, blood, and death. *What the hell?*

David followed Price to his quarters, stark compared to his digs at the facility, and he settled in. Jim brought him a meal, and Amy his e-reader, two bottles of chilled beer, and a data stick.

"So, how'd it go?" Amy asked, as she booted up the entertainment system. They were on season three of Game of Thrones.

"Not bad. The apparel specialist's a little weird." David cut a bite of steak and wolfed it down. They'd finally stopped cooking his meat.

"Fen? Yeah, she's an artist. Typical." She found the episode they'd just watched and loaded the next one. "All intensity, no social skills."

"Well, she must have *some* social skills." He cracked a beer and took a pull. "She got knocked up. That's hard to do alone."

"Actually, it's not." Amy gave him a wink. "She's not married or even seeing anyone. Doesn't like men *or* women. She wanted kids, though, so..."

"The wonders of modern medicine." David shook his head and ate. "She's got courage if she's having kids all by herself. Talk about a challenge."

He'd never had kids, at least none that he knew of, but later in his life, whenever he saw little ones, he felt a pang. If there had been a way for him to have children without the entanglement of a woman, he might have done it. Suddenly, he felt jealous of Fen. She had done something he never could. He wondered again why that bothered him.

David ate his steak and sipped his beer, still wondering why the scent of a pregnant woman would make him uneasy, and why his dream memories associated that with death.

Aleksi wore her niqab to the pickup. She arrived early and settled down in the foliage of the park to watch and wait, her nerves humming like high-tension wires.

A big SUV pulled up right on time, its windows darkly tinted. It reminded her of the government vehicles that had disgorged soldiers with automatic weapons. She tensed and waited.

The passenger door opened, and Persephone stepped out. Her eyes scanned the ballfield, the trees, the tennis courts, but passed right over Aleksi. She checked her phone, and sighed.

"Open the back door of the vehicle," Aleksi said from hiding.

Persephone started, her eyes searching the dark foliage. "Aleksi?"

"Yes. Open the back door. Now!"

"Of course." She did. It was empty. "It's just me and one of my cousins."

Aleksi eased out of the foliage and approached the vehicle, senses heightened to fever-pitch, muscles tense, ready to explode into action. Dropping the face veil, she peered through the open door, breathing deep to scent the air. *Two people, no guns.* The back was empty, and a man with short curly hair sat behind the wheel, looking back at her. There was no partition between the back and front seat.

"This is Reggie," Persephone said. "Reg, this is Aleksi."

"Hi." The man smiled and waved her in. "We should go."

Aleksi sniffed the air again, but still scented only the two. The car looked normal, and even in such a confined space, she could kill the both of them in a flash. Also, the doors wouldn't hold her if she wanted out.

She turned to Persephone. "You're getting in the back with me. If you're lying, I'll paint the inside of that car with you."

Persephone swallowed. "I understand." She got in and looked at Aleksi.

Trust... It came hard after so long being hunted. Aleksi climbed in and closed the door. The SUV pulled around, and they drove out of the park.

"Did you bring a phone with you?" Persephone asked.

"No." Aleksi had left everything but the single robe in her subway nook, everything packed away and taped closed to keep the vermin out.

"Good. We can't risk you being tracked in any way." She nodded to Reggie. "We'll be taking you to our home in Back Bay. It's comfortable and safe, and we have everything we need to treat you."

"Hutch said you live in a mansion."

Persephone smiled. "Well, it's a nice place, but *hardly* a mansion."

"And your whole family lives there?"

"No, just myself and a few cousins. A few service staff, but you won't be meeting them. We've got family all over the world."

"But Hutch lived with you there for a while, right?"

"He did, but he knew nothing of my family. That was one reason we moved into the condo. It was...difficult, keeping secrets from him."

Difficult... Aleksi thought she heard real regret there, but let it pass, content to ride along in silence. When they pulled up behind a fenced estate, she gaped in awe.

Hardly a mansion... It dominated an entire city block, one vast main house with two smaller outbuildings, all surrounded by wooded and manicured grounds. The fence stood at least fifteen feet high, steel bars with ornate pointed tips. Aleksi was long used to spotting security cameras, and counted half a dozen just within sight of the gate.

Reggie rolled down his window and swiped a card, then punched a code. A green light lit up, and he said, "It's me. I'm home," into the mic.

The gate rolled aside.

"You said no cages." Aleksi cocked one scaled eyebrow at Persephone. "Those are bars, unless I'm mistaken."

"Oh, *please*. Those are to keep people out, not you in, and they wouldn't pose a barrier to you anyway." A bit of the petulant socialite crept in to her protestation, a more familiar Persephone. "You won't be held against your will, Aleksi. I promise you. There *will* be locked doors, but I'll give you all the pass codes to get you in and out. You won't be a prisoner."

She didn't know if she could believe that or not. "So, I can go anywhere I like?"

"I didn't say that. We have things we're not quite ready to show you yet. But you can leave any time you like."

"Okay." Of course, she wouldn't know that for sure until the first door closed behind her.

Reggie drove into a cavernous garage. Another SUV, a huge Mercedes sedan, and the familiar late model Jaguar stood there. The garage door rolled down behind them, and Persephone and Reggie got out.

Aleksi followed. Habit prompted her to look for exits, escape routes, hiding places. There were three doors besides the two wide rolling garage doors. One had to open outside, while the other two must have led into the main house. Those had card-swipes and keypads.

"I'll code the main security system to you right now." Persephone fished a card from her pocket and swiped it. Another green light lit up. "You won't get a card. They aren't really necessary. If you press and hold the star key for ten seconds, it's the same as swiping. The system's coded to a numeric and voiceprint."

"Okay." Aleksi watched her tap in a number too fast to memorize.

"Persephone. Code new access. Amsterdam, Brussels, Chicago, Denver." The green light flashed rapidly, and Persephone motioned Aleksi forward. "Type in any number you like, something you can remember, then say, 'It's me. I'm home.'"

Aleksi stepped up and thought for a second, then typed in her mother's birthday in reverse, and said, "It's me. I'm home."

The panel beeped, and the green light went solid for a second, then winked out.

"Okay, try it," Persephone said.

Aleksi pressed and held the star key until the green light lit up, then tapped in her code and said, "It's me. I'm home." The green light flashed, and the door clicked.

"It'll stay unlocked for ten seconds." Persephone turned the handle and pushed to reveal a stairwell within. "This way, please."

Aleksi followed her down the stairs while Reggie closed the door and followed behind her. She felt like stopping and checking to make sure her new pass code would get her out through that door, but when she glanced back, she saw that there was no keypad on the inside.

"It's not locked from the inside," Reggie said. "Fire codes, you know."

Aleksi couldn't tell if he was being sarcastic or not.

The door at the bottom wasn't locked, and opened up into, of all things, a wine cellar.

She stopped and gaped at the rows of spotless bottles. "I've got to admit, this isn't what I expected."

"This is still part of the main house." Persephone went to the back of the low room and Aleksi followed. There, a steel door was set into a granite block wall. Beside it was another keypad and a flat, square screen about the size of a tablet computer. "This is what we call the Sanctum. The code is the same you just used upstairs, but it's verified by a hand print. I'll prime it to accept yours."

"The *Sanctum*?" It sounded too melodramatic.

"What would you suggest we call it?" Reggie asked as Persephone tapped in a much longer code and pressed her hand to the pad.

"How about 'The Place Where We Hide All The Scary Shit'?"

Persephone glanced back at her and coughed a laugh. "Well, now that *you're* here, maybe we'll rename it."

The screen came up with the text, "System Primed, Enter New Code and Apply Print."

"There you go." Persephone gestured her forward.

Aleksi tapped in the same code and pressed her palm to the screen. Of course, two of her fingers wouldn't fit on the screen, but a green outline of her palm lit up, then vanished. The single word "Accepted" flashed up.

"Try it, please," Persephone said.

Aleksi did, and the door clicked. She grabbed the handle, turned it, and pushed. Inside, warm, low light greeted her. A hallway branched left and right. It looked like a hotel, with carpeted floors, stylish lighting fixtures, and doors set at intervals with hotel-style latches, each with its own keypad.

"The door at the end of the hall to your left won't open for you, but everything else will. We have a laboratory, telecommunications, medical, and computer facilities, as well as a few rooms for guests." Persephone started down the hall to the right. "I'll give you a tour later, if you like, but right now we'll show you to your room."

Aleksi looked back at the door as Reggie followed, and noted a keypad and print scanner on the inside. She pointed at it and said, "What about those fire codes?"

He smiled at her. "They don't apply here."

"Mind if I make sure I can get out?"

He paused, then waved at the door. "Please do."

Maybe she was being paranoid, but she typed in her code and pressed her palm to the pad. The door clicked, and she opened it.

"Satisfied?" Reggie looked smug.

"Not really. You could probably lock me in with a few keystrokes. But that would be a dangerous thing to do."

His smug vanished. "I don't blame you for being cautious, Aleksi, but we're not suicidal. We know what you're capable of."

"Good." She followed Persephone to the last door to the right.

"You should be comfortable here, but once the treatments start, it may be necessary to move you to another room." She keyed the door open and went inside.

Aleksi stepped into a small suite that reminded her of a condominium. There was a sitting area, kitchen, closet, bathroom, and bedroom. Flat screen TVs hung on the walls of the living room and bedroom. She smelled food and went to the fridge. Inside, white paper wrapped packages sat in a neat row, along with bottles of white wine and milk in the door.

"There's red wine in the cooler there, and a coffee maker. If you want anything else, just ask."

"Maybe something to read?"

"The TVs have full access to an e-library, and just about every channel known to man. The menus are pretty self-explanatory. We want you to be as comfortable as possible."

"Okay, then. This is home for a while, I guess." She sighed and pulled the niqab over her head. A sharply indrawn breath brought her around. Both Persephone and Reggie stood there wide eyed, fear writ large on their faces. *Good, they should be afraid of me.* "Sorry. I didn't mean to startle you. Clothes make me claustrophobic, and…well…it's not like I'm human, so…"

"You *are* human, Aleksi." Persephone stepped forward to take the robe. "We're the ones who should be sorry. We've seen pictures, and I remember you from the Prudential, but you're…more than we expected."

"You're magnificent," Reggie added, and this time Aleksi didn't think he was being sarcastic.

"Well, I can't recommend it." Aleksi folded her wings around herself. She wasn't used to people seeing her up close. "Anything else?"

"Actually, yes. We'd like a blood sample to start with." Reggie pulled a blood kit from his pocket. "We'll want more later—muscle, bone marrow, CSF—but this'll get us started. We've analyzed the original specimen, but we've never had a live subject."

"Sure." She looked around. "Where..."

"The recliner's fine."

She sat, and Reggie chatted as he prepped her arm and drew a vial with ease and professionalism. "So, we'll see if the RNA segments that initiate the changes are still the same in your blood, then start working on eliminating them."

"How will you do that?"

"A tailored retrovirus. More than one, probably. If we don't knock out all of the infectious elements first, we won't be able to reverse any of the changes permanently."

"Because the infectious elements will just keep reasserting themselves."

"Exactly." He smiled and drew one last vial. "If you want, I can bring you up to speed on what we can do."

"I'd like that." She nodded to his hands. "You should wear gloves. You don't want this."

"No worries. Unless I jab myself with the needle, there's no danger, and if I did that, a rubber glove's not going to help." He withdrew the needle, pressing a cotton ball to the tiny wound. "Hold that there, and I'll get a band aid."

"It's fine." She pressed the cotton ball down hard then lifted it. The needle stick wasn't bleeding. "I clot quickly, and heal fast."

"Okay. Well, thank you." He smiled again and left, nodding to Persephone in passing.

"Can I interest you in a glass of wine, or a meal?"

Aleksi shook her head. "No thanks. I'll just read for a while, if you don't mind. I'm pretty much nocturnal."

"Well, make yourself at home. If you have any questions, or just want to chat, you can reach me on the intercom there." Persephone pointed to a wall-mounted pad. "Just press P." She started for the door.

"Mind if I ask you a question?"

Persephone turned back. "Not at all."

"So, your whole life, the socialite persona, your marriage, all the money and glamour, it's *all* lies?"

Persephone shrugged. "There's a difference between lies and a public persona versus a private one."

And you didn't really answer the question, she thought, deciding for a more direct approach. "And why did you *really* ask me if Hutch and I were fucking?"

Persephone opened her mouth as if to speak, then closed it and shook her head. "I'm sorry for that, Aleksi. I was…going through a rough patch."

"A *rough* patch?"

"You won't understand this, but getting a little older, being divorced, and keeping up appearances were all wearing on me. I'd hoped to get back together with Hutch, just casually, but he turned me down. We were already interested in the sample by then, and would have paid the entire research expenditure, but I was…lonely, I guess."

Aleksi felt suddenly guilty. "I didn't mean to pry. I'm sorry."

"Don't be." Persephone gave her an evil smile. "I was being a bitch that night, and Hutch was right to turn me down. You know what really pissed him off the most?"

"No." She wasn't sure she wanted to know.

"I told him if *he* wouldn't sleep with me for twenty thousand dollars, maybe *you* would."

Aleksi's mouth dropped open. "You…you didn't…mean that."

"Actually, at the time I considered it." She chuckled and shook her head. "You really wore the *hell* out of that sweater that night, you know."

"I didn't know you were bi," Aleksi blurted.

"Bi, tri, quad, whatever!" She laughed again and flipped a hand in a very Persephone gesture. "What's the point in being alive, if you can't have fun?"

"Good point." Aleksi tried to think of the last time she truly had fun, and couldn't. Flying was wonderful, but it was more of a thrill than simple fun. Then she remembered one more thing she wanted to ask. "Do you mind if I use your phone to call Hutch, just to let him know I'm all right?"

"Well, not *my* phone, but we'll work something out."

"Thanks."

"We aim to please." She waved and headed for the door.

Aleksi looked around, checked the wines—none looked familiar—peeked in the packages of wrapped meat, explored the bedroom and bathroom. There were a number of robes hanging in the closet, all with voluminous sleeves. The bed felt too soft.

She found herself pacing, nervous, anxious. She checked the door and found it unlocked, but there was a security latch that even she would have difficulty breaking. She threw it, and paced some more, wondering if they had hidden cameras watching her.

She tried the TV, surfing through the channels. *God, it's as bad as I remember.* The selection was extensive, including numerous streaming services, some of them clearly marked adult. She perused the book titles, but doubted she'd have the patience to read.

"Well, to hell with it."

She went to the fridge, unwrapped a slab of steak big enough for three, dropped it on a plate, and chose a bottle of red wine at random. Finding a corkscrew took a moment, but it popped free, and she filled a crystal glass. Inhaling the bouquet set off a riot of scent memories in her mind. She tried a sip. It was wonderful.

Dinner for one.

She sat in the armchair, sipping wine, eating raw steak, and surfing through TV channels. Among the classics, she found a trove of Alfred Hitchcock and settled in. When the steak was gone, the movie over, and the bottle of wine much reduced, she drifted off to sleep in the chair, still not sure if she was doing the right thing, but relaxed enough to not care anymore.

She felt like the night she'd smashed through the windows of the Prudential Tower observation deck. At this point, it was either fly or hit the ground.

20

Hutch sat in a packed theatre watching Julie perform in the closing night of *Ozwitch*. The audience roared with laughter and applause, thoroughly enjoying the play. Hutch would have, too, if he could keep his mind from drifting to Aleksi.

He hadn't heard from her in days.

He feared the worst, of course. How could he not? This mysterious Dr. Johansen impersonator had lured Aleksi in with the only thing she couldn't resist: the chance to be human again, to be with him again. Now she could be a captive, locked in a cage or worse, strapped to a table and vivisected. Hutch had been having nightmares of walking into a room to find her on a table, her beautiful golden skin flayed back, organs exposed, still alive and conscious, her golden eyes staring at him, pleading with him to kill her.

My fault...

The crowd erupted in applause and stood. Hutch followed a second later, tearing his mind away from his morbid musings. This was Julie's night. He was here for her. She deserved his attention.

Everyone loved her: critics, fans, theatre bloggers, students, and the faculty of the Drama Department. Hutch enjoyed her performance, and her company, but that was about as far as it went. Even their physical relationship had cooled a little, though she still came over occasionally. The initial passion had waned, as was common as relationships matured.

She felt it, too, and they'd talked about it, but there seemed no good reason not to keep seeing each other. They still found a measure of solace in one another, which was better than being alone.

But Julie was far from alone. She could have virtually any man she wanted, which had niggled at the back of Hutch's mind for weeks. *Why me? Why pick a forty-something paleontology professor, when she had her pick?*

The applause went through several curtain calls, and he smiled and clapped his hands, catching Julie's eye and giving her two thumbs up. Finally, the curtain fell for the last time, and the crowd began to bustle for the doors. Hutch waited until the rush thinned, then went around to the stage door.

"Hey, Danny." He waved to the doorman. "Quite a show!"

"Closing night's always the best." He opened the door. "Have fun!"

"Thanks." *Fun,* he thought with a mental cringe.

There was to be a cast party, and Julie had begged him to come. She'd admitted it was more to fend off men than any other reason. She knew hanging out with a bunch of drunk theatre geeks wasn't his type of event, but she'd promised to pay him back by staying the night at his place. They'd sleep late, and she'd give him breakfast in bed.

Backstage was nothing short of bedlam. Prosthetics and costumes were being ripped off and tossed about with abandon. The actress who played Evil Dorothy juggled her fake boobs like two pink volleyballs. Flying monkeys whiplashed each other with their tails. In the back, Hutch found Julie breathless with laughter, trying to keep two munchkins from playing keep-away catch with her prosthetic nose. She finally caught it, gripped the hooked green appendage like a dagger, and faux-stabbed them with it.

"The green avenger wins!" Hutch crowed, clapping at her victory.

"Hutch!" She tossed the nose aside and lunged at him.

He caught her shoulders before she could maul him. "Careful with the green, Jules."

"Oh! Right, sorry." She gave him a quick kiss and whirled to her makeup chair for the degreasing process. "Did you enjoy it? I'm afraid we camped it up a bit for closing night."

"It was great, and you were fabulous." He pulled a towelette and helped her with the hard to reach spots. "The audience was in stitches."

"Did you see the writeup in the Globe?"

"No. Good?"

"Rave." She snatched a clipping from the table and handed it to him. "I'm having that framed!"

He read it as she continued to wipe away green makeup. A glowing review, indeed, and lauding praise for the title role actress. "Miss Parks has a voice like an angel, and a stage presence that needs no spotlight to shine," he read aloud. "Wow!"

"Fuck *yes,* wow!" She finished with the makeup and jumped up. "Now, help me with this torture device, and we'll get out of here."

"Sure." Hutch held up a towel to screen her from the rest of the room while she unhooked the restrictive pushup bra and donned a Harvard Drama tee shirt.

"Done! Party time!" She lunged into his arms and gave him a real kiss, much to the amusement of the other cast and crew members.

They left the theatre and walked to the bar the director had reserved for the cast party. There were already a few cast members there, and the director greeted Julie with a hug and a kiss.

"My dear, you were marvelous! Hutch! Glad you could come! Our girl's something else, isn't she?"

"Wicked good indeed!" He wrapped an arm around Julie's waist and grinned at the man. Julie had warned him that some people got a little too friendly at these things. Having him at her side might save her some unwanted attention. "Congratulations on the Globe writeup."

"That *was* a coup, wasn't it! That hack, Westinghouse, *hates* farce!" His eyes slid past Hutch to the door and the next arrival.

Julie dragged him to the bar, snatching up finger food from a heavily laden table in passing. She was riding high and greeted the other cast members with hugs and kisses. Hutch ordered them drinks and sipped his beer, hanging at her elbow and smiling. He chatted when people engaged him, but let Julie have the limelight. This was her time, her triumph. She was the belle of the ball and deserved it.

He was on his second beer—they would ride-share back to his place, so there were no worries about drinking—when the director showed back up with a well-dressed older man at his side.

"Julie!" The director tapped her shoulder and barely avoided the spilled wine as she whirled around. "Oops! That was close."

"God! Sorry! I didn't get you, did I?"

"Near miss." He turned to the man with him. "This is Jerry Vanderwile. He's with Prendergast Productions, Manhattan."

"I watched your performance, Miss Parks, and enjoyed it very much." He smiled and held out a hand.

"Julie, please, Mister Vanderwile. And thanks!" She shook his hand and beamed. "Great to meet you. I'm glad you enjoyed the show, but we camped it up some, I'm afraid. Closing night, you know."

"Jerry, please, and you're allowed. You had a great run, and...well, the critics loved it, *and* you."

"Thanks. Good writing, great score, sensational choreography, and my director... What can I say? I just rode the wave."

"But you're a writer, too, and you've directed some smaller productions, from what I hear."

Hutch stepped back. This was clearly a rare and opportune moment, and he didn't want to interfere. New York was the epicenter of theatre as much as Hollywood was for the movie industry. If Julie had caught the attention of a production company, this could be a break for her. He sipped his beer and watched. Julie blazed with energy but handled the situation with surprising calm and grace. Of course, she performed in front of audiences all the time; keeping her head while talking to a New York producer wouldn't challenge her acting abilities.

Then the phone in the breast pocket of his jacket vibrated—his Aleksi phone.

Hutch nearly dropped his beer fumbling the phone out of his pocket. The incoming number was blocked, and it was a call, not just at text. A hundred horrible scenarios shot though his head like flashes of heat lightning. If this mysterious impersonator had hacked Aleksi's phone, had they hacked his? Did they have her prisoner? Were they holding her hostage? Was this a ransom demand? Had she died during their supposed treatment, and were they just calling to let him know?

He had no choice, he had to take the call. Hutch worked his way to the quietest corner of the bar and accepted the call. "Hello?"

"Hutch. It's me." Aleksi's voice electrified his every nerve.

"Aleksi! Thank God! Are you okay? What's happened?"

"I'm fine, Hutch. I'm safe. These people are legit. We're starting treatment today."

"Treatment? Where are you? Can I come see you?" He knew it was a stupid question.

"No. I'm sorry, but these people are secretive. They're really trying to help me, and...I think they might be able to."

"I…" Hope flared to life in his chest. "That's amazing news! How long will it take?"

"We don't know. We'll see."

"I miss you, you know."

"I know. Maybe you won't have to for too much longer."

"Can you call me again? Let me know how it's going?"

"I'll try, but the treatment's going to take a while."

"Well, call if you can. I love you, Aleksi."

"I love you, too, Hutch. I'll talk to you as soon as I can."

"Okay. Bye."

The call ended. He stared at the phone, his heart beating a tattoo against his ribs. The incoming number was still not available. He couldn't call back. He considered and discarded the notion of calling Buckmann. He didn't dare. If Aleksi trusted these people, if they really could help her, he dared not interfere. Pocketing the phone, he worked his way through the crowd, but the party and Julie were the furthest things from his mind.

Treatment… She'll be Aleksi again…

Thank you." Aleksi handed the phone back to Persephone.

"You're welcome. Now, please, just lay down and try to relax." She gestured Aleksi to the treatment table.

Persephone had given her a tour of their labs and treatment rooms, and they'd outlined the treatment plan. Their facilities left her in awe, and their capabilities to alter human genes in vivo—not to mention their ability to alter protein structures, metabolism, and treat diseases—gave her hope that this might actually work. Unfortunately, the first step was to give her another infection.

Reggie was their bio-genetics expert and had isolated four separate infectious RNA strands from both the specimen and Aleksi. They had infected virtually every cell of her body. Before they started reverting the changes in her genes, they had to eliminate the infective RNA. That was a tall order, and would have been impossible with current mainstream biomedical technology. Fortunately, Persephone's family knew far more in the field than even the most cutting-edge researchers.

Reggie had manufactured four separate retroviruses tailored to attack the transformative RNA. They were going to infuse them now, and would measure the success of the treatment over time. When the RNA was expunged from every cell, she would no longer be infectious, and they would begin reversing the changes. That could take months, but Aleksi was willing to undergo whatever was needed to be human again.

Aleksi lay back, and Reggie placed heart monitor leads on her chest, then drew a warm blanket over her. "Just relax. I want you to tell me if you're experiencing anything unusual."

"Okay." She'd come to trust him. After half a dozen different biopsies and his patience in explaining the treatment plan, how could she not?

Reggie swabbed her arm and squeezed the pressure point that would distend a vein. Her wing membranes made tourniquets impossible. "Needle stick." He slipped in the catheter, released the pressure point, and pressed on the IV. A single drop of blood escaped as he attached IV tubing to the catheter. After taping the connection down, he opened the crimp. "A little cold saline first. Let me know if it stings."

A chill tickled up her arm from the IV site. "It's fine."

"Okay, then." Reggie pulled another IV bag from a cabinet and attached tubing to it. He hung it beside the saline bag, flushed the slightly hazy liquid to the tip of the tubing, attached it to the side port of the flowing IV, and said, "Here goes."

He opened the crimp.

At first, Aleksi felt nothing, but then a rush of heat flashed through her extremities. "Hot flash in my hands and feet."

"That's expected. The viruses are crossing cellular barriers around your capillaries. It might feel prickly."

Her skin flushed with pins and needles. "Yep. All over, like coming in from the cold to a hot room."

"Your heart rate's up a little. Just relax. I can give you some Valium if you want."

"No. I'm fine. Stop telling me to relax, please." She took a deep breath and closed her eyes. The sensation eased off slowly, but she still felt warm. "I think it's okay. I'm a little warm is all. Some dizziness."

"Vasodilation, probably." Reggie attached a blood pressure cuff to her ankle and cycled it. "You're a little hypotensive. I'm going to give you more fluids."

"Okay." The chill up her arm intensified. She opened her eyes to watch the two bags flowing into her, and suddenly felt a stab of nausea. "I think I…might puke."

"Emesis basin!" Reggie snapped, and Persephone was there with a pink plastic dish. "It's a vasovagal response, Aleksi. It'll pass."

Aleksi turned her head and retched into the basin. There wasn't much since they'd cut her off to all but clear liquids, but the bile burned her throat. She retched again, harder, and spat. The head of the table hummed up to an incline, making it easier. After a third bout, she spat and nodded.

"It's easing up. Maybe a little water."

"Some ice chips," Reggie said.

Persephone supplied them, and Aleksi took a few, trying to wash the vile taste out of her mouth. The burn in her throat eased.

"You okay?" Persephone asked.

Aleksi nodded. "Marvelous. I didn't expect it to be fun."

"It won't be," Reggie agreed. "Your immune system's going to throw a fit. Maybe a few days of feeling crappy before we take some samples and see how things are progressing."

"Worth it." She closed her eyes, determined to endure this minor discomfort. To be human again, she would willingly walk through hell.

"Not exactly a fashion statement, is it?" Jim finished with the adhesive panel that held up David's new garment.

It fit like a pair of Lycra shorts split down the sides and backed with stickum at the edges. From the belt, two clips connected to a pair of suspenders with a cross strap. The suspenders were fitted with a holster and four magazine pouches. The back of the suspenders clipped to the back of the adhesive shorts.

"Considering that anyone who tells him it looks silly will probably die horribly, I don't think it looks bad at all." Amy snugged up the suspenders in back. "How does it feel, David?"

"Not as bad as it looks." He twisted and bent to the limits of his inhuman flexibility, raising and lowering his arms, extending his wings, twelve feet across now, and still growing. "It rides up in the ass."

"I'll loosen it a bit." She did. "Better?"

He moved again. The straps sagged when he bent forward, but the seat didn't ride up any more. "Better."

"If it's any consolation, your ass looks great," Amy said.

David snorted a laugh. "Thanks. I'm thinking of doing a calendar, but we need eleven more outfits."

Three weeks after beginning his transformation, David looked much like the pictures he'd seen of Aleksi. His skin was a deep golden hue, and fine scales had replaced his body hair. His face had transformed into an even more angular shape: sharper cheekbones, deeper eyes, pronounced brows, and a ridge of bone up his forehead and across the middle of his skull. His shoulders were hunched, rounded across his back with muscle. His mouth had widened, and his teeth were even more pointed, the edges serrated, canines curved and razor sharp. He ached all over, a constant background irritation that didn't help his sleep or his mood, but far less pain than he had become accustomed to. The worst side effect was the claustrophobia. His glimpses of the outdoors, the sun, trees, people, had given him a taste of freedom he hadn't known he was missing.

"Great. Let's add some weight." Jim went to a nearby table and picked up the modified Sig and four magazines. He stepped up to David and handed them over, pistol first, then the magazines. David put them in the rig. "Good, now move."

He did, following orders as always, but Jim's curt impersonality and nervousness had him on edge. The guy was terrified of him and struggled to hide it. Not like Amy.

The gear sagged forward when he bent. "Yeah, that won't do. It's going to flap around during a drop and hang up on things."

Jim scratched notes on a tablet without a word.

Amy adjusted the straps a little. "Maybe more adhesive, wider over the shoulders so it won't slip or chafe." She caught his eye and smiled. "This is just a prototype. We'll work out the kinks."

"Sure." He breathed her in, opening his mouth to take the scent deep. *Blood, meat, food, hunger...* A flash memory or dream, meat between his teeth, bone shearing, crunching, the salt-coppery sweetness. David's teeth chirped like crickets as he ground them together, the edges of his upper and lower canines grating, sharpening, preparing him. *Fight, kill, feed...*

"You okay?" Amy touched his shoulder, and he jerked, eyes fixing on her.

"Sorry. Just a little distracted." David stepped back from her. This was Amy. She was nice to him, watched movies with him, wasn't afraid of him. "Careful. I'm feeling a little twitchy."

"No problem. I get twitchy all the time." That flicker of a smile again.

"So, when can we test this rig out?" He drew the pistol. It felt better in his hand, and his claws didn't hang up on the modified trigger guard. He could tell by the weight that it wasn't loaded.

"We've got a live fire drill scheduled for this afternoon," Jim said without looking up.

"A simulation?" The VR sessions had become his only release.

"No, just a multiple target session at the range."

"That's a piss-poor test. How about you strap a VR set to this and run me through the mill?" He wasn't really talking to Jim or Amy, but the ever-present cameras and microphones. He holstered the weapon and worked the muscles of his neck. "Or better, a field test."

"Talk to the Director about that," Jim said, again without looking up from his pad.

"I *am* talking to the Director!" David flexed his hands unconsciously, looking into the nearest video pickup. "I'm tired of talking, being stuck with needles, and being kept indoors. Figure out some kind of field test! Do it now!"

"Okay, David, we'll get you outdoors." Amy looked concerned, but Jim looked like he was about ready to shit himself. "Just relax."

"Relax." He ground his teeth again. "Tell them to get me a field test, Amy, or I'm going to fucking explode."

"I'll tell them. We're good." She held up both hands and took a step closer. "Let me get that web-gear off, and we'll see if we can schedule a simulation. Get you some exercise. That'll make you feel better."

He took a deep breath of her—*blood, meat, food*—and let it out slowly. *Follow orders.* "Sure. Thanks. Sorry." David felt sure he'd just bought himself another psych evaluation. He wondered if he could make it through without ripping the guy's head off.

21

Aleksi lay curled in a fetal position, swathed in sweat-soaked blankets, shivering and miserable. Her temperature had spiked a dozen times, and they'd treated her with a plethora of drugs, but the war being waged in her body wasn't over. Three days of chills, sweats, raging headaches, and body aches, like the worst flu she'd ever experienced. She barely kept fluids down, and had started to lose weight. Still, the infectious RNA strands persisted.

Reggie and Persephone came in. She'd heard them in the outer room, talking, worried for her. It was time for a new tactic.

"Aleksi?" Persephone crouched by the side of the bed. "How are you?"

"Pretty crappy, but still here." She shivered again and opened her eyes. "I overheard you talking. An epidural?"

"The problem is the blood-brain barrier, Aleksi," Reggie said. "The RNA strands slip through with no difficulty, but our viruses don't. If we don't give you an epidural, we'll be banging our heads against a wall. You'll just continually re-infect yourself."

"Won't that be like encephalitis?" She didn't know much medicine, but brain infections were bad. Inflammation generally caused irreparable brain damage.

"We'll monitor your intracranial pressure and counteract any inflammation. If it gets out of control, we'll bail and kill the viruses." He touched her shoulder, his hand warm and dry. "Don't worry. We aren't going to let you die on us."

"Okay." She had no choice. "You need me to get up?" She started to stir, but Persephone put a hand on her shoulder.

"No. We can do it here. Just lie still."

"You're already positioned pretty well, actually. I just need to pull the covers back." Reggie moved around the bed and pulled the blankets down from her back.

Aleksi heard him peel open a sealed tray, and the cold prep solution made her shiver. She heard the pop of a glass vial being cracked open, then felt a tiny pin prick.

"Just numbing you a bit."

"It's okay." It really wasn't okay. She felt like she was being dissected, but her mind overrode the base desire to flee, fight, lash out.

"Good, now bend forward a little, please," Reggie said.

She did. Aleksi didn't feel the catheter going in. Reggie had a deft hand. Evidently, he had an MD along with his other degrees. He'd joked that he failed "Bad Bedside Manner-101," however, and had quit medicine after his residency.

"Okay, catheter's in, and I've got CSF." He pressed something to her back, tape or a bandage, she wasn't sure. "There. We're ready. I'm starting a slow infusion of the viruses. You'll probably have some side-effects. Headache, nausea, like that."

"Wonderful." Like she didn't already have both.

A warmth at the base of her skull gave her a scant warning, then pain blossomed through her head. She gritted her teeth and pressed her eyes closed, but an inarticulate cry escaped.

"It's okay, Aleksi. We're here. Just breathe through it." Persephone rubbed her shoulder.

"I..." Nausea flared. "Gonna be sick!" She retched dryly, but Persephone held a towel to catch the bitter bile. She coughed and shivered violently, retching again, the muscles of her abdomen contracting like cables.

"We've got you, Aleksi. Just get through it. It won't last long."

But it did. The pain blazed through her head continuously for more than an hour. She cried and vomited, and shivered until she felt like she would die.

"I think we should stop," Persephone said finally. "She can't take this."

"If we do, we'll just have to do it again later," Reggie warned.

"No!" Aleksi gritted her teeth. "Don't stop. My only…chance!"

After a brief silence, Persephone said, "Okay, Aleksi. We won't stop. Just hang on."

Hang on… She concentrated through the pain, the nausea, the urge to flee, fight, hide, on the only thing she had left. *Hope…* Hope to be human again.

They kept David busy. Two nighttime airdrops from a helicopter—he couldn't quite fly yet, but he could glide well enough, even with the gear on—and long VR sessions with his new weapon firing blank ammunition, had pushed back the claustrophobia. He'd gotten his psych evaluation, too, of course, and managed not to kill the guy. He'd also not quite told the whole truth. If he had, he had little doubt that he'd have been strapped down to a table and euthanized.

Still, he followed orders, the deeply ingrained training of a soldier his only solid foundation. So, when the Director paid him a visit in his quarters, he greeted him eagerly. Another man came in with him, someone he'd never met before.

"Good to see you, David! You're progressing well!"

"I hope so, sir." He stood with his hands behind his back, claws flexing and relaxing. The man with the Director looked more like a politician than anything else.

"This is Tom. He works for the Agency." He waved to the other man.

The Agency meant CIA; David had worked with them in the past. "Good to meet you, sir."

"And you, David." He didn't smile, but pulled a tablet from behind his back. "I've been asked by the Director to find something we can use as a field test for you. I think I've found something right up your alley."

"Excellent, sir!" *About damned time!*

The spook handed over the tablet. "This outlines the mission in detail. We've known about a Russian crime organization centered in the Boston area for some time. They distribute drugs, human trafficking, work in the sex trade, and have even done some contract killings. We have intel on the head of this organization, one Artyom Tredyakofsky. We've tried to approach him, but he's a… Well, he's refused our offers, shall we say."

"Sounds like a real charmer." David swiped through the screens, pictures of a well-dressed Caucasian man with Slavic features, heavily built, with a badly broken nose. In several pictures he was in the company of beautiful young women as well as obvious bodyguards. "You want him dead, broken, bent, or snatched?"

"Dead, but we could take him out ourselves without difficulty. We want to do something more subtle, and your skill set should fit nicely."

"Subtle how?" He continued swiping, and reached a set of pictures of a five-floor brownstone from several angles including from the air, then schematics of every floor.

"We don't want this to get traced back to us, so we need to implicate someone else. We'll leave evidence that it's a Chinese mafia hit. They've been squabbling over turf for a while, so it works."

"Of course. Just like we blamed so many of our Middle East ops on terrorists, right?"

"Like that, but we want a precise hit, not a bombing. Minimum collateral damage and a message left on the body is usually the Chinese's MO. We're modifying a silenced Chinese CF-98 that we recovered from an operation right here in town, so the ballistics will match previous uses. If we do this right, we'll reap more benefit than just taking out one Russian kingpin."

"Meaning it'll start a nice little war for you."

"Precisely."

David liked this guy. He didn't mince words or use euphemisms. "When?"

"Tomorrow night, weather permitting." Tom turned to the Director. "We plan to air-drop you from three thousand feet, half a mile away. I've been told that's within your glide path parameters."

"Close enough."

"So, look over the specs, and we'll meet again this afternoon for any questions you have. Your entry, approach, and exit are all you. Your record speaks for itself."

"Affirmative."

"I'll see you at fifteen hundred, then." Tom nodded once and left.

"You're okay with this?" The Director asked.

He grinned at the man with little humor. "Shit, sir, I was fucking *made* for this."

"You were made for much more than *this*, David, but the operation should be a good shake down. You're to minimize risk to yourself, of course. If things go south, the avoidance of collateral damage is secondary. We've invested too much in you to lose you to a stray bullet."

"Affirmative, sir." David nodded, his grin intact. "This is a cake walk."

"Review the mission specs, and we'll talk."

"Very well, sir."

The Director left, and David sat down to read. After two passes through the material, he had a picture in his head of the layout and started to formulate a mission plan. His stomach growled, so he called for food and got up to go to the bathroom. He'd learned to hate the adhesive backing on his shorts.

Finished, he washed his hands and, as had become his habit, examined his reflection in the mirror. *Monster...* David barely recognized himself any longer, but it was still disconcerting to see the creature he'd become staring back at him. Finally, they were going to put everything he'd gone through to reach this point, his rebirth, to the test.

About fucking time we set this thing loose.

22

At the knock on her door, Persephone stirred from a doze. She'd been reading Gi-gi's report on Aleksi's tests and had fallen asleep. She hadn't gotten much rest in the last few days.

"Yes!" she sat up and rubbed her eyes.

Reggie came in. "Hey, Seph. I thought you'd like an update."

"I would." She reached for her coffee, but it was long-cold. She got up to make another. "How is she?"

"Having a rough time of it, but the RNA titer's dropping like a rock. It's fighting us, but we're winning."

"What's the titer?" They'd been measuring the RNA load regularly.

"Down to less than four percent of baseline. When we're at zero for twenty-four hours, we'll kill the retrovirus and watch her. If she doesn't re-infect, we're golden." He nodded to the coffee maker. "You get any sleep?"

"A nap. Reading Gi-gi's report is like taking sleeping pills." She replaced the K-cup and hit the button. "I'm really worried about Aleksi. If this is hitting her so hard, how will she handle the reversal therapy?" Persephone had been through similar changes before, but to a much lesser degree. They were taxing, to say the least, and Aleksi would need extensive changes to her genome, as well. They had no way to know how it would affect her.

"We won't know until we start. Her fever spiked a couple of times last night, but she's better. Weak as a kitten, meaning still *way* stronger than me, but she's on the upswing. She kept some broth down. I've been giving her Ringer's IV for some nutrition." He sat down. "I haven't had a chance to read Gi-gi's report."

Persephone dumped sugar into her coffee and stirred. "I didn't get through all of it, but most. You want the Cliff notes?"

"Please. With Aleksi resting, I need some sleep."

"Sure." She sat down and sipped her coffee, mentally blessing the inventor of the one-cup brewer. "Aside from planning Aleksi's reversion therapy, she's mapping the entire genetic and proteogenic cascade of the transformation. There are thousands of gene activations and corresponding numbers of altered proteins. Everything from muscle to nerve conductance, to metabolism. Reverting her to her base genome is going to be a monumental task."

"Nothing we didn't already know, right?"

"Yes, but she's trying to track down every single change. If she can, it means we'd be able to pick and choose, to a certain degree, which to turn *on* in a human subject. We could, for instance, enhance vision or olfaction to Aleksi's standards separately, without altering morphology to the point that it would be easily detectable."

"Like picking only what you want from a Chinese menu à la carte instead of getting the pu pu platter."

"Exactly." Persephone sipped her coffee again and considered what attributes Gi-gi might have in mind for her. "Some of the potential applications are a little scary."

"Only a *little*? Gi-gi must be slipping." Reggie chuckled and stood. "I'm punchy. I need sleep. I'll see you later."

"G'nite, Reg." Persephone returned to Gi-gi's report, but found it difficult to concentrate. Whether it was the exhaustion or the possibility of becoming a *Homo sapiens-Homo draconis* hybrid, she had no idea.

"Eyes on target!" The flight engineer tapped David on the shoulder.

"Confirmed!" The target was hard for him to miss through the integrated helmet's display.

A high-altitude drone had painted the brownstone with a laser visible in his head's up display, complete with range, angle, and bearing. David took the helmet off and unclipped his safety belt. He could still see the laser. They'd tested his vision all through the spectrum and used a wavelength he could see but human eyes couldn't.

He nodded to the flight engineer. "Ready."

"Opening the door." The man unlocked the handle and pulled.

A hundred-knot wind buffeted the passenger compartment. They weren't in a military helicopter, but a commercial Bell 412 registered with an oil company. They were flying a commercial route, too, at a commercial altitude and commercial speed. The only thing not commercial about the aircraft were its occupants. Every member aboard was government covert ops, and they'd all been cleared to know about David.

"Step into the door!"

"Affirmative." David got up, stepped to the door, and sat on the edge with his feet on the skid step, his clawed toes gripping it firmly. "In position!"

"Cockpit; insertion is ready for drop. Confirm!"

"Confirmed! Drop when ready." David could hear the pilot even over the rushing wind with no headset.

The flight engineer slapped him on the shoulder. "Go! Go! Go!"

David stepped out of the aircraft.

He'd jumped more than a thousand times, but this was only his third without a chute. The other two had been lower, and at a hover. The hundred knot wind and propwash slammed him down and sideways, but he had the sense not to spread his wings until he was clear. When he did, the impact hit his shoulders like a three-hundred-pound defensive lineman. The stress would have torn a normal human's arms out of the sockets, but David wasn't normal, or even really human anymore.

He banked toward the target and picked his glide path, slowing his speed with a few flaps. The actions came naturally, like walking or running, but he was still learning. He didn't have to think about angles, instruments, or speeds. He just did it. He was close to being able to fly, and with any wind or a thermal, he thought that he could stay aloft for quite a while. He was also enjoying the hell out of himself.

Homo-fucking-draconis! he thought, trying hard not to grin into the teeth of the wind. *Fucking death from the sky.*

Five hundred yards from the brownstone, he banked back and forth a few times to kill his speed, indulging himself a little. A soft landing was imperative. He had to stall at just the right moment to hit the roof quietly. The building had a disused attic space, but someone would be awake, and a hard thump from the roof would be audible through the top two floors.

He banked a few more times, picked his angle, came in at roof-top level, and billowed his wings at just the right moment, killing his momentum as his feet cleared the eaves. He landed on all fours, taking up the shock easily with fingers and toes.

Light as a feather.

Keeping low, he crept to the unlit side of the house. The place was built for comfort, not security, and the attic had a short Mansard roof around the edges with shallow dormers. Those small windows were his way in.

After checking the alley below, David went over the edge head first, claws finding easy purchase. At the dormer, he leaned over the edge and inspected the window. It was barely a foot and a half across, but he could get through. His claws made short work of the window's latch, peeling the wood away in splinters. He worked slowly, making as little noise as he could. The latch yielded, and he pulled the window open slowly, wary of squeaky hinges.

Dragon eyes pierced the gloom of the attic. Nothing but dust and a bunch of junk. He crept over the edge and through the window, bending around the corner like a snake.

His web gear caught on the window frame, the holstered pistol clacking against the wood.

David froze, silently cursing the cumbersome gear. They'd resorted to two-sided tape to keep the straps in place, but it still sagged when he bent forward. He squirmed the rest of the way through the window, then waited and listened. His own heartbeat, the distant rumble of a jet landing at Logan, and someone snoring below were the only sounds he could pick out of the pervading hum of the city.

Safe... But the sagging web gear could have blown the whole op.

This shit has got to go. David drew his pistol and two magazines from the rig, then unclipped the web gear from his shorts. He peeled off the adhesive straps and lay it beside the window. The spare magazines, he tucked into his shorts. The pistol remained in his hand.

Time to go to work.

The CIA file on Artyom Tredyakofsky had many details that had nothing to do with the operation: what he ate and drank, where he went, who he met, and where and with whom he slept. The last was of use. Not the "with whom" part as much as the "where," but both were important. Tredyakofsky's bedroom was on the fourth floor in the front of the house, and he wasn't likely to be alone.

The attic accessed the rest of the house through a counterweighted drop stair located at the northwest corner of a hallway on the fifth floor. It wasn't locked. David pressed an ear to the attic floor and listened. The CIA report also said that Tredyakofsky was paranoid and had men on guard detail day and night. David heard nothing through the eight inches of plaster, lath, and R-13 insulation. Pressing down on the staircase, he leaned down to peer out and listen again. He saw nothing, but the whisper of smooth-soled shoes on carpet reached his ears. Someone was walking the floor, and they shuffled their feet. He scented the air, and knew it was only one man and that he'd had cabbage for supper.

David pushed down the stair just enough to slip through, held his pistol between his teeth, and descended. When he was still hanging by one clawed hand, gently closing the stair behind him, a tall man in a sweater and jeans stepped around the corner.

The guy's mouth dropped open, his eyes widening, and his hand moved to the pistol in a shoulder holster.

David released his grip on the ceiling, snatched the pistol from his teeth, and shot the man twice in the chest before his feet touched the floor. The silenced pistol sounded loud to his ears, but he knew it made little more noise than snapping one's fingers. A two-hundred-pound body hitting the floor, however, would. The claws of David's toes cut furrows in the carpet and the hardwood floor beneath as he dashed forward. He caught the dead man before he hit the floor and lowered him gently. A quick check confirmed that he was dead; two hollow-point rounds an inch apart had shredded his heart.

Minimal collateral damage. He moved on. *One is minimal, right?*

Still, the kill hadn't been very satisfying. As a career soldier and covert operative, David had never taken the slightest pleasure in killing. He took great pleasure in doing his job well, completing the mission, furthering the goals of his country, but the actual violence had done nothing for him. Now, however, the dragon within him stirred. The creature he had become had different urges than David Gilford, and killing a man with two bullets to the heart hadn't satisfied them.

He was here to do a job, not enjoy himself, but David saw no reason he shouldn't take pleasure in his work.

Down the squeaky stairs to the fourth floor, the dragon scented the air once again. There were more cabbage eaters on this level, and other scents, too, but those were faint: perfume, vodka, cigar smoke, sweat, and sex. And the snoring was louder.

David crept toward the front of the house. The hall T'd, Tredyakofsky's bedroom to the right, the direction of the snoring. He edged along the right-hand wall to the corner. The hall to the left opened up, empty. Turning around, he crouched and leaned out just far enough to peer around the corner with his left eye.

Two beefy men stood at Tredyakofsky's bedroom door. The nearer leaned against the wall with his eyes closed, knees locked, probably half asleep. The other rocked from heel to toe, then side to side, the age-old practice of anyone who had stood guard for long. Keep the blood moving, stay awake, work the toes to keep from cramping.

Taking them both down without waking Tredyakofsky would have been harder if not for the thunderous snoring from behind the bedroom door. That hadn't been in the CIA's file, but it worked to David's advantage. Background noise was always a good thing.

An amateur would have taken the more alert of the two first, but David was not an amateur. Taking a left-hand grip on his pistol, he set his feet, leaned out, and shot the somnolent man in the head. With knees locked, he would remain standing for about three seconds. Plenty of time.

At the crack of a bullet blowing a hole through his partner's head, the other man whirled and reached for his weapon. Turning presented his chest squarely. David dashed from hiding, shooting the guard twice through the heart. Transferring his pistol again to his teeth, he caught both men before they hit the floor.

Piece of cake.

He lowered them to the carpet and pulled his claws free. In his rush, he'd gripped more than just clothing. Well, there was no help for it, and the Chinese often used martial arts weapons. With the message he would leave, the cops wouldn't jump to any further conclusions than that.

David wiped his hands on their clothes and took his pistol in hand. There were still eleven rounds in the magazine, but he switched it out to a full one. Always best to keep topped up. Moving the bodies aside, he tried the door handle. It turned easily in his grasp and moved freely when he pushed it in. The snoring from within remained unabated.

The dragon edged into the dark bedroom, easing the door closed behind him. His eyes adjusted instantly. There were three forms in the king-sized bed. Two women lay spooned on the left-hand side nearer the windows—whores, mistresses, or wives, David didn't know or care. Artyom Tredyakofsky lay on his back on the right, snoring like a steam engine.

Perfect.

Clawed feet whispered across the carpeted floor to the right side of the bed. The man's snoring was truly cavernous. If the women could sleep through that, they wouldn't stir even if David removed the silencer from his pistol. He placed the muzzle of the silencer to the man's nose and silenced his snoring with a squeeze of the trigger.

Quiet...

The two women didn't stir.

Blood darkened the pillow behind Tredyakofsky's head, his heart still pumping away despite the lack of instructions from the man's brain. It would pump until it died for lack of oxygen, probably for minutes, but it would run out of blood eventually. But David wasn't done yet. He had a message to leave.

Opening the shirt of Tredyakofsky's silk pajamas, he carved the Mandarin character for revenge into the man's flabby chest with one claw. The tearing flesh made a sound like parting Velcro, but there wasn't much bleeding.

The sweet coppery scent of blood filled David's senses, but other scents were stronger now, too. A stubbed-out cigar lay in an ashtray beside the bed, a bottle of Russian vodka with only an inch left in the bottom beside it. The two women wore the same perfume, and the scent of sex hung on them. But there was something else there, lurking under the surface. Something that stirred a recent memory and set David's teeth on edge.

On impulse, he rounded the bed and leaned down to examine the women. He didn't recognize either of them from any of the photos in the file, but Tredyakofsky went through women like tissues. When he was done with them, they went back into the sex or pornography trade. They were beautiful, and it seemed a shame that their lives would probably end in drugs or disease, but there were sad stories all over the world. It wasn't David's fault.

But why did their scents play on his nerves like a dull razor?

Laying his pistol aside and leaning close, he drew in the nearer one's scent through mouth and nose. A memory clicked into his mind of Captain Fen, the combat apparel specialist at Natick. But why would these two remind him of...

Pregnant! Fen had been pregnant!

David still had no idea why the scent of a pregnant woman would set him off so, but there was no denying it. Both of these women were pregnant, and it ignited something deep within him that he couldn't suppress. His heart pounded in his chest, and lips curled back from razor teeth. The thought of allowing these two to bear Tredyakofsky's offspring grated against his deepest instincts. He didn't know why, but he could *not* let that happen.

And there was only one way to stop it.

Claws closed on the nearer woman's throat. Her eyes opened in shock, but she couldn't breathe to scream. As she thrashed and grasped his wrist, he reached under the blanket and raked open her abdomen. She convulsed and stilled, bright blood spreading to spill over the side of the bed in a red waterfall.

The other woman stirred. "What the fu—"

David extracted his claws from the corpse's throat and silenced the woman. Bones collapsed in his grip, and she thrashed, trying to scream through her shattered face. David ignored her flailing arms and legs. Her blows felt like the patter of rain.

Another man's seed, he thought in disgust, plunging a clawed hand into her. She bucked and convulsed as he ripped out the part that offended him so, then stilled.

David extracted his claws. It was done. The other man's offspring had been exterminated, as they had to be. As he looked at the congealing blood on his hands, a deeper horror settled into him then, the humanity of David Gilford, soldier, who had never taken pleasure in killing. But this hadn't been for pleasure, this had been necessary.

Swallowing his self-disgust, he looked around the room. His mission was accomplished, message sent, and the offending seed of this vile man had been destroyed.

David washed his hands in the bathroom, drying with a red terrycloth towel. He checked himself in the mirror, dabbed a few drops that had sprayed his chest. Clean, he recovered his pistol and slipped out of the bedroom. The scent of blood faded behind him as he crept back up the stairs to the fifth floor. Pulling down the attic ladder, he ascended and pulled it back up behind him. He then recovered his web gear and crawled out the window and up to the roof.

David put the gear back on, holstered his pistol, and took a deep breath of the sultry night air. It felt good to be outside, under the sky, instead of closed in a room with no windows. He longed to fly, but that was one thing he couldn't quite do yet. Another week, maybe, and he'd truly stretch his wings. For now, he was content, his mission finished.

Now all he had to do was make it to the pick-up point: an SUV parked in an alley three houses down.

He traversed the rooftops in a crouch, staying in shadow, and dropped down beside the waiting vehicle. David opened the back door and got in.

"How'd it go?" the driver asked, as he put the car in gear and drove out of the alley.

"Optimal," David said. The scent of blood lingered in his nostrils. "Couldn't have gone better."

23

Somebody was certainly pissed off at the Russians," Willis said as he and Jasper reviewed the Boston PD's preliminary report on the killings.

Homicide divisions in every police department in the greater Boston metropolitan area had been notified of the murders. There was little doubt that it was a gang-related hit. The local media had picked up the story and labeled it with the headline, "Gang Violence Erupts." Some were even calling it "The Brownstone Massacre."

"Somebody with a really sick streak." Jasper didn't know if six deaths constituted a massacre, but how some of the victims were killed sure earned that moniker.

The deaths by gunfire had all the marks of professionalism: nine-millimeter rounds, closely grouped kill shots. Also, there had been eight more people in the house, none of whom reported hearing gunfire, so the weapon had been silenced. The point-blank shot to Tredyakofsky's head and the mark carved into his chest were Chinese mafia trademarks. The two women, however, were another story. The descriptions gave Tony chills.

"Reminds me of what Penningly did to those two cops in Back Bay Fens Park," Willis said.

"Me, too." Penningly had surprised two female detectives assigned to troll the park for him. One had gotten a shot off and hit him in the leg, but both had been killed, the bodies mutilated. "BPD forensics is all over the building, but we won't get their report for a while, and the full autopsy reports about the same time."

"I wonder if Tredyakofsky's guys are regretting calling the cops." The forensics guys were still cleaning up the puke from the man who had first found his boss and the two women. That a member of a Russian crime syndicate had dialed 911 spoke to the horror of the scene. Willis cringed as he scrolled down to the crime scene photos. "Jesus H. Christ, Tony, you don't think *Aleksi* could have done this, do you?"

"No." Jasper reached for his coffee and washed down the lump in his throat. "No way. Not her MO at all. She's never used a gun, and hasn't *ever* harmed a woman or killed anyone. This...this is just *disgusting*."

"I won't argue that, but look at the wounds on the two guys there." Willis scrolled back up to the photos of the two men shot beside the bedroom door. "The bullet hits were all pro, but those other wounds..." He pointed to the three puncture wounds in one man's shoulder, and the same in the other's chest. "The pattern, two opposing one. That's just too familiar. Remember that rapist's ass?"

"I try not to remember men's asses, Marty, punctured or not."

"Well, if there's one thing I *do* pay attention to, it's men's asses, so let me tell you, the wounds are damn near identical."

Jasper snorted a laugh and turned away to refill his coffee. "I still don't believe it was Aleksi."

"Neither do I, really." Willis sighed and kept scrolling. "A copycat, maybe?"

"Maybe." Jasper stirred creamer into his cup and sipped. "The coroner's got a full docket, that's for sure. Let's wait for the full report before we jump to conclusions."

"Not jumping, just thinking." Willis kept scrolling, one hand raising to touch the scars on his neck. "If there's someone else out there who can do this bare-handed, we're in deep shit."

Jasper couldn't disagree, and having been up close and personal with a dragon, the last thing he wanted was to hunt one again.

Aleksi stirred under a mountain of blankets, her stomach grumbling like a starved animal. She blinked her eyes open, and found Persephone smiling at her from a comfortable chair.

"Good morning, sunshine. How are you feeling?"

"Only mildly horrible." She shifted, fighting the sweat-damped sheets. "Didn't anyone ever warn you about waking sleeping dragons?"

Persephone chuckled and stood. "I didn't wake you. Your stomach did. We've neutralized the viruses and your fever's broken." She fished a temperature probe from a pocket, and stepped over. "You mind?"

"Go ahead." The tip of the probe touched the inside of her ear. "I've got to use the bathroom."

"Sure. Your temp's normal. Well, normal for you, anyway." She helped Aleksi extricate herself from the blankets. "Hungry?"

"Starving." Aleksi wobbled when she stood but made it to the bathroom under her own power. Her urine was dark from dehydration, and her mouth tasted horrible. She washed her face and hands in hot water and brushed her teeth. The monster in the mirror looked to have lost a few pounds. Stepping out of the bathroom, she found Persephone with a meat-laden plate in one hand and a huge glass of something fluorescent green in the other. She held out the glass first. "What's that?"

"Gatorade. You're low on electrolytes, and I thought this would be better than another IV."

"Anything's better than more needles." She took the glass and drained it. "God, that's awful."

"I'll get you some water."

"Coffee, please."

"Water *and* coffee. Eat this slowly." She handed over the plate. "Your stomach hasn't seen solid food for almost a week."

"Yes, *Mom*." Aleksi took the plate and sank into the comfortable armchair. The meat, an inch-thick porterhouse that filled the plate to the edge, was room temperature, tender, and delicious. She ate slowly, savoring each bite. Persephone returned with a brimming glass of water and a steaming cup of coffee. "Angel of mercy!" She took the coffee and sipped. "So, what's the prognosis?"

"You'll live. The RNA titer has been zero for twenty-four hours."

"It's gone?" Hope fluttered around her heart. *Not infectious anymore... I'm safe! Safe to touch!*

"We hope so. We'll test you during recovery. A few days, at least. If it stays zero, we're good to start the reversion therapy."

"Best news I've had in...well, *ever*." Aleksi ate more steak, her stomach muttering happily.

"It is, but you had a rough time of it. We want to make sure you're okay before we move to the next phase."

"I'm all for that." She ate in silence, but Persephone just stood there watching her, body language screaming secrets. "What aren't you telling me?"

She frowned. "Nothing about your condition, so don't worry. In fact, nothing concerning you at all, and I don't know if *we* should even be concerned yet."

Aleksi gave her a flinty stare and ate more steak. "Not telling me something that you don't know if we should be worried about, then telling me not to worry, just makes me worry. Tell me."

"There was a murder. A mass murder, actually. It looked like an organized crime squabble on the surface, very professional, but there were… disturbing elements, and evidence that might concern us."

"What disturbing elements?"

"There were two female victims, bystanders, that were murdered by…" She sighed and shrugged. "The initial forensics reports show similarities with the victims of Derrick Penningly. We're trying to get more details."

Aleksi swallowed a bite of barely chewed meat and almost choked. "Penningly? He's dead."

"I know. I personally incinerated his corpse."

"Then who?"

"I don't know. That's what more information should help us determine."

"I see." Aleksi sipped coffee and ate another bite of steak. "Can I see the report?"

"Not today. I want you to rest, and quite frankly, if you read it, you won't sleep and probably won't eat. I'll bring it to you tomorrow. We're trying to get the full forensics and ballistics reports, and it'll be a lot easier to interpret all in one package."

"The *police* reports? How are you going to get those?"

Persephone gave her a sardonic look. "My overwhelming *charm*."

"Fine." There was no point in asking, and the issue wasn't pressing. Besides, she was still tired. "How's everything else?"

"Good."

"Can I call Hutch and tell him the news?"

"Maybe tomorrow. We'd like to take another titer tonight. I want you to call me if you start feeling feverish or get chills." Persephone pulled an afghan from the back of the couch and draped it over Aleksi's shoulders. "In your condition, if you re-infect, there could be complications."

Again, there was no point in arguing. She might not be a prisoner, but neither was a patient in a hospital. She started to take another bite of meat, but found her appetite gone, her stomach full. "Can you put the rest of this in the fridge for me, please. I think I'll try to sleep."

"Sure." Persephone took the plate and empty water glass to the kitchen.

Aleksi reclined the chair and sighed. She felt weak from the treatment and so long in bed, but on the whole, better. And the hope burning in her breast warmed her enough to let her drift off into a light sleep. Her last thought before darkness took her mind was, *I can touch him again...*

The Director sat at the head of a conference table with Dr. Price, Dr. Baker, and the facility psychologist, Dr. Helmsworthy. Two armed guards stood at the door, and David Gilford paced before a flat screen monitor that rotated through police photographs of the Tredyakofsky house.

"You deviated from mission parameters, David. Why?"

"Mission parameters called for *minimal* collateral damage." David sounded less angry than incredulous. "The three guards were unavoidable. The two women woke up when I capped Tredyakofsky. You think I should have let witnesses live?"

"No, but why the mutilations? Why not just use the pistol?" The Director had seen worse, even ordered worse, when they were trying to frame someone, but David had done this on his own initiative.

"The mission was to take out Tredyakofsky, eliminate all witnesses, and send a message." He ticked off the points on his clawed digits. "Tredyakofsky's dead, witnesses are eliminated, and the message is sent."

"But David." Helmsworthy pointed to the picture of the woman with the crushed face and abdomen torn open. "This was...*excessive*. They were merely bystanders."

David's dragon eyes narrowed. "They were *witnesses*, Doctor."

"I understand that, but you literally slaughtered them with your bare hands. How do you *feel* about that?"

Claws flexed from their sheaths, muscles bunching and writing at his jaw. "No different than I felt about the dozens of innocent bystanders I've been ordered to slaughter when the government wanted people dead, witnesses eliminated, and messages sent. Columbia, the Middle East,

China, South Korea… You gonna get all weepy over a couple of *whores*? Have you even *read* my fucking profile, Doctor?" David sheathed his claws and resumed pacing. "The CIA wanted a war between the Russians and the Chinese. You start a war by stirring up people's baser instincts. Fear, hatred, disgust… *That's* what the Russians are feeling right now, and the Chinese will deny perpetrating such an atrocity. *That's* how you start a war."

"At least we agree that this was an atrocity." Helmsworthy caught the Director's eye, and shook his head minutely.

The Director gave him a nod. "He has a point, Doctor. The mission was accomplished within parameters. Well done, David. Our field test was a success. Your evaluation of the combat gear is being processed, and we'll have some modifications for you." He stood. "You deserve a day off. Take it easy, run through some simulations, kick up your heels if you like. We'll resume tests day after tomorrow."

David stopped pacing, his eyes flicking over the faces at the table. "Yes, sir. Thank you, sir."

"You're welcome." He nodded to the door. "Just let the techs know what you want, and we'll provide it."

David left the room with the guards.

The Director sat back down. "I want honest opinions. Do we have a problem?"

"Nobody sane does that." Price pointed to the picture of the two women David had slaughtered. "Hell *yes* we have a problem."

"He was ordered to eliminate witnesses and send a message," Baker countered. "He's a covert assassin, for Christ sake, and he *certainly* sent a message that will rile up the Russians."

Price glared at him. "It's not that he killed them, Baker, it's *how* he did it. He eviscerated them. That *screams* psychosis."

"Helmsworthy, your assessment."

"Price is correct, sir, but there is the stipulation that he was told to leave a message that would start a war. We've ordered operatives to commit atrocities before." The psychologist shook his head. "I'm just as concerned that he's obviously not telling us everything. This was *not* a calculated killing, sir. This was…something else. He *wanted* to do that, or maybe needed to. The forensics reports pointed out similarities between the victims' wounds."

The Director looked at the image on the screen, but all he saw were two dead women. "I'm not seeing the similarities, Doctor."

"The facial and neck injuries were to silence the victims. The abdominal injuries were similar in that the entire lower pelvic region was removed."

"You think that's significant?"

"Absolutely. He could have shot them or killed them with a blow to the neck. He silenced them, then destroyed their ability to procreate. As Price stated, it *means* something. Exactly what, I'm not sure yet."

"What's more, David's lying about *why* he killed them, sir," Price cut in.

"About what aspect?"

"He said they woke up when he shot Tredyakofsky. What he did to those women took both hands. He did one, then the other. If they'd both woken up, one would have been screaming while he killed the other. The whole house would have heard her."

The Director looked from face to face. "Agreement?"

Baker and Helmsworthy nodded.

"I believe that something prompted David to lose control, sir," Helmsworthy added. "The predator took over. What exactly elicited such an act...I don't know, but we *damned* sure better find out, and make double-damned sure it never happens again."

"Agreed."

"I'd also like the staff to be warned, sir," Price suggested. "Everyone working with David should see that." She pointed to the picture on the screen.

"I don't know if that's wise, sir," Helmsworthy said. "We know that David can smell fear. If everyone around him is terrified of him, it could set him off. He's like a cat, sir. If something runs, he'll chase it. It's instinct."

"You're saying *that* was instinct?" The Director pointed to the screen.

"Yes, I believe it was. It certainly wasn't David Gilford."

"All right. I'll warn the staff to be more careful around David, but we won't show them the report. He's still following orders, and nobody can debate his efficacy." The Director nodded to the three doctors. "If any more details come to light that suggest his motivation for this deviation, I want to know."

They all agreed and left the conference room.

The Director turned back to the screen and resumed the slide show. He watched it through twice before he said, "What the hell were you *thinking*, David?"

24

Good news!" Reggie smiled and pointed to a monitor on his lab bench. "The titer's still zero. If you were going to re-infect, you would have by now."

Aleksi examined the table of figures over time. The last four measurements of the RNA load were nil. "Thank you!" She sat down heavily in one of the lab's swivel chairs. *I'm not infectious... I can touch him again!* She turned to Persephone. "I'd like to tell Hutch before we start the reversion therapy."

"By all means, but I'd like to get your opinion on this first." She handed Aleksi a tablet. "This is the complete police file on the murders I told you about. A Russian crime boss was assassinated, but there were two women murdered with him, and the circumstances of their deaths, and some of the other evidence, point to someone like you."

"Like *me*?" Aleksi swiped through the report, skimming through the text. She came across pictures of four men, all shot, two with shallow three-fingered puncture wounds, and another with some kind of Asian character cut into his chest. There were also close up photos of thin carpeting torn in five parallel lines, the hardwood floor underneath splintered. Then she swiped to the next victim and caught her breath. "Oh, my *God*."

"Yes, and I've culled out the worst of the photos. There's no need for you to see them."

"What could be worse than—" Aleksi swiped to the next screen, and choked on her words. "Jesus!"

"The evidence points to someone with your strength and physical attributes. There were five-digit claw marks on the floor in several places, the three-fingered wounds on the other victims, and the force used to crush bones pretty much cinches it. We've got another person in the city who's been infected with same thing you were. My bet is that the government is behind it."

"Buckmann. I fucking *warned* them!" Aleksi fought the urge to crush the tablet in her hands.

"I know. You actually warned *me*, remember?"

"Right." She kept forgetting that Persephone had actually been the Dr. Johansen she'd spoken with. "So, what did you want my opinion on?"

"Two things, actually. The first is simple. After you read the details, I want you to tell me if this was really someone like you, someone transformed, or if it could be something else."

There was an easier way to tell that, but she nodded. "Okay, what's the other?"

"The two women were sleeping in the same bed as the Russian kingpin, the man who had the Chinese character cut into his chest." Persephone spoke didactically, her face a mask of control. "They were both killed similarly, but with some differences. The most disturbing element is that both were eviscerated."

"*Eviscerated*?" Aleksi swallowed hard.

"Yes." Still, Persephone's face showed no emotion. "The head and throat traumas silenced the victims. The...abdominal injuries, however, prompted the medical examiner to run some other tests. As it turns out, they were both pregnant."

"*Pregnant*? That's...weird." Aleksi shook her head.

"I know, but I need your opinion on this from your *specific* perspective, both as a...as someone with the senses and impulses you have, and as an evolutionary biologist."

"Okay. What do you want to know?"

"Can you tell if a woman's pregnant by scent?"

Aleksi thought about the question, and shrugged. "I've never noticed it before, but I've never tried to. Maybe."

"We can run some tests later to find out." Persephone took a deep breath and let it out slowly. "Second, as a scientist, can you hypothesize why someone like you would murder pregnant women?"

"Maybe you should talk to a psychologist."

"Maybe, or an animal behaviorist. Don't some species, male lions, for instance, kill the offspring of rival males?"

"Yes." Aleksi considered, thinking back to everything she'd learned about animal behavior and evolutionary biology. "As weird as it sounds, it's genetic. The new dominant male is deleting the genes of the previous pack leader and replacing them with his own. Killing young offspring forces the female to go into estrus. It happens to a lesser degree in primates. Male macaques will harass a female that's pregnant with another male's offspring, sometimes forcing a miscarriage."

Persephone nodded. "But killing the female. What about that?"

Aleksi shook her head. "No, unless it's accidental. The male needs them. Without them, he can't spread his genes."

"That makes sense." She nodded to the tablet. "So, why would someone with your attributes do that?"

"As I said, there's no evolutionary rationale for this. Could he have been...punishing them for being pregnant?"

Persephone arched an eyebrow. "He? You think it was a man?"

"Without a doubt." Aleksi stared at the pictures on the tablet and tried to imagine doing something like this. She couldn't. "My...urges have always been protective toward women. Penningly killed indiscriminately, but his motivation was food. Were there any signs of cannibalism?"

"None. He even washed his hands in the bathroom afterward."

Aleksi examined the facial and neck wounds again. "This was for spite. He was angry, maybe compelled to eliminate another male's offspring, but killing the women doesn't make sense."

"It doesn't make sense to me, either."

"Unless this is a...unless he was doing this on purpose, if he was ordered to."

"To frighten or anger someone?" Persephone looked introspective. "Possible. If the government wanted to create a conflict between the Russians and Chinese crime syndicates, this would certainly prompt a violent response."

"Let me look into it, Persephone." Aleksi stood and dropped the tablet on the chair. "I'm feeling better, and I'll be able to tell if this was done by someone like me."

"I don't know if that's a good idea. They'll be watching the house."

"Maybe, but I won't have to go inside. If a dragon was anywhere near it, I'll be able to tell." She flexed her claws and stretched her wings. "I'm also feeling cooped up. I need to get out."

Persephone exchanged a look with Reggie, but he just shrugged. "It's not like we could keep her here even if we *wanted* to, Seph."

"No, but we can certainly caution her." Persephone fixed Aleksi with a level stare. "If the government's put this in someone, they no longer need nor *want* you at large. Be careful."

"Trust me. I've been hunted by them before, remember?"

"I do remember."

"I'd also like to tell Hutch about this if I confirm it was someone infected by the specimen. He can rattle Buckmann's cage a little."

"Very well, Aleksi, but they're also probably watching him, so be careful."

"I'll phone him. No worries." She wanted to see him, too, but couldn't argue her point. Persephone wouldn't want her to take the risk, but it was Aleksi's risk, not hers.

"Okay. You can leave after dark."

"Thank you." Aleksi put a hand on Persephone's shoulder, her claws retracted. "And thanks for curing this thing. I can't ever repay you enough for this."

"You're welcome, Aleksi, but we're not done yet. We've got a lot of work to do."

"I know, but this is a start." She smiled, thinking forward to going out tonight, a thrill warming the pit of her stomach. "It's enough to give me hope."

Hutch dropped his keys into the bowl beside his door, and Iggy rattled his cage. "Oh, be still you crocodile!" Doffing his sport coat and tossing it in the general direction of the couch, he went to the kitchen and began his evening ritual, opening Iggy's cage to let the lizard roam the condo while he made dinner for both of them.

The iguana bolted as soon as his clawed feet hit the kitchen floor, but Hutch knew he'd come running when he rattled Iggy's food dish. After throwing the old food out and cleaning the bowl, he rifled the refrigerator for fruits and vegetables for both of them, and some bleu cheese and a beer for himself. Drawing a knife from the block, he started making a salad for himself and a smaller one for Iggy. He booted up some music on his phone and Bluetoothed it to the stereo, a local improv jazz group Julie had taken him to see. Sipping beer and dicing strawberries, grapes, and some slightly rotten banana for Iggy, he focused on the rhythms of the music, not the worries that had been plaguing him. Work and routine had become his meditation. He went on because he had hope, though every day that hope dwindled.

"All right, Iggy. Dinner's ready." He put the bowl down and rattled it against the floor. "Come and get it!"

Iggy came running, and Hutch grabbed his salad and beer and started for his favorite chair. Halfway there, something buzzed on the couch. His phone was in his pocket, but his other one still sat in the inside pocket of his sport jacket.

Aleksi! He put the food and beer on the coffee table and rooted the phone out, his hands shaking. It was her.

"Aleksi!"

"Hi, Hutch."

"How are you? God, it's been forever!" He fished his other phone out and killed the music, sinking onto the couch, his heart hammering in his chest.

"I'm good. Great, in fact. I've got good news, and some not-so-good news. The good, I'd like to tell you in person, if you don't have plans for tonight."

"No plans at all. Just me and Iggy rattling around the house." He took a deep breath. "What's the bad news?"

"Did you see the news about the murders of some Russians? There were links to organized crime."

"Yeah. It was all over the news. Pretty sick."

"Yes, it was." She paused, and he could hear the tension in her voice. "The police reports, the wounds, and some gashes in the floor, looked like someone like *me* might have done it. I paid the house a visit, and it's true. I can smell him. There's another dragon in Boston, and I can only think of one way that could happen."

"Buckmann!" Hutch gritted his teeth. "God*damn* it! They put this in someone!"

"Maybe not her, but the government. I think they might be trying to create something like a soldier or assassin out of this."

"That sounds like something our tax dollars would be used for." He took a breath and tried to find calm. It wasn't there. "They're playing a dangerous game."

"More dangerous than they know, I think. Hutch, can you call Buckmann, tell her this is risking the human race?"

"We've already warned them more than once, Aleksi."

"I know, but..." Another pause. There was something she wasn't telling him. "Tell her this: their dragon slaughtered two women because they were pregnant by another man. Think about macaque behavior for context. He's going to try to exterminate any offspring who don't share his genes, then create his own lineage."

"Can he even *do* that?"

"I don't know. I don't want to think about what would happen if he inseminated a woman. The thing is, he'll see every male on the planet as his genetic competition, and every female as a vehicle for his lineage. Maybe not intentionally, but just like I have urges to protect, he'll have urges to spread his genes. Think about what will happen."

"The infection will spread like a COVID pandemic! Worse, because he'll be *trying* to spread it, and any male who gets infected will do the same."

"Yes, and the human race will cease to exist."

Mary Buckmann sat at her desk reviewing the very same police reports that Persephone and Tony Jasper were scrutinizing. She had also come to the same conclusion.

A Homo draconis did this. But Buckmann knew something the others didn't. There were two possibilities. *The human trial...or Aleksi's gone over the edge.*

But she also noted that this didn't resemble Aleksi's pattern. She'd never used a gun and had never hurt women. Also, the precision of the gunshot wounds suggested a professional. *They put this thing in a soldier.*

Her phone rang, and the caller ID read "Hutchinson."

"Well, well..." She accepted the call. "Dr. Hutchinson. Thank you for calling."

"Thank me by telling your government friends they're risking the entire human race by putting this thing into another human being." He was angry, and she couldn't blame him. So was she, but she couldn't let him know that.

"What makes you think they have?"

"Don't *bullshit* me, Doctor. The murders the other day were perpetrated by someone like Aleksi. A male."

"And how do you know that?"

"Aleksi just phoned me with the news."

"And how do you know this wasn't her? If she's finally lost it, she could have—"

"You *know* it wasn't her!" he bellowed.

"The pattern doesn't match hers, I agree."

"Look, deny all you want, but you need to tell your friends to end this. He sees every male human who doesn't share his genes as a threat, and every female as a potential vehicle for progeny he can't have."

"An interesting theory, Doctor, but you have no evidence."

"You're a *scientist,* Doctor. Look at the facts! The two women were pregnant. He didn't just kill them, he effectively aborted their pregnancies."

"How do you surmise this?" she asked.

"I know evolution, Doctor. He's acting like a male macaque taking over a troop from a rival male, but the entire male population of the planet are his rivals. Look, fifty thousand years ago, when human population was thinly spread over the world in primarily interbreeding groups of related tribal units, this strategy would have worked. One male dragon to ensure no other males with completely dissimilar genes invaded the group, and one or more females to protect the human females from him and other males. *That's* why Aleksi sensed danger from Penningly by his scent alone. That's why she has the urge to take out men who hurt women. It all fits!"

"An interesting theory," she reiterated. It was more than interesting, it made perfect sense. "I'll forward that on to my superiors."

"Good. Thank you." He heaved a breath. "But there's also the risk of spreading the infection. The incubation time is days, and the symptoms mimic the flu. It'll spread before it's recognized, and any male infected will be *trying* to spread it."

"I've seen the simulations, Doctor." She wasn't an epidemiologist, but she didn't have to be to understand the potential for world-wide spread of the *Homo draconis* infection.

"Good! Then you know that if this gets out, it'll make the zombie apocalypse look like a peace protest. It's the end of the human race and civilization as we know it, Doctor."

"I'll forward your recommendations. That's all I can promise."

"Thank you."

The call ended, but Mary Buckmann stared at her phone and the crime scene photos for a long time. Finally, she put in a request for a private video conference with the Director.

25

Aleksi spent an hour surveying the area around Hutch's condo building before she felt certain it was safe. Persephone's warning rang true, but she didn't think the government would try to kill her, at least not yet. Buckmann had told her they still considered her a potential asset, and they didn't waste assets.

And the risk was worth it.

Landing on Hutch's balcony, she slipped through the door in a flash, crouching in the corner beside the drapes. She breathed in his scent, her dragon eyes piercing the darkness. He sat in his favorite chair, an empty glass on the arm. It smelled of whiskey. He thumbed a remote, and the curtains hummed closed. The lights came on low.

"Aleksi." Hutch stood from his chair, his face alight. "God, it's good to see you."

"It's good to see you, too, Hutch." She stood, still reticent, hope and loneliness burning a hole in her heart. "Did you call Buckmann?"

"Yes, and she seemed…receptive to the warning. I think you're right. She's not behind this."

"Good." She gauged him critically. He didn't seem drunk, but she had to ask. "You've been drinking?"

"One. I couldn't think straight." He took a step closer. "You're thinner. Are you okay?"

"The treatment they put me through was…taxing. I just got out of bed a couple days ago."

"And?"

She smiled at the hope in his voice. "And the infectious RNA that started this whole thing is gone."

"That's…" His jaw dropped with the implications. "Aleksi, that's wonderful! You're not infectious anymore!"

"Yes, but that was only the first step. There's a lot more to do." She spread her wings. "I'm still a dragon."

"But you're not *infectious.*" He stepped slowly toward her, lifting his arms toward her. "You can touch me. There's no danger."

"But I'm still…" She lowered her wings and looked at the floor. "I'm still a monster."

"You're *not,* Aleksi!" He stepped closer, his hands on her shoulders. "You're beautiful, and I love you."

"Hutch, I… You don't have to…"

"Shut up and give me a hug." He pulled her in.

For a long moment she just let him hold her, then she lifted her wings to enfold him. He felt good, safe, human. A sob wracked her, tearing at her like claws.

"Oh, *God,* Hutch, I've missed you."

"Shhhh." He pulled away and lifted a hand to wipe away her tears. "It's okay. We don't have to miss each other anymore, Aleksi. It's safe."

He leaned in to kiss her, but she pulled back reflexively. "Hutch, are you *sure* you want to do this?"

His eyes searched her face. "I'm sure, if you want me to."

"I've wanted to be with you for *months,* but I…" More tears poured down her scaly cheeks. "I don't know how you can stand to touch me."

"I *love* you, Aleksi." He kissed her then, tentatively at first, then with more passion, fingertips tracing the tracks of her tears.

A moan of longing escaped her chest. She kissed him carefully, held him like she would a fragile vase, a butterfly in her grasp. His fingertips quested down her neck, her chest, lingering, caressing, igniting her every nerve. She caught her breath as he ran his fingers down her abdomen. Her claws extended of their own volition, but not to rend flesh. She held him close, shuddering as his fingers explored the smooth scales where her legs joined, caressing, teasing.

Hutch pulled back. "Do you want this, Aleksi?" His eyes sought hers, an earnest plea writ on his face. "If you don't…"

"I *do*! Please!" She caught her breath again as he ran a finger down farther. "Oh, *please*! Yes! More!"

He gave her more. He gave her everything she asked for, and Aleksi immersed herself in his touch.

When he arrived at his office, the Director began weeding through his overnight messages. The news from the team was good. Price reported that David was stable but tense, keeping himself busy with simulations, exercise, and bugging everyone for a new mission. Then he found Buckmann's request for a private conference.

Five keystrokes opened an encrypted video connection, and she answered immediately. She didn't look well-rested. "Mary. You look exhausted. What's happened?"

"You put this thing into a soldier, didn't you?"

The Director glared at her accusative tone. "The details of the human trial are not up for discussion, Doctor. Where did you hear this rumor?"

"It's not a rumor. The hit on Tredyakofsky had *Homo draconis* written all over it, and Aleksi confirmed it."

"*Aleksi* confirmed it? How, exactly, did she do that?"

"She *smelled* him. Dr. Hutchinson relayed her message and gave me a warning, a repeat of the very same warning I gave you, sir. This is dangerous in the extreme. The epidemiology analysis of an outbreak should have been warning enough! I strongly urge you to end this trial. Your subject is infectious, and behavior analysis of this attack paints the picture of a deranged mind. I'm sending you Dr. Hutchinson's analysis. Your dragon's behavior makes evolutionary sense in a world with scattered populations of interrelated tribes, but *not* with a population of seven *billion* people who aren't genetically related to him. He's compelled to kill rival males to protect his genome and proliferate. He has no family, sir. He'll see the entire human population as rivals."

"The subject is under control, Mary. I've got teams of psychologists analyzing his every move."

"It's not psychologists you *need*, sir, it's behavioral scientists, evolutionary biologists, and animal behaviorists. Your subject isn't *human* anymore. Human psychology doesn't apply to him any longer."

The Director gritted his teeth, but Mary had a valid point. David had shown signs of instability. The murders of the two women and how he'd done it now began to make sense, but David was still in control, still following orders. And the potential for more like him outweighed the risk.

"I'll take your warning under advisements, Mary. That's all I can promise."

"Very well, sir, but I hope to *hell* you have him under control. If he gets out, we're *all* in trouble, and I don't mean our department, I mean the whole human race."

"I *understand* that, Doctor." He broke the connection and pulled up the latest reports on David.

Thirty-five days had passed since his fever broke, and his evolution was nearly complete. His behavior was stable but worrisome. He had been complaining of claustrophobia, and was really amped up, spending all his waking hours either exercising or running through simulations. He wanted another mission, insisting that they allow him to do what they made him to do.

Buckmann's warning settled into the Director's threat assessment like oil into a bubbling cauldron, roiling on the surface, volatile, waiting for one spark. If she was right, if David had become more animal than human, they had a serious problem.

The Director called in his team; it was time to make sure this thing couldn't get out of hand.

Persephone stood beside Gi-gi's bed, staring in rapt attention at the scene playing on the flat-screen monitor. She didn't know if she should be appalled, fascinated, or aroused. She did know that placing a camera in Hutch's bedroom had been the worst idea she'd ever had.

"Why are you showing me this?" She tried to look away, to ignore the interplay of writhing human and slightly inhuman flesh, skin and scales, fingers and talons, arms and wings. Her eyes remained fixed, her mind reeling.

"To show you that love transcends the flesh, my dear." Something akin to reverence filled the ancient woman's voice.

"So it would seem." Persephone marveled at them, the ecstasy on Hutch's face, and the shudders of pleasure rippling Aleksi's wings. *Love... transcends everything.*

"We've given them this gift."

"Yes, but we didn't know what we were giving them."

"Nevertheless, it is given. Aleksi will be grateful."

"And if she ever finds out we watched this, she'll rip this house apart from rafters to foundation, and everyone inside with it." Persephone tore her eyes away from the display and fixed her great-grandmother with a warning stare. "You *know* that, don't you?"

"Yes. Yes, I believe she would. We must be careful that she never finds out."

"Is that all?" Persephone tried to keep her eyes averted and failed. A deep, burning arousal began to smolder in the pit of her stomach, a dark desire she never knew she'd been capable of. *God help me...*

"No, it's not. There is the matter of Dr. Hutchinson to consider."

That jolted Persephone out of her fascination. "What about Hutch is there to consider?"

"Aleksi and he are in love. That will never change. Aleksi knows our secrets. You, of all people, know how difficult it is to keep secrets from the ones we love."

"Yes, I know." She knew where this was going now. "What do you propose we do?"

"Nothing yet, but there are only two options: bring him into our confidence, or eliminate him."

"I will *not* allow you to kill him, Gi-gi!" Persephone snapped, harsher than she'd intended.

"Will not *allow*?" The piercing lavender eyes swiveled to fix upon her. "It's not your choice."

Love transcends...

"If you choose to kill Hutch, I'll leave." Leaving the family was a one-way ticket; a new identity, enough money to live comfortably on, and utter exile. There was no coming back, ever. Defiance? Maybe, but she couldn't allow him to be harmed.

Gi-gi's ancient eyes narrowed. "You *know* how I dislike ultimatums."

Persephone met Gi-gi's cold stare with hardening resolve. "Nevertheless, that is mine. If it comes down to it, we take him in, or you lose me. Figure *that* into your risk analysis."

"Very well, I will." Gi-gi's hand twitched and the screen went black. "You may go."

Persephone left the Sanctum, unsure if she'd done the right thing. *Love transcends...* She'd either ensured Hutch's survival, or sealed her own fate.

26

David heard the two armed guards with Amy and Jim from halfway down the hall. The guards would stay in the hall while the techs came in. That had become the norm anytime anyone came to see him now, and it had begun to irritate David on a visceral level. They didn't trust him. He'd become moody, quick to anger. He knew this, but if they'd just let him out of this goddamned cage to do what he was made to do, he'd be fine. Of course, he was a dragon, and they feared him, which was only right. He still looked forward to seeing Amy, though she'd become more distant, more afraid of him after the mission. He suspected they'd all been told about the killings.

They knocked, and David got down from the stair climber. "Yes." The door opened and Amy and Jim came in.

"Hi David! We've got your new gear." Amy held up a small satchel.

"And another field test. Hope you're up for some travel." Jim waved a data stick.

"Excellent!" He went to the mini fridge and pulled out a cold water as they donned their protective gear. "About damned time!"

"Let's try on your new suit of clothes first." Amy put the satchel on the table and unzipped it. Web gear, wider suspenders with tapered edges, adhesive backing, and a separate collar with a clip in the back and two more on the straps. "This shouldn't sag. We'll run you through some simulations this afternoon to make sure."

David drank deeply and examined the new rig. "What's the collar?"

"GPS tracking, radio telemetry, and biometrics transmitting at low wavelength," Jim explained. "All in a stylish package."

"They worried I'm going to get *lost*?" He didn't like the idea of being tracked and monitored, but it could have been worse. Price had wanted him to wear a body cam.

Jim barked a laugh, but there was nervousness in it. "No, but if something happens, we can't let the bad guys get their mitts on you. They'll have an extraction team ready, and with this, they can find you."

"Makes sense." But it didn't. If he was captured or killed, an enemy would strip him of anything that might be used to track him. *Probably some REMF's bright idea,* David thought, but orders were orders.

"Let's try the web-gear on." Amy came around and clipped on the front suspenders. "We're going to have to wipe you down or these won't stick."

"I'll grab a towel from the bathroom." Jim put the collar on the table and headed for the bathroom. He'd always been jittery, but seemed really twitchy today, too chatty. His fear hung around him like flatulence in the air.

Jim came back with a towel. They wiped off the sweat, and then Amy swabbed him down with alcohol where the adhesive would stick. She avoided his eyes.

Something's wrong, David thought, though what it could be he had no clue. Amy had never avoided his gaze, and Jim was too talkative. Both were scared, more than usual.

"Okay, just duck through, and we peel and stick." Amy held the harness, and he ducked under the back's cross strap. Jim clipped it to his shorts, and they both peeled the plastic backing off the adhesive and pressed it to his chest and back. The glue smelled strong, like resin.

"How does it feel?" Amy asked.

David twisted and turned, bent and flexed. "Better."

"Good! Now let's try on the collar." Jim lifted the device and unclipped the back of the collar. It bulged slightly, made of ballistic cloth with more adhesive backing and two clips that would connect to the suspenders of his web gear.

"I told them something with little metal studs would make you look like a badass, but they nixed the idea." Amy's joke rang hollow.

"I'm glad they did. I'd look like a drag queen."

"Ha! Or a *dragon* queen!"

"Oh, please stop it. You're making me ill." Jim held the collar up. His hands were shaking and sweat had broken out on his upper lip. Fear wafted off him in waves.

Then David caught the scent of something else, something familiar, something dangerous. He had worked with every type of explosive the military employed, and had investigated blasts from even more. He could have smelled the difference between a grenade blast and a C-4 charge by the residue when he was still fully human. This collar they were putting on him reeked of pentrite, probably primer cord. There could only be one reason to put primer cord in a collar.

They're going to kill me!

Claws ripped the collar away and tore it open. Six loops of primer cord and a detonator, enough to blow his head off nicely.

"Fuckers!"

"Guards!" Jim shouted, backpedaling, but David was faster.

The dragon threw the explosive collar away and lunged, grasping Jim's face in one clawed hand and ripping out his throat with the other. Blood and meat painted the wall. One twist and a kick, and the body flew at the door, minus its head. David flung it aside and whirled on Amy.

"David! Don't!" She backed away, hands up, eyes wide with terror, helpless. "We were just following orders! You know about following orders, don't you?"

"Yes, Amy, I know about *orders*." He strode toward her. Outside the room, the guards chambered rounds in their carbines and turned to face the door. They were going to gun him down. "I won't kill you, Amy, but I need your help."

"Anything!"

"Walk to the door ahead of me. This was an accident. I lost my temper, but they were trying to kill me." The door clicked, but the headless corpse blocked it. David loomed over Amy. "Now!"

"Okay! I'm sorry, David." She edged around him. "I didn't want—"

One of the guards kicked the door open wide enough to level his weapon through. "Don't move!"

Amy turned, hands out. "Wait! It was an accid—"

David carefully grasped Amy between the shoulder blades, his claws plunging in to grip her firmly by the spine.

She screamed, and the guard fired.

True to his word, David hadn't killed Amy, but the three-round burst in her chest certainly did. He felt the shock of the first round hitting her, and he was moving before the second.

The world slowed, the sound of the first shot echoing around the room, his ears ringing. David watched the carbine's action eject the spent round, the brass cartridge tumbling, the recoil lifting the muzzle minutely. He lifted Amy to intercept the next bullet. That one blew all the way through, painting him with her blood and holing his left wing. Another spent cartridge tumbled, and he'd halved the distance to the door. The third round smashed into bone under his fingers.

The echoes of Amy's scream fell silent.

David clawed the door open and threw the twitching corpse at the guard. The other had his weapon aimed, but David grasped the barrel and thrust it aside as the man's finger moved from safe to the trigger. Three rounds blasted into the wall and ceiling, and three claws plunged into the guard's throat. He tore the gun away and flung the guard around like a flail into the other man. They both went down, another burst from the first guard ripping holes in the floor.

David was on them before either could react. *So slow, so weak...* The first guard was only stunned, the second bleeding out from his neck. David tore the stunned guard's helmet off, grasped his skull with one hand, and squeezed. Bone collapsed like an egg in his grasp.

The dragon stood there for a moment, panting, seething with rage. *Fuckers tried to kill me!*

The guards' weapons weren't made for him, but if he was going to survive, he would have to use them. Already, alarms were sounding, booted feet pounded through the facility. They were coming for him.

But they should have known better than to try to kill a dragon.

The two carbines felt awkward in his altered hands, but they would do for now. He turned to face the onslaught, lips pulling back from razor teeth.

"It's about goddamned time I set this dragon free!"

Mary Buckmann's phone beeped and vibrated in her jacket pocket, interrupting her conversation with the Boston Police Department's chief forensic scientist. She had silenced her phone, but emergency messages broke through with an audible alarm. This was important.

"I'm sorry, but I have to take this."

"Of course, ma'am." The man smiled and gestured to a door. "Use my office if you want some privacy."

"Thank you, but I shouldn't need…" She faltered as she swiped the screen.

The header said it all. "Containment breech of *Homo draconis* subject."

"Shit!" She stuffed the phone away and turned to the scientist. "I'm very sorry, but this is an emergency. I'll have to get back with you later."

"I understand completely." He waved her to the lab's exit. "I hope everything's okay."

"So do I." Mary thanked him and bolted out of the building. Only when she reached her car did she pull her phone again and read the entire message.

It read like an epitaph for the entire human race. The *Homo draconis* subject had broken containment and killed at least seventeen armed and unarmed government personnel, the Director among them. The subject had escaped the facility entirely and was at large, whereabouts unknown. She was to report immediately to the facility and take charge of the situation.

"Shit, shit, shit!" Mary punched in the address and drove, cursing Boston traffic and the fools who had put this thing into a soldier. *What were they fucking thinking!*

Stuck at a stoplight, wishing her car had lights and a siren, she made a decision and pulled her phone once again. She put it on speaker and punched Dr. Hutchinson's number.

He answered on the third ring, "Dr. Buckmann? What's wrong?"

"I'm breaking just about every rule in my department and probably a few laws by telling you this, but the higher ups at DHS have done a human trial. They inoculated a soldier about a month ago. He's fully transformed, and has broken containment. He's on the loose."

"Oh *shit*!"

"Exactly what I said." She pulled around a slow car, hammering her horn and squealing tires. "If you're in touch with Aleksi, tell her she was right. He's on the rampage. He's already killed, and will likely kill again. If we're going to contain him and prevent an outbreak, I'll need her help."

"You…" A long pause, then he came back on, sounding angry. "I'll tell her, Dr. Buckmann, but this isn't *her* mess to clean up. It's *yours*!"

"I realize that. Please, just tell her. You *know* what will happen if there's an outbreak."

"Yes, I know." The call ended.

Mary drove, following her phone's directions to the facility where the dragon had escaped, praying to God that the infection hadn't already spread.

Hutch dropped the phone and rolled over to face Aleksi. "You heard that?"

"Yes." She stirred, lurching up from the bed. "We're in trouble."

"We, as in the entire human race." Hutch got up and rounded the bed to intercept her. "Aleksi, this isn't your fight."

She folded her wings, her beautiful yellow eyes piercing him. "It is. I found this thing."

"But *they* stole it and put it in a soldier. That's on *them,* not you." He put his hands on her shoulders. "Please."

"Please what, Hutch? Let the world burn?" She shook her head. "I can't do that."

"This is worse than Derrick Penningly, Aleksi," he pleaded. "This man was a *soldier,* a trained killer. You can't fight someone like that."

"Maybe not, but I can find him, lure him into the open."

"You want to *trust* Buckmann?"

"*Want* to trust her? No, but—"

"Well, if you're planning to lure this maniac out of hiding for them to kill, you're trusting them not to kill you, too."

She shrugged. "What other choice do I have?"

"Let them handle it." Hutch knew she wouldn't, and even knew he was being selfish, but he couldn't stand the thought of her facing someone like this.

"I *can't,* Hutch. I wish I could, but I can't." She started to step around him, but he caught her arm.

"Wait, Aleksi. You can't go out now. It's the middle of the day! You've got to wait until tonight."

"Shit." The muscles of her jaw bunched. "I've got to risk it, Hutch. I've got to find out about this man. If I'm going to find him, I've got to *know* him."

"But flying around in the middle of the day will get you shot!" He rubbed her shoulders. "Stay here, and I'll get hold of Buckmann. She can send everything they have on this guy, and you can study it and leave at dusk."

She considered, then nodded. “So much for your day off. Sorry Hutch.”

Hutch laughed and pulled her into a hug. He’d taken a personal day to spend with her. So far, it had been wonderful. “Well, the day’s not over. I’ll make us some coffee and call Buckmann.”

“You should probably call Jasper, too, and warn him all hell’s about to break loose.”

“Good idea.” He grabbed his phone and started for the kitchen.

“And you may want to put some pants on.”

“Nah! Pants are highly overrated. Besides, you’re not wearing any.”

“I’ve got wings.” She followed him. “And you’re just teasing me.”

“Not teasing.” He shot her a smoldering glance. “But we *do* have all day…”

27

Jasper pulled his phone and stared at the caller ID. "It's Hutchinson."

"What do you think *he* wants?" Willis took the driver's side and put their lunch between the seats.

"I almost don't want to find out." Jasper got in and put their coffees in the holder then took the call. "Dr. Hutchinson. I hope this is a social call."

"Sorry, Tony, but it's not. There's a serious situation."

"Is this about the murders?"

"Indirectly, yes. I'll probably go to prison for this, but the government's put this infection into a soldier. It's not hard to figure out what they're trying to do."

"Shit." The implications hit him like a freight train. "A *soldier*? Those stupid fuckers!"

"It gets worse. This thing is infectious, Tony. Aleksi's been very careful not to transmit it to anyone, but this guy's on the loose, and he probably won't care. He may even *try* to infect others on purpose. He's broken out and killed people."

"Son of a *bitch*! How contagious is this thing?"

"Not airborne, and not through touching. But a bite or blood would probably do it. The government's on this, and they'll probably contact the CDC and FBI as well, but I thought you should know. This could be bad."

"Okay." Jasper cleared his throat, trying to wrap his head around all this. "Okay, thanks, Hutch. Does Aleksi know about this?"

"Yes."

"Okay. Stay in touch, please. You're my only contact on this. I'll try to keep your name out of it. Confidential source, you know."

"Thanks, Tony."

"Take care." He dropped his phone and looked to Willis. "We are so fucked."

Mary handed her ID to the gate guard and waited while he checked it and brought a print scanner. The perimeter was heavily manned by soldiers in full combat gear. They looked nervous. She pressed her hand to the pad and waited.

"Thank you, Dr. Buckmann. You may proceed. Dr. Price will meet you at building two, main entrance." He pointed.

"Thanks." Mary took her ID back and drove. She didn't bother finding a parking spot, but just pulled up to the entrance. By the time she got out of her car, a woman in a blood-spattered lab coat with two more guards stood at the door. "Dr. Price?"

"Yes. You're Dr. Buckmann?" She didn't offer to shake hands, which Mary found refreshing. Pleasantries at a time like this seemed inane. She also seemed remarkably calm considering what had happened here.

"Yes. I need to see everything, and I want you to fill me in on the project, the subject, his behavior, and every detail you can think of while I try to absorb exactly what the *hell* happened here."

"Yes, ma'am." Price waved her through the door, and the guards fell in behind them. "The subject's name is David Gilford. He's career military, covert ops rated, and highly skilled. He was chosen because he was the most psychologically stable candidate. Fifty-eight years old and facing forced retirement."

"Psychologically stable, and he just slaughtered seventeen people?"

"Nineteen. Two of the injured have died. You'll see from his file that he was an exemplary candidate."

She didn't bother to tell the woman that if their best candidate resulted in this clusterfuck, they needed better exclusion criteria. Recriminations were pointless at this stage. The potential for infection loomed like a storm front. "How many more injured?"

"Twelve, ma'am. They're being treated here under full precautions."

Mary looked the woman over. "That blood on your coat isn't yours, is it?"

"No, ma'am. It's Dr. Baker's. He...I tried to help him, but he passed."

"Okay. Keep talking and take me to where this breakout started."

"This way."

Price led her through the facility to the room where they'd housed the subject. The bodies had been removed, but Price filled in the details. Gilford had torn through the place like a bull through a china shop. Forensics teams were going over everything, but there seemed little point to blood spatter analysis at this point. Mary stared at the supposedly "secure" doors that had been ripped off their hinges, claw marks in the steel, gouges in the concrete floor.

"Is there any indication that the subject was injured?"

"Nothing concrete, but as you can see, a lot of rounds were fired at him. Our people are all combat veterans, ma'am. They reported that he moved too fast to effectively target." She guided Mary through the mangled door into the open field behind the facility. "We used this area for the initial field trials, air drops, and the like, so he knew his way out."

"Field trials. The assassination of the Russian, Tredyakofsky. That was him, right?"

"Yes, ma'am. The target was selected by the CIA, the operation coordinated by the Director."

"Who is now dead."

"Yes, ma'am."

"And how the *hell* did he get in the way of this...of Gilford during the breakout?"

"He did it intentionally, ma'am. He tried to reason with him. That was when Dr. Baker was killed, too."

"And this is the last known position?" Mary shaded her eyes and scanned the trees.

"Yes, he flew southeast and vanished. We've had helicopters searching for him since the incident."

"Gunships?"

"No, ma'am. Commercial aircraft with marksmen aboard. We don't want to start a panic."

"Very well." She took a deep breath and let it out slowly. "Take me to the Director's office. I want clearance to all project files. Everything. If Gilford took a shit, I want to know about it."

"You've already been cleared, ma'am. This way." She waved her back through the demolished door.

Halfway to the Director's office, Mary's phone vibrated in her pocket. She pulled it out and stopped. The call was from Dwayne Hutchinson. She held up a hand for quiet and took the call.

"Dr. Hutchinson. Thank you for calling."

"This is Aleksi."

Mary's blood froze in her veins. She was using Hutchinson's phone. "You've heard the news, I gather."

"I *warned* you people, and you did it anyway." Aleksi sounded angry.

Mary couldn't find fault with that. She was angry, too, but a shouting match would solve nothing. "The person in charge of the project was killed, Aleksi. I'm now in charge, and my only goal is to clean up this mess. I'd like your help in that effort."

"So you can put a bullet in my head?"

"Of *course* not! You're our best chance of finding and neutralizing this threat."

"Why do you use euphemisms, Doctor? You want me to help you kill the man who *volunteered* to be made into something none of you even understand! He *trusted* you, and now he's a fucking *monster*!"

Mary had to admit, that was the absolute truth. "Sorry. Yes, Aleksi, we want your help to kill him. His name is David. David Gilford."

"Send everything you've got on him to this phone, including the latest photos you have, his capabilities, everything!"

"That's classified."

"Then fuck off and deal with him yourself!" The call went dead.

"Fuck!" Mary returned the call immediately. It rang six times before Aleksi answered.

"Change your mind?"

"Yes. I'll send you everything we have on Gilford."

"Good."

"I have to stress to you, Aleksi, this man is a soldier, one of the best. He's an experienced killer. You can't fight him."

"I'm not *stupid,* Doctor. I don't intend to, but I can find him. I'll need his last known location."

"I'll send it with the data." Mary paused, but she had to ask. "Do you think you *can* find him?"

"Yes."

Mary didn't ask how. "Then what?"

"If I call you on another phone and leave the line open, you can track me, right?"

"Yes."

"Then I'll find him and lure him into the open for you."

"That'll be dangerous."

"You *think*?" Aleksi actually growled over the line. "I only have one advantage over him, Doctor. I've been a dragon for half a year, he's only been one for a few days. I know how he thinks, what he can do, and where he'll go better than he does. Send me the files."

"It'll be on your phone in five minutes," She promised. "Please be careful, Aleksi."

"Yeah, that's what I told you people, and look what the fuck happened!" The call went dead.

"Take me to the Director's office." Mary stuffed the phone into her pocket.

"You're not really going to send the project files to a civilian, are you, ma'am?" Price looked horrified.

"No, Dr. Price, I'm going to send them to a *dragon*, and she's the only hope we've got! If you've got a problem with that, please file a grievance with my supervisor."

Of course, Mary's supervisor was dead.

Aleksi stood staring out Hutch's window at the sunset, his arms clutched around her. He felt good, warm, human. *So strange*, she thought, remembering the day, his relentless tenderness, her careful passion. She had never thought she would ever experience intimacy again. It was almost more than she could take.

"This has been the best day of my life, Hutch."

"Mine, too." He squeezed her tight.

"It's time. I have to go."

"I know. I don't want you to."

"Neither do I, but I have to."

"I know." He let go, and she turned around to face him.

"I'm sorry, Hutch."

"For what?"

"For ever agreeing to be your student, for discovering this thing, for getting infected...and for falling in love with you."

"I'm not." He kissed her. "I'm sorry this happened to you, Aleksi, but I'll *never* be sorry for loving you."

"Thank you." She wrapped her wings around him and held him, maybe for the last time. "I have to go."

"I hate this. I don't want to lose you. Promise me you'll be careful."

"I promise." *As careful as I can be hunting a dragon.* "I'll call when I know something."

"Okay. I love you."

"I love you, too." Aleksi smiled and went to the back door without looking back. She couldn't bear to see the heartbreak on his face.

She leapt into the sultry night and soared at treetop level above the streets and houses of Cambridge, heading west. She'd texted Persephone a few times, letting her know her findings at the brownstone and that Buckmann had been notified. She hadn't told her about the rest, only that she would return soon. She didn't want to hear the warnings, the admonitions, the promises.

Banking and dipping under a bridge, she crossed the Charles River, then wheeled west, staying low, weaving amongst the trees. The thought that this all might be an elaborate trap had occurred to her, and she wasn't ready to trust Buckmann implicitly. She'd find out soon enough if she was telling the truth.

Google Earth had supplied her with satellite photos of the government facility where they'd made their dragon. It was listed as a military contractor's R&D facility.

Aleksi approached cautiously, staying low. A thousand LED streetlights lit the scene like day, and Aleksi spotted patrols of soldiers walking the perimeter with dogs and rifles. Vehicles with roof-mounted cameras drove around inside the fence line, undoubtedly scanning the skies with night-vision. If this was a trap for her, they weren't being very subtle. She landed in the trees and scented the air.

The wind wafted from the west, bringing her the scents of blood, gun smoke, and human fear, but no dragon. Buckmann's report had said that Gilford had flown away to the east, toward the city. Aleksi had little doubt that he was there now, maybe coming out of hiding. He'd be hungry, and there was only one type of prey in the greater Boston area.

I've got to stop him... Her first step, however, was to pick up his scent.

Aleksi worked her way back and forth through the trees east of the facility, far enough away to avoid the night scopes of nervous soldiers.

On her third pass, an alarm went off in her head. She dove into the nearest tree out of instinct, hunkering in the crook of the huge oak to listen and scent the air. Nothing reached her ears above the ambient roar of the city, but on the wind, she caught a whiff of danger. Following the scent upwind, she found its source. Another tree, claw marks, and the biting scent of urine. She sniffed the marks and knew she'd found the dragon.

Closing her eyes, Aleksi concentrated on the scent, imprinting on it, picturing the photos Buckmann had sent her. *David Gilford...soldier, assassin, dragon.*

With the scent firmly fixed in her mind, Aleksi began a careful search pattern to the east, toward the city of Boston and millions of unknowing humans, hunting for the dragon who could end the human race.

28

David clung to the side of a building somewhere in the downtown area, a mixture of elation and frustration battling within him. He was free, but what exactly to *do* with that freedom he hadn't quite figured out yet. Forty years of following orders, and now there was no one to give him any. He was also undoubtedly being hunted, and he was still getting used to being a dragon.

The flying thing he was learning fast, experimenting with his capabilities, and he was still growing. Stealth, fortunately, he was well versed in. He'd evaded governments before, deep in hostile territory, alone and with far fewer resources, but never his own government in his own country. He didn't know Boston very well, either. The streets were confusing, nothing square, with three and five corner intersections, like it was designed by an artist instead of an urban planner.

For now, he lay low and watched the teaming crowds of humanity: the bars, the clubs, the couples and groups, drunks, students, business people, construction workers, rich and poor side by side. The city was a tapestry of skin hues, faces, body shapes. *Such diversity, such beauty, and such weakness...* And cops; there were cops everywhere. He didn't think they were looking for him yet. Homeland Security wouldn't put an all-points bulletin out on their secret weapon, not even if word got out. They'd deny ever creating him and lay the blame on someone else, terrorists, rogue governments, mad scientists...

And still, he had to decide what to do. David was a soldier with nothing to fight, an operative without a mission, a dragon without a lineage.

His stomach growled, reminding him of one more problem. A dragon needed to feed.

The smell of food from a thousand restaurants grilling meat competed with the millions of scents of living flesh. To his dragon senses, it was hard to separate the two. Flesh was food, and the scent of burning meat was less appetizing than the live kind. But he was still David Gilford, and the thought of consuming human flesh repulsed him.

More frustration mounted, instinct battling human memories, new impulses battling fifty-eight years of learned behaviors. He was trapped in a cage, starving, and surrounded by food he couldn't eat. In the end, need and instinct won out over his reticence.

David didn't even realize he'd picked his first victims until he moved to follow them, a woman and man leaving a restaurant. Something about the couple clicked in his mind. Maybe she reminded him of Amy—*I didn't kill her; they killed her!*—or maybe it was the guy that set him off. She wore black jeans and a white blouse, probably a waitress' uniform. He was soft, well-dressed, slick, maybe a lawyer or businessman. Not good looking, a little pudgy, shitty posture, but he had money. Men like that took all the good ones.

Well, not tonight. Without knowing why he felt the urge to do so, David began a slow, careful stalking.

Following them was easy. His claws found purchase on the older buildings' ornate facades, and he knew to stay above the street lights. Anyone looking up would be blind to the shadow among shadows. He followed them for a few blocks, listening to their inane conversation about marriage, decorating their apartment, maybe trying to find someplace closer to town. He wanted her to quit her job and have kids, she wanted to get her degree and have a career. He wanted a cat, and she was a dog person. He wanted Italian for dinner, and she wanted to go home and cook.

Do people really care about all that shit?

Finally, they cut through an alley toward the nearest transit station. There was nobody else around. David released his grip and fell from the sky, banking into the alley, wings billowing at the last moment to soften his landing, the wind buffeting them.

"What the fu—" The man started to turn, but David's claws caught him just behind the ear, ripping off a hand-sized flap of scalp and sending him crashing into a wall.

The woman screamed, but he cuffed her. The scream, however, ignited him like a drug. She lay there clutching her face, stunned, helpless.

David's mouth flooded with saliva, but it wasn't hunger. Something else had hold of him now, something new, yet familiar. Something so deep he couldn't understand it. *Dreams of biting, grasping, fucking...* He wasn't in danger, his dinner lay waiting, but the woman lay there helpless, healthy, young, in her prime. Killing her would be a waste of something precious. Primal instinct took hold of him like the jaws of a beast.

He lifted her, breathed her in, his tongue tasting the sheen of sweat on her neck. *Yes! Perfect! Pure! Mine!* Her eyes fluttered open, and her mouth opened to scream again. The pure note of her terror sent him over the precipice. He buried his teeth in her, but not to kill, not to feed. *Mine!*

Then the man behind him stirred and lunged up, a feral cry tearing from his throat.

David turned and caught the haymaker punch in one clawed hand, his bloody teeth bared. "Not smart," he seethed, letting go of the woman he'd marked. She collapsed, still screaming, gripping her bloody blouse where his teeth had pierced. David ignored her for now.

He squeezed, pulping bones in the man's flabby hand.

A scream rose, almost feminine, but his victim flung another punch out of nowhere. David wasn't expecting so much fight from such a soft one, and the punch landed, not really hard enough to hurt, but enough to transform his pleasure into anger. Again, something deep within him tipped over a precipice he didn't even know was there.

"How *dare* you, you pissant little *puke*!" David released the guy's broken hand, gripped him by the throat, and tore his ribcage open with a single swipe of his claws. Then, standing there with shattered ribs and quivering heart in one hand, the twitching corpse in his other, David heard the most curious sound.

The woman behind him uttered the strangest cry, one stuttering, wailing word over and over. "N…n…nooo! N…n…nooo! N…n…nooo!" She stared in blank-faced horror, not at David, but at the corpse dangling in his grasp.

"Yesss!" he countered, his mouth flooding again with saliva, but this time it *was* hunger. The handful of meat in his right hand still quivered with the last pulses of life. David raised it to his mouth and tore off a bite, wolfing it down.

Glorious!

He fed on his kill, bite after luscious bite, gorging himself while the song of the woman's screams played his nerves like a violin.

This! He realized, ripping off another bite. *This is what I was made for!*

Jasper and Willis arrived at the scene as the ambulance pulled out, siren wailing. They'd been scanning for just this type of incident and knew before they got out of the car what they'd find.

"Cambridge Homicide." Jasper showed the street cop standing at the yellow tape barrier his shield.

The uniform nodded and let them through without a word. He looked a little pale.

"Who's in charge?"

"Detective Blake." The cop pointed to a middle-aged woman in a pantsuit.

Jasper knew her. "Thanks." He strode up and caught her attention.

"Jasper! What are *you* doing this side of the Charles?" She pronounced it "Chaals." Boston to the core.

"Slumming." Jasper gestured to the crowd of cops and forensics people wearing blue gloves and booties going over the scene. Between them, he caught a glimpse of a mangled corpse. "Sounded like shades of Penningly."

"Spot on. Gruesome shit. The guy's heart, liver, and most of his chest are missing. Also wounds to the head, throat, and hand. Looks like he tried to put up a fight."

"Jesus." Willis swallowed audibly. "What about the ambulance? Were there two victims?"

"Yeah, a woman." Blake pulled up her phone and swiped the screen. "Loretta Watkins, cohabitating with the deceased, one Charlie Fenwick, a financial analyst. She was in shock. Had a nasty wound, but not life threating."

"What kind of wound?" Jasper asked.

Blake leveled a stare at him. "The truth? It looked like a fucking shark bite on her right tit."

Jasper traded a glance with Willis. "That's a new twist."

"One hell of a hickey," Willis quipped.

"Right?" Blake pocketed her phone. "Forensics is on this right now. I can't let you touch the crime scene, but I'll forward everything to you. Fair?"

"More than fair. Can we talk to the first cops to get here? Ongoing investigation and all."

"Sure." She pointed to the forensics van where two cops sat on the rear bumper. "Henderson and Vicks. Careful, Vicks is a rook. He kinda lost his shit."

"Probably no worse than I lost my shit the first time." Jasper had tried long and hard to forget that day, and had failed miserably. Some things branded you to the bone. "We'll be gentle."

"Thanks." Blake went back to work.

Jasper and Willis approached the two street cops slowly, gauging them. The older of the two, an African American who looked like he spent time as a prize fighter, seemed solid. The younger guy beside him clutched a cup of forgotten coffee like it was his only lifeline to sanity.

"Evening guys. Tony Jasper, Cambridge Homicide. Mind if we chat?"

"Sure." Henderson stood, towering over the two detectives and taking point to shelter his fragile partner. "What do you want to know, Sergeant?"

Sergeant, Jasper thought. He hadn't introduced himself as Sergeant Jasper. The guy must have heard his name and remembered it. After what they'd just been through, that meant he was sharp. That was good; Jasper needed him to be sharp. "You were the first on the scene, right?"

"Yes. Someone called 911, and we were half a block away. We arrived on foot from the east."

"And you found both victims?"

"Yes. We called EMS for the woman, and my partner applied pressure to the wound. The guy was already dead." Henderson watched Jasper's eyes drift toward his partner and took half a step to block him. He shook his head minutely.

"Sounds like Officer Vicks saved her life," Willis said. "Well done."

Vicks looked up. "I… Maybe. I don't know. She was out of it."

"Did you see the woman's wound, Henderson?"

"Yes, sir. An oval of punctures to the pectoral. She was breathing fine, so we knew there was no lung puncture. She also had a facial contusion, but nothing broken."

"Good work. Where'd they take her?" Jasper wanted to talk to this woman very badly.

"Mass Gen, but she was almost catatonic. Probably won't be able to give you a coherent account of what happened, at least not for a while."

"Well, she's alive, and that's something. Good work, guys."

"Thank you, Sergeant."

Jasper nodded to Willis, and they went back to their car. When the door closed, Tony pulled his phone.

"You calling Hutchinson?"

"Yep."

"What are you going to tell him, exactly. That there was a shark attack in downtown Boston?"

"Give me a break, Marty. We both know what did this!"

"Yeah." Willis touched the scar at his neck. "Yeah, we do. But why a former soldier turned dragon would bite a woman on the chest is beyond me. The doesn't fit Penningly's MO at all."

"Maybe he wasn't breast fed as a baby." Jasper punched Hutch's contact and held the phone to his ear. "Not my area of expertise to psychoanalyze someone like that. I'll leave that to Aleksi."

Thanks, Hutch. You should call Buckmann, but she probably already knows. I'll have a look." Aleksi hung from the Suffolk University building by her toes, scanning the street and park below and scenting the air. She'd heard sirens, but that was nothing new for Friday night in Boston.

"I'll call Buckmann. Listen, Aleksi, Tony said the cops are freaked out. They're talking about the Penningly murders. Be careful, please."

"Always. Gotta go. Love you."

"Love you, too."

She ended the call and taped the phone to her leg, then pulled another one free. Carrying three phones, she'd have to be careful not to run out of duct tape. She tapped Persephone's contact and opened a call. She answered breathless.

"Aleksi! What's wrong?"

"We're in some really deep shit. The government put the dragon infection into a soldier. They're calling it the HD infection, for *Homo draconis*. Anyway, he went berserk and killed nearly twenty people breaking out of their facility."

"Oh my God."

"No kidding. He just killed a man and injured a woman downtown. I'm going to have a look at the site, see if I can pick up his scent."

"Aleksi, do *not* try to find this person! He's a soldier!"

"Yeah, I thought you'd say that. Look, I'm not going to fight him, but I told Buckmann I'd lure him out for them. I've got my old phone, so they can track me. This guy might be a soldier, but he's new at being a dragon. He won't catch me."

"Don't *do* this! *Please*, Aleksi! Let the government clean up their own damned mess!"

"And if they don't, and the HD breaks out into the population?"

Persephone had no answer for that.

"Listen, the surviving victim had a bite wound. Chances are, she's infected. It sounded like a superficial wound, Persephone. He's *intentionally* spreading the infection, making more like himself. Whether he knows what he's doing or not, he's trying to procreate the only way he can. They took her to Mass Gen. Her name's Loretta Watkins. You're the only person on Earth who has a chance to cure her."

"Yes. Okay. We're on it. Thank you, Aleksi." She still sounded pissed, but obviously knew she couldn't talk Aleksi out of anything.

"I'll call you when I know more." Aleksi ended the call, taped the phone to her leg, and released her grip on the cornice.

After six months flying through the canyons of Boston, she knew the streets and alleys like the ridges on her claws. She landed in shadow atop the apartment building abutting the alley where the attack had taken place. There were cops all over the place, half a dozen police cars and two vans, all with lights blazing. She couldn't risk getting much closer.

A team of people in white Tyvek suits, blue gloves, and booties were lifting a bagged shape onto a gurney. It wasn't hard to figure out what was in the bag. She could smell the blood on the air. But had this really been the handiwork of a dragon, or just some sick psychopath? She had to know for sure.

Aleksi crept down the wall at one end of the alley, head down, wings folded, her body close to the bricks to reduce her profile. Getting shot by a nervous cop would be embarrassing. Halfway down the wall, she caught Gilford's scent, strong on the porous bricks.

Danger flashed through her mind, then the memory of fighting Derrick Penningly in Hutch's apartment. He'd seemed psychotic, but he'd been after her not just to kill her. He'd tried to sexually assault her. He, like Gilford, had been impelled to procreate. Aleksi wasn't even sure if that could happen, and if it could, what the result would be, but she knew one thing: this was the result of evolution, not just psychosis. Male dragons needed female dragons. Why, if not to procreate?

She needed more data to formulate a hypothesis, but decoding this evolutionary riddle wasn't her job here. She needed to stop a killer.

Aleksi released her grip on the brick facing and spread her wings, hot on the scent of the only other creature like her in the world...so far.

29

Reggie strode out of the hospital entrance with two of Persephone's other cousins, Ed and Carrie. They all looked grim and determined, and since they didn't have an injured woman with them, Persephone could guess why. They'd failed.

They all piled into the back of the van modified to look like a CDC ambulance. Persephone wore a uniform with CDC markings and a nametag, but her face was far too recognizable for her to walk into a hospital and make off with a patient.

"Well?" She asked over her shoulder.

"No dice. She's gone." Reggie worked his way forward to the passenger seat.

"Gone dead or gone missing?" Aleksi had said the wounds were superficial, but shock could do strange things.

"Missing. Federal agents whisked her out of the ER even before they were done treating her."

"Fuck!" Persephone pulled the van out of the rotunda and onto the street. "God*damn* it! They beat us to her!"

"Yep, and they have no way to cure her," Reggie met her eyes. "If we don't intervene, they'll have another dragon on their hands in a matter of days."

"I know, but we can't exactly walk into DHS headquarters and ask Mary Buckmann to hand her over."

"I know, Seph, but we do have one other option."

Persephone didn't like the sound of this. "What option?"

"Give them the cure."

She thought about that for a while. The danger of giving Buckmann the manufactured retroviruses and the tailored cure to those retroviruses would be extreme. Not only would it tip their family's hand in the biotechnology department, but there was a chance they'd track the delivery back to Persephone's family. Also, there was no guarantee that they'd use the cure on Loretta Watkins in time. They'd analyze it first, probably try to reverse engineer it to crack the underlying technology. And, of course, if they could make future dragons non-infectious, they wouldn't hesitate to make an entire army of them.

But it wasn't really Persephone's decision. "Above my pay grade, Reg. We'll have to pitch that one to Gi-gi."

"I thought you'd say that." He sighed and shook his head. "She won't do it."

"I know." The woman was protective of their family secrets to the point of paranoia. "I don't like it either. We can do one more thing to try to keep this from happening again, at least."

"Aside from killing David Gilford?"

"Yes. Text Gi-gi and tell her what happened. Next time, we have to get to the victim first, not at the hospital, but at the crime scene."

"That won't be easy," Carrie said from the back. "Ambulance response time is only minutes."

"That's why we're not leaving this van until morning. We'll sleep during the day."

"I call dibs on a stretcher," Ed said, probably trying to lighten the mood.

No one laughed.

They drove back to the storage unit where they'd switched vehicles in silence, each deep in their own thoughts. Homeland Security would sequester the Watkins woman, so there would be no chance of an outbreak, but they couldn't treat her. They'd have another dragon within a month.

How is she?" Mary asked, as she strode into the operating room. Price and two other doctors were there, a host of nurses and medical techs assisting them. All wore surgical garb and protective gear. Mary didn't, but she stayed well back from the sterile field.

"Alive, sedated, and infected with HD." Price didn't even look up. She was stitching up a wound.

"Damn." Mary put on a surgical mask and approached the table.

Loretta Watkins lay there, a surgical drape obscuring her torso save for the injury site. Warming blankets covered her from waist down, as well as her outstretched arms. An anesthesiologist held her head behind the surgical drape, pressing a breathing mask to the woman's battered face. She was breathing fine on her own, so they hadn't intubated her. The monitor showed her breathing fast, her heart rate steady, and her temperature elevated. Price was stitching up an oval of puncture wounds on the woman's chest. The injuries looked remarkably minor.

"We've loaded her with antibiotics and antivirals, but, well, you know."

Mary knew. Nothing they had would touch the HD infection "I just got a call from Hutchinson. It's confirmed. This was Gilford."

"Thought so." Price finished with one wound and took up a new needle from the tray with the bloody hemostat. "He was being careful when he did this. He wasn't trying to kill her. The injury is healing already. Remarkably fast, in fact."

"Do you have any idea why he would do this?" Mary had heard Hutchinson's theory, but she wanted Price's unadulterated opinion.

"He's either got a breast fetish, or he was actively trying to infect her with HD." She secured another stitch, and her assistant clipped it short. "*Why* he would want to infect her, is beyond me."

Time for some prompting. "Could he be trying to procreate?"

"By *biting* someone? I don't..." Price paused mid stitch and turned to stare at Mary. "Shit! Yes! He inoculates a female, she evolves into a full *Homo draconis*, and he's got a *mate*!"

"That was Dr. Hutchinson's reasoning."

"You know what that means, don't you?"

"Yes. He'll do it again soon."

"You've got to neutralize him, ma'am. This will get out of control if this continues!" Price's hands were shaking.

"I *know*, Dr. Price. We've got teams in place to intercept any more victims, and someone trying to find him."

"Who the hell..." Price's eyes widened. "The other *Homo draconis?*"

"Yes. She's agreed to help."

"Warn her, ma'am." Price went back to work, but kept talking. "Tell her that Gilford will go after her. If he gets her scent, he'll stop at nothing. That's what he was trying to accomplish here! Something deep in his psyche needs a mate!"

Mary was counting on exactly that. "I'll tell her. See to your patient, Doctor. When she's out of the OR, I want her isolated, sedated, and restrained. Twenty-four-hour monitoring, and armed guards in the room at all times."

"Yes, ma'am."

Mary left the OR, her mind racing. The question she had to face now was whether or not to warn Aleksi about Gilford's motives. If Hutchinson knew, Aleksi probably did, too, but if she hadn't figured it out, the news might scare her off, and Mary needed her on the job. Aleksi was their only chance to lure Gilford into the open for the kill.

Hungry again already?" David hunkered in a massive oak tree on the verge of the Esplanade, watching the eastern sky lighten with the first shades of predawn. "It's like eating Chinese food."

The city had quieted down after the bars closed, but there were a few early risers out already. Lone cars drove along Storrow Drive, and health freaks ran and rollerbladed along the park's paths, more than he thought possible for so early on a Saturday morning. As before, the sight of humans running tweaked his instincts to chase, to hunt, but David wasn't stupid. Everyone carried phones these days, and the last thing he needed was his picture on the news. He needed someone isolated, someone alone, or even another couple. Yes, that would be perfect.

The memory of the woman's screams, her wide eyes, her flesh beneath his teeth sent jolts of sensation through him. He had made her his own, possessed her, branded her with his mark, then, as she watched, he'd killed and eaten her mate. At the time, he hadn't been thinking it through, but now, that primal instinct unsettled him. David was a trained killer. Taking a human life was nothing new. But eating human flesh...that was unthinkable. But he'd done it, he'd *enjoyed* it. He'd crossed the bridge and blown it up behind him. He'd truly become a dragon. And even more disconcerting: eviscerating the woman's boyfriend as she lay there helpless, watching him, bleeding from his mark had given David a carnal satisfaction he'd never known. Even now, thinking about it, he had to shift himself under his shorts to alleviate the strain.

But why would killing a man in front of his woman give him a hard-on?

He had met soldiers who admitted to sexual arousal from killing, and had always thought they were insane. *Is that what I am? Another lunatic killer? A Jeffrey Dahmer?* The thought repulsed him, but he couldn't deny the urges he was feeling. And why bite that woman like that? He could have killed her, probably should have since she was a witness, but he hadn't. He only knew that biting her had been *exactly* the thing to do.

But why?

David's stomach rumbled in complaint. He would have to go into hiding during the day, so he needed to feed now. But where, who, and how? He hadn't gone so primal that he wasn't thinking.

Two women and a man ran past him together, chatting and laughing. He watched them, listened, and swallowed the saliva flooding his mouth. They turned off the path and crossed the street into a more isolated area.

Perfect! He launched himself after them, closing in for the kill.

I'm getting too old for this shit, Marty. Maybe it's time for a desk job." Tony Jasper rested his head back on the driver's seat and rubbed his eyes.

"You're kidding me." Marty Willis licked the icing from his fingers and reached for his coffee. "And give up all this? Fine cuisine, great company, ambiance..."

Jasper snorted a laugh and sipped his coffee. "No, I mean take the lieutenant's exam. Fisk's been begging me to for a while."

"For real?" Willis gaped at him.

"The hours are killing me." He shifted in his seat, trying to work the kinks out of his ass. "Sitting in a car all night waiting for the call, I just feel useless. I mean, we can't tell anyone what's *really* going on without losing our jobs, and we can't find this...guy ourselves. This isn't police work, it's..." He flailed around for an answer and realized he had no idea what they were doing exactly. That was part of the problem.

"Spy shit," Marty finished for him. "With some science fiction thrown in for color."

Tony snorted again. "Right. Government conspiracies, genetic experiments, monsters killing and *eating* people. It's like that old show, *X-Files,* but this isn't TV."

"That's the *point,* Tony. This *isn't* some TV show. This is all too fucking real. This is the only reality we've got, and this thing could rip the guts out of mankind just like Penningly tore out my throat." Marty put his coffee down and reached for the bag of donuts. "Besides, you're no Fox Mulder, and I'm *way* less pretty than Gillian Anderson. So quit whining, have a donut, and save the fucking world, all right?"

Jasper snorted a laugh. Leave it to Willis to put things in perspective. "Yeah. All right." He picked a jelly-filled heart attack out of the bag and held it up. "Here's to saving the fucking world."

Willis picked one out and toasted him. "To saving the fucking world."

As the two donuts touched, the police radio erupted with a near-hysterical cop calling for help: two injured women, one man killed, suspect sighted, location. Lastly, he called for a helicopter. The suspect had flown away.

"Call it in!" Jasper took a bite from his donut, slammed the car in drive, and flipped on the lights and siren. "And call Hutchinson!"

Willis called in on his handheld that they were responding to a BPD call for assistance, then pulled out his cell phone. The BPD dispatcher was questioning the cop's claim that the perpetrator had actually took wing. "That poor bastard just bought a psych eval."

"Maybe we can talk him down if we get there before they put him in a straightjacket." Jasper concentrated on driving, trying to forget that they were literally rushing into a dragon's den.

30

Persephone pulled their CDC-labeled ambulance up to the scene and surveyed the situation. Four police cruisers and one unmarked car, but no ambulance yet. Four cops wearing gloves were pressing bandages to two women who were obviously alive and bleeding, one from a shoulder wound, the other from her leg. The rest stood around another shape, twisted and torn limb from limb. Thankfully, there weren't many bystanders, and no one looked to be recording the scene with cell phones. Gi-gi had been scanning every police frequency in the greater Boston metropolitan area since the first attack, and they'd been waiting for the call.

Then she recognized Tony Jasper. "Shit! That's Jasper! What the hell's he doing here?"

"Hunting dragons, maybe. He's out of his jurisdiction. Does he know you?" Reggie motioned Ed and Carrie to pull the gurneys out of the back.

"No. Well, at least not with this face. You do the talking, I'll play the CDC rep. We've got to get those women out of here before EMS gets here. Try to keep his attention on you. I don't want him remembering me."

"Will do."

"And, Reggie, he knows what *really* happened here. Use that."

"Got it."

Persephone followed Reggie to the cordon of yellow tape while Ed and Carrie pulled gurneys from the back of the ambulance. As the uniform confronted them, she showed her fake ID while Reggie took the lead. "I'm special agent Winston, FBI, and this is Dr. Nelson with the CDC. Who's in charge here?"

"Sergeant Wilks. Right there." The patrolman pointed to a portly uniformed cop with chevrons on his arm. He was talking to Jasper and Willis.

"We need to speak with him right away. This is a contagion situation, officer."

"Contagion?" His eyes widened, and he lifted the tape for them. "Go ahead."

Again, Persephone followed Reggie as he squared off with the police. Ed and Carrie wheeled their gurneys straight over to the injured women. She tried to listen to two conversations at once while keeping out of anyone's attention. The two women looked disoriented, in shock maybe.

"Sergeant Wilks, I'm Special Agent Winston, FBI." He showed his ID, the best forgery Gi-gi could manufacture. It would probably have gotten him into a federal building. "This is Dr. Nelson with the CDC. We have every reason to believe that the perpetrator of this and other murders is infected by a variant of rabies. We need to take the survivors into quarantine immediately. We have a treatment, but it has to be administered within ninety minutes of infection, and the clock is ticking."

"CDC?" The sergeant sounded worried.

"It's not rabies, Agent Winston," Jasper cut in. "It's *way* worse than that, and you know it."

Reggie faced Jasper. "And you are?"

"Sergeant Jasper, Cambridge Homicide. We're carrying on an investigation with the BPD into these murders."

"I recognize your name, Sergeant. You took out Derrick Penningly."

Nice move, Persephone thought. It told Jasper that they knew exactly how much he knew.

Jasper stiffened. "That's right."

"Then you *also* know what's at stake here. We need to treat those two women immediately."

Jasper traded a look with the uniformed sergeant. "Your call, Jim, but he's not lying about the infection. I'll guarantee you that."

Wilks nodded. "Okay, but I'll need a signed release with contact information."

"Right here." Reggie pulled out the prepared document and handed it to him, another convincing forgery with the local CDC facility's address right on the header. Unfortunately, the BPD would probably follow up on the women, so this trick would only work once. On the upside, if Buckmann and her team from Homeland Security tried to steal away any more victims, they'd run up against the same roadblocks.

Persephone turned to the two women being loaded onto the gurneys. They were listless now, which wasn't surprising. Carrie had given them injections of Ketamine mixed with Versed, a general anesthetic and an anxiolytic that also provided retrograde amnesia. They wouldn't remember anyone they'd met for the last five minutes.

If only we could administer the same to all the cops.

They wheeled the injured women toward the van with the aid of the four attending officers, and Persephone turned to follow. The less time she showed her face, the better. Reggie continued his spiel, assuring the two sergeants that they would keep them appraised of the situation. With luck, they'd treat the women and drop them off somewhere with no infection, no residual genetic disorders, and no memories of what had happened to them. They'd get their lives back.

In passing, she got a good look at the other victim. The wounds showed the same pattern as the others: throat torn, chest flayed open, but there was one difference: the man's right arm was missing. Gilford had taken a snack for later. Persephone swallowed hard and got in the front of the van.

"How are they?"

"Alive. The wounds are superficial." Ed continued his work affixing pressure dressings to the wounds. "They seemed confused already, and seriously freaked out."

"Nothing pharmacology can't remedy." Carrie showed her an empty syringe before she dropped it into a sharps box "We'll get IVs going in transit and start administering Reggie's viruses."

"Good." Persephone watched Reggie disengage with the cops and start toward the van. She had the vehicle in gear when he got in. "Good to go?"

"Yes." He took a deep breath and let it out slowly. "That Jasper's a bulldog."

"I know. He's also the reason Derrick Penningly's nothing but a stain in a landfill. I just hope he doesn't remember my face. He's pretty good friends with Hutch."

"You'll have to make sure you're not on the same guest list at the next

Policeman's Ball, then." He chuckled and looked over at their patients. "How are they?"

"Good. Starting the infusions now."

"Excellent!" He laughed and chucked Persephone on the shoulder. "Cheer up, Seph! Mission accomplished!"

Persephone nodded and drove on, the exhilaration of the mission fading fast, exhaustion setting in. She couldn't force herself to laugh. "I'll be cheerful when they're cured and the monster that did this is in a body bag."

They were *what?*" Mary stared at her monitor in open-mouthed shock.

The field operative shrugged helplessly. "Taken, ma'am. They never made it to the ER. When EMS arrived, they were gone. Some people posing as FBI and CDC took them away. Their ID's were bogus. Evidently it all looked official."

Gone? Dread welled up in her gut. Mary leaned into the monitor pickup. "Check with our other sections! Call CDC! I want to know who the hell took those women!"

"We're already checking, ma'am. Nobody at the CDC even knows about this contagion yet."

"Then I want video footage! The police have body cams and dash cams. Scour traffic cam footage, too. I want plates on the vehicle. It shouldn't be hard to spot."

"We've hit a snag there, ma'am," the operative said. "There was a system failure in city-wide traffic CCTV, and the police footage has a three-minute gap. Someone hacked it."

Goosebumps rose on Mary's arms. "Someone *hacked* the entire city's CCTV network and the police system simultaneously?" It seemed an impossible task to accomplish so quickly.

"That seems to be the case. We've started looking for independent security camera footage, but there are thousands of cameras in the greater Boston area. We're looking for a needle in a haystack without a magnet."

"Someone's *really* on their game."

"Affirmative, ma'am."

"Keep checking, and monitor all police radio traffic. When Gilford hits again, we need to be at the crime scene before the dispatcher even calls for an ambulance!"

"We're on it, ma'am."

Mary broke the connection and leaned back in her chair. "Hell of a way to start a morning."

But she hadn't gone home last night, so this didn't feel like morning. It felt like a nightmare she couldn't wake up from.

The couch in her office where she'd gotten two hours of sleep was still warm, but she doubted she'd get much more. Mary got up and jammed her empty coffee cup in the brewer, stabbing the buttons like they'd offended her. She had little doubt that this mysterious "CDC" intervention and computer hack had been perpetrated by the same group who had abducted and impersonated her. Finding and neutralizing Gilford was job one, but she'd be damned to Hell if she'd let these people undercut her.

"I'll find you," she promised herself. "I'll find you and lock you in a cell for the rest of your fucking *lives*!"

Aleksi caught traces of Gilford around the murder scene, but dared not get close. It was getting light, and there were way too many nervous cops around. She would have to go into hiding soon. The scent of blood hung in the air around the scene, but a stronger whiff caught her attention, blood mixed with the now familiar scent of another dragon. *A blood trail? Did he take something with him, or was he hurt?*

Following the scent of blood, keeping to the shadows, she caught more of Gilford. Six blocks away, she found the source atop of one of the apartment buildings across the street from the park, a denuded human arm with the marks of dragon teeth scoring the bones.

He's hungry, she thought, *but he's not a fool. He'll find someplace to hole up for the day.* Unfortunately, she had to do the same.

Aleksi looked to the east, gauged the light, and decided to call it a night. She might be able to track Gilford and find his hiding place, but she couldn't risk being spotted by the police. At this stage of the game, twitchy cops were probably a bigger risk to her life than a rogue dragon. She headed for the nearest MBTA tunnel entrance. It was time to bed down.

Bed... The urge to bank back to the north, across the Charles, and go back to Hutch's condo welled up in her. Resisting that urge felt like cutting off her own arm, but she knew if she went there, she'd not only not get the sleep she needed, but would also be risking his life. The images of the murder scenes flashed into her mind along with the all too clear memory of fighting Penningly in Hutch's apartment. *Been there, done that. Hell, no!* Gilford tracking her to Hutch's home was not an option.

Aleksi wheeled for home. She'd call Hutch from her subway nook and find out what he knew. *And sleep,* she resolved. *You need to get some sleep if you're going to find Gilford.*

31

Got to find someplace better than a damned tree, David resolved. Not that he hadn't been perfectly comfortable hunkered in the nook of an oak the previous day. He'd slept in far worse places with people trying to kill him, but in a city of four million, he ought to be able to find an empty hotel room. The sky was getting light fast.

Skulking from rooftop to rooftop, he started looking in top-floor windows along the streets that had markets and shops on their ground floors. The housing market in Boston was insane, studio apartments going for thousands per month. Even crappy mom-and-pop walk-ups above coffee shops and bakeries were going condo. Everything was occupied.

Then a scent he'd never encountered before hit him. David froze, every nerve, every sense tingling. Dropping to a lower rooftop, he breathed deep through nose and mouth. The scent was here, strong and electrifying. It smelled familiar, like the perfume of an old girlfriend.

Visions raked through his mind: warm flesh, scales against scales, scents, tastes, carnal desire… His knees shook with it.

What in the name of... Why would a scent hit him so hard? He didn't understand.

But as he closed his eyes and steadied himself on the rooftop, the visions settled down: scales smooth against his hips, sharp teeth in his shoulder, claws raking his back, a warm release. Instinct told David what reason could not: it was the scent of another dragon, and there was only one other.

"Aleksi Rychenkna." All the pictures and footage of her that the Director had shown him came back. Now, however, recalling them with that scent in his head grabbed him by the balls. She was here somewhere. If he could find her… No, not if. *When* he found her.

David followed the scent like a bloodhound, traversing two more rooftops, then it ended. She'd taken to the air, or… The rumble of an east-bound train, the first of the morning, drew him like a magnet. *Of course! The perfect place to hide.*

The train shot into a tunnel, and David launched himself into the air after it.

Inside, in the dark, he landed and breathed deeply. Amid the stench of garbage, ozone, and a million humans, he picked out the scent he had to follow. David started along the tunnel at a jog, listening for trains, sniffing the air, watching for movement. She was here somewhere, but where? He had no choice but to follow.

The subway stations were challenging. He crept along the juncture of the platform and the railbed. Trains passed him by twice, but the roar and the light gave him plenty of warning. He hunkered down, drawing his wings up to look like a bundle of discarded canvas.

Then the scent faded.

David backtracked and found an old disused access door. The lock was rusted. It looked secure, but Aleksi's scent hung on it like an invitation. He opened it carefully and slipped inside. An old, disused station, arched brick, old wood, broken glass…

Yes, her scent was strong here. The space didn't look like it had been used for years, but the dust on the floor was scuffed away by the passage of many feet, or perhaps the same feet over and over again. He followed the spoor, turning and twisting through the labyrinth until he finally found her lair.

A blue cooler sat in one corner, and another Styrofoam one in the open. The tops were duct taped closed. An old piece of orange construction netting hung from a wall, a backpack, blankets, and a rolled sleeping bag packed inside. Not exactly what he expected for a dragon's lair, but it was secret, secure, and relatively clean.

Home sweet home. He felt a flush of admiration; she'd made the perfect retreat, a secret nook in the middle of a city where no one would find her.

David inspected everything, breathing her in, going through her things. The coolers were mostly empty save for one smoked ham and some bottled water. The pack held a computer, several phone chargers, and an extension cord. He booted the computer up, but it was password protected. He also found an outdated audio player and a pair of ear buds, several rolls of duct tape, an old coat, a sleeping bag, several hoodies, and four carefully folded garments. Unfolding one, he chuckled. The niqab would cover her from head to foot.

"Oh, you're a smart one..." David pressed his face to the fabric and drank in her scent like sweet liquor. Yes, this was unmistakably one of his kind. She had found the perfect hiding place, the perfect lair, and the perfect disguises. She'd lived here for half a year, and no one had been the wiser.

But she's been alone, he thought, refolding the cloak and putting it back. That was about to change for both of them.

David sat down on the blue cooler, folded his wings, and waited for Aleksi to come home.

Aleksi smelled him long before she arrived. He'd tracked her just like she'd tracked him. At the disused access door, she stood for a while considering what to do. Confronting him in a confined space had not been her plan. She had little doubt that he was bigger and stronger than her, and he could undoubtedly outfight her. She only had one advantage: she'd been a dragon longer than he had. Flying had taken time to perfect. Aleksi was betting her life that she could outmaneuver him.

Besides, she was curious about David Gilford. She'd read everything Buckmann had sent her about him. He'd been a dedicated soldier and government operative longer than Aleksi had been alive. She'd been a neurotic scientist plagued by social anxiety disorder; he was a veteran of war and covert operations all over the world. What motivated a man like that to kill as he had, when she could suppress her violent urges? Had her psychological abnormality somehow protected her?

The scent of him set off a hundred danger signals in her head, but she had to know what was going through his mind. He wasn't a borderline psychopath like Penningly. Maybe she could talk to him. Until now, she only had theories why he'd done what he had. To learn what made him tick, what urged him to kill men, but only injure women unless they were pregnant...she had to meet him.

Aleksi backtracked down the tunnel to an electrical access panel. There, she took off her phones and hid two of them behind the box. With the third, her old one, she called Mary Buckmann. Then she muted it and taped it to her leg, leaving the line open. Creeping back to the access door that led into her lair, she cracked the portal an inch and scented the air. Yes, he was still here. She stepped through the door, eased it closed behind her, and crept forward, ready for an ambush, scenting the stale air and listening with every step. She could hear him breathing from ahead, could smell the blood on him, the human blood.

Steeling her nerves, Aleksi stepped into the open. "Hello, David."

He sat on one of her coolers, wings folded, eyes fixed on her, nostrils dilated wide, breathing in her scent just as she breathed in his. She wondered what she smelled like to him.

"Aleksi Rychenkna." He stood, unfolding his wings, lips pulling back from his dragon teeth. "I should have known you'd smell me, but I didn't expect you to know my name."

"Buckmann told me about you." She took him in, trying to hide her awe. Broader and thicker than her by far, muscles rippled under his fine scales. He probably doubled her weight, and it was all muscle. She couldn't let him get hold of her. He also wore a strange pair of shorts that looked to be stuck to his skin. They fit like bike shorts and looked painted on. His wings, however, weren't quite fully developed, the long finger bones thin and shorter than hers.

All that weight and smaller wings... It's a wonder he can fly at all.

"Who's Buckmann?" He took a step forward, just one.

"DHS. She took over the project after you killed everyone."

"They tried to murder me, Aleksi. I had to get away. You understand how they work. They tried to kill you, too."

"Once, yes, before they knew me."

"And now you've come to clean up their fuck up?" He spread his wings, muscles writhing across his chest. "No offense, but I don't think you stand much of a chance."

"I'm not here to kill you, David." That was the truth; she was here to lure him out so somebody else could kill him.

"What then?" He took another step, still far enough away that she felt she could evade him, but too close for comfort.

"I'd like to know what motivated you to bite those women last night and to kill the two pregnant ones when you murdered the Russian."

His face hardened. "That wasn't murder. Those were orders."

And you didn't answer my question. She took another tack. "What about the two innocent men you killed last night? Those weren't ordered."

"That was survival. Guy's gotta eat, doesn't he?"

"You don't have to kill humans to feed, David. I'm proof of that."

He paused and shook his head. "No, I know. I didn't want to, you know. I'm a killer, but not… I don't know why I did it. I had to."

Aleksi recalled dreams of feeding on humans. "The dreams. You have them, don't you?"

"Yes." His lips curled back again. "Some very interesting ones, lately. While I was waiting for you, breathing in your scent, I had just a snippet that you might like to hear about." He took one more step, and Aleksi backed away.

"Just stay there. You're close enough."

"Oh, I'm not *nearly* close enough." He breathed in, and then frowned. "But you've got another scent on you. A man. A *human*." He breathed deep through nose and mouth. "Really, Aleksi? You found someone to fuck you? He must have a kink for reptiles."

He can smell Hutch on me! She took another short step back and changed the subject. "You shouldn't have let them do this to you, David. I warned them not to, but they don't listen to me."

"I had no choice." He spread his wings again. "It was either this, or die of old age and decrepitude. I've been *reborn*, Aleksi."

"I know people who can reverse it," she said. "They can cure this."

"I don't *want* a cure. I'm better now, stronger than ever."

"But you're *infectious*, David! Those women you bit last night are infected! If this breaks out into the human population, the human race will—"

"The human race is fragile and stupid. We can create a *new* race of human. *Homo draconis*, they're calling it." He grinned, and she heard a note of revelation in his voice. "*Think* of it, Aleksi! A race of us to protect them from themselves. I spent my *life* protecting them, fighting their wars, killing their enemies, and now I really can, but on my own terms!"

"By killing anyone not like yourself? That's not a very protective strategy."

"Well, some have to die so others can survive. Collateral damage." He shrugged. "One of the rules of war."

"But this isn't *war*, and you can't procreate!"

"You're sure about that?" His claws flexed out of their sheathes.

"Even if you could, you'd only make more like us! You'd spread the infection, and *everyone* will be a dragon. You have no family, no genes to protect! You won't have the drive to protect *anyone*! This evolved in a world of one ten-thousandth of the current human population, David. Small tribal societies of interrelated individuals. That's not the way the world *is* anymore."

He huffed a disgusted laugh. "Maybe that's the way it should be again."

"But it *can't* be! They'll hunt us, exterminate us, just like they did before." It made sense to her now. "They don't need us, David."

"I don't care what they do and don't need, Aleksi." He took another step forward. "I know what *I* need."

It all made sense to her now, Penningly's behavior, the danger she sensed whenever she caught the scent of a male like her but not like her, unrelated, a rival. What she was feeling made sense now: one primary male and one or more females of similar genetic relatedness to protect a breeding population of *Homo sapiens*. The female dragons kept the male from destroying the least related humans. That was why she felt protective and he didn't.

An idea blossomed in Aleksi's mind; maybe a way to persuade him.

"They're going to kill you if you don't come in, David." What was it that Persephone had told her when she was posing as Buckmann? "They don't waste assets, and you're an asset! If you agree to come in without hurting anyone, I'll...go with you."

"What?" he froze, his eyes narrowing.

"You don't have to kill anyone else to get what you want. We can be together. We're the only two of our kind, David. It'll be enough. It's either that, or they end their experiment, and both of us with it." It was a lie, of course, but a believable one. "They've been hunting me for half a year, but *I* don't kill people. You crossed the line. It's either come in, or die."

"I've got a better idea: let's you and me create our *own* race." He stepped forward, but didn't stop this time. His claws tore away the strange adhesive shorts, and she saw exactly what he had in mind.

"Oh, *hell* no!" Aleksi whirled and dashed for the exit, but he was right behind her, faster than she'd bargained for.

She had no time to look back, but could hear his claws tearing at the floor, cutting furrows in the concrete, just like hers. She smashed through the access door hard enough to bend the metal hinges, and billowed her wings to turn. Something caught her leg, a single jerk, but she was free. A howl of rage from behind drew a quick glance back. He'd hit the far wall of the tunnel, unable to bank as hard as she. He was bigger, stronger but a lot heavier, and his wings were undersized. He could fly, but she had better aerodynamics.

She was also bleeding.

One of his claws had caught her calf, but she'd torn free. The pain arrived as if on time-delay. Aleksi gritted her teeth and flew for everything she was worth.

They raced past a train parked at Arlington station, drawing a few gasps from early morning travelers on the platform. Luckily, it was Saturday. On a weekday there would have been two hundred people there. They blasted through the station before anyone got a clear look, let alone raised a cell phone, and plunged back into the dark tunnel.

Daylight loomed ahead, predawn still, but light. Another glance back confirmed that David was behind her. He could nearly match her speed in the confines of the tunnel. Once they were in the air, she'd show him some tricks.

Aleksi hit daylight and banked as hard as she could, wheeling back around toward downtown. Behind her, David turned wider, clipping a street lamp with his wingtip. She skimmed the apartment rooftops, diving and ducking into alleys, among trees, dipping low over a park, then back up, gaining a slight lead, but a glance back confirmed that he was still there. She was faster and more maneuverable, but he was stronger, and would probably outdistance her. Aleksi had just spent days in bed, and she could feel the lingering fatigue dragging at her wings. If she tired, he would catch her.

Come on, Buckmann! This is your chance!

She flew on, ducking and diving, trying to foul him with wires and poles, trees and buildings, but she couldn't lose him. She was tiring, and he was gaining. More than once, she heard a startled cry from below as someone caught sight of the two winged shapes soaring through the sultry morning sky. If someone caught them on a cell phone, there would be hell to pay.

Then she heard it, the distinctive roar of a helicopter flying low over the city, far lower than usual. Aleksi caught a glimpse of a blue and white aircraft in the gap between two buildings, the side door open, a man there with a rifle.

"Yes!" She banked up, gaining altitude to give him a shot.

"Stay down, you idiot!" Gilford growled from behind her, even closer now that she wasn't dodging and weaving.

Aleksi ignored him, flying as fast as she could for the canyons of downtown. The helicopter's engine screamed, echoing off buildings. Heading south, she banked around a tower, perilously close to the corner.

There! The helicopter broke into the open. The rifleman raised his weapon just as David soared around the corner of the building. The sniper fired, the muzzle flash bright in the dim light. The bullet buzzed past less than ten feet from Aleksi, the report hammering her ears. She glanced back, hoping beyond hope that the bullet found its mark.

David must have banked the moment he saw the helicopter. The bullet zipped past his torso, holing one wing. He barrel-rolled and turned hard, diving low beneath the helicopter's path. The sniper leaned out the door, his feet on the skid, the strap to his harness keeping him from falling. Another shot echoed off the buildings, but David didn't fall.

Instead, he banked up right under the helicopter.

"Oh God, no!" Helpless to affect the outcome, Aleksi wheeled to watch.

David struck the underside of the aircraft hard, claws piercing the aluminum skin like paper. The sniper turned, trying to aim his weapon beneath the helicopter's belly, but the strap attached to his harness was too short. David's hand lashed out and took the man's leg off at the knee.

Even over the rotors, Aleksi heard the scream. The sniper fell, slamming against the side of the aircraft, blood spraying the blue and white paint into a caricature of red-white-and-blue. He lost his grip on his rifle, but it, too, was tethered. As David scrabbled up and into the side door, the man pulled a pistol from his chest, but even as he took aim, the dragon slashed once again, taking the hand and the pistol away.

Then David simply grabbed the man, jerked him free of his tether, and flung him up into the helicopter's rotors. Flesh, bone, Kevlar, and all the man's gear didn't react well with the spinning blades. Pieces flew in an arc from the impact, and one of the aircraft's rotors snapped, spinning away like a deadly boomerang to impale the glass side of a building.

The helicopter spun madly as the pilot tried to save their lives, but David wasn't through. Aleksi caught a glimpse of the front windscreen as the aircraft spun around to face her. Blood and gobbets of meat spattered the glass as the dragon ripped the flight crew to pieces.

The aircraft rolled and plummeted nose first, but wings billowed from the door before impact. David pulled out of his plunge fifty feet from the pavement, and Aleksi lost sight of him. The explosion rocked downtown Boston, shattering windows and sending the few Saturday morning pedestrians scrambling for cover.

"Well, shit! *That* didn't work so well, did it?" Aleksi soared through the steel and concrete canyons, looking for a place to hide. A catholic church caught her eye. She snagged the spire and ducked into the shadows of the bell tower. She hunkered and checked the tear in her calf. It hurt like hell, but wasn't deep. The bleeding had stopped already.

Pulling the phone from her leg, she saw that the call had ended. Buckmann knew her team had failed, and didn't want to hear recriminations from Aleksi. *Well, fine. Two can play that game.* She turned off the phone, found a comfortable nook, and settled in. Somewhere, she knew, David was doing the same.

He knows what I did, Aleksi realized. *I won't get that chance again.*

She wrapped her wings around herself like a blanket and tried to think through the haze of fading adrenaline. Buckmann had made good on her word, or at least tried to, but she'd failed. Now it was up to Aleksi, but she knew she didn't stand a chance in a fight with David Gilford. What she had proven she *could* do was outfly him. But how could she use that to kill him?

"Sleep on it, Aleksi. You can't think exhausted. Sleep and let your brain unpack this." She closed her eyes, and the airborne chase played back through her mind in slow motion.

Then another memory arose like a harbinger of death: *He smelled Hutch on me.* If David Gilford found out where Hutch lived, the man she loved would die.

32

Hutch sat staring at the television, forgotten breakfast shake in one hand, his mouth hanging open. He was supposed to be out running with Julie, but she was late, so he'd turned on the news. Usually, he avoided news on weekends, but with a rogue government dragon on the loose and Aleksi out trying to find him, he thought he might find out if something had happened in the night.

Something had. In fact, all hell seemed to have broken loose.

The news networks couldn't get out of each other's way reporting two gristly murders and a helicopter crash in Downtown Boston. The crash was so far being called a massive mechanical failure, and the rotor blade sticking out of the side of a building corroborated that theory. FAA, Homeland Security, and the police had cordoned off a two-block radius around the crash site. News jockeys were trying to make terrorist connections, but so far it was just conjecture. They'd made no connection to Aleksi either, which was good. He'd tried her phone but got no answer.

Earlier, she'd confirmed that the two murders had been the rogue dragon. Eviscerations, dismemberment, and pieces of anatomy missing had brought every conspiracy nut out of the woods. Derrick Penningly's name was bandied about along with theories of cannibalistic cults and even an outbreak of rabies. That oddity had gotten traction when an unnamed source told a reporter that a CDC ambulance had taken away two women injured during the second attack. The theory had gotten even more support from an ER nurse at Mass General who said an injured bystander of the first murder had been swept out of the hospital by government officers with no explanation whatsoever. Both sounded like Buckmann cleaning up her mess. Hutch wasn't about to call her to find out.

Flipping through channels for more information, he found a local station running a seemingly unrelated story of a pair of hang gliders flying over the city. At the blurry cell phone video of two shapes wheeling through the air, Hutch sat down hard and put his breakfast shake on the coffee table before he dropped it. The video was horrible, but he knew it was Aleksi. She'd found the rogue dragon.

When his phone rang, he was off the couch in a flash, the TV forgotten. He snatched it off the counter, but instead of Aleksi, or Buckmann, or even Tony Jasper, the screen displayed a picture of Julie in her *Ozwitch* makeup.

"What the…" They were supposed to have gone running a half an hour ago, and he'd completely forgotten. He muted the TV, tried to calm himself, and took the call. "Hey! Did you sleep late?"

"Hey, Hutch. Not really. I'm going to have to take a raincheck this morning. Sorry, but something really big came up last night, and…" She sounded almost hysterical, prattling without a breath. She took one now, and dropped the bombshell. "Well, I'm catching a train to New York in twenty minutes."

"New York, like *Manhattan*?" His mind raced and came up blank. "What happened?"

"So, you remember that producer guy, Vanderwile, at the cast party the other night?"

"Yeah."

"Well, they want to produce *Up and Down*. *My* play. On *Broadway*! With *me* in it!" Her voice rose an octave with every clipped sentence.

"Like, *on* Broadway, not off Broadway?"

"On… Fucking… *Broadway*!" She laughed hysterically. "Can you *believe* it? I'll be getting double credits as writer and the lead role!"

"Julie, that's amazing!" His mind spun. This was unheard-of. He didn't know much about the New York theatre industry, but he did know that new talent had to pay their dues. For a writer to star in her own play for her Broadway debut, without any previous credits other than school-related productions, just didn't happen.

"It's un-be-fucking-lievable!" Julie screeched.

"Congratulations! You *so* deserve this!" He didn't know what else to say. It was a huge break for her, but, quite frankly, he had so much more on his mind at the moment that he felt a little guilty for not being more elated.

"Thanks. Yeah, so, like, train in twenty minutes. I've got to take some time off from school, but…I can't pass this up." She was still breathless.

"Of *course,* you can't pass this up. Breaks like this don't just fall from trees. You can get an extension, and it's only summer term."

"Yeah, I may even transfer to NYU. I don't know yet. The schedule's still up in the air. Hell, *I'm* still up in the air! I haven't slept, and I've got to get to the train, and…" She hesitated. "And I had to call you to say good-bye. I don't know when we'll see each other again, Hutch. I feel like shit for leaving like this, but I can't pass it up."

"Of course, you can't! Don't feel guilty for going after this, Julie! Don't you *dare*! This is what you've worked your whole life for!"

"I know, but…I'll miss you, Hutch. We had something going, and…" She choked up.

"Hey, don't. You're exhausted and wired, Jules. Catch the train. Call me from New York. I'll come down to watch the play, and we'll paint the town. We're *friends*. We always will be." *And I don't love you,* he didn't say.

"Friends." She sniffed. "Yeah, but, I…"

She sounded strange. "Julie. It's okay. Catch the train."

"Yeah. The train." She sniffed again. "Look, I'm sorry, Hutch, okay?"

"Don't be. You've got to take this opportunity. Go."

"Yeah. Okay. Bye, Hutch."

"Break a leg, Jules."

She laughed, and said, "Thanks."

The call went dead. Hutch stared at the phone for a minute, wondering about Julie. Why she would be so broken up about leaving for an opportunity like this didn't make sense. She knew what their relationship was, had known it from the start. Why would she apologize for grasping the chance of her life?

The TV flashed up another video of the helicopter crash scene, and his thoughts returned to Aleksi. Then he looked back at the phone in his hand and remembered all of Julie's questions about her. Could that have been why Julie was apologizing? Something to do with Aleksi?

Impossible… But in a world where dragons battled in the skies over Boston, nothing was really impossible anymore.

Mary Buckmann paced the control center, watching four monitors at the same time and talking to a senior FAA official on the phone. She'd been running damage control all morning, and they had a handle on every leak. The FAA, however, was being a pain in her ass.

"This was a DHS operation, sir, and quite frankly, you're not cleared to know the details."

"Not *cleared*? That's bullshit, Doctor! You crash a helicopter in the middle of a city, it's *my* business! We will investigate this! You don't have the authority to stop us!"

"I may not, but in matters of national security, we hold all the cards. If I take this up the chain of command, you'll lose."

"Matters of national security! That's *always* your bail-out line when you people screw up and risk the lives of innocent civilians!"

"We're protecting innocent civilians, sir, *millions* of them! This operation cost the lives of three of our best people. They were doing their job on *my* orders! I take full responsibility. Now pull your investigation team out of the crash site, or I'll have your fucking job roasting on a spit!" Mary ended the call before he could respond and cursed herself for losing her temper. She didn't have time to get angry.

Turning back to the monitors, she ran through another risk assessment in her head. The murder investigations were under control, but they had no lead on the missing women. Loretta Watkins was under sedation and running a high fever. Price was monitoring her constantly. Mary had ordered her kept under sedation for now, restrained, and tended by only female staff. She'd also had her moved to another facility, one that David didn't know about. If he could track down Aleksi in a city of four million people, he might come after his other victims. They couldn't afford to fuck this up before they'd even cleaned up their last fuck up.

Mary focused on the video leak, the only thing still pending that she had any control over. Tapping the IT supervisor on the shoulder, she asked, "Progress?"

"Yes. We're in the guy's phone, and the video's been sanitized. The news station now has an altered copy. We got lucky there. They tried to enhance the images, but we caught it and enhanced it for them. They now have video of two hang gliders doing stunts." He looked over his shoulder and cocked an eyebrow. "You going to spin this as the cause of the chopper crash?"

"That's the plan. Send the doctored video to me. We can leak it to a major network with eyewitness reports."

"Yes, ma'am." His fingers flew over his keyboard. "It's in your folder."

"Thanks." Mary turned to another analyst. "Any hits on that CDC ambulance?"

"Nothing good." She pulled up a split screen on her monitor. "Exactly two frames from a convenience store security cam. Blurry and side on, so no plate. Can't see the driver through the glare on the window. We're working on make, model, color, tires, paint, and the modifications."

Mary clenched her hands behind her back. "But there are thousands of vehicles like that, and the mods could have been done anywhere, right?"

"Yes, ma'am."

"And there's no other video of this vehicle at all?" That seemed impossible in a city like Boston. There were cameras everywhere.

"Not anymore, ma'am. Whoever did the scrub is really top notch. They're freaking everywhere, and they leave *zero* tracks." The tech sounded more awed than angry.

"Any indication that they're in our system?" Mary asked.

"None yet, ma'am, but like I said, they don't leave tracks."

"Run a database analysis of current files compared to the last encrypted backup. If we spot differences, we'll know they were in our system."

That was a monumental task, but the specialist just nodded. "Yes, ma'am."

"Thanks." She turned to yet another desk. "How's the subway story?"

"Squashed." The guy flashed her a smile. "Two drunks and a stripper. A little money, a little pressure, and they're gone."

"Excellent." That was the best news she'd had all day. "We need a team in that tunnel posing as a routine MBTA inspection. That could be where Aleksi's been hiding."

"We're on it."

"Good." Mary tried to think of anything she could have missed but came up empty. She checked her phone for the hundredth time since the crash, but still had no call from Aleksi or Hutchinson. They'd both gone dark. She called Aleksi's number and got an out of service reply. She'd already left a message.

Come on, Aleksi, turn on your phone. She pocketed hers and resumed pacing. They were running damage control, responding instead of planning, reacting instead of being proactive, but right now they had no idea where Gilford or Aleksi were hiding.

Come nightfall, she thought, *that's going to change.*

How are they?" Persephone asked as she entered the treatment room.

"Remarkably well, all things considered." Reggie rubbed his eyes and sat down on a swivel chair. "Sedated, running fevers, but the infection titer is low. We caught it early."

"Good. Any signs of DNA damage?"

"None that I can see, but I don't have baselines. The cascade hadn't really started yet. The fevers are in response to my viruses as much as the RNA infection. They'll have some weird proteins, maybe a few gene switches in time, but we'll see those if they crop up and do some clipping. They should be okay in that regard." Reggie shrugged. "We'll know more in a couple of days, but they should wake up none the worse for wear."

"Good." Persephone stepped up to the two hospital beds and looked over the women, both young and healthy, breathing fast, sweating profusely, eyes closed but moving around under their lids. She wondered what they were dreaming about. "And their injuries?"

"Superficial and healing *really* fast! There's something about the *draconis* RNA that triggers localized tissue regeneration at inoculation. Gi-gi's analyzing it."

"Gi-gi's analyzing *everything*. She also refuses to sleep, and absolutely will *not* give the cure to the feds. I'm worried about her."

"We've got a lot of things up in the air."

"True." *Including two dragons...*

"Any word from Aleksi?"

"None, but that helicopter crash this morning *has* to be connected to this. She's out of her league going after this guy."

"Don't sell her short. She's been a dragon a lot longer than he has."

"Yes, and he's a trained assassin."

"But he's not going to try to kill her, Seph. He *can't*. She's the only person in the *world* like him. He wants a mate to start a lineage."

"That's what's got me worried." She turned to face him. "What if he succeeds?"

"Then, we've got a much bigger problem." He rubbed his eyes again. "Did you get any sleep?"

"Maybe an hour. I'll get some this afternoon." She started for the door. "You should, too. We're on call all night."

"What's our cover this time?"

"Regular EMS service. We get to the scene first, scoop up anyone injured, and vanish."

"If there *is* a scene. You think this guy will hit again?"

"Yes." Persephone opened the door and looked back at Reggie. "Unless he finds Aleksi first."

"Or she finds him, you mean."

"Yes, or that." She didn't know which she dreaded more, another murder or another battle between dragons in the skies over Boston.

33

With the fall of night, David stirred from his hiding place beneath the I-93 bridge. The roar of traffic overhead and the pain of his injury had kept him awake through most of the day. He wondered how Aleksi slept in a subway station with trains passing by every ten minutes. *Well, you can get used to anything in time,* he supposed.

Right now, David was still getting used to being a dragon.

The things Aleksi told him had haunted his troubled sleep. For a man who spent his entire life in control, dealing with trauma, violence, war, killing sometimes innocent people to further the greater good, he found his current inability to control his urges more disturbing than the urges themselves.

You don't have to kill people to feed. I'm proof of that. You crossed the line...

David had read every scrap of information they'd had on Aleksi Rychenkna, and recalling all of that now left him scratching his head. How could a neurotic scientist with social anxiety disorder deal with the violent urges he was feeling? How could she resist them, when he, a hardened soldier with a lifetime of dealing with violence, couldn't? It was like she understood herself better than he did, not her human self, but the dragon, the dreams, the violent yearnings, the impulses. Maybe they made sense to her from a scientific perspective. To him, they were just violent impulses without any underlying reason or purpose. When the human

David had violent urges, they'd been in response to real-time or post-traumatic threats or stresses, and he dealt with them. Now he was dealing with a thousand lifetimes of violent impulses that he could do nothing with. They weren't his. He didn't want them, but couldn't delete or ignore them.

And to top it all off, the very government he'd devoted his life to was hunting him, intent on erasing their mistake. David fingered the wound along his ribs, the track of the bullet that had almost ended him. Two inches left, and it would have fractured bone, pierced the lung, and sent him plummeting to the street. Instead, he had sent the assassins plummeting. But Aleksi was right, he couldn't fight them all. He knew their capabilities, their weapons, their tenacity. Dragons had been eradicated by humans with lesser technology, poorer weapons, and no modern communications. They had been exterminated by the sheer will of mankind because they weren't needed or wanted any longer. In the end, he had little doubt that humans would exterminate David Gilford, but that was an eventuality every soldier learned to deal with.

But not before I find Aleksi.

David released his grip on the pitted steel girders and unfolded his wings. The laceration across his ribs tugged, but pain meant nothing. Pain was his oldest friend. It meant you were still alive.

He wheeled west, downwind now with the evening sea breeze, and began a careful, low-level search pattern. Not a visual search, though he did watch the humans as he soared just above the street lights, but an olfactory one. He breathed in the night air, testing it, tasting it, analyzing it for the one scent he could pick out from the millions of others.

Aleksi... Where are you?

The memory of her scent surged through his brain like a drug, but he wanted more than to make her his mate; he wanted what she knew. She understood what it was to be a dragon. Maybe she could teach him how to resist the impulses. If only he could talk to her without losing his mind this time.

There! The alarm went off in his brain, and he wheeled into the wind. He lost it, but as he banked back across his path, he caught it again. *Aleksi!*

Like a shark following a blood trail in a current of water, David banked back and forth upwind, zeroing in on the scent trail. It was getting stronger, cleaner, fresher each beat of his wings. He fought to keep his mind clear, his thoughts human, but the dragon inside him battled his every effort.

Then, when he wheeled around a church steeple, the scent vanished. Banking back and forth, he still couldn't regain the trail. *The church!* David turned hard and swooped around the belfry tower. A flicker of movement in the shadows within caught his eye, and her scent hammered into his brain on the downwind side. He'd intended to approach from downwind, invisible to her senses, but he'd blown that attempt.

Circling closer, he tried the direct approach. "Aleksi! Don't fly away. I want to talk to you."

More movement, her golden eyes reflecting the lights of the city, tracking him.

"Can you talk without your dick getting in the way this time?"

She sounded pissed off, and she had every right to be.

"I'll try. Let me land."

"I can't stop you, but you only get one chance."

He banked to the upwind side and landed in the narrow aperture, crouching on the sill like an overgrown pigeon. Her scent was weaker here. He could think. "I'm sorry about before. I'm…not used to these impulses. I lost control."

She moved into view from behind the bell, tense, ready. "You need to work on that."

"I do." He looked her over, slimmer than he, sinuous, fragile, beautiful. "I'm sorry for hurting you. I didn't mean to. Your scent…the dragon took over."

"*You're* the dragon, David," she said. "You have to own it."

"*Own* it?" He gritted his teeth. "How do I do that? How do *you* do it?"

"I accept what I am, but remember what I was. It's probably harder for you. You were a soldier before."

"I'm *still* a soldier."

"Okay, then *be* one. Follow orders. Do your job. Answer to your commander and do what they say."

"They'll kill me."

"They'll kill you if you *don't*, and probably me, too." She pulled something from her leg, and he tensed, wary of a weapon, but it was a phone. "You can call Buckmann on this. Talk to her. Convince her that you'll follow orders. Or, you can come with me and meet the people who have helped me. They can reverse this. They're going to make me human again."

"*Human* again?" He coughed out a laugh. "Old, weak, infirm… Those aren't very attractive options."

"Life's *full* of shitty options," she replied scathingly. "I was a scientist. I was in love. I had a fucking *life*!"

"Okay, you look at this thing as a loss of your life. I did it to *regain* mine. My life was over, Aleksi." David clenched his hands into fists, his claws piercing his palms, the pain clearing his mind like a slap in the face. "I can't get back what I was, and if I go back, they'll kill me."

"Then I can't help you." She took a short step back, slapping the phone back to her thigh.

"You *could* help me, Aleksi. You've lived out here among them without becoming a monster. Show me how! Teach me!"

"I can't. Men react differently to the changes than women do. They become...dangerous. A million years of evolution is screaming at you to kill every rival male you can get your claws into and slaughter any female carrying the child of someone not related to you. I can't teach you how to fight that."

"But if we were together, I'd *have* someone! *Be* with me!" He stepped down from the sill, the movement involuntary. "You could make me sane, Aleksi!"

She stepped back to the aperture opposite his, her eyes flicking down, then up. "You're thinking with your dick again, and I'm not about to fuck the crazy out of you."

David glanced down and cursed his body under his breath. "Aleksi, please. I don't want to hurt you, but I can't hold back the dragon!"

"'I couldn't control myself' is the argument of every rapist who ever abused a woman, David. Try harder!"

"I *can't* try any harder!" He clenched his fists tighter, his palms slick with blood.

"Then I can't help you." Aleksi twisted and dove out the narrow window.

"Wait!" He lunged after her, clipping the window frame hard with his wings. Her scent slammed into him again, stoking the furnace in his gut. He couldn't stop, couldn't hold the dragon back any longer.

Own it, he thought, wheeling after her, diving into the darkness, hot on her scent. *I'll own it, all right! I'll show you what a dragon really is!*

For a fleeting moment, Aleksi had thought David might be able to control his impulses. He was at least trying. When he stepped down from the window, she realized that he might be trying, but he would fail. Danger wafted off of him in waves. The dragon in him was too strong, or maybe it was the lifetime as a soldier, a killer. The HD transformation had hit him like throwing gasoline on a smoldering fire.

Diving from the window, she caught a glimpse of the clocktower. Eleven fifteen. The timing would work, but she'd have to stall for a few minutes. She'd left her phone off. To hell with Buckmann; she'd do this her way. Her only advantage was that she could still outfly David. She'd had a good day's sleep, and he was wounded. She'd smelled his blood, and his flying was even more erratic than last night.

One chance, Aleksi. Make it count!

She dove for the street, folding her wings for speed, then pulled out just above the streetlights. The city was busy. Like most Saturday nights, rivers of people crowded the sidewalks. They didn't look up, of course. *Bad evolutionary gap there, not looking for predators from above.*

A glance back confirmed that he was right behind her. *Good.* She needed him there. She dodged and ducked into an alley, then up and skimmed the rooftops. Another glance back. David hadn't handled the maneuver as well and had fallen back a few yards. That gave her hope, but she had to keep him close. That meant slowing down, but he was smart. She had to convince him that she was trying her best to evade him.

She dove into another alley, then, blasting out onto a wider street, turned hard and struck a support cable for an awning with her wingtip. The impact shook her, but didn't break the bone. She'd been ready for it, and bent her wingtip back like pulling a punch. Now she had to convince David that she was hurt.

She wobbled and dipped, favoring her left wing, wiggling her longest finger. A glance over her shoulder, and David was only yards behind her, lips peeled back from his teeth, nostrils wide. His eyes burned like beacons, flashing with reflected light, pupils wide.

Come on! She mentally urged him. *Catch me!*

A glance at a bank's clock told her it was time. Veering onto Gainesboro street, she wobbled and swerved erratically. She could hear him behind her now, close, lungs pumping like a bellows, gulping in her scent. At the corner of Huntington street, she wheeled to the east, banked up into a roll, and dove for the subway tunnel entrance. The light from within told her she was right on time.

Swooping into the tunnel, she squinted into the lights of the oncoming train.

Aleksi banked up and rolled, flattened her wings, and dipped one wingtip to spin like a frisbee. Her claws raked the tunnel ceiling, chips of concrete raining down as she pressed herself flat. The train blasted past inches beneath her, the wind of its passage buffeting her, trying to tear her free, but she clung for dear life. She heard a cry of terror, and looked up.

David tried to mimic her maneuver, but instead of grasping the ceiling, he'd bounced off. He hit the roof of the train and tumbled, wings flailing, claws lashing out, trying to grasp something, anything. Bones snapped, wing membranes tore, a leg bent the wrong way.

Aleksi cringed and closed her eyes until the train had passed.

When it was gone, she dropped to the tunnel floor and looked at what she had done.

David lay in a crumpled heap between the rails, broken, battered, but still breathing. She approached carefully.

A broken arm moved, a feral growl of agony escaping his throat. He pushed himself up and turned his head to look at her with one piercing yellow eye. The other was gone, the orbit smashed to ruin.

"I'm sorry," she said.

He coughed a laugh and spat blood. "Nice move."

"I wish I could have saved you, David. This wasn't your fault. HD changes men into monsters. Derrick Penningly wasn't crazy, he was just doing what came naturally."

"I wish…" He coughed again, thrusting himself up on his elbows. "I wish you didn't have to be the one to kill me, Aleksi. I should have died last night, in combat, like a soldier."

"Maybe, but nobody made anything happen by wishing for it." Aleksi stepped forward, unsheathing her claws.

"Wait! One last question. Please." He thrust himself up to his knees and elbows. A bone in his thigh was broken, the splintered end showing through torn meat.

"Ask."

"Who is he? The man you were with?"

Suspicion and protective instinct surged up in her. "Why do you want to know?"

"Because you should keep him. Anyone willing to love someone…like us… He's…special."

"Yes, he is. His name is Dwayne. We were together before. Once."

He nodded and coughed again. "Good." He looked around, then back to her. "I can't let you do it, Aleksi."

"You can't stop me."

"Yes, I can." He lunged, but not at her.

"David!" Aleksi reached for him, but he had been right. He could stop her from having to kill him.

David Gilford landed right on the third rail. Electricity arced through him, convulsing his broken limbs, blackening his golden scales. Flesh caught fire, sputtering and popping, charring on the bone.

Aleksi stared on in horror until it was over, forcing herself to watch. When he stopped twitching, and the fire finally subsided, she pulled her phone and turned it on, walking past the smoldering corpse to the entrance of the tunnel where she could get a signal. When it came up, she punched Buckmann's contact. It only rang once before she answered.

"Aleksi!"

"It's done. David's dead."

"Where?

"Find this phone, and you'll find him. You should hurry. You've got fifteen minutes before the next train."

"Train? Oh. Okay, I understand. We'll take care of him, Aleksi."

"You should. He's one of yours." She started to put the phone down, then, on impulse gave Buckmann one more piece of her mind. "I know you've got one of David's victims, Mary. There are people who can cure this infection, maybe even reverse the changes. Give her up. Check her into a hospital where they can find her. No more dragons. Please."

"We can't do that, Aleksi. It's out of my hands."

"Then may God have mercy on you, Mary, because I won't. If you continue trying to make this into some kind of weapon, the human race will end as we know it. I can't let you do that." Aleksi didn't bother to listen to the woman's answer. She dropped the phone and took to the air. She had a promise to keep.

34

Hutch bolted up from a dead sleep as the sliding glass door to his balcony opened. Iggy's claws dug in as he leapt from Hutch's chest to the floor and scrambled away. He'd fallen asleep with the iguana on his chest.

The door slid closed, and a shadow moved into the corner, a pair of golden eyes reflecting the dim light.

"Aleksi?" He thumbed the drape remote and stumbled up. "Is that you?" Of course, if it wasn't, he'd be dead in seconds. There was, after all, another dragon on the loose.

"Yes. Sorry I startled Iggy." She stood, and he reached for the lamp.

Beautiful golden scales reflected the light, but she was scratched all down her chest and legs, her claws filthy, and there was blood on her leg. "You're hurt!"

"It's not bad. I'll live."

"And the other…"

"His name was David. He's dead." The remorse in her voice staggered him. "There was no other way."

"God, I'm sorry, Aleksi." He took her in his arms, holding her tight. "You shouldn't have had to kill him."

"I didn't, actually. In the end he killed himself." She drew a deep rattling breath and folded her wings around him. "He didn't want me to have to do it, Hutch. I think he was a good man once, a good soldier. The changes made him into a monster, just like they did Penningly."

"Well, it's over." He squeezed her tight. "I have a steak in the fridge and a bottle of red wine, if you're interested."

"That sounds good, but I need a shower first." She released him, and he saw the tears streaking her cheeks.

"Then come with me." Hutch took her clawed hand in his and pulled her toward the bathroom. "I'll wash your back."

"Thanks."

She went with him, and he made good on his promise, gently scrubbing away the grime and blood. The wound on her leg was shallow and scabbed over, so he just rinsed it. Then he held her in the warm spray and let her cry into his shoulder until the tears ran out.

"Do you think I'll ever be human again, Hutch? I feel like I want too much."

He couldn't lie to her. "I don't know, Aleksi. I only know that I'll love you whether it works or not." He released her and kissed her. "If it does work, will you come back to Harvard?"

"I don't know. So much has happened. You've got a full crop of students, and no research project for me."

"Well, the university would probably have issues with a graduate student and her advisor in a relationship anyway. I'm sure you could find someone to take you on." He smiled and chuckled. "Maybe Dr. Oliver."

"Ha. Funny, but not really." She ran clawed fingers through his hair, her dragon eyes searching his face "I just don't know if I'll ever be what I was before. It scares me, Hutch."

"Aleksi." He kissed her again. "You'll always have a home here, no matter what happens."

"Good, because I can't go back to my other one. Buckmann knows where it is now."

"Oh?" Hutch stroked her cheek and trailed his fingers down her neck. "So, you're asking if you can move in with me?" He caressed the shallow rise of her breast, teasing the sensitive circle of scales there. "I'll have to ask Iggy. He's pretty territorial."

She shuddered and closed her eyes. "You're driving me crazy, you know."

"No, I'm not. Not yet." Running his fingertips down her flat stomach, he explored the smooth scales where her legs joined. "But I could, if you want me to."

She leaned back against the tile and closed her eyes. "David was right."

"David?" Hutch paused, uncertain. "About what."

"You're special." Aleksi opened her eyes and reached for him. "You're mine, Dwayne Hutchinson, and I intend to keep you."

With a call from Dr. Hutchinson assuring them that the threat of the rogue dragon had been put to an end, Tony Jasper and Marty Willis had gone back to investigating mundane murders. Unfortunately, there was no shortage of work to do. They were reviewing an unending pile of crime scene evidence and constructing a murder board on their latest case, a serial killer preying on social security recipients, when Jasper received a most curious text.

It simply read, "Twin Oaks Hotel, room 302. Missing persons."

"What the hell?" He showed Willis the text. "You know anyone looking for missing persons?"

"Aren't we?" Willis pointed to the picture of a seventy-four-year-old woman who was still missing, the suspected victim of their latest psychopath.

"True." Jasper looked at his phone, but there was no return number. "The sender blocked their number." He shrugged and looked to his partner. "Wanna go for a drive?"

"Sure. This is depressing, and I could use a real coffee."

"I'll buy, but no donuts. Those things are killing me."

"Killjoy."

"Yeah, I take no pleasure in life at all."

Willis drove them through Starbucks, and Jasper directed him to the Twin Oaks Hotel. It was a nice place near MIT, catering to visiting faculty and the families of students. The manager was more than cooperative, but insisted that nobody had rented out room 302.

She opened the door with her pass card and caught her breath. "Oh, my God!"

Tony stepped past her into the room, pulling his weapon, but he knew instantly that he wouldn't need it. "Call an ambulance, Marty."

"On it."

Tony stepped carefully forward, checking the closet and bathroom in passing, cautious to avoid stepping on any evidence. The main room sported two beds, and each one was occupied by a woman. They lay atop the covers, clad in running gear, including shoes. They were breathing, and looked healthy, but didn't respond when he announced himself or even when he checked their pulses.

"Ten minutes, Tony." Marty joined him, peering at the two women. "You recognize them?"

"Nope." He holstered his Glock and checked their pupils with a penlight. "Drugged." One wore a fanny pack. "I'm going to check for ID."

"Okay." Marty checked over the other woman as Tony unzipped the pouch. "Hey, this one's got a needle mark in her arm. An IV."

Tony checked, and nodded. "This one, too." He found a driver's license in the pack, along with forty dollars, a bottle of perfume, a Chapstick, a small pack of panty liners, and several folded tissues. "Roberta Stewart. Why does that ring a bell?"

"Wait! That's it!" Marty snapped his fingers. "I *do* recognize them! The two injured bystanders from the second murder! The ones the CDC took away!"

"But they were injured." Tony inspected Roberta Stewart's shoulder, then her leg. He couldn't remember which one had had which injury. Below the line of her shorts, he found a faint scar, a circular ring of healed tissue. "Jesus, Marty, this is fully healed! It's only been a week."

"Not even." Marty checked the other woman's shoulder. "Yep, this must be Sally McMaster. She's got scars here."

"Well, son-of-a-bitch!" He pulled out his phone and called up Detective Blake's number. It rang four times before she answered.

"I'm in no mood, Jasper. This better be important."

"I'm the bearer of *good* tidings this time. We found Roberta Stewart and Sally McMaster in a hotel in Cambridge."

"What? How? That's not your case!"

"So, jump down my throat for getting an anonymous tip, for Christ sake! How about a little gratitude!"

"Sorry. I'm up to my ass in alligators right now. Tell me they're alive."

"Alive and drugged. They look perfectly healthy. We've called EMS and will take them to Cambridge Hospital. I'll give you a call when they wake up. Looks like you'll have to take Wilks off the desk job."

"Looks like. Thanks, Tony. I owe you a beer."

Tony? She's never once called me Tony. "I'll collect on that." He thought about it for only a second. "How about tonight?"

"Um...yeah. Okay. About eleven? I'm swamped."

"Great. I'll meet you downtown, save you the drive."

"O'Brien's then. See you there."

"See you there." He hung up and caught Willis starting at him with a furrowed brow. "What?"

"Blake? *Really*?"

"Hey, be nice. I like her. She's a no bullshit kind of woman."

"And you're *all* bullshit, so…"

"So, we ought to balance each other out nicely."

"Suit yourself." He waved a hand at the occupied beds. "I'm actually disappointed that you didn't recognize these two at the first glance. You're seriously slipping."

Tony snorted a disgusted laugh. "I was looking at a dismembered corpse at the time, Marty. I barely glanced at them."

"But recognizing healthy young women in skimpy outfits is usually your forte."

Jasper glared at him. "Don't be sexist."

"Hey, just stating facts. I recognize men's asses, Charles can spot a Pierre Cardin a block away, and you notice young healthy women. It's just the way the world is. But if you're losing your edge, maybe you *should* take the lieutenant's exam and start driving a desk."

"Fuck you, Marty. I like my job." And he realized that despite the shitty hours, bad food, cold coffee, and dealing with death on a daily basis, he did.

"Good. I like my job, too." Willis gave him an evil grin. "Now if I could just find a decent partner."

Mary Buckmann sat at her desk reading reports. It seemed that was all she did anymore, read what others had done. She was in full charge of the *Homo draconis* project now, not just cleaning up the previous Director's mess. There was a new Director, of course, but Mary had full autonomy on this project. She'd expected to feel better about it, but there were still too many unanswered questions.

One of the more troubling reports was the one from the Boston Police detective in charge of the murder investigations. They'd found the two women Gilford had bitten alive and well in a hotel near MIT. Blood tests confirmed that they had no HD infections. That left only two possibilities: they either hadn't been infected in the first place, which wasn't likely, or there really was someone out there who could cure this thing. The women were recovering with no ill effects. Mary was betting that Aleksi had told her the truth. She was also betting these were the same people who had impersonated her.

"Who the hell are you?" she wondered, reviewing the assessment of her genetics team's analysis. They'd hypothesized methods of neutralizing the infectious RNA, but hadn't had any luck in any of their animal trials. Mary wasn't about to risk trying something untested on Loretta Watkins. She also wasn't going to give her up to some unknown terrorist group.

With that thought, she pulled up Dr. Price's latest report. Loretta's fever had broken two days ago, and they were easing off the sedation. They had a full dossier on the new subject. Lori had no family in the area and had moved to Boston from the west coast after a falling out with her parents. She was a part-time student at Boston College studying hotel and restaurant management, worked as an assistant manager at a sports bar, and had lived with her boyfriend, Charlie Fenwick, who was killed by Gilford. With few other friends, she had no one missing her, no one inquiring as to her whereabouts, and the police had been told to drop the investigation. Homeland Security had paid off her credit cards, her student debt, and removed her personal effects from Fenwick's apartment.

Loretta Watkins had vanished from the face of the Earth.

"Maybe this time we can do it right." If HD created monsters out of men, but Aleksi was still psychologically stable after so many months, a female candidate seemed more likely to succeed.

She looked at the list of medications Price had prescribed, a reduction of the dosage of Versed, followed by benzodiazepines to keep her anxiety under control. By all reports, she'd been hysterical at the murder scene, but she'd watched Gilford murder her boyfriend, so that was understandable. She showed no signs of previous psychological instability, so she should recover in time.

The only other issue on her plate was Aleksi Rychenkna, and her warning. *Then may God have mercy on you, Mary, because I won't. If you continue trying to make this into some kind of weapon, the human race will end as we know it. I can't let you do that.*

Her team had found her hiding place in the disused subway station. They'd recovered a computer, an audio player, clothes, food, and a few other items. The computer yielded little of any use. A lot of paleontological research, an unremarkable browser history, and a few emails that were months old. Where Aleksi was now remained a mystery.

Once again, Mary was betting that the same people who had abducted and impersonated her now had Aleksi. They had promised her a cure, and for all she knew, they might be able to deliver.

If it works, she thought, pursing her lips, *her threat will be impotent. There will be only one dragon in Boston.*

On a whim, she pulled up the real-time CCTV monitor in Lori Watkins's room. She lay in an inclined hospital bed, soft restraints on her wrists and ankles, an IV in her arm. She was awake, but listless. A female attendant in full protective gear stood beside the bed spoon feeding her something from a blue plastic bowl, wiping her chin between bites. Lori shook her head and turned away from the spoon. She said something to the attendant, but Mary had the volume turned down. She'd read the transcript later. The attendant took the food away and left the room.

Lori tried to lift her hand to her face, but the restraints stopped her. She turned her head toward the camera, and Mary saw that she was crying. Her lips were moving, so Mary turned up the audio.

"I don't want to sleep. Don't make me sleep. Please. I don't want to see it again..."

The dreams, Mary thought. *They've started.* She opened a message window and typed in an order for Price to increase the anxiolytic dosage and consult with a psychiatrist.

The last thing they needed was another nutcase dragon on their hands.

EPILOGUE

Aleksi landed by the back door of Persephone's mansion and waved to the camera. She tapped in her code and said, "It's me. I'm home." The light flashed green, and the door clicked.

She opened it and stepped into the garage. The lights were off, but she didn't need them. *Home,* she thought as she strode past the two SUV's, the Mercedes, and the Jag. *Is that really what this is? My new home?*

She'd spent almost a week with Hutch and felt more alive than she had in half a year. David had been right. He was special. Aleksi didn't feel like she deserved him. She'd hated to leave, but this was her only chance. Maybe, if this worked, she could be with him again.

Tapping her code in again, she opened the inside door and descended the stairs. At the bottom, she stepped into the wine cellar and found that someone had seen her come in.

"Welcome home." Persephone leaned against a rack of wine bottles with a satisfied smile. "I was worried you'd left for good." She didn't sound worried.

"I had to tie up some loose ends." Aleksi regarded the woman and decided it was time for the inevitable confrontation. She'd finally made the connection with the scent she'd detected in Hutch's condo and Persephone, and her hacked phone. "But then you knew where I was, didn't you?"

"We knew, yes." Persephone turned toward the entrance to the Sanctum.

"Tell me the truth. Were you watching us, or just listening?"

Persephone froze, then turned to face her. "We were watching, but only once. I had the cameras turned off."

"Well, then you know how special Hutch is to me." Aleksi stepped up to the woman who could make her human again and grinned a dragon grin. "If you or your family harms him in any way, I'll tear everything and everyone connected to you to pieces."

Persephone's face paled. "We won't, Aleksi. I loved him, too, you know."

"But you said—"

"I couldn't have you tell him about us. I had to convince you that I was serious somehow."

She'd lied? Aleksi chided herself; the woman lived a lie every day. "Okay, fine. I won't tell him, and you won't hurt him. Do we have a deal?"

"We have a deal."

"Good." She took a deep breath and let it out slowly. "Okay. I'm ready. Let's do this."

"Reggie's got everything ready for you." Persephone punched her code into the Sanctum door and opened it. "Just step inside, and we'll begin."

Trust... She'd already crossed that bridge with Persephone and her family, but there were levels of trust. Reversing her condition would make curing the infection seem like a three-day flu. Still, to be human again, to regain her life, to be with Hutch, it was worth the risk.

Hope... Steeling her nerves against the bone-deep instinct to flee, Aleksi stepped into the Sanctum.

To Be Concluded

ACKNOWLEDGMENTS

Many thanks as always to my wife for her patience and support through this and all of my other works. Being married to a writer is not an easy indenture. Also, thanks to John Hartness for his support, fortitude, and excellent input in the story, and the editorial help provided by Falstaff Books.

FALSTAFF BOOKS

Want to know what's new & coming soon from Falstaff Books?

Join our Newsletter List
& Get this Free Ebook Sampler
with work from:
John G. Hartness
A.G. Carpenter
Bobby Nash
Emily Lavin Leverett
Jaym Gates
Darin Kennedy
Natania Barron
Edmund R. Schubert
& More!

http://www.subscribepage.com/q0j0p3

ABOUT THE AUTHOR

Born and raised in Oregon, Chris met his wife and soulmate, Anne, while attending graduate school in Texas. Since then they have been gaming together since 1985, sailing together since 1988, married since 1989, and writing together off and on throughout their relationship. Most astonishingly, they have not killed each other during the creation or editing of any of their stories...although it was close a few times. Since 2009, the couple has been sailing and writing full-time aboard their beloved sailboat, *Mr Mac*. They return to the US every summer for conventions, always happy to sign copies of their books and talk with fans.

Find him on Twitter here: https://twitter.com/ChrisAJackson1

Or on Facebook here: https://www.facebook.com/chris.a.jackson.967

Check out Chris's books on Goodreads https://www.goodreads.com/chrisajackson or on https://www.jaxbooks.com/

ALSO BY CHRIS A. JACKSON

From Jaxbooks

A Soul for Tsing

Deathmask

Blood Sea Tales

The Pirate's Scourge

The Pirate's Truth (coming 2019)

The Pirate's Curse (coming 2020)

Weapon of Flesh Series

The Cornerstones Trilogy

(with Anne L. McMillen-Jackson)

The Cheese Runners Trilogy

(novellas – also on Audible)

From Dragon Moon Press

The Scimitar Seas Novels

From Paizo Publishing

(also available as audiobooks)

Pirate's Honor

Pirate's Promise

Pirate's Prophecy

From Privateer Press

Blood & Iron (ebook novella)

Watery Graves

From Fantasy Flight Games

The Deep Gate (Lovecraftian horror novella)

www.ingramcontent.com/pod-product-compliance
Lightning Source LLC
Chambersburg PA
CBHW030424310726
48979CB00009B/1603/J

* 9 7 8 1 6 4 5 5 4 0 5 7 1 *